Return to the enchanted islands of Naipon, and the acclaimed hero of Jessica Amanda Salmonson's wondrous saga

THOUSAND SHRINE WARRIOR

"Admirers of the filmmaker Kurosawa will see some similarities between movies like *Yojimbo* and (Salmonson's) blend of lyricism and violence."

—Carol McGuirk,
New York Daily News

"Sandwiched between bloodbaths and grotesqueries are finely etched passages of introspection, with flourishes as delicate as hummingbirds..."

—Don Strachan,
Los Angeles Times

"The sf reader will enjoy the parallel universe idea employed by the author, who uses an island nation that 'bears a striking resemblance to old Japan' as the setting for the heroic tale of a female samurai who will delight feminists and martial arts enthusiasts with her unflinching courage, strength of will, and perseverance in the face of wondrous and horrific challenges..."

—*Library Journal*

The Tomoe Gozen *Saga by Jessica Amanda Salmonson*

TOMOE GOZEN
THE GOLDEN NAGINATA
THOUSAND SHRINE WARRIOR

Edited by Jessica Amanda Salmonson
HEROIC VISIONS

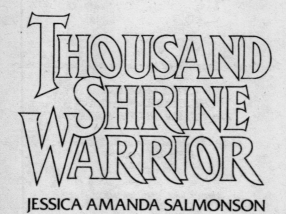

THOUSAND SHRINE WARRIOR

JESSICA AMANDA SALMONSON

Illustrated by Wendy Wees

ACE FANTASY BOOKS
NEW YORK

THOUSAND SHRINE WARRIOR

An Ace Fantasy Book/published by arrangement with
the author

PRINTING HISTORY
Ace Original/March 1984

ISBN: 0-441-80761-5

Ace Fantasy Books are published by The Berkley Publishing Group,
200 Madison Avenue, New York, New York 10016.
PRINTED IN THE UNITED STATES OF AMERICA

To history's Tomoe Gozen—
different from her Naiponese counterpart
but just as strong

LIST OF ILLUSTRATIONS
by Wendy Wees

PROLEGOMENON

Naipon the Anchored Empire
the Land of Marsh and Reeds.
Naipon of peak and valley
river, stone and tree.
Naipon of the Thousands of Myriads
who animate the world.
Naipon between the Heavenly River
and the lands called Roots and Gloom.
Naipon where warriors stalk
and are stalked by
the invisible and the seen.
Naipon where good and evil meet
exchange identities
and meet again.
Naipon where strange beasts roam
and stranger men.
Naipon of the Sun's womb.
Naipon of steel.
Naipon in glory and pathos
sweetness and terror
Naipon.

PART ONE

The Nameless Nun

The woman, pale with fright, hurried through moonlit woods, stumbling, breathing heavily, trying not to cry out. The cloth *obi*, which ordinarily wrapped around her waist several times to hold her kimono together, was half undone. It trailed the ground behind her, catching on fallen branches. Her kimono threatened to open altogether. Behind her, she heard rude laughter. One of the three men called to the others,

"Takeno! Yojiemon!"

"This way, Chojiro," a laughing voice replied. "Over here!"

"No!" shouted the voice of the one called Chojiro. "This way! I see her!"

Panicked, she fell, drew her long obi inward so that it would not trip her again, then rose and dashed onward. The laughter behind her grew louder. She could not outdistance them.

Somewhere up ahead she heard the mournful notes of a *shakuhachi,* a heavy bamboo flute. She ran toward the sound, thinking it might be a priest playing for the moon's sake or for his night's meditation. But the sound echoed weirdly under the canopy of evergreens, confusing her about the direction to run. She dropped the end of her loose obi and it caught on something, coming off entirely. She did not try to retrieve it, but held the front of her kimono closed with both hands and continued forward.

When the three men happened on the obi, one of them— Chojiro, the thickly built fellow—picked up one end. He sniffed it, grinning some more.

"Now she will be easier to get at," said Yojiemon, a man younger and prettier than the other two, but somehow more cruel in appearance. Chojiro let go of the obi and tried to scan the dark woods. Due to the fact that he was somewhat over-

3

weight, he breathed harder than the others. The third man, Takeno, was the least winded by the chase. He was the strongest in appearance, in a lean and wolfish manner.

All three men bore two swords apiece, proof that they were samurai and not common ruffians. But they were drunk, as befits no samurai of merit. Takeno, the quieter of the three, raised his hand and pointed in the direction of a momentary flash of color in the moonlight. The three were off again, leaving the woman's obi snaked across a bush.

She was hiding behind a thick tree, trying not to let her breath be heard. The men passed by, so close she smelled their sweat and the wine they had been drinking. They did not go far before stopping, looking left and right.

Chojiro was the most befuddled by the saké. "You saw her go this way?" he asked, panting. "You're sure?"

Takeno did not answer.

"What Takeno sees is certain," said Yojiemon.

"Where can she hide?" asked Chojiro. "A matter of pride that we catch her! Especially after she kicked Takeno that way!"

"Takeno has an iron groin," said Yojiemon. "Still, she escaped before we could finish our business with her. Not real men if we let her go!"

New notes from the shakuhachi drew the woman out. She ran toward the sound again, and the men saw her. "Hoi! Hoi!" shouted Chojiro who led the chase in clumsy bounds. The sleek samurai and the one with young, cruel visage and mirth followed casually.

The echoing music confused her again. She dashed in a new direction and was cut off. The three men surrounded her. Yojiemon's laughter did not abate. Chojiro smacked fat lips lustfully, nearly drooling. Takeno kept quiet but was the most frightening for that.

"You want her, Chojiro?" asked Yojiemon. "Prove you know how!"

"I will!" said Chojiro as he untied his *hakama*, the split skirt worn over his kimono. He placed his long and short swords against a tree while doffing the hakama, then began to untie his kimono's obi. The woman lunged not away from Chojiro, but toward him, grabbing for his swords by the tree. Takeno was quick to kick her away, but she had managed to get the shortsword in her hand. She unsheathed it. Yojiemon's cruel laughter was louder. Neither he nor Takeno moved to help Chojiro.

"To lose your sword is to lose face!" chided Yojiemon. "How will you handle her now, Chojiro?"

She stabbed and stabbed, but Chojiro evaded her easily. He was not in as good shape as a samurai should be, but he was battle-trained nonetheless, and she was helpless against him. She stabbed again, but missed her mark as before. The other two men began to approach, seeing that Chojiro could not take the knife away without some help. It would not be possible to fend off all three at once, so she darted around the tree, then took off through the woods again.

As she had Chojiro's shortsword, it became a matter of honor for him to get it back without his friends' help. They might not hold back to give him the chance, however, for they weren't the sort to be concerned with Chojiro's loss of face. They would probably tell everyone about it, too, unless he got the weapon back immediately. The woman was uncertain if grabbing the sword had improved or worsened matters for herself.

Chojiro's headlong rush was reckless. His obi had been half-untied before the woman caused so much trouble, so he was not in the position to catch someone. Still, he almost had her—except that she reeled about and slashed blindly, scratching him by sheer luck.

"Shimatta!" he cursed, lurching back and inspecting his minor cut. He said again, "Damn!" His friends caught up with him, one carrying his hakama, the other his longsword. He took the hakama and threw it away angrily. Yojiemon said, "A crime to steal a samurai's sword. You will have to kill her now. No other way to regain face." Chojiro tied his obi quickly and took his longsword from Takeno. Takeno said to Yojiemon, his voice strangely gentle,

"We would have killed her anyway. What would happen to us if she told?"

"Yes, but now Chojiro will have to do it. I don't think he has killed a woman before."

"Can you?" asked Takeno quietly.

"I can."

"Good," said Yojiemon. They heard a fallen branch crack under a footfall and were after her again.

At the wood's edge, she stumbled into a cemetery. She hurried along paths between small stone gods and monuments. She kept running until she came to a section of the cemetery where the poor were buried close to one another. A thousand sticks poked high into the air, bearing the names of the individuals whose ashes were in the pots below the ground, or bearing sutras for those whose names were unknown. There was barely room to run between these high slats.

A strap of one of her sandals broke. She fell hard against a little stone deity, nearly losing consciousness. She heard the men close by and it shook her from her daze. Rising, she stumbled onward, hobbling with one foot bare. She had dropped the shortsword and her head hurt so much that she hadn't thought to look where the sword had fallen.

A cloud passed before the moon. In the darkness she could not keep to the narrow paths through the forest of slats. She knocked the closely placed markers awry; they rattled like bones as they struck eath other. She was sorry to desecrate their sad, destitute graves, but too frightened to stop and apologize to the spirits whose places were upset.

The sound of the shakuhachi ended abruptly. Yojiemon's laughter behind her was much closer; of the three, he seemed to enjoy this the most. She looked back to see them as the cloud moved away from the moon. Takeno moved swiftly and with grace, making no sound. Yojiemon bounced as he ran, like a child on a lark. Chojiro huffed and puffed, red-faced and angry about his sword. When she looked forward again, she saw that she had nearly run into a toolshed at cemetery's end.

She banged on the door, hoping a caretaker or vagrant or someone was inside. She finally cried out, "Help! Help me!" She could not get the toolshed door to open, not that it was a wise hiding place if she succeeded.

"Hold there!" shouted Chojiro, coming up behind her. He grabbed her shoulder, spun her around, struck her with the back of his hand. "Where's my sword!" he demanded, but she could only stare at him, dumb and petrified. She knew she could not escape them a third time. She resigned herself to her fate, letting him strike her a second time.

"Beat her up later!" said Yojiemon. "We want her fresh right now."

"But my shortsword!"

"Look for it," said Yojiemon, pulling Chojiro away and looking at the woman eagerly. At that moment, the door of the shed flung open. In it stood a dark shape no one could quite make out. The three men backed away, hands to hilts of longswords.

Chojiro demanded, "Who is in there!" sounding less belligerent than he might have wished.

The dark figure stepped out.

"A woman!" said Chojiro.

"Our lucky night," said Yojiemon. Their hands moved away from their swords. The woman who stepped out of the shed was a nun, but not of an ordinary sort. She wore dark, unpatterned hakama over a kimono neither bleached nor dyed, therefore the natural cream color of raw silk: strong cloth, and suggestive of high station before she became a Buddhist nun, yet not a pretentious cloth, nor soft. Over this she wore a long, black vest, which looked to be made of hemp but was a loose, coarse weave of silk. Her sandals were made of straw; they tied around her ankles. She carried two swords through the straps of her hakama and the obi underneath. A martial nun, then, perhaps the retired wife of a slain general.

The three men could not tell if she were beautiful, for a large *amigasa* or "incognito hat" of woven bamboo hid her face. In her hand was the shakuhachi, a thick bamboo flute nearly as long as a shortsword.

The nun was unperturbed by the three men facing her. She seemed to ignore them as she put the shakuhachi in a silk embroidered bag, then placed the bagged instrument through her belt behind her back.

"*Bikuni!*" said Yojiemon, recognizing her as an esoteric nun. "Tell me what convent you belong to, so I will know which order I defile!"

"I have no convent," said the woman, her voice even and deeper than expected. Perhaps she was older than they thought. They could not see any feature of her face, so dark were the moonshadows beneath the large hat. "I am of Thousand Shrine Sect, a wanderer."

"Beggar-nun!" chided Chojiro, having heard of this mendicant sect.

"I play my shakuhachi at city gates and temples, it is true, and before the kitchen doors of houses and fronts of stores. I am paid by whoever has been pleased to hear me."

"Same thing!" Chojiro said with a childlike spitefulness. "A beggar!"

A long breath issued from under the hat, as though the woman's patience were beginning to feel tired. "If you catch me begging," she said, "I would be grateful if you put me out of my misery. I would do the same for you."

"Big talk for a woman!" said Chojiro, but he seemed a little cowed.

Takeno whispered something to Yojiemon, so softly no one else could hear. Yojiemon nodded, then said to the nun in a tone of magnanimity, "Since you are Buddha's woman, maybe we will let you go. But the girl at least is ours."

The frightened woman moved away as Yojiemon tried to grab her. She scurried to the bikuni's side, then behind her, hidden by the long sleeves of the nun's kimono. "How is she yours?" asked the bikuni.

"We caught her in a tryst with a peasant," Yojiemon revealed. "She serves the daughter of our Lord Ikida Sato. A bad example to other maids that she has mingled with the lower class."

"It should be taken up with your Lord," said the nun. "Perhaps she should be dismissed for her behavior, forced to marry into a peasant clan."

"That would not be punishment enough!" exclaimed Chojiro, puffing. "She would probably be happy if that happened!"

"So you would punish her yourselves? Before your Lord and his daughter know anything? What if you are found out? It soils the honor of samurai that you become drunk and unseemly then threaten a girl. She'll lose her position in Lord Sato's house for her tryst; but if you complicate the crime yourselves, you may find that *seppuku* is your own reward. Are you brave enough to slit your bellies? Already it may be too late for you."

"Cheeky nun!" exclaimed Chojiro, but he was beginning to sober up a little. His upper lip was sweaty and quivering. His hand moved toward his sword. He exclaimed to his two friends, *"Kiru!"* meaning, "Kill her!"

"Agreed," said Yojiemon, flashing a smile. Three swords slid from their scabbards. The three men readied themselves to attack. The nun did not draw her sword. She said,

"I came to this place to honor one among the thousand shrines I must visit on my ceaseless pilgrimage through the sixty-six provinces of Naipon. It was my desire to play my shakuhachi for the spirits here tonight, especially for those who died by violence. It would dishonor them if I fought you in their graveyard. Please do not make me fight."

The bikuni started to bow politely. Chojiro used this chance to try to cut her. She stepped backward so that he missed. She turned quickly and pushed the frightened maid into the cemetery's toolshed. When her back was turned, Chojiro struck again, barely missing her but clipping the shakuhachi, which she had put behind herself in the silk bag. She reeled about and her sword was suddenly in her hand. Chojiro had not seen the swift draw. He stepped backward, suddenly afraid.

The nun looked at the tip of her shakuhachi on the ground and sucked in a long, angry breath. "That was made by my instructor, who taught me to play," she said. "He is dead now and it cannot be replaced. Your lives are like that, too. There is still time to run away."

Her arm raised slowly. Moonlight played up and down the length of the sword's polished steel. "Careful," Takeno whispered as he and Yojiemon attacked together. She stepped sideways, evading Takeno and slicing Yojiemon from shoulder to opposite thigh. His body fell two ways at once. Takeno was quick to attempt vengeance for Yojiemon, but the nun did not even turn to face him. Her sword reached sideways and he stuck himself on the weapon's point.

Chojiro saw his second friend spitted through the throat, saw him stand there making gagging sounds while the nun held her sword motionless, still looking another direction. The spitted Takeno dropped his own sword, reached up to grab at the blade in his voice box. He gurgled and blood gushed from his wide-open mouth. Finally the bikuni pulled the sword out and let the man fall to the ground to die. Chojiro threw his longsword away and fell onto his knees, realizing the terrible error in attacking this woman.

"Please!" he said. "I was led astray by these other men! I will abide by the Way the rest of my life if you will pardon me tonight!" He bowed several times, striking his head on the hard, cold ground.

"A tragedy that you have become a beggar," said the nun. "I will keep my promise to you!" Her sword swept up and down and the craven samurai's head rolled between grave markers. The nun took a piece of paper from her kimono, wiped the blade of her sword clean, and dropped the paper on one of the corpses. As she sheathed her sword, the woman in the shed came out and fell before her savior, saying over and over, "Thank you! Thank you very much!" The nun picked up the clipped mouthpiece of her shakuhachi and started to walk away, but the woman she left behind ran after her, threw herself down to block the path, bowing again.

"Don't bow to me!" said the nun. "Go home!"

"I am too dishonored!" said the woman, who began to weep horribly. "I disgraced myself and my family by having that affair! Those men found me out and captured me afterward. How can I live? You must complete your duty and kill me, too!"

"Did those men touch you in the woods? No, do not tell me; no one needs to know. Why should you die for it? Once I was a samurai and as such would have killed you for the sake of your own honor. That was a long time ago. Life is too precious; so much so that I will feel compelled to build those three men a shrine to atone for what I have done tonight. But since they are dead, who will know your secret?"

"I will know!" said the woman, no longer crying, but aghast. "How can I live with it?"

"Tell your master and his daughter about your illicit affair. Maybe Lord Sato will have you beaten for it, and your family will disown you for mingling below your class. Then, divested of all privilege, you will be free to marry the peasant boy. You will work hard and your beauty will fade from struggling in the rain and sun. You will have many brats and that will be painful, too. Women suffer a thousand times in life! Do you think yourself so different from the rest? It is boastful to think you deserve to die! Now, run away and see what you can do about yourself. If you follow me again, I may kill you after all!"

The woman did not move as the nun walked away.

The night had not been quite as cold as the dawn. The path began to sparkle with frozen dew. The cold did not appear to perturb the traveler, though certainly it did not make the morning pleasant.

Deciduous trees had lost their leaves, for autumn came early to the mountain region of Kanno, and winter already approached, though in lower domains, maples were bright red and gingko yellow. The leaves that softened her path were already devoid of color, mildewed, rotting.

To the south were high hills, the tops blanketed with snow. There was a stillness in the air broken only rarely by the wind's hissed deathhhh, deathhhh, chilling the bikuni to the marrow. Her hands ached from the cold, so she kept them inside her kimono, next to her flesh.

In a while she stopped, pushed her hands out from the warmth of her kimono's interior, and looked at the ground to one side of the road, seemingly at nothing. Then she knelt near a tiny patch of brittle grass. The grass was white with morning's frost. Beside the stiff, dry stems there reposed a small serpent, coiled upon the ground. It was a white snake with pink eyes. It was scarcely able to move. Doubtless it had misjudged the weather due to the night's relative mildness, and, foraging at dawn, became ensnared by the frost.

The bikuni cupped her hands around the white serpent and lifted it to her hat-shaded face, breathing moist air between her thumbs. The pitiful, small thing coiled more tightly about itself, perhaps understanding that its life was being saved. The bikuni talked to it briefly. "The wrong day to bask in sunshine, Snake. The sky is clear but Amaterasu's light is colder than that of her moon-brother. As you are a white creature, I will take you to a Shinto shrine, where you will be honored."

Shintoists considered unpigmented creatures of any sort to be holy and supernatural. Though tradition among warrior-widows dictated that such a woman become a nun of a Buddhist sect, in the wanderer's heart she sympathized more strongly with Naipon's older faith, and was eager to save the snake for this reason.

The wandering nun owned little. Besides her two swords, deep bamboo hat, and damaged shakuhachi, she also had a pouch, which hung loose from her neck. It was an alms-bag, in which she was supposed to receive payment for playing shakuhachi at doorways and gates. Though the alms-bag was intended to take a cup of rice or small coin or other donation, the bikuni could not expect to make her living properly until her shakuhachi was repaired or replaced. So she used the alms-bag to hold the snake. She placed the creature in the pouch with utmost care, then pushed it halfway into the fold of her kimono, to assure the small occupant warmth.

Along the way was a Shinto shrine with a *torii* gate facing the ridge highway. The bikuni stood at the road's high point, where the view was remarkable. The pretty, rustic shrine-houses formed a fairly large compound, far enough away that they could all be framed within the tall torii, which was nearer the road. The gate itself was ceremonial rather than functional, inviting rather than a barrier, consisting of two vertical poles thick as logs, and two horizontal beams near the top. There was an old, worn, moss-grown staircase leading sharply downward, the torii being halfway down the slope. There was no fence from this approach, though the shrine grounds were somewhat protected by the natural wall of the mountain's slope. She could see, far across the compound, where two sides of the grounds were protected from desecration by high walls; but there were numerous entries, as though none would really desecrate such a place, and everyone was welcome.

Beyond the torii and at the foot of the ancient staircase, there stood two stone guardians so worn by time that it was impossible to say if they had once been lions, or dogs, or foxes. The fangs of one were broken out; the other was clamp-mouthed. If the guardians had ever been fierce, their current weathered softness had erased all ferocity.

Beyond stair, torii, and featureless knee-tall guardians, the path was winding and indirect. It passed amidst blossomless lily ponds, grottos, carved bridges, and small cascades artfully improved, with numerous tiny streams rushing from high ground to lower. In spring, this place was surely gorgeously ablossom. Even now, mouldering leaves on paths or floating on ponds, naked branches twisting upward, it remained a pleasant sight to soften one's heart. As winter hurried nearer, the grounds would become more and more stark; but there were evergreens both large and dwarfed, well-situated rocks, and stone lanterns on gravel jetties, so that the sanctuary would be beautiful even at the height of winter, when everything would be dulcetly muted by blankets of snow.

Some of the auxiliary buildings were in extreme disrepair. Large areas of the gardens looked wilder than they should. It was not a rich shrine, to be sure, but a haven nonetheless, and the nun liked the looks of it. She said, "A good place for you to live!" and had anyone been close enough to hear her words, it might have seemed she meant herself, though a Buddhist nun living at a Shinto shrine would be unusual. But it was the serpent she addressed. The occupant of her alms-bag moved almost imperceptibly.

A group of children were running through the gardens of the sanctuary. A white elk fled the racket of rowdy, ill-clad youngsters, bounding out of sight. An old man came running out from somewhere, beseeching the children not to bother the holy creatures who lived in the sanctuary, bowing to the scamps several times as though they were his elders. Their response was to run and dance around the old fellow, making a lot of noise, calling him names that were more whimsical than disparaging. Soon he seemed dizzy from trying to catch this one or that one, and staggered like a scrawny, drunken ape, to the heightened amusement of the peasant brats.

The watcher on the upper road lifted the front of her big hat, to better observe the comical business among the shrine-houses and gardens. She descended halfway down the steep stairs, then stood in the frame of the torii gate, her usual solemn expression betraying amusement.

The children had bundles of twigs and bags of leaves tied to their backs, light enough loads that the weight did not slow them down too much to avoid the priest. They were slender children, too hungry-looking and small to be sent out in the mornings to gather fallen limbs and leaves that would be used to kindle charcoal in the firepits of peasants' houses. But such were their duties, young though they were for it, and they obviously wished to turn their hard work into moments of wild freedom—at the old priest's willing expense.

They relieved the harsh tedium of their morning chore by meeting at the shrine, attempting to infuriate the tiny, elderly man. From the bikuni's vantage point, it was clear the priest was not easily annoyed, but was more like one of the children himself, participating in a silly game he could never hope to win. In this way, he brightened the dark lives of poor mountain children, encouraged their laughter, and at the same time eased his own lonesome life.

Eventually the children tired of their sport and ran off in the direction of a village, screaming laughter as they went. The Shintoist stood watching them leave by way of back exits. Then, shaking his shaven head, he went into one of the main shrine-houses and closed the door against the cold.

The bikuni went down the rest of the steps, passing between

the gently observing guardians, scabrous with lichen. She sauntered along the winding approach to the buildings. For a moment she stood near a bridge and watched a little cataract tumble over stones and spill into a pool. White fish rose to the surface, then dropped into murky depths. She was surprised to see a pink-eyed turtle with a carapace white as a mound of snow. At first she had thought it a stone, until it looked at her then slid into the chilly pool.

She came in due course to the door of the sanctuary's caretaker. Before she could slap the door, the entry slid open and there stood the wizened Shinto priest in stiff green cloth. He said,

"I saw you on the high road enjoying the nonsense. You are Buddha's woman, I can see; but all pilgrims are welcome here. Please enter. I have already prepared a morning meal. Perhaps you will be kind enough to play your shakuhachi for me before you're on your way."

The mendicant entered, the odor of the promised meal inviting. She doffed sandals and hat, listening to the sound of baby birds, hatched out of season, peeping in the warm rafters. Before making herself comfortable at the fireplace, she bowed deeply and said in an apologetic tone, "I fear there was trouble in the night and my instrument was damaged in a scuffle. Yet fortune saves me from becoming a true beggar, for I have come upon a thing which should prove valuable to your shrine and gardens."

She removed the small serpent from her alms-bag. It was livelier for its warmth and wrapped itself tightly about two of the bikuni's fingers. The Shintoist could barely contain himself. The deep creases of his aged face traced his delight. He took the serpent from the bikuni's fingers and let the small thing rest in his two cupped hands. Then he looked up into the rafters and made chirping sounds. Directly, six small white birds fluttered down to the Shinto priest's shoulders and arms. There were three species represented, but the bikuni could not identify them with any certainty, for they lacked familiar colors. They blinked red eyes and turned their heads from side to side to inspect the creature in the priest's hands. He said to them,

"We have a new friend!"

Then he bowed to the bikuni, showing his gratitude, while the birds on his shoulders were unsettled only a little bit. He said, "You have saved this serpent's life and enriched this shrine by far."

The six white birds returned to their nests and their peeping chicks above. The priest set the white serpent on the floor and let it crawl off wherever it desired, to search the cracks and cubbies of the shrine-house for crickets and spiders. Perhaps it would decide to hibernate beneath the floorboards of the house and not come out until spring, when the gardens would be their liveliest and most beautiful; or it might choose to live near the warmth of the fireplace and not hibernate at all, losing track of seasons as the mating birds in the rafters had done.

Though the bikuni had saved the snake within the context of Shinto belief, it was at the same time an act of Buddhist compassion. The bikuni and the Shinto holy man sat together before the firepit in the center of the room, understanding one another well enough. He was old, shriveled, bowlegged due to rickets in childhood, a trait which lent him a sort of monkey-grace when he was running through the gardens trying to catch the children. He said,

"I am originally Yano of Seki, but the village children call me Bundori-sama, 'Honored Mister Paddy-Bird,' because I live with sparrows in my house. It has become my favored name."

The Buddhist bowed and addressed the priest by his favored name, then introduced herself somewhat cryptically. "I am a retired warrior upon an endless pilgrimage to pray for those who've died in battles. I have given up my station and family ties, thus I have no name to offer you in return."

"Ah. I see," said the old man, handing the nun a bowl of soup, then sipping from his own. "I had thought you might be a famous person I have heard about: Tomoe Gozen of Heida, who fought in the great battle of Heian-kyo, where her husband died. Of course, there are more widow-warriors than just that one in this sad world, but an old man such as myself sometimes dreams of meeting a few famous people before he dies."

The bikuni seemed uneasy, so the priest laughed at himself and added, "It is rude of me to pry into your past! Please forgive me." He set his bowl aside and bowed. The bikuni said,

"If it pleases you in your old age, feel free to think I am a famous warrior. And my sword by the door is famous, too."

"Ah, *soka,*" said the priest, and laughed at himself again.

"Will you take some more soup?" His spidery hands moved to the ladle, then to the pot hanging above the firepit. The bikuni held forth her emptied bowl between two hands. They spoke of various matters of varying importance as they ate, and afterward, she sat as near the firepit as possible, holding her hands over the glowing coals. The Shintoist had been watching how she used her hands, how presently she kneaded each finger one by one. At last it caused him to remark,

"Your hands appear to ache. I've knowledge of herbs if you need something."

"It's a minor thing," she said, drawing away from the firepit and placing her hands on her knees, sitting more formally than before.

"Don't mind me at all," said the Shinto priest as he scooted on his knees and came close enough to reach for her left hand. She let him take it, though it made her uncomfortable that he was solicitous. He poked at her knuckles, finding them slightly puffy, then bent her fingers backward until she winced. He shook his head a little and said,

"I sympathize with you. It must hurt a lot."

"It doesn't."

"You must use your hands for hard work," he said. "Usually hands don't wear out like that until someone is older."

She could not hide a startled emotion. "Worn out?" she asked.

"Joints creak and get stiff every morning, especially in cold weather. The fingers sometimes swell up, not so most people could notice, but it's a nuisance." He wiggled his own gnarled fingers as if to say he shared the problem. "It happens to all of us when we get old. Sometimes it happens to younger people, too, especially if they use their hands more than average for hard labor. Perhaps you practice with your swords too much!"

His last remark seemed partially in jest, but the bikuni was silent for a while. The priest looked at her with a kindly expression, and his concern unsettled her more than the pain she had experienced off and on during the last two years or so. At length, she felt compelled to ask, "Will it get worse?"

The elderly fellow nodded. The bikuni cupped her hands one inside the other, looking upset. The Shinto priest said, "I'll give you an ointment that will help; and I can counsel you to rest your hands as much as possible, and keep them warm. It could be that the problem will not progress too rapidly. But I'm afraid I cannot tell you the pain will ever go away."

After a while, the wandering nun took her leave in order to visit the village. She had arranged to return to the shrine at a later time, with Bundori's promise to aid her in the task of carving a stone lantern for the sake of the three men she had killed the night before. Her immediate concern was with her shakuhachi, which by some means would need to be repaired.

When Bundori was certain the nun was far enough along the path to the village that she could not possibly hear anything untoward within his house, he became an industrious fellow indeed. He went bowlegged about the interior of his dwelling double-checking locks, doors, and windows. He hung a large kettle over the firepit for tea. He gathered up a few utensils and set out a tray of small cups. He unrolled a long, narrow straw mat. He put everything into a precise if puzzling order.

He dragged a storage chest out into the middle of the floor and climbed on top of it so that he could reach inside the nests of the birds who had hatchlings. Two of his three pairs of birds had one youngster apiece. The parents did not mind that he was handling their babies. He took the tiny birds—one with pinfeathers, the other still a homely thing with bulbous red eyes on its featherless head—and placed them with utmost care on the woven straw mat. They seemed tinier than tiny at the mat's center.

The mother birds and father birds, as well as the pair who had no hatchling, flew down to the mat to be with the chicks. They preened their feathers, devoid of surprise regarding current affairs.

Bundori pushed the storage chest back into its proper place. Then he took out a special box and set it beside himself on the floor. He gazed upon the six adult birds and two babies on the mat, and his expression was one of extreme delight.

Removing the lid from the small wooden box, Bundori took from it a brass bowl and a little mallet carved of wood, a bit longer than a chopstick. The mallet was intended to strike the bowl for the sake of a pure, sweet knell. The old priest looked comfortable on his knees before the bowl-bell, striking it over and over again, as rapidly as he could manage. The birds enjoyed the knell, matching the note with their chirping.

At the same time, Bundori chanted a pretty Shinto incantation, quite different from most incantations, which had a more dour sound to them. The combined effect of the knell, the chirping, and the chanting caused the interior of the shrine-house to feel warmer and more pleasant. The very floors and rafters resonated. The walls of the place began to shine in a subtle manner. A glittery substance rained down from nowhere, disappearing before it struck the floor.

Priest Bundori recited his spell so swiftly, and beat the brass bowl so fast, it did not seem possible that he could increase the pitch or pace. Yet he did so. It was a mad, merry sound. The birds, with their two small chicks, bobbed their heads up and down and from side to side in time with the rhythm of the priest's activity.

The raining glitter began to swirl about the happily peeping chicks and the twittering adult birds.

The birds began to grow.

Caught in the vortex of a powerful magic, the white birds were nevertheless devoid of fear. They acted as though this strange business was something to which they were accustomed, something they found to their liking. Perhaps they were helping to cause the event, rather than being the passive recipients of Bundori's talent.

Bigger and bigger they became, growing up and up. As they grew, they changed in shape and substance. Their contours altered by degrees until they looked no longer like birds, but like human beings. Their feathers became regal finery. Kimonos were of the most extraordinary, shimmering quality.

The mother bird named Shiumi, whose chick was youngest, became a beautiful woman holding a sweet infant. The infant was clad in a child's kimono, embroidered white on white with crane designs. Shiumi's strong husband Omo looked on with pride at the nicely clad infant.

Iwazu was somewhat older, and her child was near the toddler stage. As she held her son, the tiny fellow gazed about with wonder as he grew and grew. Iwazu's husband Guma laughed at their child's surprise.

The childless couple were younger than the other four bird-folk. Uda was as handsome as a castle page. Akuni might well have been a famous courtesan instead of some bird's wife, and in fact had a courtesan's coiffure. The manner of them both tended to the sensual. They were vain but gentle.

The white hair of the two mothers was arranged like that

of court ladies. The fathers wore high-peaked hats shaped like the black hats of noblemen, except these hats were white. Uda wore no hat; his neatly tied topknot stood up straight like the crest of a bird.

When they ceased to grow and metamorphose, six adults and two children of utterly human appearance sat on the long mat before Bundori. The raining glitter began to fade away as the priest slowed the pace of his frantic spell. In no time at all, he had fallen silent, and gazed with a grandfather's affection on his six friends and their children. These men and women gazed at Bundori with equal love, eerie only because their faces were so pale and eyes so red. As one, they bowed to the patriarch of the holy sanctuary.

"How glad I am to see you," said Bundori with tears in his eyes.

"It is good of you to invite us here today," said Guma, senior among the bird-folk. He was a Lord among birds and held himself regally. He was handsome in a mature manner completely different from the attractive Uda, who was practically a boy, or Omo, who was strong and calm and silent like a warrior.

Iwazu, wife of Lord Guma, was, through association with Guma, boss among the women. She indicated to young Akuni that she ought to prepare tea for everyone, for the water was steaming. Pouting a bit, Akuni nudged her husband Uda, who yawned as though he didn't notice she wished he would help, but then he got up and helped her anyway. Soon everyone had nice cups of tea before their knees, but none began to drink until Priest Bundori had taken the first sip. When he had done so, everyone laughed merrily and drank leisurely from their teacups.

Akuni had settled down next to Bundori, leaning toward the priest in a sexy way. As he sipped his tea, he tried not to let his eyes linger on the back of Akuni's lovely, slender white neck. It was hard not to admire the faint tracings of blue veins beneath her perfectly alabaster complexion. Bundori felt somewhat flustered. Uda seemed not to mind Akuni's flirtations. He was not of jealous propensity and may have been himself a bit like his wife.

Bundori was a gray cloud amidst the ethereal snowiness of his friends. To an outsider, his strange company might look all alike; but to Bundori, the whiteness of their skin and the redness of their eyes provided the most superficial of similarities. They were as different from one another as any other group of people could possibly be. Flirtatious Akuni and her girlish husband Uda; haughty Iwazu and her imperious husband Guma; contrary Shiumi, attentive of her infant, next to her quiet husband Omo. The child of Iwazu and Guma was in some ways Bundori's favorite. He took the fellow onto his knees and grinned at the cherubic, laughing face. Tiny fingers clung to the priest's old gnarly ones. Bundori realized the power of childhood was greater than any magic of his own! When the boy wiggled and wanted to go exploring some more, Bundori was sad to let him go.

Everybody talked of many things and were generous with compliments for one another. It was a nice party. After a while, Bundori bacame serious and asked everyone if they would help him with some important business. They became quiet and attentive so that they could find out what the business was about.

"I thought this might be my last chance to speak with you for a while," he said, looking sad about it. "The nun who was here today is liable to find it difficult to travel beyond this mountain province, for the freezing storms will start soon. I have it in mind to ask her to stay at this sanctuary until after winter, when it will be easy to travel again. That would mean I could not beckon you to visit me, it being against the rule of Shinto priests to let this magic become known. I will be lonely without you, especially since the nun is of melancholy disposition and won't help cheer things up.

"Still, I am thinking I should convince her to stay. As you know, that weird priest up in Lord Sato's castle, claiming to be of the Lotus sect, has beguiled the Lord and caused some trouble within the castle walls. If it continues, the trouble will spill out into the town. The best retainers have already left Lord Sato's service, and those prone to cruelty have remained, in order to have a good time for themselves. This is coupled with a short summer and the early arrival of fall, meaning there may not be enough rice to eat this winter. Either Lord Sato's men will get hungry and become dangerous nuisances, or extra rice-tax will be levied out of season so that villagers will starve. It is regarding these things that I have summoned you, seeking your wise counsel."

"You have a good idea!" said Akuni, still leaning scandalously close to Bundori as she praised his thinking. "That nun looks like a strong fighter to me, too. If you can keep her here until spring, she could be a lot of help if there are problems in the meantime."

Uda, as pretty as his wife, agreed easily with Akuni. "That priest of the Lotus sect has been a bad influence," he said, shaking his shoulders like a bird ruffling its feathers with annoyance. "Most Lotus priests take such names as 'Sun,' and 'Light,' but this one calls himself Kuro the Darkness. I wonder if he's a priest at all, or some creature out of Hell! An esoteric nun with swords could take care of such a fiend as that."

"I could tell at once," Iwazu added, her haughtiness giving way to momentary awe, "that the nun had killed a lot of people. It made me frightened for my child, until I sensed the poor nun's heart and knew she wouldn't harm a bird."

Shiumi, ever a cynical woman, said, "I'm not so sure it's a wise idea. You think she will help people out, but she's a Buddhist after all."

"Such a prejudiced statement!" complained Uda, sensitive about such matters. "Not all Buddhists are like Kuro, and not only Shintoism is good. Buddhists can be compassionate, I'm convinced. They talk about it a lot."

"Yes they do," agreed Shiumi, but there was still an edge to her voice. She adjusted the infant in her arms and pulled her kimono open so that her babe could suckle a moon-white breast. Shiumi's good looks belied her contrary nature. "That nun," she said, "wants to carve a lantern for some men she killed. Is that compassion? It won't bring them back to life! My husband is strong enough to fight Kuro. We don't need a Buddhist nun at all!"

"There is no need to argue loudly," said imperious Guma, causing Uda and Shiumi to settle down. He said to Bundori, "It might be that a killer is exactly the thing the villagers will require. It takes more than compassion to help beleaguered people. It takes anger, too, or else all that one can do is feel sorry for everybody, and watch things happen."

Bundori sighed. He said, "You're talking about murdering that troublesome priest, but I am thinking of a more defensive posture. The villagers don't understand how bad things may yet become. They are resigned to a little trouble and can live with that. If someone stands between the people and Lord Sato, maybe things will stay the way they are, neither worse nor better. In that case, no one will need to suffer very much."

Guma's wife caught her small son before he could crawl too near the firepit. She wanted to disagree with Bundori, but respect for his opinion made her venture her own feelings at first tentatively and then with more conviction. "Lord Sato's retainers listen more to Kuro the Darkness than to their own master," Iwazu said. "He will compel them to do burdensome things until he has whatever it is he seeks. Without a strong master to hold them in check, some of the retainers may begin to kill at random, with Kuro's blessing."

Priest Bundori did not like to listen to this, and he wondered aloud, "Am I wrong to think that it is possible to gain a champion for those people without it causing a lot of bloodshed?"

Iwazu continued, "The influence of the weird priest is the cause of your having to go hungry. You eat nothing but thin soup because the people are afraid to make donations to any shrine or temple, as it makes him jealous. He has frightened off or caused the death of every priest in Lord Sato's fief, and would like for you to starve to death or leave your place as well. This being so, it is natural that you should wish ill on Kuro. We wish him ill ourselves."

Bundori looked more and more upset. Guma wished to reinforce his proud wife's strong sentiment, so he spoke intensely: "You are really the source of our concern. I believe Shintoists and Buddhists should live in harmony. It is not Lord Sato's faith, but his clerical advisor that is the source of the belligerence against the native gods of Naipon. The zealous attitude of Lord Sato has made the people afraid to honor Shinto gods except in secret. It angers the Thousands of Myriads that this is so, and they will send a revengeful agent one way or another. If the nun uses her swords to cause Lord Sato and his privileged priest annoyance, maybe you can regain your health."

"I am used to hunger in my life," said Bundori. "If I thought my motivation was to improve my own situation, to receive good rice and better donations for my shrine, then I would cease at once to consider my plan. But this imbalance of faiths concerns everyone. There is always some kind of response when significant numbers of gods are denied their due."

Quiet Omo made his feelings known at last. His voice was nearly as soft as girlish Uda's, but more self-assured and devoid of vanity. "Shiumi was correct when she said I could be of help. It is not necessary to look beyond our very home for the revengeful agent of the Shinto gods. I need only to acquire a sword and your permission to pit myself against Kuro the Darkness. If I die, only then will it become necessary to consider help from outside."

Priest Bundori's usually gleeful expression was now much tortured. "It is a terrible thing for us to wish death on another human being. I cannot let Omo go into the world with vengeance on his mind. I can involve the nun only if I truly have no ulterior motive for myself, only if my exclusive wish is for the villagers' safety in a worsening situation." Bundori's emotional pain was evident. He concluded, "I cannot decide what is right."

Someone not seen previously ventured out from a dark corner. The bird-folk and Priest Bundori were surprised to realize someone had been hiding in the shrine-house the whole time. He was an extraordinarily slender man, albino like the others, his kimono having the pattern of a serpent embroidered in the faintest yellow, winding around and around himself.

"Our new friend!" exclaimed Bundori. "I had forgotten all about you!"

The thin fellow was not as beautiful as the bird-folk. He had a sallow complexion and a long face. But he had a look of sincerity that suggested a purity of heart. He came out from where he had been listening to everything and bowed in an apologetic way. He said,

"Forgive my eavesdropping so carelessly, but I did not know what had happened to myself and could not move for the longest while."

Bundori returned the bow and reassured the polite fellow, "That's how it is the first time. I know you meant no harm by staying hidden."

"I was encouraged to come out because of your discussion," he said. "I believe you have failed to consider the needs of the bikuni. She should not be encouraged to kill, for it has become distasteful to her. She should be helped along her way as soon as possible, lest she become caught up in the way things are or may soon be."

The bird-folk chattered in hasty disagreement, but Bundori held up a hand until they were silent. He said to the serpent-fellow, "The nun saved your life so you alone have her best interests in mind. I'm afraid you are correct. My own thinking has been self-deluding. I was hoping my friends could talk me into having the bikuni cause Lord Sato and Kuro trouble, though foolishly convincing myself that my only concern was for the village. You have helped me see the falsehoods and selfishness I have pursued today. I am indebted to you."

The priest bowed again, and deeply, and the serpent-youth seemed embarrassed by it. Bundori eased the embarrassment by insisting the young man join the rest of them for tea. They spent a pleasant afternoon together before Bundori could no longer put aside necessity.

Bundori left the shrine-house and started off along the path toward the village. He must find the bikuni before there was any kind of trouble.

In the village, the bikuni found an artisan who repaired musical instruments. The front of his shop was open despite the chilliness of the day. He sat in plain view of the street, on the raised wooden floor of his shop, working on the bridge of a koto. He was a man of middle years. Judging by his clothing and his shop, he was not a particularly successful businessman, but managed to get by. His features were hard, pale, and etched by concentration. His fingers were long and thin.

She stepped over the threshold into the shop, but did not step onto the raised portion of the floor or in any manner interrupt the artisan. When he seemed finished for the moment, she placed her silk bag on the platform and pushed it toward him. Without word, he opened the damaged bag and removed the body of the shakuhachi, then reached deep into the bag to get the clipped mouthpiece. He inspected the angle of the cut and pursed his lips disapprovingly. After a careful look at the entire instrument, he looked up, but could not see the bikuni's face beneath her hat. He said, "Did you think it would stop a sword? It's an excellent piece of work. Too bad someone treated it badly."

The woman accepted this chastisement, bowed very slightly, and asked, "Can it be repaired?"

"It will never have the timbre of before," he told her, "but it can be put together."

"I regret my carelessness has spoiled its perfection. Perhaps flawed it will better suit my talents. What would it cost to make it work again?"

The artisan pursed his lips as before, looking pensive. Then he raised five fingers. It was not such a high price to ask, but the bikuni had no money whatsoever. She looked at the five fingers a long while without comment. As her face was hidden beneath her hat, the artisan could hardly be expected to read her thoughts by her expression; but silence can convey a lot. He said, "As you are Buddha's woman . . ." then made his five fingers three.

For a samurai, it would be inconceivable to barter. The activities and behaviors of artisans and merchants were totally at odds with the ways of the *buké* class. Although the woman had left samurai privileges behind to become a strolling nun, it was still a distasteful matter. Awkwardly, she asked,

"Could it be done on credit?"

The artisan placed the mouthpiece and then the body of the shakuhachi in the silk bag, tied the end as best he could, considering the rent left by a sword's cut, set it on the floor before himself, and pushed it toward the end of the platform. It seemed a mean act, yet the bikuni saw there was guilt in his expression.

"I understand," said the bikuni, for a traveler was a risk for extending credit, and the man's shop did not reflect an income that could well afford charity. "If I forfeit my instrument should I fail to pay you for the repair, would it then be possible? I will find some work to do to raise the small amount."

"Who would buy it, even repaired, if it made a damaged sound?" The artisan looked most put-upon, but his hard expression could not disguise a well-intending heart. "Very well," he said, not allowing her to humble herself further. "Leave it with me a while. There is work which must come first. But I will get it done."

The bikuni bowed deeply and turned toward the street. She stood a moment, a motionless silhouette at the entrance, then looked back at the artisan to ask, "Will this road lead me to Lord Sato's castle higher on this mountain?"

His answer came reluctantly. "It's no place for a nun to seek even brief employment."

"I hear he is a convert to the Lotus sect," said the bikuni, encouraging the artisan; but he would not say more about Lord Sato, no doubt afraid of who might overhear any criticism. She could not believe Lord Sato was especially wicked, as provincial rulers go, but there was something about the artisan's attitude that seemed dark and moody, and she had seen this in the faces of everyone on the street. The village was not prosperous, but neither was it destitute. Thus Sato's taxes must be neither slight nor excessive. She wondered what it was, then, that made the townsfolk act as though a pall hung over their lives, that made them leery of a Lord who didn't seem to practice common tyranny.

She stepped out onto the street and continued through the town. She stopped here and there to see what various merchants and artisans were doing. They went about their lives in an ordinary enough way, but at a slower pace than usual, and that gloomy aspect was in everybody's disposition. It was a subtle thing, more related to an absence of cheer than to any excess of fear or visible sorrow.

As she strode along the main street, she found herself nearing the end of the village proper and approaching the wide, cold creek that separated the village from the numerous small estates of Lord Sato's retainers. Sato's fief was indeed provincial, so nothing as elaborate as a castle-town had grown up around his fortification. Rather, there was a densely forested area surrounding his most private lands. Interspersed throughout the ancient trees were the homes of samurai owing Lord Sato allegiance.

A bridge connected the village street with the road winding through that forest. On the samurai side of the bridge, there was a squat little guardhouse, its front doors opened so that the two men within had a clear view of who came and went. Under the usual order of things, strict rules were observed, which governed the comings and goings especially of townsfolk and farmers. Whatever an individual's business, ranging from charcoal delivery or payment of the rice levy to fetching away fecal matter from toilets or fulfilling each year's quota of forced labor, it was required that identification tags be presented. On them was engraved one's name, position, and business. Such information was cross-checked with a ledger in the keeping of the guards, and thus little was allowed to happen around the castle that was not controlled. Such typical regulations were not being observed at this small checkpoint, however. What few people passed over the bridge were virtually ignored by the two guards, who seemed more concerned with staying near the warmth of the coal-pot resting between them. Perhaps it was because they knew everyone by sight, the village being small. The guards disposed of what struck them as meaningless tasks. But it struck the nun as evidence of laxness regarding duty. It caused her to wonder.

It was equally customary *not* to hinder the passage of pilgrims, particularly one with two swords, hence an ex-samurai with every right to visit temples, shrines, and graves of a samurai quarter. It was the nature of Buddhist mendicants to give up their names, families, and positions, and thus there would be nothing left to record on an identification tag. But once again things were contrary to the norm where this mountainous fief was concerned. The two guards, though careless of the few townsfolk who passed by, were suddenly less lazy when they saw the bikuni. They hurried out of the guardhouse and took up a posture with spears crossed, keeping her from stepping foot off the far side of the bridge.

She stopped at the bridge's edge and did not say a word for a long while. They seemed to expect her to turn and cross back over to the village. Instead, she acted as though she were waiting for them to uncross their spears to let her pass. Her utter silence made the two men nervous, for surely they had measured her bearing and guessed her skill with the swords she wore.

They broke the silence first. The one with a mustache demanded identification and statement of business. Still the nun did not move or reply. Surely they were aware that a bikuni by definition had neither name nor business. There was nothing she could tell them.

The two men became more irritable, unable as they were to see the face beneath her hat of woven bamboo. When they were sufficiently unnerved, the bikuni's voice issued from beneath her amigasa.

"You dispose of the formality of checking the business of what few townsfolk dare your bridge, but forego tradition to bar a mendicant from her Way."

The younger of the two samurai, his face smooth and hairless, tried to sound as severe as the nun as he responded; but there was a quavering edge in his voice. "Only Lotus mendicants beyond this point! Do you know the Lotus Sutra?"

"Namu myoho-renge-kyo," the nun intoned.

Both guards sighed with relief and started to lower their spears, but the nun added,

"Anyone can say it."

The spears went up again, this time not crossed to bar her path, but leveled at her abdomen.

"I am of Thousand Shrine Sect," she said, seeming unthreatened by the spears. "As my allegiance is to no specific temple, it can be said that my bond is with all temples."

This might well be a good rationale for not fighting, as far as these particular guards were concerned. Their post was not impressive to begin with, certainly not worth a duel over particulars. They glanced quickly at one another, then allowed the bikuni to pass. They returned to the warmth of their coal-pot in the guardhouse, and did not hear the nun whisper to herself, "Sloppy men."

She wondered why they had been so uncertain of their duties. There would be another bridge and checkpoint before she reached the castle itself; the guards stationed there doubtlessly would be more capable, it being the final point before the castle's gate. Still, she began to think there'd be less trouble meeting Lord Sato than she had first imagined. Patience would answer that question for her.

Evergreens shaded the winding lane. It was no longer possible to have a clear view of the castle, though periodically she saw a part of it higher on the mountain side, through breaks in the roof of the forest.

The houses of samurai families were small but attractive, tucked at intervals between old trees, protected by those trees from autumn and winter storms. As the estates were on relatively steep ground, numerous rushing streams came down from higher areas, on their way to the gorge and torrential river far down the mountain's eastern slope. These streams provided excellent excuses for the many artful bridges, some of them no larger than four or five short steps.

Some of the homes were so far back from the road that the passing nun could not see them well. Several of them seemed run-down, from what she could see; but the neglect was recent. A few places appeared as though abandoned. She passed a temple that was even more clearly abandoned, though it might well have been important to certain samurai families before Lord Sato's conversion to Lotus Buddhism. The Lotus sect was by nature a belligerent one, but Sato's zeal was rather more extreme than usual. By the evidence, his zeal might well be considered irrational.

Though Lord Sato's fief was small in terms of rice production, by which the size of fiefs was measured, in terms of area it was the largest in Kanno province. It seemed odd that so many of the samurai estates were ghostly and deserted. Retainers should have been quite busy with the policing and administration of the fief's widespread holdings, and their homes should have reflected a constancy of comings and goings. Instead, weeds clogged the paths between the narrow, winding road and the small estates. Only once did anyone share the road with her; he was a townsman on some errand, and he stepped off the road to let her pass when he saw she had two swords. For the rest of her casual walk, it seemed a haunted forest, diffuse light barely penetrating the trees or the overcast sky. It was, at least, a little warmer than it had been earlier in the day; that, or climbing the upward grade of the road was work enough to keep her warm.

She began to put a few things together in her mind as she passed through that forest: the laxity of the bridge-guards, the estates in disrepair, the minimal activity, the perfidy of the three retainers she had been forced to kill . . . clearly Lord Sato did not have a firm control of his men. Everything was odd! The bikuni's deep hat moved from side to side as she shook her head in heightened consternation.

At an unexpected sound, the bikuni stopped on a flat part of the trail, waiting to hear further movement. She appeared relaxed but ready. Yet there was no need for readiness this time, for the sound came again, and she recognized it as the *clip-clippa* of gardener's shears. She raised the front of her hat so she could see up a path leading to one of the estates. This one was better cared for than most of the others, though it was also about the smallest. There, amidst a stand of leafless plums, was a rotund young man trimming away the tiniest stems of a particular tree. Further along the path was someone else in identical industry; he was older and rawboned, but otherwise the bikuni could not make out much about him, for foliage obscured her view.

The rotund fellow stopped working and looked toward the road. He grinned foolishly. He was apparently one of the gardener's helpers or his son, as he looked neither bright enough nor old enough to have much direct responsibility for anything. The grinning, oversized youngster waved his hand up and down until the nun felt it was rude not to wave back. She raised a hand in a slow greeting, which encouraged the large, happy fellow to wave all the harder, rather than quit. Not until the older man higher on the path yelled something at him did the fellow return to his labor, gazing covertly at the bikuni as she continued her way.

She came to a knoll where trees were stripped away and the view in every direction was spectacular. Not much further up the way was a long, wide bridge, far larger than the one separating the village from samurai estates. Three separate roads came out of the woods and met at that bridge, and the nun realized she had taken a lesser route. On the far side of the bridge were Lord Sato's most private lands and, in the middle of those lands, a castle impressive in design if not in actual size. Snow-covered barren peaks provided a gorgeous backdrop.

Halfway between bridge and castle were a group of samurai riding across wide fields in pursuit of a hind. The nun could not hear them; it was eerie to see the hunt go so swiftly and soundlessly. The man in the fore of the group was exquisitely clad. The party was armed with longbows and arrows and wore high, narrow hats. Running along behind, and looking slightly ridiculous, were several servants, who could not possibly keep up with the mounted hunters. They brought replacement arrows and other equipment for the convenience of the hunters and their steeds.

The man in the shining silver hunting cloak, probably Lord Sato himself, unleashed an arrow, which found its mark in the rump of the hind. It staggered, fell, but was on its feet almost immediately, and bounded into a wooded area. It could not go far, as Sato's private lands were surrounded by bodies of water, either natural rivers or moats. The hunting party vanished into the wooded area, after the unfortunate beast.

Such was the view in the direction of the castle. The opposite direction provided the bikuni a clear view of the village, for she could see right over the top of the forested samurai estates. The low-built homes of samurai were hidden; but here and there, the tiled roofs of temples poked out from the trees.

To the east of both the forest and the village, she saw where the creeks and rivers poured into a deep, tremendous gorge. A vast number of waterfalls vanished into mist. Far, far along the gorge she could see a rope bridge, thin as a thread from so far away, traversing the wide gorge. A miniscule guardhouse stood on the nearer side.

Beyond the gorge was another inhabited area, still well within Lord Sato's fief. The bikuni saw farmhouses scattered at intervals, smoke rising from roof-holes, going straight up into the clouds. Fine mist made the picture look flat, more like a painted screen than reality. Between the poor, thatched homes, every bit of arable land had been cleared for agricultural use, leaving the farmers vulnerable to highland storms. They must have replaced their roofs very often! Most of the fields, staggered up and down that further mountainside, already lay fallow. A few farmers were still busy on the land, preparing it for its winter's rest. From the bikuni's vantage point on the knoll, the industrious farmers looked like ants.

She imagined that the view from the castle was even more extraordinary. A full third of Sato's fief would be visible from that high place.

The mountainous regions of Kanno were harsh areas to live, it was true, but that gloominess that confronted her time and again was not explained by common hardship; for there was beauty all around, and enough arable land that peasants oughtn't suffer to excess. She was hard put to understand the source of the emotional shadows she sensed reaching out from the castle, affecting samurai estates, townsmen, temples, and farmers.

She looked again at the tiled roofs of temples, which stuck out from the forest where samurai homes were interspersed. Were they all abandoned or impoverished by Lord Sato's late decrees? If that were the case, it might explain everyone's reticence, having only lately been denied their usual avenues of worship. Nobody would elaborate the situation for her, not even Priest Bundori. She could not shake the feeling that something evaded her understanding, something that did not fit the most obvious explanation.

As she went down from the knoll toward the river, she saw beyond the bridge, where the hunters had come out from the woods. Servants afoot carried the downed hind by means of a pole cast through its bound legs. The creature's limp head bobbed from side to side. The fellow who was almost certainly Lord Sato rode to the fore of his entourage, his posture that of a conqueror home from wars. The bikuni was not impressed.

The guardhouse at the long bridge was capable of housing

a lot of men if such were required, but presently there appeared to be only about a half-dozen lounging within. They were drinking saké from small cups, but didn't talk to one another very much. They shouldn't have been drinking while on guard, but they didn't seem to mind that Lord Sato had passed by, close enough to catch them in the act, had he been less absorbed in his hunt.

The guards saw the bikuni approaching and pointed at her. Two of the men looked annoyed, then put down their cups and came out of the building to bar her from the bridge.

"None pass without Lord Sato's invitation!" one of the men shouted. The other added, "Monks and nuns are especially unwelcome!"

The former rule was common enough, but the latter surprised the bikuni. It would be too audacious of her to question Lord Sato's policy, however. Instead, she spoke to the two guards in a courteous manner, though they were samurai of low status and red-faced from what they had been drinking.

"I have come to Kanno province," said the bikuni, "in search of a young samurai of Omi province. He was rumored to have been adopted into the service of Lord Sato. That samurai's name was Yabushi when I knew him before, but no doubt he has changed it by now."

As she spoke, the four samurai inside the large guardhouse slowly put aside their cups and came out to join the first two. Three additional men, who had not previously been visible when they were sitting within the open-fronted building, took up long spears and came out with the rest. All of them looked edgy, none was completely sober, and they watched the bikuni closely.

The two men she had been addressing did not reply. One of the other men, who seemed to be in charge, despite his youth, stepped in front of the others to say,

"Lots of samurai work for our Lord." His implication was that the nun's query was too vague and stupid to be answerable.

"Still," she said evenly, "not many from Omi province." She watched the nine men carefully, for they were moving apart from one another, trying not to be obvious, though it was rather too clear that they were fanning out to surround her. She tried to clarify her query: "The friend I mentioned was of the Rooster Clan, an impoverished family despite a noble history. He had been able to maintain a 'sympathy' allowance of less than fifty rice-shares of land only by continuous bribes to certain officials. You can imagine it was hard on his dignity. It was his good fortune, I was told, to make the acquaintance of one of Lord Sato's ministers who was on a mission to Omi. The minister was impressed by the young fellow's intelligence and swordsmanship, and hired him as a retainer in some high post almost immediately. That's the story I was told."

"No man of Omi across the bridge," said the leader among the nine.

"He would be younger than you," said the bikuni. "He was small when I knew him."

"No such man," the head guard reiterated. He looked at her sternly. Though her own face was hidden beneath her amigasa, it yet seemed as though he looked her straight in the eyes, daring her to doubt his information.

"If you say it is so," she replied, "there is no need for me to seek audience at the castle."

"I say it is so," he answered.

"Then I won't bother Lord Sato or his minister about it," she said evenly, for if it turned out the guard was incorrect, he would lose face and be embarrassed. By his tone, she suspected any error was willful; but she must not prove him false in front of his men, even if they knew he lied. Also there was the matter of the other eight men's current position. They had her surrounded. A misstatement, and she could be forced to fight.

The guard said nothing more. He did not move. The nun spoke quietly:

"If you hear of such a fellow, perhaps you can tell him to visit a strolling nun at White Beast Shinto Shrine."

She turned to start back along the road through the samurai estates. The men surrounding her on that side let her pass. She did not look back at the men guarding the bridge, but was aware they watched her until she was out of their sight.

Bundori rarely came into the village, for he was ascetically minded and tended exclusively to his duties—exhausting duties, since he was the sole caretaker of an ancient mountain shrine. Usually he was welcomed heartily whenever he did decide to come into town; in fact, his visits used to be an event. In recent months, for the most part, he went ignored on his rare trips, except where children were concerned. Children were too innocently disreputable to understand or obey decrees that forbade catering to the needs of any priest. As they seemed disrespectful in their actions toward the priest, any spy for Lord Sato or Kuro the Darkness would not complain about the children's attention to Bundori.

It was a bleak-spirited village and Bundori was like a patch of light hurrying up the street. Children flocked to that light the way moths gather around a paper lantern in the night. Their dirty faces grew smiles. Their little voices rose up in laughter. Their tiny, calloused hands fluttered about, trying to touch the green-gray garments of the Shinto priest. All the while they teased him about living with birds, and being like a bird himself, or half bird, the other half monkey. He didn't mind them at all, although he pretended to be annoyed, since that was the response they were seeking. He looked like some sort of mother duck, chased about by her rambunctious youngsters. The merry sound of their silly parade was the first evidence of happiness the emotionally repressed village had experienced since the last time Bundori had paid a visit.

Yet all this happy noise came to a sudden halt when a mounted samurai appeared at the low end of the street. He was a huge man, made monstrous on his big horse, a wide wicker hat upon his head, and a longbow sticking up high at his back. He rode into the village slowly, and had a second horse tethered to the first. Strapped upon the second horse were three dead men. They were twisted, hideous corpses. One had his head completely severed, tied to a saddle, jostling from side to side. The staring eyes of the dead men were white as porcelain.

The mounted warrior passed slowly through the village, as though wishing everyone to see that three samurai had somehow been slain. He did not stop anywhere, but continued right up to the bridge leading to the samurai estates. There could be trouble about the dead men, unless someone confessed right away.

The terrible sight sent the children fleeing into their dark houses, and mothers sealed the doors. Shop-owners closed their businesses. Priest Bundori stepped into a teashop just as the maid there was closing up. Perhaps the shops would reopen in a while. More likely, fear would keep the village silent for the rest of the day.

It had not been necessary for the samurai to come through the village. There was a larger, straighter road, which bypassed the village, a more direct route to the castle, if that were where he was heading. But the samurai had wanted the villagers to fret, to wonder what would happen, to wait in gloomy anticipation for Lord Sato or his religious instructor Kuro the Darkness to propose some scheme of retribution. Then again, there might be no repercussions at all. Such uncertainty only increased everybody's tendency toward discouragement.

When the mounted samurai and the second horse burdened with corpses had vanished over the bridge, Priest Bundori came out of the inn to find he was the only one to brave the cold light of day. Even his visit could not cheer the town now.

The green-clad Shintoist scurried bowlegged along the street and came to the establishment of the artisan who repaired musical instruments. The door had been closed only a few moments before, along with the rest of the shops in the village. Bundori found it wasn't locked and opened it without calling for permission. He stood inside the door for a couple of seconds, bowing like a pecking duck, and made a loud greeting. The artisan was in a bad enough mood because of the passing samurai, and was twice-irritated by the priest's uninvited entry. Thus the artisan continued working nimbly and quietly on a certain instrument, as though nobody stood in his door.

Bundori slipped off his sandals and leapt onto the raised part of the floor, oblivious to the artisan's attitude. He burst into a string of queries: "Did a strolling nun by the name of Tomoe Gozen stop by here by any chance? Ah! That's her flute-bag over there! Where did she go from here? I must find her right away! How soon will you have her shakuhachi repaired? I've got to keep her at my shrine for a while before she gets mixed up in any trouble!" He tossed his hands about as he talked, the very epitome of an hysterical fellow. He hovered over the artisan, who sat working busily on the floor. The artisan managed to get a reply in edgewise:

"I can't answer everything at once!"

"You should be working on her shakuhachi right this minute! She has to be on her way before the windstorms start up! What if it snows? She'll be stuck here through the winter! Why are you bothering with that silly koto?"

"This koto belongs to Lord Sato's daughter, who broke it in a fit of unhappiness," said the artisan. "One of her personal guards brought it to me and paid me in advance to repair it.

Even if I had not been paid already, it does no good to put things off where the castle is concerned."

"I've heard about her ladyship's sadness," said Bundori, "so I'll forgive you wasting your time like this. But what about that shakuhachi?"

"The nun hasn't any means of paying me at all, but I agreed to do it somehow when there's time. Did you say her name was Tomoe Gozen? I've heard of her before!"

"Well, she didn't exactly say that was her name, but she said it was all right if I go ahead and think that's who she is. Don't tell anybody! I think she's had some trouble in other provinces and doesn't want people to know which way she goes. I've heard of a Lord Wada, favored by the Shogun, who collects warrior-wives like they were rare swords. He would like to add Tomoe Gozen to his collection, though she might not willingly return to the world from her retirement."

The artisan was interested in this gossip, and, much as the children of the village, he was glad of the warm-hearted glow Priest Bundori brought with him everywhere. The artisan said, "But it could be that she's just an ordinary wandering nun. She has two swords, it's true, but not all retired women warriors were once famous. Why would she come to a backwoods fief like this one if she were Tomoe Gozen?"

"Maybe she doesn't require a reason. Maybe I'm wrong about who she is. But that is not what I'm here to talk to you about. You must fix her shakuhachi in two or three days at the most. Without fail! She wants to make a stone lantern before she is willing to leave this place. If she lets me help her, it won't take more than three days. I've already arranged to have a soft piece of stone delivered to White Beast Shrine, after dark so that Lord Sato's spies won't see the stonecutter make his overdue offering to me. You haven't made an offering to the shrine in a long time either! What will it cost to fix the flute? One zeni? Two?"

"Ordinarily it would cost five!" said the artisan, suddenly indignant, though only half as upset as he acted, since indignation was a better feeling than the gloom he had felt before Priest Bundori had started being typically a nuisance. "I told her she should try to raise at least three!"

"Well, raise your price to ten zeni and I'll write that in my ledger as your contribution to the shrine. Erase your sin!"

"Don't write me in your ledger!" the artisan argued. "What if Lord Sato's spies steal it? Can't give anything to any shrines or temples because it insults the Lotus sect! A sin to disobey one's Lord!"

"I'll write in that you gave one hundred zeni unless the shakuhachi is done in a couple of days!" the Shinto priest threatened. "Where did the nun go when she left here?"

"I didn't ask her!" the blackmailed artisan said testily. "She asked about Lord Sato's castle. Probably she went up there, but nobody will let a vagrant like her inside unless she is a Lotus mendicant. She looked like an esoteric nun to me. Some hair showed under her hat. She doesn't shave her head."

Bundori looked upset. "She shouldn't have gone there. Well, maybe they'll treat her like they do me. Send her away without letting her talk to anyone! I hope she doesn't tell them what she did."

"What did she do?" asked the artisan.

"Nothing."

"You said she did something! If I'm giving you a hundred zeni, I should get something for it! Tell me something else about her! It's interesting!"

"Nothing to tell. She's not even who I said she was, so don't tell anyone about it. Anyway, it's only two zeni, you said so, not worth even as much attention as I've given you already."

"Three zeni!"

"I'll write it in my ledger."

"No need to do that."

"All right, I won't." He jumped off the raised wooden floor into his sandals sitting on the packed ground, and was out the door before the argument could be continued. He scurried up the street again. He did not go so far as the bridge, for the two samurai guards would never let him cross. He stood outside a small saké den in view of the bridge, rocking on his heels, looking agitated. Suddenly he spun about and slapped a hand on the door of the saké den, shouting rudely, "I'm coming in for something to drink!"

The maid who unlocked the door was pretty. She looked around to see if the samurai with the corpses was gone and, seeing the way clear, left the door open and invited Bundori inside. There were a couple of customers within, sitting at rustic tables and benches on a dirt floor. Not a comfortable place at all. The owner had been a friend of Bundori's until Kuro the Darkness started influencing Lord Sato's decrees. The maid was the daughter of Bundori's friend, and she was aware of her father's obedience to the awful decree against donations to temples and shrines. She could see how skinny the priest had gotten since the last time she saw him. Her eyes were sad because of this.

"Old priests shouldn't drink," she said, and smiled at the funny fellow. He brought good feelings with him, even into such a poor little den. "Sit in a nice place and I will make you something good to eat."

"That's all right with me, but bring saké too. The best you have! Not that it will be very good. I'm not paying for anything, mind you. Erase your sin!"

The maid laughed at that, and the sadness vanished from her eyes. She went into a back room to get the priest some noodles. Bundori sat on a splintery bench and the humor that usually marked his face was weakened. He craned his neck so that he could see out the den's entryway, wishing the wandering nun would appear at any minute.

The nun, in charcoal and cream, moved like a specter midst the shadows of the evergreen-shaded lane. When she came around one of the many turns along the way, there stood the overgrown boy she had seen before. He was directly in her path. At close quarters, he was even larger than she had supposed. He held his gardener's shears at his side, but there was nothing threatening about him. The nun bowed respectfully. Quite likely, no one had ever bowed to the big fellow before, and he was inordinately pleased to be treated with courtesy. His grin could not have gotten any larger without touching his ears.

"Are you the gardener's son?" she asked, watching him through the loosely woven window-section of her bamboo hat. "Or are you the son of some low-ranking samurai?" The boy's eyes gleamed, but he did not reply. There was a family crest on his kimono, by which the bikuni deduced his *buké* or warrior-class lineage. He opened his mouth as if to try to say something, but his mouth was full of saliva. He had to wipe his mouth on his sleeve, looking somewhat embarrassed. The bikuni asked, "Can't you speak?"

"Muh. Muh."

The fellow had some deformity of the palate. He was clearly a child in mind, though physically he outmatched most men.

"Whu-*rhens!*" he exclaimed loudly. He used his gardener shears to point down a narrow, little-used path. He said again, practically shouting, "Hur-RENDS!"

"Friends," the bikuni said softly. "Friends of mine?" The fellow became excited because she had understood him. He pointed more exaggeratedly. The bikuni nodded curtly and started to walk the direction indicated by the big, stupid fellow. He ran to get in front of her on the weedy path, leading the way.

They went by a back path to the smallest of samurai estates, the very one she had earlier passed in front of and had thought was better cared for than the rest. The rear gate was locked from within, so the big fellow shouted, "Tah-neh!" and a moment later, "Tah-neh!" in his deep, awkward voice. Already there was someone rushing to unlock the gate.

When the gate opened, the nun saw before her the woman who had been attacked by three men the night before. She looked about nervously, then grabbed the big boy's fat arm and pulled him into the enclosed garden, indicating to the bikuni that she should enter as well.

They went into the house by way of the kitchen door, as though they were servants. The bikuni was used to back entries, as mendicants commonly came by kitchen doors; but the young woman and the retarded boy were of samurai caste. This was their house. The bikuni wondered if their furtiveness in their own house was due to the likelihood that the young woman belonged in the castle serving Lord Sato's daughter, but was a runaway, having returned without permission to her parents' home.

"Tah-neh!" the huge boy exclaimed. The young woman shushed him sternly and made him sit down in the kitchen. She bowed in an embarrassed manner to the nun, then gave the big boy some rice balls and told him to stay in the kitchen to eat them.

The bikuni had left her sandals by the door. She had removed her hat and carried it under her right arm; in the right hand she carried her sheathed longsword, for it was rude to wear any but the short one inside a house. The young woman failed to indicate a place to leave hat and sword. In fact, she had not as yet made any kind of formal greeting or introduction. Rather, once the slow-witted youth was settled down, the young woman indicated by posture that the bikuni should follow her toward another room. The bikuni did so, taking hat and sword along.

Only their toe-socks were between soles of the feet and the cold, hardwood hallway. The two women passed several doors. Then the younger knelt before a certain door and asked permission to enter. No one answered, but she slid the door open, then bowed to one side of it, allowing the bikuni to enter first, stepping foot on the soft tatami matting of the room.

Inside, an old man lay on his deathbed, a thin futon mattress beneath him, another on top of him. To one side of the bed there were three family members with mournful expressions. Nearest the head of the dying man's bed was a man perhaps twenty years younger, but still elderly. Beside him, there was a woman as ancient-looking as the man who was dying, undoubtedly the reposing man's wife. Near the foot of the bed was a young man wearing a peasant's field jacket, and this was most unexpected, except that the bikuni recalled that the young woman had been attacked by samurai who had learned of her involvement with a peasant youth. His mere presence in the samurai house was a punishable crime. Yet it appeared as though the family accepted him, however fugitively, as their son, inviting him even to the deathbed of the family patriarch.

It was clear, too, that it was a small family on the verge of extinction. There were no young sons present. If the foolish fellow in the kitchen was the family heir, then essentially there was no family heir. The aging father appeared to be a widower, for he had no wife nearby. The entire clan might well be embodied by two grandparents (one of them dying), a father, a slow-witted son, a daughter, and an unofficial son-in-law whose blood would not allow the family name to be carried on. No peasant could be adopted into samurai lineage except by the most unusual of circumstances. The family had a cowed look because of all this, as though only recently aware of the extent of personal, and clan, mortality.

The bikuni had an uneasy feeling, for she began to suspect why they had brought her here in quiet. When the grandmother, father, and peasant youth saw the bikuni enter, they bowed with faces to the floor, although they did not owe a bikuni such obeisance. When the old, old woman's face looked up at last, her eyes were wet and shiny, and her creased expression was one of gratitude, but the bikuni had done nothing to merit such a look.

The man at the head of the patriarch's deathbed, soon to be the family's patriarch himself, was immeasurably sad as well. He looked as though the weight of the world were upon his shoulders. He said to the bikuni,

"I am Kahei Todawa, a low-ranking samurai in the service of Lord Ikida Sato, presently under house arrest for misspeaking myself as regards the Lotus Sutra. It is the measure of Lord Sato's goodness that I was not executed. Please forgive the shyness of our invitation. It is not really that we are ashamed to invite you here. We had very little time to prepare, having only seen you pass the other way a short time ago, and realizing you would be turned away and would pass our house on your return."

"Please don't feel embarrassed for my sake," said the bikuni, settling on her knees near the foot of the deathbed, setting her sword and bamboo hat at her side. "I am aware that Lord Sato has decreed only the holy men and women of the Lotus sect may be invited into any house."

"I am chagrined to go against my Lord's wishes," said Kahei Todawa. "But it is an odd thing that Lotus mendicants have not heard of Lord Sato's favor. They have not rushed to this fief at all. Only a priest named Kuro the Darkness represents that order, so that my Lord's decree means, in essence, that there are no priests to whom anyone might turn legally, save Kuro alone. Due to my comments regarding this very observation, Lord Sato placed me under house arrest, although at least I can still wander to the edge of my small estate, and my doors have not been barred with bamboo crosses. Again I ask you to see in this the goodness of my Lord's true heart. All the same, I find it difficult to be entirely obedient in this particular instance, when my father is dying and in need of a small service.

"My daughter, Otane, informed me previously of your effort in her behalf, only last night. It was my decision, on seeing you pass my estate while I was pruning trees, to quietly invite you here. A brave and martial nun might not fear Kuro the Darkness, and would be willing to recite the sutras of Amida Buddha before my father breathes his last."

The dying old man's eyes opened for the first time since

the bikuni entered the room. He turned his head weakly, looking straight at the nun. She could not look away. A withered, spidery hand slipped out from under the quilt, clinging to a Buddhist rosary, shaking with palsy.

The bikuni was extraordinarily ill at ease. She scooted away from the foot of the dying man's bed, bowed with forehead to floor, and whispered, "Forgive me, but I have never learned Buddhist sutras of any sort. I am a Shintoist at heart." When she raised her head from the floor, the old, old woman was looking at the straw matting at her own knees, her face blandly unreadable, devoid of its former and premature gratitude. Otane, who was sitting on her knees just inside the door as though she were still only a servant in the castle, finally spoke.

"Surely you know a few! How can you walk about the country as a nun and never learn the sutras?"

The bikuni's eyes were again caught by those of the dying old man. It was impossible to turn her face away from his. Still, she was able to answer Otane's harsh query.

"Buddhist doctrine is as the leaves of a tree, but Shinto is the tree itself." Her voice was small when she added, "Think of me as a poor, dry autumn leaf."

Otane was indignant and angry, perhaps embarrassed as well, if she had been the one to suggest to her father that the martial nun be brought in the first place. "A bikuni can't think like that!" she exclaimed.

"It is the essence of esotericism," said the bikuni, "that we think as we please."

"It's too much!" scolded Otane, but Kahei Todawa shushed his daughter, and the room became deathly still. Deathly. After a long, cold, lonely silence, the dry lips of the dying man began a pitiful recital in his own behalf: *"Namu Amida Butsu . . . Namu Amida . . . Butsu . . . Namu . . ."*

The nun could not remain composed in the face of this wretched encounter. She bowed again, this time to the dying man in particular. Though it was unlike her, she made an excuse for herself: "It has been my way to play my shakuhachi for the sick at heart or the dying. This has been my excuse for never learning the sutras. But my shakuhachi has been damaged and waits this very moment to be repaired in the village. Please live two or three more days and I will come back to do my best for you!"

With so much pain in her gut she felt as though she had

committed seppuku, the bikuni grabbed hat and sword and hurried out of the room. Otane bowed to her grandmother, father, and dying grandfather, and she left as well. The unobtrusive peasant youth followed after Otane.

For the majority of her life, the bikuni had been a samurai. Among samurai it was generally felt that there was nothing so terrible as retirement from worldly life. Honorable, valorous death was vastly preferred to lost privilege, glory, and class standing. Yet the bikuni had taken the tonsure voluntarily. She had not regretted it until this day. Only now did it seem she had given up less of the world than previously believed. She had lost status while retaining responsibility; given up glory though deeds were still required. It had always been easy for her to face her own death as a samurai. But it was terrifying to be asked, as Buddha's woman, to ease another's dying.

She went as far as the kitchen, trying to erase from her mind the image of the dying man and his watchful mourners. In the kitchen, she saw the huge boy with bits of sticky rice all around his mouth. A grin widened in his pudgy face. The bikuni stood over him, looking at him strangely. Otane came up behind her, the handsome farmboy in tow. Otane said softly,

"Let me feed you before you go."

The nun sat by the firepit and held her hands above the coals, trying to look at none but the foolish boy, whose innocent spirit was a healing thing, untouched as he was by remorse or sorrow. This boy and the priest called Paddy-Bird were the only two individuals she had seen in the whole mountainous fief, aside from small children, capable of smiling.

"Tah-neh!" the huge fellow exclaimed, seeing she was after food again. Otane shushed him with a not-too-harsh look, and for a moment he didn't smile.

The farmboy sat down near the nun, warming himself by the kitchen firepit as well. The nun didn't look at him, but noted his appearance from the corner of her eye. There was no denying his beauty. His lips were full and small, his chin round, his eyebrows long and thin. It was a wonder no one in the castle had noticed him among the fields, and made him a minor page at least, for he was prettier than those pampered youths. Yet there was something disrespectful in the manner of his expression, something perhaps not attractive to many, suggesting as it did a dislike for authority.

"Iyo there is Otane's brother," said the farmboy. "He has a lot of trouble understanding things and being understood, though he's good for a few sorts of errands and chores. He doesn't know his grandfather is dying, though it's been explained to him once or twice. You're a stupid fellow, isn't it so, Iyo?"

Iyo realized this last was addressed to him, but didn't know that he had been disparaged. He grinned hugely as always, and exclaimed, "Shin Ji! Tah-neh's Shin Ji!"

The farmboy laughed, yet there was a joyless edge to it. "That's right, Iyo," he said. "I'm Otane's Shinji, not Shinji's Shinji."

The nun had been near the verge of disliking the youth, if for no other reason than his easy mistreatment of Iyo. But she quickly detected Shinji's self-deprecation. She realized he did not hold himself in as much esteem as he would like to project. For all his physical beauty, Shinji yet seemed to think of Iyo as a kind of mirror. When he teased Iyo about things, it reflected on himself. Certainly Iyo absorbed none of it and felt no injury.

Otane was hurt by it, though. She cringed at Shinji's last remark, but hid her mortification as she went silently about her task of preparing fresh rice balls for the nun. Shinji continued talking boldly to the bikuni.

"Though Iyo isn't very smart, he is nonetheless of the buké class. Even a fellow like him is more important than a farmer's son. Otane's parents condescend to treat me like a son at times, and I remind myself to be humble and appreciative. But they are lost in their sadness and have forgotten that I am here. They never think I might have feelings as real as their own, that I might share their sorrow, or comfort them, given half a chance. Samurai are good at not noticing peasants, don't you think? Just like crickets on a path. Who sees if one is underfoot?"

Otane moved about the kitchen in speechless trepidation. Was Shinji so blind? Didn't he see that she was affected by his tongue? Such a good-looking fellow should learn to notice the feelings of others, or his beauty didn't mean a thing. That's what the nun was thinking. But she didn't say a thing.

"Even if you keep a cricket in a little cage," he said, "and feed it and write a poem about how nice the cricket is . . . if it gets loose, or if it dies, pretty easy to replace it with another one. Hard to tell the difference."

Otane dropped the rice spatula. Surely Shinji noticed, but hardly skipped a beat in the rhythm of his lecture.

"Despite this, Otane and I have decided we will live together someplace. Isn't it funny? A samurai and a cricket. Maybe just a worm! Feel free to laugh at us." Shinji's eyes glinted as though to convey the jesting nature of his words, yet the words were far too harsh to be accepted as humor. Otane was visibly shaken, but had no doubt heard it all before, and offered no criticism of anything her illicit lover said.

The bikuni turned her face from Iyo's to the farmboy's and looked at him without the least emotion. Her thoughts were many, but she would not let him know her feelings about his callousness and insecurity. He'd been respectfully silent at the deathbed of the patriarch, and was doubtless grateful that they had not shut him out altogether. Yet he was simultaneously bitter about many things. He had not been raised like a samurai and could not hold back his feelings for long periods of time. As he was more comfortable in the kitchen, as opposed to the private rooms of samurai, Shinji felt at ease to speak his mind, especially as he was only talking to a mendicant.

He matched the nun's gaze, but as she did not reply to his frank speech, the humor in his eyes began to fade. He looked away from her, uncomfortable or ashamed. As he wished her opinion, the bikuni searched for some honest response, and said,

"Surely Lord Sato's daughter has noticed that Otane did not return to her duties as lady-in-waiting. Someone will come to this house looking for her. A lot of trouble if it seems a peasant is living with a samurai family as though he were a son-in-law. Her family risks a lot in your favor."

The farmboy was unmoved by this. He met her gaze again, then leaned her direction to share a secret. "If Otane's grandfather had not gotten so ill unexpectedly, we would already have run away together! When Otane told her father about your helping her, we all agreed you must have been a famous samurai before you were a nun. We thought you'd be brave enough to give a dying fellow a nice service despite Lord Sato's decree favoring Priest Kuro exclusively. So Otane and I delayed our plans a while. Well, how could we know you lacked knowledge of the sutras? If you hadn't left the room so fast, I'm sure Mr. Todawa would have apologized for bothering you. I know Otane is embarrassed to have put you in such a spot. But there is another matter Otane and I talked about privately, another reason for hoping to talk to you."

Otane brought a tray of fresh rice balls and some hot tea to the bikuni and placed these at her side. She slapped Iyo's greedy hand, then produced some walnuts from her sleeve for him. These kept him busy, albeit noisily, cracking and eating the nuts. Otane was tense, but let her beloved farmboy handle the matter he had brought up.

"It's like this," said Shinji. "When Lord Sato finds out you killed three of his retainers, he'll send more than three to punish you. The corpses may already have been found. It's best you run away with Otane and me! After Otane has made enough prayers for the sake of her grandfather's spirit, we intend to sneak across the river gorge. I have a pass to do so, since my family farms across the bridge and we must always bring a certain percentage of our crops to the castle. Otane has secretly taken her grandfather's pass, since he will not require it. I altered it a bit so that she can use it to cross over the rope bridge with me."

Their plan was a terrible thing. They could be crucified just for running away in the first place. Altering a fief pass was also a punishable crime.

"As a mendicant," said Shinji, "you can come and go as you please, more or less. The three of us could meet at the rope bridge and not have any trouble. If the single guard stationed there suspects something, we can give him some money. Most of the samurai serving Lord Sato these days are corrupt and easy to bribe."

"Many illicit lovers try what you suggest," said the bikuni. "Most of them are captured by and by. Do you know you could be crucified? I don't think you've exhausted other avenues as yet. A special petition could be set before Lord Sato, who might make an exception for your case."

"You haven't been here long enough to know how things are!" exclaimed Shinji. "In other places, such special dispensation can sometimes be acquired. Otane's father is very low-ranking for a samurai. In fact, before he was placed under house arrest, his main duty was caring for Lord Sato's plum trees. Practically a farmer himself! Otane and I would have a good case with any other lord, but Sato has no concern for people's happiness. We know exactly what he would say. 'Recite the Lotus Sutra until you have gotten over your desire for one another.' If we argued, he might have us killed, our corpses buried in Priest Kuro's horrible cemetery at the Temple of the Gorge, where already several of Kuro's victims now repose. Nobody petitions Lord Sato for anything anymore, nor complains about the way he governs things—or fails to govern. If there are no complaints, things aren't too bad. Otherwise, Priest Kuro whispers in Lord Sato's ear, and the advice is no fun for anybody."

The bikuni was beginning to have very strong doubts about the dark priest's motivations. She said, "A priest should not be so drunk with power. I would like to know more about this Kuro."

"Better not to deal with him at all!" said Shinji. "Accompany us away from Kanno province, *neh?* It's selfish to want you to help us, but it's for your sake too."

"A bikuni travels alone," she said. "I will go my way after I have carved a stone lantern for the men I was forced to kill."

"Someone will have to carve one for you!" said the farmboy. When she did not comment, his face became clouded with anger. He said, "Are you too proud to keep us company? An ex-samurai like you can't be concerned with lovers intent on breaking the law!"

She studied his expression a long moment before speaking. "You dislike samurai a lot," she said. "But you want to marry one."

Otane knelt at Shinji's side and pulled on his sleeve, keeping him from saying something angrier than he already said. She whispered, "I told you she was too severe. She won't help us. We must run away without her."

"Tah-neh!" exclaimed Iyo, having run out of noisy walnuts.

"Shut up!" the farmboy scolded, making Iyo stop grinning, making him upset. Otane went nurturantly to the big fellow and soothed his hurt feelings. The bikuni didn't like to see a samurai daughter jerked back and forth like that, meeting the needs of others and never really stating her own feelings. Perhaps it was true, though, that all she required was the presence of the handsome, if somewhat rude, Shinji.

"If your plan is to succeed," said the bikuni, "you must be calmer in your hearts. Fear makes people angry. Anger makes people careless."

Shinji folded his arms and turned his back on the bikuni and the firepit. Otane's large, hurt eyes watched the bikuni' profile. She said, "I've caused him a lot of responsibility." Her tone was apologetic. When she said this, Shinji turned back to face his lover, and his anger had dissipated. He looked miserable and forlorn. He virtually leapt in Otane's direction, to fall beside her and cling to her sleeve, weeping like a child. Bowing his head, he wailed, "It's I who have caused you the trouble!"

They were pitiful to see. The bikuni began to tie her hat upon her head, indicating her intention to leave, but also to hide her face lest they notice her reluctant concern. She stood, saying, "Is Lord Sato as heartless as you say? Villagers seem to dislike him, but I saw no particular evidence of cruelty. If his men catch runaways, however, he is justified in applying the law, though laws are often cruel."

"Really it isn't Lord Sato so much as that dark priest," said Otane, extricating herself from the clinging Shinji and hurrying to the doorway to place the bikuni's sandals where she could step into them. "Since Kuro came, there have been numerous bad omens, poor crops, illness, deaths, and Lord Sato's retainers have become unruly. In past years when things were bad, taxes were reduced, but this year they were raised a little bit. It's not that things have become untenable, but happiness has been erased from the land. It's much worse in the castle than in the village. But a shadow cannot fall upon the lord of a country without the country feeling it as well."

The bikuni placed her longsword through her obi and stepped out into the back garden. Otane hurried on ahead to get the rear gate. The bikuni stood beneath the gate's roof while the young woman held the gate open. The nun asked, "I did not want to pester you with my own problem while your family could overhear. But as you were a lady-in-waiting for Lord Sato's daughter, perhaps you can help me with something I need to know, even though I have been no help to you."

Otane's eyes conveyed her willingness to help.

"I came here looking for a man of Omi in the service of Lord Sato, but was informed that no such man is in the castle. I can well believe the one I seek would not work for Lord Sato if it could be helped, since things are as they are. But I think there is more to it, or the men I talked to would not have been so upset about my query."

Otane, too, appeared upset by the query, but she took a deep breath to calm her feelings, and spoke confidentially.

"Ordinarily a lady-in-waiting knows little about what men of the castle do. But the man you speak of was Lady Echiko's betrothed, destined to become Lord Sato's son-in-law!"

The nun replied, "I'm surprised," though there was no hint of shock in her tone.

"He was Lord Sato's favorite retainer and achieved a high rank among castle men. Though his clan had declined in his native province, still he had a good family tree and might well have been a minor Lord himself, had he been a more ruthless fellow. Lord Sato was glad that his daughter noticed this man above others. We ladies-in-waiting conspired to help Lady Echiko have secret meetings with him from time to time. All of this was when it was still nice to live in the castle, before Priest Kuro possessed our Lord's heart.

"I don't know exactly what happened, but some while later, Lord Sato announced that Heinosuke, my Lady's betrothed, was to be exiled for some petty reason. Everyone knew it was on the advice of his Lordship's new cleric, who certainly did seem to dislike Heinosuke and some other good men.

"On the same night as the proclamation of exile, someone made an attempt on Priest Kuro's life. A week or so later it was finally announced officially that young Heinosuke had gone wild and made a foiled attempt on the priest, then ran off. We ladies-in-waiting knew it wasn't exactly like that, for Heinosuke had come to Lady Echiko the very night of the assassination attempt."

"Do you know if he really tried to kill Priest Kuro?" asked the nun.

"He did!" said Otane in a harsh whisper, her eyes large when she confessed her knowledge. "I remember Lady Echiko was playing her koto, when suddenly a string snapped—a bad omen! She had been singing a sad song because of the news of her betrothed's pending exile. It was a cold, cloudless night and all the doors were shuttered. Yet there was a cold wind from somewhere, which ran through Lady Echiko's chamber. We ladies-in-waiting looked around to see what door had been opened. The oil lantern suddenly went out, as though Fukkeshi-baba the fire-extinguishing hag had slipped in and blown it out. We were as frightened as little children by then, until we were relieved to hear Heinosuke's voice in the darkness.

"'Please don't light that,' Heinosuke said as I was about to fix the lamp. So we sat in the dark and could not help but hear what he said to our Lady. 'I have failed to kill that fellow and he has had his revenge on me for trying. Now there is no help for me. I will escape tonight, Echiko, and you must forget me.' Our Lady was most upset, as you can imagine. She moved her koto to one side—I heard it slide across the tatami mat— then scooted toward the place in the darkness where Heino-suke's voice could be heard.

"He avoided her and said harshly that she should not come near him. She would not listen, so Heinosuke drew his sword! We heard it slide from the scabbard and we held our breaths. Echiko stopped where she was, shocked beyond belief that her beloved could threaten her! 'Believe it!' said Heinosuke, his voice devoid of its usual gentleness. 'There is nothing between us anymore!' I thought I heard a catch in his voice; and Echiko must have known he was lying about it, too, since she knew him better than anyone. 'I only came to say goodbye,' said Heinosuke, then opened the sliding door to Lady Echiko's garden.

"Lady Echiko ran out into the moonlight to stop him, but something startled her, and she cried out and fainted. We brought her in and put her to bed, fussing over her because she was delirious. Her betrothed never returned and our Lady remained inconsolable. She took ill and only rarely left her bed in the months that followed. There is a rumor that Heinosuke is still somewhere plotting revenge, but surely there is nothing to it, or he would get word to Echiko so that she doesn't pine to death.

"Only two nights later, she had a horrible nightmare and could not be restrained from getting up at the Hour of the Ox, wandering madly around her chamber. She ended up smashing her koto, which reminded her of her last unhappy meeting with Heinosuke. I sympathized, thinking how I would feel if Shinji vanished from my life! The next morning, she had no memory of damaging her koto, and was distraught that she could not play it. She has been irrational like that for a long time now.

"When I left her side yesterday, seeking relief in a secret tryst with Shinji, I could hardly believe Lady Echiko's ap-pearance. She has become like a skeleton of herself, a shadow of the beauty that was. The horrifying part is that Lord Sato has shown a lot of concern, sending Priest Kuro every night to chant the Lotus Sutra for her. It's been too much! I don't care if Shinji and I are caught and crucified. I won't return to the castle."

The bikuni mused. "A strange, sad story," she said, then turned away from Otane as though to leave without further word. But she stood in the gate a while longer. When her voice issued again from beneath her hat, she said, "If you and Shinji must try to find a better place, I suggest you go in the direction of Shigeno Valley. It's a long journey for you, but the lord of that valley is a woman named Toshima. You may have heard of her, since women rarely rule a fief alone, and it has made her famous. Under her protection, you can work hard as farmers in her valley. Tell her a strolling nun with two swords said so on her honor! If you are caught before you reach there, you'll be brought back here and killed."

The nun stepped out onto the path leading to the main road. Otane bowed behind the departing nun, then closed the gate, a barely audible "Thank you" reaching the bikuni's ears. As the nun made her way back to the road and started toward the village, she could not unburden herself of thoughts about Otane. "How sad she is," the nun said to herself. "I hope people help her and her lover along their way."

Under the protection of a thatched lean-to that had been propped up by Priest Bundori for the nun's sake, a stone lantern was slowly taking shape. The nun worked diligently, oblivious to the chill, heavy rain outside her tiny cover. The priest had loaned her mallet and chisel, and gotten her started with numerous verbal instructions, for she had not made such a lantern previously. "You must bore the horizontal holes first, while the stone is strongest," he'd advised. "Then shape the outside of the lantern. The top is made separately. Don't worry if it stands straight or not; the ground where you put it won't be flat in any case."

Most of the time she was left alone to this labor, though often she could see Priest Bundori working about the shrine compound and grounds. He wore a coat made of grass, which caused him to look like a spiny animal, and a wide hat, these protecting him from the elements. With a long rake, he swept leaves from the surfaces of ponds, and unclogged the various miniature cataracts and tops of tiny waterfalls. Some of the streams were already swollen to their limit and parts of the gardens would surely become flooded, even with Bundori's best efforts to keep the water flowing smoothly.

The leaves he removed from waterways became mulch and compost in other areas of the grounds. Leaves collected in dry weather had been placed in sheds to use as fodder and fuel, but this wet stuff would be saved for next year's gardening.

When the rain became heavier still, Bundori vanished into one of the buildings for a while, performing what chores the nun could not tell. It was comforting to see the fellow scurrying about, but sometimes the nun felt she should be helping him rather than chipping at her stone creation. But Bundori had been most insistent that she adhere to her own labor.

She whacked hammer against chisel against stone. It shook the length of her arm and caused wrists especially to ache. She set the tools aside a bit, reaching inside her pocket-sleeve to withdraw a thin, stoppered bamboo tube. She removed the plug and stuck a finger in the opening of the tube, taking out a helping of salve. It was the medicine Bundori had mixed for her, smelling of knotweed and shepherd's purse and clove. She rubbed it on the backs of her swollen hands and around her wrists. It created a warm sensation and did indeed ease the ache.

Later in the afternoon, rain still falling in sheets, Bundori brought a meal to her from the main shrine-house. She ceased chipping at stone, greeted the priest, and accepted the bowl of coarse millet and some kind of stringy, tough root he had dug up from somewhere. He had brought a bowl for himself, generously keeping her company rather than eating in the comfort of his home. The stuff he was forced to eat out of poverty was not especially tasty, but both Bundori and the nun were grateful for what there was.

"I don't blame your pushing me to get this work done quickly," said the nun, it not evading her notice that twice the priest had fed her outside so that she would have minimal excuse to interrupt her task. "If I stay too long, I'll eat you out of home."

This was not Bundori's reasoning at all, and he was chagrined to be misunderstood. "If you don't mind the poverty of our meals, it is no bother to me that you eat a lot," he said. "But it is true I am trying to be particularly helpful so that you can finish your lantern in a hurry." He gazed out from under the lean-to, beneath which he crouched alongside the nun. He held the bowl of food in one hand, chopsticks in the other. The sky was dark and foreboding, promising worse rain than what presently fell. "Hard to say when the first high winds will start. Harder still for you to travel if they start up soon! Please don't misunderstand me; I would be glad to have you stay the rest of autumn and the whole of winter. But it would be a long time for you. I think you'd rather continue your thousand-shrine journey. Life is short, after all. Not enough time for you to finish your atonement if you dawdle here and there."

"You think I travel to atone for something?" asked the feasting nun.

"Isn't it so?" he asked. There was not the least antipathy in his remarks, but he sounded pretty sure of himself. "You killed a lot of people in the past, is that right? Now you're sorry for it. That's why you walk about Naipon the Anchored Empire, too modest even to tell your name to anyone."

"Maybe it's true I'm sorry about some things I've done," the nun allowed. "But I'm not sure I am. You think me humble to live this life, but it may well be that I've become addicted to freedom. Once I was a retainer to a certain lord, then I was wife of another, and always I pursued my duty with utmost vigor, except once or twice when I strayed for the sake of adventure. On reflection, I realize that when I did not stray, it was because duty itself led to adventure. I never did like the ropes which bound me, even the ropes of samurai fame and duty and face and honor. Now I have given up family, masters, even my own name. To whom am I answerable except my inner self? It is supposed to be a tragedy for a samurai to fall as I have fallen, to 'leave the world' as a nameless wanderer. I haven't yet experienced the fullness of the tragedy. If I atone for something, I do it badly. Life interests me too much."

Bundori had a capped bamboo container full of tea, and two matching cups. He poured a little for the bikuni. Then she took the container and poured for him. The brew warmed their insides. "The tea is a herbal remedy," he remarked, smacking his old lips. "It will help your fingers and my knees!" He poured a little more for her. He pondered the things the woman had said to him, then added his own thoughts: "I traveled around a bit myself, when I was young. I suppose I was not doing any particular atonement either. I was looking for someplace better than dear old Seki. Now I've a nostalgia for the place I felt critical about in youth!"

"We're all looking for a better place," the bikuni mused. "Even those of us who don't go anywhere."

"That must be true! Therefore I may not have given up, even though I haven't traveled in so long. I'm still looking!"

"Looking for Seki you left behind?" she asked wistfully. "As I, perhaps, seek my native Heida, as though it could exist the way it existed for a child."

"Seki has grown better in my memory, no doubt. Have your travels taken you there as yet?"

"I was in Seki when very young, visiting a warrior's shrine with my father and younger brother. The shrine faced the sea and was on a windy hillside. That's all I can remember. I was pretty small, but I did learn something important while there."

"It's so?"

"Yes. Until I went to Seki, the first place I can remember visiting, I had always thought the moon shone only in Heida. I was surprised to see the moon favored Seki as well!"

"The moon favors it very well!" said Bundori, misty-eyed. "The thought of it makes me want to make a poem." He started to recite something on the spur of the moment, putting it to a rough tune:

"What a splendid place, Seki!
I should go back there someday
Stand upon the hill and smell the sea
Oh, but it's far, and I am old
ha ha! What a splendid place, right here!"

He laughed at himself, a crooked-mouthed and clownish laugh, but his brow knit upward in a sad way. It was hard to say if he was happy or sad. It seemed he was both. He said, "You should go see it for me! See if it isn't even nicer than you recall! Think about me when you go there. That way, Seki will be in my dreams."

"I will do it," said the nun. "I'll play my flute before the very shrine my father took me to when I was little. I will play for the warrior buried there, and for the memory of my father and younger brother."

"Your brother is dead too? Must have been he died of war!"

"Yes, he died of war. He died bravely." Her expression was

vacant for a moment, her mind wandering off into memories of the men in her family. Then she said, "My father died of a mean horse, though. He had a long life."

"I'm glad," said Bundori.

Bundori's white stag came into the gardens from a wooded area. The beast drank from a cold, shallow pool, then raised his red eyes to look straight at the two people sitting under the lean-to. He seemed amused by them, but who can say what a stag may think? The rain ran off his pale fur in rivulets. He had already grown his winter coat and didn't mind the chill of autumn.

"As you were a traveler before," the nun asked, "what convinced you to settle down at last, in such a place as this? I can't imagine giving up the freedom!"

"Ideas change as one grows older," said Bundori. "Especially with bad knees like mine, which always did make wandering a nuisance. Maybe I had a reason for staying at this particular shrine; maybe it was an accident. I came here as you did, by chance, many years ago, not intending to stay long. Twenty years have passed. Maybe more! I've lost track. There were five old men living here at the time, and the gardens were nicer than nowadays, there being more hands to take care of things. They had lived at this shrine since they were young men, more than sixty cold winters! I was appalled by the very notion. I told them stories about my travels. I was rude enough to suggest they had wasted their own lives by staying put like they did. They didn't mind my saying so. After a few days, they decided to go on a pilgrimage together. That's how much my stories impressed them. I promised to take care of the gardens and the compound for them while they were away. But even then, watching them hobble down the mountainside, holding onto one another's sleeves, going in search of they knew not what, I didn't think they'd live long enough to come back. I hope they had at least one good adventure before they died!"

"So you've been here ever since," said the bikuni.

"I was glad to trade my way of living for theirs. I've not regretted it a moment, even lately when things are not so easy."

"You never miss adventure?" she asked.

"In my case, I was not after adventure in particular, unless I've forgotten. I was only searching, as I said. You said we all search, even if we don't travel. I must have started searching long before I left home. I searched for joy in a world filled with cruelty and stupidity. At first I thought I could be happy if only I could count on a few friends. But friends can be contentious, so I thought ideal friendship could be found in the classics, and I read a lot. But old books are often hard to comprehend, so I decided anthologies of poetry were best, for anyone can understand the poems in any manner they decide to understand them. Yet poems prey upon emotion, so it struck me that a rural life would be more conducive to restful joy. Thinking so, I set out in search of a restful place, but never could stay anywhere too long. Little towns were dull. People were no different than in bigger places. For a long time I believed music and dance were the only things to ease the heart. As I traveled from place to place and festival to festival, I listened to the folksongs and watched the regional dances. I even wrote a treatise about it, though I've no idea what became of the manuscript. Songs and dances were nice to see, but in the long run it was only my special interest, and not the road to joy. I had lived this fickle life for many years when I stumbled on this shrine. When those five old men left me here by myself, I soon realized that seclusion in a mountain shrine, attending to the Thousands of Myriads, cleanses the impure heart and makes us whole. Nothing else can do it. This is the only thing. Before I die, I expect to find a wild retreat higher in the mountains, and that shall be the most complete seclusion, the final ecstasy of my life!"

The bikuni could not suppress a smile, for Bundori had as much as confessed that his fickle nature had not really changed, that he still felt there was something better in the next field, or higher on the mountain.

For a while, the Shinto priest and esoteric nun were silent together, warm cups in their hands, staring out at nothing, their hot breaths little clouds before their faces. It was a peaceful comraderie. Far, far away there was a flash of lightning, so far away it made no sound for a long time; and when the sound rolled up the mountain at last, it was muted, like the weary sigh of gods. The sun could barely penetrate the clouds. The world was diffuse and dreamlike. Despite the rain, the edgeless quality of everything was pleasant.

After a few moments of listening to the rain upon the small thatched lean-to, the nun asked carefully, "Tell me about the Lotus priest who instructs Lord Sato."

The question stilled Bundori's breath. The nun saw that she would have to encourage him better.

"You have managed never to mention him to me yourself. But yesterday in the village, and at a place I visited among the samurai estates, it became clear to me that Priest Kuro is uppermost in everybody's mind. His influence seems not to be a good thing, although to tell the truth, I've seen fiefs in worse condition than this one, even without untoward clerical influence. It makes me wonder about the real purpose of Kuro's machinations."

"He's a monstrous fellow," Bundori whispered. "He hasn't done much for a while, but when he first appeared at the castle last autumn, several priests of the area took ill and died. The rest left shortly after Lord Sato's terrible decree against worshipping Amida or Kwannon or the Shinto gods, or anything but the Lotus Sutra, as though the sutra were itself a god. Now there is only Kuro the Darkness—and me. His influence cannot reach me directly, because the Thousands of Myriads of Shinto deities protect me from Buddhist demons and magic. Also I have the white buck. He's a good luck charm, as are my white birds, fish, turtle, and a family of voles who have already hibernated so you haven't seen them. I fear, though, that someone will defile my shrine by some physical act, if Kuro cannot reach it with his spells. If someone had the nerve to pee or spill blood or throw some dead things on these grounds, then evil spirits would be able to take control of the fouled spots. I am prepared at any moment to fight Buddhist monsters with Shinto counter-spells. But I'm an old man, to tell the truth. I don't look forward to what Kuro might do."

"Has he done anything to you so far?"

"Not much. Several samurai came once and tried to claim my white buck, so that Lord Sato could hunt it to the ground. I think Kuro sent them, but Kuro does everything through Lord Sato and cannot insist too much. I couldn't have stopped them from taking my buck if they'd been more resolved. When they tried to catch him, they realized how difficult it would be. He's only gentle when he wants to be, and his antlers are sharp. So the samurai went higher in the mountains and caught an ordinary deer for Sato's hunt. When the weather changed recently, numerous deer started for low ground, passing through local places. Sato's retainers have caught several of these for Lord Sato's purposes. Kuro hasn't had an excuse to worry me about my buck since then. As I don't interfere with anything, Kuro has overlooked me for a while. But it's only a matter of time."

"Why would the stag be important to Kuro?"

"Well, he's a big fellow, and even the smallest of white beasts constitute Shinto charms and magicks of the highest order. Probably I would have to leave here if not for the buck, or risk the sickness that took care of Kuro's rivals."

"It's interesting," said the nun. "If he's a sorcerer, as you say, why does he fear priests?"

"Not a sorcerer," said Bundori. "He's a monster. A devil out of Buddhist Hell. I have no proof of it, but I think I'm right. He seems immune to the Lotus Sutra for some reason, so it's the only one he will allow. He acts ambitious, and pretends to be devoted to the Lotus Sutra, but these things will prove to be a ruse in the long run. Ambition disguises an even more unholy purpose, though I don't know what the purpose might be. Why else has he slowly rid Lord Sato's fief of the holy men who might exorcise a devil in a confrontation? Kuro will worry about you for the same reason he didn't like the priests. He can't risk his plan by ignoring someone strong enough to fight a devil."

"You assume he has some plan," said the nun. "But would a devil need one?"

"This one does," he answered. "Or else he would already have wrought random havoc. He has something in mind and is careful about his moves. He awaits the proper moment, and has been patient. I'm sure of it, though don't ask me to be specific, for it is only how I feel."

"Do you plan to stop him if you can?"

"No. I don't," said Bundori, without the least hesitation in his reply. "I'll defend my shrine, that's all. Does it mean I'm a coward? What happens happens. The most I can do is keep White Beast Shrine a haven for the villagers and farmers in the event of something awful coming to pass. All I need to do is keep blood and urine and rotting flesh away from here, and this place will be a fortress against whatever Kuro the Darkness might conjure."

The nun picked up her borrowed tools and made as though to start on her lantern again. But she stopped a moment and looked at the priest who was sitting on his haunches looking out at the rain. She said, "As a matter of fact, I've fought devils before. My sword is a famous one, as I told you, though like myself, it does not boast about its name. It is haunted by its maker, who died for love of swordsmithing and Naipon. A ghost-haunted blade is a good weapon against a monster."

"I was afraid you would say so. That's why I did not want to tell you about Kuro." Bundori mechanically stacked the bowls, cups, and utensils they had used as he continued, "I didn't want to convince you to try something I myself would not attempt by any means. It's also possible that Kuro is a mortal sorcerer after all, in league with devils but otherwise like most men. And as for those Buddhist priests who suddenly died, maybe it was because most of them were already old. I've never set eyes on this Kuro myself, so I assume a lot. Think of everything I say as senile ravings! Nothing worth concern."

"I won't meddle if you insist," said the nun, catching his real point.

It seemed Bundori wanted her to meddle, for he was slow in his response. But his soul-searching did not take long, and he said, "Then I will insist. You must complete your work on the lantern quickly, and not worry about Lord Sato's fief when you are gone."

The nun bowed slightly. Something startled the huge stag. He leapt, landing gracefully in another part of the gardens. The nun returned to the lantern-in-progress. The sound of her hammering and chipping melded with the hard rain and the sound of Bundori's tramping away through puddles.

It was not the hail that awakened her. The pelting on the roof of the shrine-house had been a pleasant music, which became, in her dream, the festival drums of a warm province in the south. When the hail ceased (she had no way of knowing how long it had fallen), the bikuni opened her eyes. The next moment, she had rolled out of her bedding onto the hard floor, crouching in darkness, listening. There was the sound of birds roosting in the rafters. They went *pipa-pipa* as they slept and jostled one another in their nests. Outside, the branches of old cedars whispered *sawa-sawa* in the rising and lowering winds. She heard nothing untoward and did not know what had interrupted her sleep. There had been something, she was certain.

On the other side of a standing screen (painted with white cranes), Priest Bundori slept, breathing lightly, curled into a ball beneath his futon covers. Without a lamp, she could not see him very well, but could tell by his breathing that nothing had bothered his rest. Silently, she put her outer kimono over the one she had been sleeping in, but did not bother with her hakama trousers. She tied her obi hastily, put her shortsword through it, and carried the longsword with her to the door. She slid naked toes into straw sandals and, thrusting longsword through obi alongside the short one, stepped out onto the porch of the shrine-house.

The wind was a cold slap against both cheeks. Everything was white outside, covered by a layer of ice pellets. The sky was overcast, hiding moon and star, but the covering of hail made things visible despite the depth of night. The ponds and miniature lakes had a thin glaze of ice, hardly enough to hold the weight of a pebble, but enough to support the fallen hail. How eerie everything appeared, bumpily whitened!

She stepped away from the shrine-house onto the path. Pellets of ice crunched underfoot. She stopped, listened, for she had recognized the crunching sound as something that had provided a note of discord in her otherwise pleasant dream of the warm south. She looked about for footprints, but nothing marred the fresh layer of hail.

Bundori's stag stood quietly, head bowed, sleeping under the cover of a small, open-fronted barn. Nothing had awakened him. The bikuni could see no sign that he had been wandering anywhere since the hail-fall.

Looking more carefully at the ground for sign of activity or intrusion, she noticed an odd-shaped mark, partly hidden by hail. About half the small balls of ice had been crushed. Those that had fallen afterward made the track uncertain. As near as she could make out, they appeared to be the footfalls of a child, although the stride was too long for a child.

The bikuni followed the track between two outbuildings and away from the shrine compound, through a wild and ungardened section of the grounds, toward the *mizugaki* or rustic Shinto fencing marking the rear edge of the sanctuary. As she went along, she was shocked to see the dimensions of the footprints grow larger with each step, until they were no longer child-sized, but the same size as her own.

There were a few small gates at intervals along the mizugaki. Near one of these she lost the original track amidst several others. It appeared as though more than a half-dozen men had entered by one of the back gates, but been driven back by something or someone.

So attentive had she been regarding the curious footmarks, she had not noticed what was against the tree just beyond the fence. She stood off the edge of the shrine's land, trying to see what direction the footprints led, but could only make out that there had been a scuffle. When she looked up, she was startled, although she conveyed no outward evidence of this surprise. A samurai stood tied to a tree by a length of sacred rope. His own shortsword had been taken from him and used to pin him through the throat. The fellow had died with a terrified expression.

The sacred rope was a specially woven kind kept in Bundori's shrine-house. It had tassled threads hanging from it at intervals. It was a pretty rope, generally reserved for innocuous ceremonies, to mark off places that were especially holy, or to link a pair of trees or a pair of boulders in marriage. It was unsettling to see the rope used inappropriately.

The nun wondered how someone could have taken the rope from the shrine without waking either herself or Bundori.

She looked higher into the tree. A second samurai was hanging by his neck. Another length of sacred rope had been used.

She stood motionless, again attentive for sounds. The wind rose so that it was hard to hear any sign of movement anywhere. Still, she heard something strange, and her whole body was readied for any surprise. Slowly, she moved further from the Shinto fence, away from holy ground.

Only a few steps on, she was able to see the others. There were eight in all, counting the two nearest the fence. She recognized them. They were the bridge guards she had encountered a day-and-a-half before. All of them were tied to the trunks of trees or hung from limbs. Some had been badly cut with their own swords. Three had been pinned through the throat—*after* having been tied with sacred rope.

It seemed likely they had been sent to the shrine for some mischief. Perhaps her queries about the man of Omi had been passed on to Kuro or Lord Sato. The intent might well have been to kill her in the compound, not incidentally despoiling Bundori's shrine. Someone or something had intervened! Judging by the footmarks upon the hail-strewn ground, the scuffle had been swift and heated. There was evidence that struggling

men had been dragged across the ground, caught no doubt in ropes slung from darkness around their necks or shoulders, hauled away to be bound to trees. It must have taken supernatural strength to accomplish!

Again she heard the eerie moan. She was close enough to recognize it as the sound of a man in agony. She found him, the ninth victim. His longsword had been taken away from him and used to pin him through the stomach, a slower death than the strangulation and throat-piercing granted the others. He'd been tied to the tree with a length of the rope wrapped under his arms, so that both hands were free to clutch feebly at the blade stuck deep into the bark at his back.

The bikuni recognized him as the young leader of the bridge guards. Whatever power punished these men so cruelly had been most cruel to the leader. His eyes were closed and he was mumbling the Lotus Sutra. When he heard the crunch of ice, he opened frightened eyes and grew still. He seemed relieved to see it was only a woman with shoulder-length hair. He wouldn't recognize her, as she had worn the hat when they met before, but he would be able to guess who she was. She introduced herself nonetheless,

"I am the one who came to your bridge not long ago. Did you come to cause Bundori trouble?"

The fellow turned his head from side to side in negative reply.

"Then you came to kill me, which is trouble for Bundori anyway. Who stopped you? Trussed up and stuck like a pig . . . even a villain deserves better. Tell me and I'll avenge you!"

The fellow mumbled. His lips and chin were bloody. He made a coughing, spasmodic sound, which caused more blood to gush forth. His feet slipped at the icy base of the tree, causing his sword to cut upward to the base of his diaphragm. Still, he wouldn't die. He reached out his free hands and the bikuni did not evade his grasp. His left hand caught the shoulder of her kimono and drew her near. He said, "Seek . . . the man . . . of Omi."

The bikuni drew a breath, regretting her promise immediately.

"Heinosuke, who I knew as Yabushi!" she exclaimed. "Do you name him out of obedience to your master? Or is he really the one who did this awful thing to you!"

The wounded man grinned, his bloody mouth an ugly, gaping hole.

"Kill . . . the man . . . of Ohhh . . . mi."

She grabbed the wrist where he clutched her kimono and pulled him loose of her, but kept her grip on him. She looked him in his wild eyes and said, "I promised you revenge, so I must be sure! How could he have such strength against you?"

The dying man's lips twisted in greater, horrifying glee. He would not be more specific with her. He gave her the name of a place: "Temple . . . of . . . the Gorge."

Then he was dead, that look of ironic glee and victory frozen upon his face.

She wondered if a dying man would lie. If he served a master who demanded it, a samurai might tell mistruths even on his dying breath, all for sake of fealty, which was foremost in the mind of any good retainer. Yet Sato's men weren't famous for their devotion to him. Everyone agreed his men were more obedient to Priest Kuro. By all that she had heard, it did not seem likely that Kuro was the sort to inspire fealty in men faithless to their actual lord. Perhaps a glamor was on Sato's men after all, encouraging them to do and say things that served Kuro's secret purpose.

She had barely heart enough to work on the lantern that next morning. She quit after a while, setting aside the tools that helped her shape the stone. She busied herself helping Bundori gather the tree limbs that had blown down in the night. She helped cut these into short lengths and stack them in a shed with other twigs and limbs, which would eventually be used in Bundori's firepit and hibachi.

The temperature had risen to slightly above freezing, so most of the night's thin ice had vanished from the ponds, hail balls survived only in the shaded areas of the gardens, and the ground was muddy and uncomfortable. The priest had loaned the nun a pair of high wooden *geta* to keep her feet dry, but she accidentally stepped in an unexpectedly deep puddle, and her toes curled with chill as she worked moodily.

She brooded about the promise she had made the dying man in the night past. She was afraid she would find out there was no lie involved, no occult imposition on the samurai's last words. In that case, she had indeed bound herself to fighting a friend unseen in years. The nuisance of the thing was that she had spoken so swiftly and boldly, without thinking first, and had no one to blame but herself. Her samurai spirit had been outraged by the unclean nature of the nine killings. She had spoken as a samurai would speak, though she was no longer a samurai. Was her promise then binding? It could be argued that, as a nun, she was unqualified to make an oath of samurai vengeance. But such excuses did not sit well with her.

Late in the morning, a mounted samurai appeared on the high road. He had two more horses tethered to the one he rode. The short parade moved slowly, dreamily, along the route. The samurai carefully made his horses step down the staircase toward the torii gate. The horses took each step almost daintily. Bundori saw the man doing this and was immediately annoyed. "No horses here! Only sacred animals allowed! If your impure animals excrete, it's trouble for me to repair the desecration! Go back! Go back!"

The samurai stopped at the first landing beneath the torii. He raised the front of his wide hat and said, "I promise my horses won't excrete."

"You can't promise that!" said Bundori, standing in the way. "I know horses can't control themselves!"

"I know these horses better than anyone," the deep voice of the big samurai calmly asserted. "They are old and useless girls, but my friends for many years." He urged his steeds onward in spite of the priest who stood in the path. By this time, the nun had crossed a small drum-bridge and hurried along the path, in case the samurai meant harm to Bundori. She was wearing only her shortsword, the long one being kept indoors while she worked about the gardens or on her lantern. She did not wear her hakama either, but only a nun's kimono, and overall did not look like a warrior-widow. It was just as well. Now that the samurai was within the shrine grounds, it was not feasible to fight with swords. But she would protect Bundori somehow, if the trespasser meant ill.

"What do you seek?" she asked, standing beside the priest.

The big samurai studied her a moment, then let his hat slip from his thumb to cover his face again. It was not as deep a hat as the one the bikuni often wore, but it was almost as good at shadowing his features. He said, "My master says there are nine men for me to take to a private cemetery."

Bundori was aghast at the very thought. "No dead men at

my shrine!" he exclaimed. "I'd know if such defilement occurred!"

"How does your master know about the men?" the nun
inquired, causing Bundori to look at her with sharp amazement.

"My master is aware of many things," the booming voice
replied.

"Your master is not Lord Sato, then, who pays little attention
to what his men may do," said the bikuni. "Do you owe open
allegiance to Kuro the Darkness?"

"For the time being, that is true," said the mounted man.

"Corpse-collecting is a job for outcastes," she said. "What
outcaste has two swords?"

"This outcaste does," he said.

She said, "The corpses you seek are beyond the back gate,
bound to trees grotesquely. Pass through these gardens carefully
if you must, but don't try to come back into the shrine with
the dead." The mounted samurai nodded acquiescence.

The nun followed along behind the slow horses, to make
sure they did not soil Bundori's shrine, and to be sure the
samurai did not try anything unwarranted. Bundori hopped
alongside the nun, whispering excited questions at her: "Who
was killed? What's going on? Who is that samurai? I saw him
bringing corpses through the village the day before yesterday.
Funny job for a warrior! Why are you trusting him this way?
Aren't you worried about this? Pardon me, I should let you
answer. Nothing to say? Well, that's all right. A bother all the
same."

She did not try to edge in a reply to any of his myriad
queries, and was uncertain she had answers even if he calmed
down enough to listen to her. "That way!" she shouted to the
horseman, indicating the gate he should pass through with his
horses. She didn't go out with him, but heard him cutting ropes,
piling the bodies on his three horses. He would have to walk
alongside the steeds to wherever he wanted the heavy loads
taken. His third horse had looked decrepit as with old age, and
might have trouble hauling more than two dead men at once;
but one of the others might be able to handle four, the bikuni
reasoned. In whichever case, the samurai would be left afoot.

In a few moments, he appeared inside the gate, leaving his
horses outside. He had removed his hat, so the bikuni saw his
face clearly now. He had a dour look, which made him un-

appealing, but a vulnerability in his expression made her think he was an honest man. He seemed unperturbed by the dreadful manner of the nine slayings outside the gate.

Though built hugely at waist and shoulders, his face was almost gaunt, cheeks high-boned and rough-hewn. She oughtn't trust him, considering his professed alliance with Kuro. But she had known too many warriors in her life not to be able to judge one fairly.

He had come back into the shrine-grounds to say something to the nun, but looked at her a long time before doing so. She saw in his gaze an unaccountable nostalgia and melancholy, as though he were a man who chanced to sight a lover from his youth standing far away.

"I remember you," he said at last.

She could not say the same, so did not speak.

"I fought with Kiso Yoshinake's armies at Heian-kyo a number of years ago."

There were thousands upon thousands involved in that terrible war. She still could not recall him.

"Since that time," he said, "I have been unemployable, stigmatized as a supporter of a fallen general. Not that I blame anyone. It was a chance worth taking at the time. There are few wars nowadays, and sometimes it is hard for me to eat. I see you've become a mendicant nun, but I'm too proud to get my meals in that way. I trained warhorses for Yoshinake, but recently I was barely able to live by selling my services to carry goods through these mountain passes on some horses which were my last treasures. One of them died recently, and one of my remaining three isn't strong. I was resigned to a quick death by my own shortsword rather than live another year in such poverty." He punctuated this last remark by running his little finger across the front of his stomach. "Priest Kuro discovered me as I prepared to die. He berated me for my weakness. I don't like him in the least, but he offered me a chance to be a retainer once again, to regain my samurai dignity. It is said, 'Who serves a cruel master well is the best retainer in Naipon.' I am obedient in my humble station. I'm Kuro's only direct retainer, though somehow he gets Lord Sato's men to obey him and trusts them more than me. He trusts no one really, but I don't mind that he thinks I could turn against him. It's enough that I know in my own heart that

I'm a samurai capable of fealty under severest conditions, not a beggar or a packhorse driver."

"I understand," said the nun.

"You think you do?" He sounded as though he doubted it were so. "He tests me with repulsive labor, but I don't complain. He pays me well enough. I save what I can and may one day be freed of Kuro, with enough funds to purchase a better retainership in some city. It galls me, but gifts, not skills, pave a man's way in this corrupt world. Don't look down on me for it!"

"I don't," she said.

"I admired you a lot in those days," he said, the source of his nostalgia finally understandable. "Now you are nobody, like myself. Maybe from now on, you'll remember me. My name is Ittosai Kumasaku."

"I will remember," she promised.

The man turned to go. Soon, she heard his horses trotting at a slow pace into the deeper woods, going along back routes. Bundori, who had listened to their cryptic dialogue, was somewhat subdued from his previous overexcitement. Still he could not stand long in one place. "He knew you at the Battle of Awazu and other places like that, is it so? You are Tomoe Gozen, like I thought you were!"

"Don't be too certain," she said, passing him and starting back toward the compound. She added, "Everybody changes a lot. If I was such a famous warrior as that, it doesn't mean that's who I am today."

Bundori clapped his hands and hopped happily, feeling adulation for his famous visitor. But she stopped on the path and wheeled to face him so swiftly that he was frightened of her for that moment, and he stopped in his tracks as well. She said, "I must see a pawnbroker in the village and sell my vest. Can you recommend someone? It'll be a hard winter, but I must give up my vest for the sake of a little money to get my shakuhachi. An old, dying samurai of low rank promised me he would live two or three more days until I could play for him. The artisan must be finished now."

"That's been taken care of!" said Bundori, waving a hand. "He decided to fix your shakuhachi as an offering to this shrine."

She looked at him evenly. "How did he decide that?"

"It was only his idea," said the priest innocently.

"Since you've meddled about that," said the nun, "I needn't feel guilty where I meddle from now on."

Bundori knew her meaning at once. She had promised him not to meddle where Kuro the Darkness was concerned. Her retraction caused him to look distraught. "How was I meddling to help you out?" he said defensively. "You won't have to sell your vest!"

"My meddling will help you out, too. But that's not the point, is it? It was rude of you to interfere without permission. Now I will do as I please, just like you. Don't think it's for your sake! Those men who died outside your shrine—I didn't kill them, though you may have thought I did. Somehow Kuro learned of my presence here; someone with a loose tongue must have said he thought I was someone famous while he was in the village, and Kuro's spies overheard the gossip, so he sent nine men to kill me." Bundori looked at the ground when the nun made her speculation. She continued, "But someone else killed them before the nine men could try to use my blood to despoil your shrine. I promised them revenge, and I can't evade it. I will find out what is going on in this mountain fief, so that I will know how best to avenge those men, or if indeed I was misled about the need for vengeance."

When she walked on, the priest stood crookedly, turning his head sideways and saying to himself, *"Shikata-ga-nai,"* it's too late to be helped now.

No one greeted her at the back entrance to Kahei Todawa's house. It was so quiet that the nun feared death had proceeded her, that she was too late to play her newly repaired shakuhachi for the household's patriarch. Then she realized the family might well be shy two members, presuming Otane and Shinji had acted on their plan to flee the fief. They might have had a good chance of getting away undetected during the previous night's bad weather. If they did happen to make their way to another part of the country, and settled somewhere without anyone betraying them, then it could be rumored in Kanno that Otane must have fallen into the gorge or met with some similar mishap. As for Shinji, it would take longer for any authority to miss a farmer's son; by the time it was investigated, some excuse could be invented to infer a pitiable fate separate from Otane's. If some evidence were uncovered to prove they had actually left Kanno illegally, it would mean trouble for their families, and possible pursuit of the couple themselves.

There was no wooden bell at the back entry, and no watchful daughter to see the bikuni's arrival. Yet it would be rude to enter unbidden, and uncouth to shout. For this reason the nun stood at the open gate a long while, fretting about things. At length the kitchen door slid open and an old, withered face peered out. It was the Todawa matriarch, whose widowhood approached swiftly, if her husband were not already dead.

The old face was like crinkled parchment on which nothing had been written. She turned away as though unconcerned with a nun at the gate. But in a few moments, Kahei Todawa came personally, for his impoverished house could afford no servant.

Formal greetings were exchanged. Then Kahei Todawa led the nun along an inner garden wall, until she saw the opened sidedoors to a certain room. From that room wafted the scent of old man's flesh, hair, nail clippings, urine, and nearness to death.

The doors had been opened in spite of the chill, for the old man wished to view the world from his bed. As Kahei Todawa and the nun approached, she could not be certain that the patriarch in his bedding really did look worse than he had looked before; but each step rendered the situation more certain. With his sallow complexion, bony cheeks, pain-creased expression, and the palsied hand clinging to a rosary, he looked as close to death as any living man may come.

His eyes were open and glistened black. He watched the nun weakly. She came to the step leading from the garden to his private chamber. She left her wooden footgear on the stone step as she placed one foot, then the other, upon the deck outside his door. Then, upon her knees on the platform, she bowed fully.

With her hat and longsword to one side of the doorway, where they could not be seen from the inside, she seemed a common nun and not a warrior. But it was an uncommon instrument she bore, the shakuhachi being considered a somewhat masculine instrument, and the side-blown flute more appropriate for women. Her shoulder-length hair framed an ageless face, so that she seemed a boyish apparition, a ghost-page come for an old man's spirit.

Kahei entered the room, leaving the bowing nun upon the

deck, framed in the doorway, the garden behind her. About the same time, the elderly wife of the dying man came into the room by a different entry. She led foolish Iyo by the hand, sitting him near the bed and bidding him be very still. He lacked solemnity, but was an obedient boy, and did not move. His anile grandmother knelt beside him.

A frigid breeze passed over the nun's shoulder and entered the room, but the dying man did not seem to wish his door slid shut, having as he did such little time to see even so small a portion of the world. Though the garden was bleak due to the winterlike qualities of highland autumns, it was yet a soothing sight, well cared for by Kahei, who knew much of trees and flowers.

Kahei Todawa, who also was not a young man, knelt close to his father's head, then lifted him by the shoulders until the old man was in a sitting position, leaning against his son. It was a sorrowful picture, an aged son serving to prop up his exceedingly old father, striving to keep his father's frightful shaking from negating their mutual sense of dignity and earnestness. In a moment, the shock to his body—caused by being lifted, however gently—had passed, and the withered samurai tried to speak, possibly in greeting to the nun. He was unable to squeak forth even one word. To save his face, the nun bowed anew, with head to floor, so that she would not appear to witness his infirmity and embarrassment.

It was hard for a samurai to die slowly and of old age. Some old men were ashamed to do so. It must have been an imposition to live these extra days, at the bikuni's request, that she might uphold her own duty.

When she lifted her face, she said, "Please pardon my lack of skill," and raised the shakuhachi to her lips. The patriarch let his head roll against his son's shoulder. He closed his eyes to listen.

The bikuni had been unnecessarily shy about her skill with the instrument; and the household soon believed her efforts were a fine substitute for a recitation of one or another sutra. The instrument had only four holes on top, one on the back, but by half-holing there were many variations to the notes. The sound of an end-blown flute, particularly a large one such as the nun held, was unequaled in its mournfulness and expression of tranquility—most appropriate for so funereal an occasion.

As she began, the sound swelled at once and enclosed the

listeners as in a fog risen from the mountain's valleys—a muted, melancholy bass, which broke at last into a metallic forte, then fell anew to an almost inaudible, quavering note. Her intake of breath was a note in itself, followed by the swell again, this time cut short and, as an artful afterthought, a grace-note was added. The loose tune changed dramatically, becoming a fluttery whisper, conveying vague reassurance, before lifting sharply into a shout or a knell—then, that same grace-note as before.

She was playing not merely for the dying patriarch, but also for the spirit of her instructor, who had taught her all she could learn of the instrument, who had loved her as his most sincere if not always his most gifted pupil. The shakuhachi had been his present to her on the day he died. That she had allowed it to be damaged in a foolish battle had caused her guilt and grief. She made amends for her error by duplicating the very melodies and rhythms of nature, in the manner she had been taught, creating songs in harmony with the universe, in apology for and admission of her personal insignificance, inadequacy, and obeisance.

Her music became a wind passing through the last crisp leaves of autumn's maples, then going up, up among the crags and dwarf pines of the highest peaks of Kanno province. The listeners felt the coldness of their world increase, due to the altitude at which their spirits soared. Everyone felt alone in the cosmos, alone on the edge of an icy precipice, certain they would be thrown down by the frightful wind, dashed into darkness and annihilation.

They felt they would die for the terror of that music, except that it changed by subtle stages, until they were certain they had already died, but of the music's beauty.

The mood and sentiment began its change, notes descending the further side of the mountains, striving for a place and time of greater kindness regarding its vastness and intentions. The rapt listeners, and the player as well, were carried gently first upon the sweet wind, then upon a quick river, for the sound was now swift and wet. And they came unexpectedly to a placid lake in summer!

The musical wind hung quietly, quavering upon the infinitesimal waves of the huge, supreme ocean.

The world was warm and comforting. It would not be surprising if a peony burst into blossom, in the very garden behind the performing bikuni. She held everyone in the spell of kinder days, gentler dramas, and the dream of dreams fulfilled. She took each of them along paths of mercy and oblivion, taking especially a dying man, who wished to know, more than did the others, that life had had some meaning and reward, and some regard for him.

All felt poised no longer on the brink of disaster, but on the brink of ecstasy, pinned to a climactic moment until it was unbearable and each craved release from beauty.

It took a while for them to realize, one by one, that the music had ended; it took a while for each to return from far-off places. Even foolish Iyo had been caused to ponder things profound, although already these were fading, as do all dreams of enlightenment.

They opened their eyes to the world as it actually exists, but were not disappointed. The illusions of terror and of beauty lingered just enough that everything was sharper and more thrilling—though paradoxically there had grown within them a vacuum where once reposed their hearts. No one in the world could truly recognize the empty corners of their spirits, unless once those corners were filled by some kind of magic; and the music was, above all, a kind of magic.

Each sighed unobtrusive sighs as their attention returned to the patriarch, who had a fierce, strong light in his dark eyes, and a peaceful look that had not been there before. Death no longer mattered; it held no fear, and no regret. He was made calmer and more powerful by the dream of deadly heights and gentle summers, and thus was able to speak, though in a voice as quavery and faint as the bikuni's subtlest note.

"Just now," he said quietly, "I was walking in a summer field, and friends I used to know were calling out to me. Or was it only the sound of cicada? I would like to know."

Then he was no longer shaking with palsy, for he no longer lived. The tearful old son laid his father back upon the quilt; and then the son hid his face behind a sleeve of his kimono, lest someone see the tracks upon his cheeks or the sadness of his expression. Iyo, rendered momentarily wiser by the spell of the flute, knew at last that his grandfather was gone; and he wailed a heart-piercing lament such as some would say only a shakuhachi could convey, and threw himself upon the old man's corpse in disbelief and sorrow.

The decrepit widow sat very still, her expression the same

as always, the music not enough to unburden her of life's
tumult, or to free her from pent-up emotion. That she was
sorrowed could not be doubted. But her will was like a sword,
her face a tarnished mirror, reflecting nothing.

The bikuni placed her shakuhachi on the platform and bowed
to the instrument, keeping her eyes upon the grain of the deck's
wood, so as not to impose upon the family's mourning.

She chose not to tarry in the house of Todawa. Their mournful disposition combined with her own sense of inadequacy as
Buddha's servant; and this made her uncomfortable in their
presence. She accepted from the aged widow a portion of un-
cooked rice for the alms-bag; then she set out into the gray
afternoon.

The silent old woman had also given the bikuni a letter. It
was addressed by Otane to the nameless nun, and was intended
to be read after Otane and her peasant lover had fled the fief.

The day grew colder, though not so bad as the past night.
Judging by the dismal sky, the weather would certainly worsen.
For the moment, the chill was bothersome, but sufferable.

Her breath came out from under her hat in small steaming
clouds, which she left behind like fading and unwanted memories. Dampness made her clothing hang heavily from her
shoulders. She walked as though burdened with woe, each step
hard and careful, her arms folded inside her kimono to embrace
her own slight warmth. The colorless and foreboding sky
matched her mood. It was not possible to tell where, behind
the clouds, the sun might be.

Along a seldom-used path, she came upon a neglected drum-
tower, in the woods east of the Todawa family's small estate.
She sat on a step of this secluded structure, her amigasa and
longsword at her side and Otane's letter on her knees. The
bikuni sighed deeply and turned her head from one side then
the other, a motion of despair.

Though she had been reluctant to read the missive, it turned
out to contain little more than idle praise and gratitude. Otane's
choice of words came close to endearments. The letter increased
the nun's sad feelings, for she did not think she had betrayed
sympathy for the lovers, and certainly had not helped them
regarding their pitiable situation. Otane's letter suggested she
had seen the heart of the bikuni and knew what was hidden
there.

Otane's quiet wisdom did not lessen the bikuni's sense that a generous appraisal remained unearned.

"Maybe we will meet again in Shigeno Valley," the nun said to the letter, moved despite herself by Otane's poetic calligraphy. She hoped the couple would find happiness and live long lives of devotion to one another. As she refolded the letter and touched it to her forehead, she said, "I will try to merit your high estimations." She looked about, half in embarrassment, then sniffed to clear her nose.

Inside her kimono, held to her body by the tightly wrapped obi, the bikuni kept a cloth wallet. A traveler could not keep many mementos, but she could not hastily cast away the sensitive letter. She put it in the flat, silk folding wallet alongside a few other items—miniature sewing utensils, a wrapped lock of hair which was not her own, one or two other private things of negligible size—then tucked it back within her kimono, where it was undetectable.

She picked up hat and sword and entered the darkness of the pagoda, sitting upon her knees to meditate. She was not eager for her next destination. Thus she lingered in the tower, playing the shakuhachi for the same forgotten war-dead for whom the pagoda had been built long ago. The plaintive notes of the instrument echoed the bikuni's sentiments.

Her mind would not become clear of all thought, for some fragment of consciousness refused to submerge itself in a melody that was overly aware of its own notes. She could not remove herself from various desiderations: longing for enlightenment, for comprehension of life's complicated events and windings, for some honorable means by which to avoid what appeared to be an inevitable duel with Heinosuke of the Rooster Clan.

It was difficult to believe the boy she had known as Yabushi could have grown into a cruel killer. Yet she had seen good men become contrary, and indecent fellows become repentant and benevolent. The world was not static, though things might be more comprehensible if it were. It was possible that her dislike of change had driven her to tonsure, though she was unsuited to its meaning, and inept at its keeping.

Because of life's vicissitudes, she must prepare for the possibility of finding not an old friend, but someone wicked, or desperate, or misled . . . someone who could pin vassals of Lord Sato to trees, with or without justification, denying them their coups de grace. It was an act of infamy so out of keeping with samurai ethos that even a nun felt drawn back into the affairs of the world. Though temper abated, yet had she bound herself by an unchecked moment of anger and anger's oath of vengeance.

Considerations such as these kept her from becoming utterly clear of mind, therefore less ready for anything that might occur during the promised encounter. It was necessary to enter each aspect of one's life guiltless in order to come out of it the same. It was necessary to begin a task with perfect emptiness, rather than encumbered by doubt, or fear, or hatred, or anything other than a selfless sort of intuitive control and readiness.

She was not ready for much today.

But it was time. And for all that she could see, it was inescapable.

A gulleyed byway led in and out of an ancient forest and near the dangerous brink. Here and there the route was marshy. Her borrowed wooden geta kept her feet above the ground, except once or twice when they sank into mud, allowing her feet to become wet and cold. She ignored the discomfort. Warped and half-rotten bridges saw her across narrow streams, which were numerous, spilling into the gorge.

When the path took her near the cliff's edge, she could see to the monstrous, frothy river far below. From some points along the way, she could see as far as the curve of the gorge, atop which perched the sullen temple between high falls. Funguslike patches of fog clung to the temple. Toward the base of the stony cliffs, numerous wide falls collided into an ultimate, single entity and continued downward. The river was entirely obscured where this entity struck. There might have been no river at all in that spot, for all one could see through the roiling, billowing clouds of mist. It looked as though the waterfalls spilled straight into Emma's Hell, and smoke was seeping out. The smoky mists swirled up and away, forming grotesque visages, which dissipated, then reformed into shapes more hideous than before.

At other points along the route, she could see only the ancient cedars all around, a forest virtually untouched by woodcutters, who shunned it. Her mind could not help but compare these trees to those surrounding White Beast Shrine west of the village. There, around Bundori's refuge, a sad nostalgia weighted moist branches, heavy with old dreams and new tears; whereas here, the trees were bowed beneath terrifying secrets, and their tears were thick as blood.

Above her head, branches brushed against one another, whispering dour warnings in a language she could not comprehend. The sky's illumination was, within the cold embrace of these cedars, mostly blotted out. There was little underbrush beyond luridly colored toadstools, spidery moulds, fleshy lumps, and darksome mushrooms whose wrinkled caps resembled devilish faces.

Nor were there beasts in this portentous wood, possibly due to nothing more untoward than the early hibernation patterns in the highlands. But one could well believe the animals, like the woodcutters, were reluctant to disturb the atmospheric glumness.

What was more, one could sense that this appalling essence of the unknown exuded outward from the Temple of the Gorge. It became more intense as one drew nearer that cheerless hold. And though another traveler might have turned and fled the very scent of the macabre, the bikuni, she knew not why, was strangely attracted to that temple's odor.

She did not know what was more wisely dreaded: the sinister, whispering forest; the roaring visages below the harrowing cliffs; or the waiting temple, at once beckoning by means of malign magnetism and auguring doom for all who were drawn near.

When the path led out of the forest again, she saw the place loom close. A sudden high wind tore upward from the gorge, heralding her arrival, gusts pressing her from behind. A slight but unpleasant drizzle was driven sideways. A full-scale storm seemed unwilling to touch the vile earth, despite increasingly dark and menacing cloudcover.

The temple enticed. It dared.

She passed between two stupendous warriors carved of pine, their faces threatening scowls stained red, their wooden swords held high as to sever the heads of whoever proved foolish enough to enter the temple grounds. Angry—or laughing?— gusts whistled by the lips and swords, but could not stir the wooden gods to life.

The bikuni approached the entrance of an outer temple. She stopped to listen, thinking something echoed off the face of

the monastery: the faint, weepy prayer of a ghost. It might
have been the wind, or a hungry crow's distant complaint. She
could not hear the exact sound a second time.

Standing before the entrance, even damp and wretched,
there was an heroic mien to the bikuni, a musing quality to
her posture. She lingered on the steps merely to appreciate the
fineness of the weathered, derelict structure, the ingenious mood
of horror invoked by the surroundings and the architecture. She
was not commonly of dark disposition, and ought not to find
such a place familiar to her soul; even so, the site held some
attraction. If it were other than haunted, she would be surprised.
If a great priest exorcised the vicinity, it would be almost a
pity.

She removed her amigasa for vision's sake, held it in her
left hand, and stepped across the threshold. Her charcoal-and-
cream colors caused her to blend into shadow. The gale had
risen to such pitch, no one was apt to hear her, even though
she strode overtly, investigating unlit chambers without regard
for whom, or what, she might disturb. The building was deserted, apparently for decades.

She passed through a back exit and was about to cross a
muddy court, thence to the main temple, a frowning structure;
but a sparkle of light captured her attention. She turned her
face slightly to look back, and saw a lamp's gleam through the
crack of a loose shutter.

The bikuni retraced her steps to see what room she might
have missed. It turned out that one corner of the monastic
dwelling was divided into more parts than she had realized.
Approaching this previously overlooked cell, she tried to catch
any sound, but the wind raged more and more, sounding of
celebration, so there was small chance of her hearing every
movement.

When she slid the door aside, there sat a man upon his
knees, in the center of the room, hunched over a table, his
back to the intruder, ink and brush to hand. As the door slid
in its dusty track, the fellow ceased writing and sat bolt upright.
He did not turn around to see who entered, but moved his
writing brush from right hand to left. His right hand then moved
toward the floor, where a longsword rested at his side.

The bikuni said, "Man of Omi?"

The youthful fellow leapt upward with alarming speed, sword

in hand, but did not turn to face the intruder even then. Rather, he bounded over his table, kicking the lantern so that its own oil doused the flame. He vanished in the darkness.

The bikuni dropped her bamboo hat, took one step forward, and drew steel. She heard no panel open, no indication of the man having left the room. With the gale's racket, she might have missed the sound of retreat, especially if he had prepared in advance by oiling the track of some secret door. Yet she suspected there were only two routes of escape: the shuttered windows, or the door she stood before. The man of Omi likely lurked invisibly in some corner of the room, whereas the bikuni stood in diffuse light from the crooked shutter.

She moved forward, her face tipped downward, listening intently, apparently calm. She approached the small table, beside which were three stacks of thin, worm-eaten books. Upon the table, a long sheet of paper was partially unrolled. The bikuni lowered herself into a squatting position next to the table, her whole posture still conveying readiness. By the negligible illumination, she could see that the books were family genealogies of the sort kept by priests responsible for regional documentation of clans. The books must have been filched from various surrounding temples—temples more recently vacated than the long disused Temple of the Gorge.

Her left hand raised the long sheet of scroll-paper from the low table into a slant of vague light, which filtered between the shutters. Because she had to remain sword-ready, it was difficult to concentrate on what the man of Omi had been writing. She was able to tell that the scroll included family names, which served as main headings; and beneath these main headings were the given family's individual members, along with the rank and position of each. The Sato name headed the list, and the bikuni was surprised to see how few members there were in the present generation. Sato's line seemed near extinction, as were many local families, if the scroll was accurate.

She had seen the format of the scroll only a couple of times in her life, when powerful warlords had their clerks draw up charts to aid in the extermination of enemy clans. This was done either for purposes of revenge, or to circumvent revenge from one's foes. Once begun, the process would not stop until every member of the indicated families, from infants to dotards, were eradicated. There had been such a hunt for members of her husband's clan, after his failed treachery against the Shogun's government. It was generally considered an extremist measure and not entertained lightly even by the military authority of Naipon. That Heinosuke should have use for such a compilation was inconceivable.

Here and there, names were already deleted by means of a simple character, which meant "complete." This indicated a death, or a death so certain to occur within days or hours that the individual required no further attention.

As she was ignorant of most local family names, the greater portion of the scroll was meaningless to her. But she did recognize the style of names taken by Buddhist priests and scholars. These had already been systematically marked "complete," which did not surprise her, given what the Shinto Priest Bundori had said about the fates of local temple men. Most of the names awaiting the cruel mark were followed by ranks or titles that were associated with castles and vassalage—Lord Sato's men, no doubt. Among these, the bikuni was surprised to see three she recognized: Takeno, Yojiemon, and Chojiro. These were the men she had slain, and for whom she had lately been carving a lantern. It was disconcerting to see that she had slain men whose deaths were already plotted.

Unrolling the scroll further, a startled breath escaped her, for she saw the major heading "Todawa," beneath which were placed the members of that family, whose members equaled the fingers of one hand. Two names had already been stricken. One was the family patriarch, whom the listmaker might well have known had been close to death for several days. The other name dealt the grievous stroke was what shocked her. The bikuni had believed Otane had fled safely from the fief, for love's reason, yet Heinosuke's list deleted Otane's name with the word "complete."

Despite an outward calm, the bikuni's breath had quickened. She had just about concluded that Heinosuke was plotting one of the most vicious and extensive schemes of revenge ever undertaken by a single man, for what reasons she could not begin to guess. However, her first conclusion was shattered as she eyed the scroll further and found that it included a heading for the Rooster Clan, beneath which heading had been scribed the family's last two members. The Rooster Clan was another clan near extinction, though once it had been large and distinguished, before wars brought its numbers, and politics brought its power, steady decline.

What was most alarming was that of these two names—one being Heinosuke's, the other being his sister Oshina's—Heinosuke had already marked his own name "complete," as though he counted himself as good as dead. His sister's name was not deleted, for Heinosuke had no way of knowing his sister's fate; it was, in fact, this very matter that originally had brought the bikuni in search of Heinosuke. If he knew that he and not his sister was the family's sole remaining member, and he its only chance at future progeny, then he might not treat his own life so hazardously. For surely he had marked his own name "complete" not simply because he knew his life was wanted, but because he intended to give his own life in an effort to foil the villainous plan of Kuro the Darkness.

It became clear to the bikuni that Heinosuke's research in stolen genealogies, and the making of this scroll, were endeavors undertaken in order to establish the full extent of the felon's vengeful targets. The Rooster Clan was only one among many marked for doom. The genealogies were required in order to find a common link, and thereby, perhaps, a common reason, for Kuro's hatred for so many unknowing objects of revenge.

Even though many facets of the conspiracy evaded her understanding, the bikuni's racing thoughts were eager to vindicate Heinosuke. Priest Kuro, not Heinosuke, sought the deaths of Lord Sato's vassals and sent them on deadly errands. The man of Omi had uncovered at least part of the reason; thus Heinosuke's moment of "completion" had gained high priority. The bikuni nearly had become the unwitting tool of Kuro's plot.

She was about to call out to the man of Omi by his childhood name of Yabushi, so that he would know her for a friend; but at that moment, a shutter was torn away from the window. Wind raged into the room with a hateful shout, drowning her cry to Heinosuke. Her attention was diverted to the window, for she thought it was the man of Omi seeking egress, not the wind tearing loose the shutter. But he was elsewhere, noting her every move, realizing the moment when her readiness focused in a direction contrary to his position. He leapt out of deepest shadow with a bat's swiftness, his longsword scraping through the bikuni's alms-bag. Raw rice scattered through the air, sprinkling the floor. The length of paper was snatched from her grasp, leaving her but one small fragment.

The man of Omi was through the door.

She pursued him to the muddy courtyard, where she was struck by cold blasts of wind. The man of Omi was already across the court, too far to hear her shouting that she was his friend. She saw him enter the maw of the main temple. Though she was at the same door in an instant, already he had vanished, knowing the buildings and the grounds too well.

Something intangible stroked her neck as she entered; and the wind outside, raging the moment before, became a silent zephyr, as though to inform her that some portion of the performance was over. Now she stood in a vast hall where sound was absorbed and rendered mute. She knew she had stumbled into the vortex of whatever malignance ruled the forest and the falls; yet she could give no great thought to the matter, not in the wake of more personal revelations, and on the heels of a friend nearly treated as a foe.

She spied his footmarks, left by muddy, unshod feet. The track ended less than halfway through the building, having gotten cleaner and dryer with each step of his flight. If he hadn't changed direction, she calculated his arrival at the lap of the blasted Buddha seated at the far end of the hall.

The Buddha looked to be the survivor of conflagration, his once-holy visage reduced by the ravages of decay. Now he frowned malevolently upon she who approached.

Nearing the altar, she saw that there was a separate room behind the large wooden Buddha. Ready for a new attack—for Heinosuke might well regard her as an emissary of his worst enemy, as indeed she had almost been, through clever and depraved machinations—she stepped into the small back room. It was relatively well-lit, for a side door had been left open onto a graveyard.

She stood in the doorway and looked at gulleys, rivulets, and paths leading in several directions, none betraying Heinosuke's quick route. Far to the left was a wide, rushing river which, beyond her view, leapt into the void of the gorge at the temple's rear. Before her was a heavily overgrown cemetery. Many cedars had been left throughout the grounds to provide shelter of sorts from the mountain winds, so that graveyard and forest were poorly delineated.

Because of seepage from higher ground, many of the cedars'

roots were weirdly exposed by runoff. Purulent, mildewed soil
gave rise to disagreeable odors, despite the present drizzle's
efforts to cleanse the air. Nearly every Buddhist temple was
associated with a graveyard, which were by their nature on the
darkled edge; but the sight before her now was much more
evocatively evil, though less so, she thought, than the main
temple hall overseen by the blasted Buddha.

A distant voice weakly intoned a sutra addressed not to Priest
Kuro's favored Wonderful Law, but to the wargod Hachiman.
It was a prayer of vengeance, though the voice was thin and
reedy. It was the voice of an old woman.

The bikuni descended a steep, wide, slate stairway, the sides
of which were impinged upon by worn figures of buddhas and
bodhisattvas, their eyes shut, their visages complacent. Water
cascaded over the steps, splashing beneath her geta. Springs,
which ages anon had woven their way through the graveyard
in a managed, controlled manner, after decades of neglect had
made their own wild courses. Numerous graves were washed
away, ashes carried into the muted gorge. The bikuni passed
a stone bodhisattva that had had the soil washed from underneath. It had tipped sideways, revealing bones.

Both wind and drizzle subsided, though the sky rumbled
distantly, still promising ferocious weather. The sound of prayer
was somewhat louder. The bikuni took a side path over slippery
clay. She wove between additional monuments, many of them
leaning. At last she came to an area devoid of monuments, but
recently cultivated with graves, few of them marked, proof that
the old cemetery was still used.

She pushed through brittle, dead weeds higher than her
shoulder, finding grave after unmarked grave, and hoofmarks
which she took to be the tracks of Ittosai Kumasaku's cherished
horses. This would be the very place into which Kuro the
Darkness instructed Ittosai, his only true retainer, to place the
uncremated victims of monstrous and curious schemes.

She found a certain grave, one of the few with any kind of
marker, albeit a marker of little merit, its inscription apparently
made by an unsteady hand with a worn-out brush; the bikuni
could not read the sloppy characters. Before this grave knelt a
woman whose bent posture and ragged brown clothing conveyed old age. Her face was mostly swaddled, the slits of her
closed eyes the only portion revealed. She seemed a very mountain spirit, a ghostly hag, hunkered in front of the recent grave,

calling out to the wargod in her weak voice, muffled by wrappings; pleading for revenge. Omnipotent revenge. Purifying revenge. Glorified and holy to gods, devils, and humankind: *revenge!*

"Grandmother," said the bikuni, shattering some spell. The old woman grew still and opened her eyes. "It's too cold to stay out here. Can you pray before your houseshrine for a while?"

The old woman's wrappings hid her hair and ears and nose and jowls and chin...everything but those pinched, narrow eyes. A knife was sheathed at the front of her obi. Her muffled voice replied,

"Here lies the last of my kin. I've made this marker with his name upon it, in my own broken calligraphy. I couldn't find a priest to do it properly. I couldn't have his corpse taken for interment at our traditional grave sites near a temple distant from here." She pointed vaguely south with a bent finger, then continued. "I am cast from my home, in which I could live only while my nephew had the rights of a castle retainer. What is there for me to do but die in this place, begging Hachiman for revenge against Lord Sato's hellish cleric?"

"What good is dying here alone?" the bikuni asked, pitying the old woman. "If you have no home, why not live secretly in one of the abandoned temples? You can pray for your nephew's spirit anywhere."

The oldster turned her swaddled face away and said vehemently, "I will die right here! Don't try to make me fail! You shouldn't bother me like this. Even that villain Ittosai, who buried nine more men this morning, does not interrupt me, does not try to sway me, does not show me such disrespect. You know it's impolite to meddle! Go away quickly!" Now she glowered at the bikuni and insisted that she "Go! Go! I pray for only one to come to me before I die!" She gripped the handle of her sheathed knife and added, "The one I wish to see is the slayer of my poor Chojiro."

Only when the woman said her nephew's name was the bikuni able to decipher the barely intelligible calligraphy on the wooden slat marking the grave.

"Grandmother," she said, head hung low. "Hachiman has answered your prayer just now."

The old woman's vein-mapped hands clutched at the knife's

handle, ready to unsheath it. She stared up at the bikuni, demanding, "You are Kuro's handmaiden of death? You killed my poor Chojiro?"

"I have never seen this Priest Kuro. I fancy myself his foe; although I wonder how deeply his intrigues are rooted. I begin to wonder if anyone can die within this fief who does not do so by the design of Kuro the Darkness. Whoever slays anyone may serve Kuro, though not knowing how or why."

The old woman tried to stand quickly, but was too feeble, and found her unsteady legs by awkward stages. Her hunched spine kept her from standing tall. Her fingers were knotted and deformed; she could not draw the knife very well. Her eyes conveyed a fierceness all the same. The knife was raised to the side of her head and she appeared willing to dash forward at any cost.

But she did not move. Momentarily, her expressive eyes broke from ferocity into shame and sorrow. She confessed, "I knew Chojiro was too much influenced by Priest Kuro. I knew it would undo him in the end. He was a good boy all the same, if you can believe that. He did what others told him, but never thought up anything evil on his own. I can bear the truth, if it comes from a nun with so guileless a face. Tell me: Did my Chojiro die bravely?"

The bikuni had to turn her face away in order to reply. "He was not such a brave man, if I must tell the truth."

A cry caught in the old woman's throat. She took one step forward and managed to ask, "Did he commit some misdeed in Kuro's name that required your cutting off his head?"

The bikuni was bitterly ashamed, and barely able to respond. "I don't know that he did," she said. "I gave in to the irony of the moment. He begged mercy, but I had none."

The old woman's knife raised again, aiming shakily at the bikuni. She demanded, "Then how can I let you off for killing him?"

The bikuni squared her shoulders, looked the woman in the eyes, and replied, "I don't believe you can."

The old woman hobbled forth, striving for swiftness, knife stabbing the space the bikuni had already vacated.

"Grandmother, your vengeance is a just one. If I give my blood to any, I promise it will be yours. Yet I am not ready to give it to you now."

The old woman struck again, but the bikuni stepped aside, evading her easily.

"Take care of your health," said the bikuni, "in case it takes a while for you to have your wish."

Then the bikuni wheeled about and hurried back toward the Temple of the Gorge, quickly outpacing, and losing, her elderly foe.

As she backtracked, intending to reclaim her hat, she found, in the muddy courtyard between buildings, the same scrap of paper that had torn in her hand when Heinosuke snatched his scroll, and which she had dropped in pursuit of him. It was wet and dirty, but after she straightened it out a bit, it was easy to read. It contained part of another list of names, a peasant clan, and one of them was Shinji's. As was the case with Otane's name, Shinji's had already been given the mark that implied completion of revenge.

The bikuni stood in the courtyard, pondering the variety of families on Heinosuke's scroll: a lord and his relatives; vassals of various posts, with their kin; local holy men; and here, she found, even a farm family. All their fates were intertwined for some reason that the bikuni could not penetrate. A strange mystery! She wished she had been able to speak with Heinosuke, for it was possible his research had already resolved Priest Kuro's purpose and the connection between such divergent and unsuspecting families.

As her mind struggled with the fragments of information she had acquired, the dark sky became extremely pale and unleashed not a deluge, but snow. The day's long promise of tempest would not be met after all. Snow clung to her shoulders and hair; but that which touched the ground melted at once. It was a light snow and had the beneficence of making the temple less overtly grim.

That which she had felt in the main temple hall—a hand placed lightly at her nape—she felt a second time in that courtyard. It was eerily unnatural; she might have dismissed it as a snowflake or breeze had she not felt it once before. Yet the touch was not entirely threatening. She looked about, seeing no one. She crumpled the paper, then opened her palm; and a slight gust stole the scrap, losing it among flakes of snow. *How odd I feel,* she thought, gazing at her palm, on which snowflakes danced as within a miniscule tornado.

The peaked, tiled roofs around the court were swiftly becoming white-on-rust. Menace was certainly not erased, but snow's deathliness was more comprehensible, muffling the temple's native strangeness. The bikuni felt once more a fascination with or attraction for the macabre, a thing usually contrary to her disposition, or so she felt. Sometimes she was moody or withdrawn, but rarely grim or haunted. All the same, the monastery made her think about the tragic beauty of things grotesque, not about their frightfulness.

Perhaps this was in her nature, she reflected, only she refused to embrace it with full honesty. Her past was rife with gory deeds, dark battlefields, calm strokes of steel. She had been less reflective in those days. Even now, despite a discrete sense of criticism regarding herself and others, her dreams remained peaceful ones, more than not, never filled with severed limbs groping for the life her own sword had denied them. Because she had fallen from high station and become humble, some might think she suffered, battling a corrupting ego or a pitiful sense of inconsequentiality. Really she reveled in such feelings in a self-indulgent manner, and was quite happy to evade peace of mind. This being so, both her occasional sense of inadequacy and her questioning of the necessity of violence in no way caused her sensations of guilt for things past, or things that yet might happen.

In all, it would seem her life was a kind of supernormal force that meant no evil, destruction and slaughter notwithstanding. The malignance of the Temple of the Gorge was like this also. What really separates a hero from a villain where death is concerned? Is a righteous slaying less irrevocable?

She entered the long, narrow building, treading the corridor in search of the room where she had first spied Heinosuke and where she had dropped her bamboo amigasa. Her thoughts still rushed about her like the flurry of snow outside the monastery. She knew that of late her own cruel blade had swung less easily, not for loss of valor or vitality, but out of some sense that life was precious. Thinking about life was too interesting. The snuffing of such thoughts was too sad. Did the thing that was hellish about this Buddhist compound ever have such doubts? Probably it did not. Maturity had made her more conscious of herself, but the haunted temple was something frozen in time, mindless of itself and therefore, like a young warrior, able to destroy without shame. It was, then, her own violent youth she felt amidst the haunting: a loving recollection of the terrors she had witnessed, wrought, or survived.

And wasn't that the same thing that caused her to slay those three roguish samurai? She hadn't thought they merited death for pursuing a harmless girl through the night; so far as she had been able to tell, they had not even consummated their infamous intent. But she had been caught in the mystery of steel's strength, eager to recapture the innocence of the naive warrior who ceases to be a thinking entity but is only a part of a sword. It was easy to apologize afterward; to play her instrument for the dead, or buy a priest's prayers, or carve a lantern of stone.

Yet she would not give up what she had learned in order to be innocent again; and innocence is as ongoing a process as gathering knowledge. It was unlikely anyone ever knew herself completely. Still, some aspect of herself, out of her past or hidden within herself at all times, grazed off the walls of the Temple of the Gorge and echoed though its corridors. Though others would regard this place as horrific, the bikuni found in it something that was comfortably familiar and singularly splendid.

From a long way off, she heard the whinny of an aged horse. The bikuni thought it might mean Ittosai Kumasaku was bringing another corpse for Priest Kuro's cemetery. It might even be the corpse of the Todawa patriarch, for Priest Kuro, through Lord Sato, would doubtless cause the beleaguered family to give up any notion of interment elsewhere.

She found the room and reclaimed her hat. It was less dark, for the shutter was gone from the window. Snow reflected into the chamber like myriad small white flames. She noted that Heinosuke had also returned, at least momentarily. The books containing genealogies were gone from beside the table. The bikuni knelt before the table, removed a piece of rice paper from her sleeve, and lifted the inkbrush Heinosuke had left behind. She wrote:

Yabushi: We've much in common, I think.
We both take comfort in this haunted place.
Please think well of me until next we meet.

Then, from within her kimono, against her belly, she extracted her silk wallet. From this she withdrew a woman's hair, held fast by a tube of paper on which was written the name "Oshina," Heinosuke's sister. She placed the hair upon the short missive and said to Oshina's spirit,

"I was nearly fooled into fighting your brother." She bowed to the hair and asked Oshina's forgiveness, adding, "He considers himself to be dead to the world, so I must try to save him, fearing he will not save himself. As it stands, I don't understand the whole mystery yet. But I feel some resolution is pending. In the meantime, please look over Heinosuke for both of us."

When she stood, taking up her hat again and leaving Oshina's hair for Heinosuke to discover, she turned and saw a shadow hulk in the door, a wide straw hat upon his head. Ittosai Kumasaku came into the room and looked about, as though the nun were not his primary concern. Finding nothing of greater interest, he acknowledged her by saying,

"My master told me to come and bury the corpse of a troublesome fellow named Heinosuke of Omi. For once, Priest Kuro seems to have guessed wrong. Have you noticed such a body?"

"One of the men you buried this morning," she replied softly, "requested, on his dying breath, that I slay the man of Omi. But Heinosuke was shockingly quick and evaded me. Your master's ploy went awry, for I no longer think Heinosuke killed those nine men. If I find out who really slew them so obscenely, I will yet consider myself bound to avenge them. Could it be that you were sent to commit the inhuman act? Certainly you weren't shocked by their conditions."

"I am shocked by nothing," said Ittosai deeply, walking about the room, his manner apparently intended as a threat, though the bikuni was uncowed. "If my master had asked me to slay in that grim manner, I would have tried, as I am his one faithful retainer."

"A devoted vassal might prefer to take his own life as a form of criticism," said the bikuni, speaking of *kanshi* or remonstration suicide, practiced by retainers bound to tyrannical masters and otherwise unable to disobey. Ittosai grunted at the very implication, and replied,

"I will rise in the world instead. In any case, he has not

asked me to commit cruel acts, only to perform degrading chores. It might be that cruelty in his behalf would be more appealing to me, rather than continuing at the lowly tasks assigned me."

The bikuni was bold enough to say, "I think better of you than that." Ittosai responded with bitter, momentary laughter, his deep voice failing to convey true mirth, but only anguish. He ceased striding about the chamber and stopped in sword's reach of the bikuni, glaring at her from under the shadow of his wide hat. His eyes were as white as the snowflakes clinging to his hat. He warned,

"Don't imagine sensitivity where there is none. The years have driven me mad, I promise you." The high-cheeked, hardened prettiness of his face became, for a moment, sallow and almost like a skull. His lips formed a line of anger not so much aimed at the bikuni but at the whole of Naipon, the universe, or himself. She backed away from him and bowed slightly, an act of obeisance that made Ittosai turn from her with a nervous look, his anger, or his madness, abating like a tide, and as surely liable to return.

The bikuni spoke again, softly, as to a wild animal that was known occasionally to allow itself to be stroked. "I have recently found out that three men I killed in a cemetery along a pass leading to White Beast Shrine were men your master Kuro did not wish alive. The nine men sent to fight me this morning were also, I believe, meant to die by my hand, though some supernatural agent intervened to do the work instead, for reasons that elude me. I begin to fret that some fate of mine is bound to Kanno province and that I was drawn here for other reasons than to inform Heinosuke of his sister's death. Am I somehow your master's pawn but cannot see it? Is there some connection between myself and his malevolence? If he seeks to use me in some way, it will be his undoing, I am sure. I would like to meet your master and find out his intent!"

Ittosai said, "You cannot ask his vassal's aid."

"Do you refuse to comprehend your master's villainy?"

"That is not for me to judge."

"Even if it can be proven that he is a monster escaped from Emma's Hell, born of this strange temple?"

"I wouldn't know about such things," he said flatly.

It was years since she had personally counted on the regulations of vassalage for the definition of her own conduct, and the bikuni was irritated that Ittosai was not similarly able to think for himself. She was free and a wanderer; he had wandered too. His stubbornness made her tell him hotly, "It annoys me that you feel the way you do!"

"I'll tell you what I know," said Ittosai, his voice gone throaty and strange, his white eyes turning on her again. His expression was at once calm and maniacal. He did not seem the same fellow she had met that morning, or who had entered the chamber moments before. In this unexpected persona, Ittosai spoke with greater self-assurance. He said, "What I know is this." When the nun was attentive, he continued, "You, woman of Heida, are the nearest living relative of Kuro the Darkness."

The bikuni was plainly shocked. Her throat was instantly dry. Ittosai continued to speak.

"Through you, Kuro will have vengeance, for reasons that are not my business to ask about. You say you are annoyed with me, but consider my position; I have greater reason for annoyance. You unwittingly perform services I would do with open eyes. You do against your will that which I would count proof of my worth as a vassal. I admired you before, but look how far you've fallen! And still I am a shadow in your wake. I wish Kuro would order me to kill you! But he values my strong arm for the way it holds a shovel. When at last your eyes are opened, you will know that you, more than Kuro the Darkness, were the monster of the play."

"What you say is senseless!" the bikuni challenged, backing to the wall as though attacked. "You're vicious to invent such a story! How could I be Priest Kuro's servant and not know it? How could he be my relative, when my clan lives far in the east of Naipon? I am a slayer of monsters! I am no beast!"

She staggered backward through the door, feeling again that nearly loving stroke at her nape, slapping at it with her hand, finding nothing. Ittosai's words could not be revelations, but only mistruths meant to confound her! He stood against the window of the chamber in which she might have slain Heinosuke. Snow fell behind the outline of Ittosai. He began to walk forward, following her down the corridor. He had become a dark shape inside a golden outline, glowing, a frightful vision though making no physical threat.

It was true she had felt something of madness in the haunted, derelict temple, and had nurtured some affection for the echoes of cruelty that made its presence known for miles around. Now the temple's malignance rang in her ears. Her hand covered her mouth and nose, for some spell descended upon her, along with sickness. She strode backward, keeping the glowing shape of Ittosai in her sight. She came out of the monastery onto the path, which had frozen, the snow beginning to stick. She continued as far as the wooden guardians, on whose heads sat small coronets of snow. The sound of the river and the falls could not drown the throbbing, knelling sound, which originated with Ittosai or the temple or from within her very skull.

She stopped between the tall wooden gods, took a stand, hand to hilt of sword, menacing Ittosai while shouting hoarsely,

"What have you brought me!"

"Truth."

"Or Kuro's magic! I have done you no harm. How can you make me think I am a monster? The trouble in Kanno province never began with me!"

"It will end with you. It will end badly."

"Because of truth or beguilement?" she demanded hotly. "You cannot charm me!" She began to calm her spirit, straighten her posture, but kept her hand to hilt as she said with a forced quiet, "I won't let it happen."

Ittosai was himself in the grip of some spell, standing as an automaton without emotion, betraying none of his anger, none of his pride, none of the goodness she had felt could not be long suppressed. He raised his hand, in which he held a small wooden plaque, which she had not seen him holding before. He recited the sutra inscribed thereon, his white eyes glaring at her from under the edge of his hat.

"Namu myoho-renge-kyo. Namu myoho-renge-kyo."

"Stop it!" she demanded, sounding stern, but he did not stop. Her sword came from its sheath and she ran along the snow-sprinkled path toward Ittosai. Steel slashed across the top of his hand. In a moment, the top of the plaque fell off, landing between Ittosai's feet. The bikuni growled, "I cannot be made to do a dark priest's bidding!" She was panting and felt that she was not talking to Ittosai any longer, but through him to Priest Kuro himself.

"Ho ho," was Ittosai's response. The amusement and sarcasm of his tone and look was definitely not in keeping with the nature of the man. "If what you say is true," he said, "then you should experiment with it and find out. Last night, a runaway maid from the castle was found trying to flee the fief, a crime punishable by death. She was aided by a farmer's son. At this moment they are being tied head-down to the cross. They will die in a fenced enclosure outside the village. Criminals are commonly exposed there, to die slowly, as examples to others. It's a hard way to die. Sometimes people last for days. On the other hand, with the sudden snow, they could freeze to death in one night. How unfortunate! And weren't they pretty lovers?" Ittosai, or whatever made him speak, laughed again, this time without bitterness, without anger, without sorrow. There was only joy. He said, "If you are strong enough, if you are independent of Kuro's whims, why not save the pitiable couple? They are among Kuro's foes, after all. If you can get them out of their trouble, then you will have proven Kuro has no hold on you, no plan for you. Can you do it? Why not try?"

When the bikuni was gone, Ittosai Kumasaku strode bearlike over the thin blanket of snow. He went to the place where he had tethered the old mare. He stroked her muzzle, took hold of the reins, but did not mount. Instead, he looked about in confusion. Somehow he had forgotten why he had come to the temple.

His brain ached. He took off his wide straw hat and wiped his forehead. His hair was soaked, his face hot. Snowflakes steamed into nonexistence as they brushed his cheek.

He leaned hard against the flank of his mare; and with wild, forlorn expression, he began to bellow as with pain. The horse, old but battle-trained, was frightened, but did not move as Ittosai continued yelling, and yelling, and yelling.

She hurried to the edge of the mountain village, then strolled with a forced casual air through its center street. It was early in the evening. The sun, though nearly invisible, had not as yet gone below the mountains. The weather, as well as fearful sentiments, had sent most of the villagers indoors. Most of the shopkeepers had taken in their signs, somewhat prematurely. A tea and noodle shop remained open. A young woman stood in the doorway, gazing toward the farther edge of town, her expression tense, rice-floured hands worrying the apron hanging from her obi. As the nun passed by, the young woman averted her eyes and withdrew into the interior of the noodle shop.

Two middle-aged men in peasant blues came down the middle of the street. They were squat fellows conversing with one another rapidly, making vague comments about pitiful this and pitiful that. Their conversing halted when they saw the nun in her incognito-hat and two swords at her side. She appeared to them out of the swirling snow, causing them to draw aside and stand motionless, mouths open, eyes round. When she had gone by them without taking much notice, they renewed their jabber. She overheard a reference to the Battle of Awazu. Then she caught another snatch of their discussion, predicting warm blood on fresh snow. They knew much, these peasants! Priest Bundori's tongue had wagged through the town, and the nun's present nonchalance fooled no one.

She saw eyes peeping from windows that were opened the barest slit. The whole village expected carnage. What else was in their minds? Did they think her the gravest part of their misfortune, or their salvation?

Fires burned in the homes, but the snow cleansed the air of smoke or scent of cooking. There was a deadening of all the senses, due in part to the muffling snow; and there was a quietude about the village that smacked of held breaths. Somewhere nearby, the silence was momentarily interrupted by a door slamming adamantly—against the cold, and against expectation.

As she neared the further edge of the village, the bikuni took a narrow alley off the center street, circling about in such a way that she could investigate the punishment-enclosure without the guards noticing her presence. The enclosure was made with thick, sharp strips of bamboo, loosely laced from one vertical pole to another. There was a gate that could be removed altogether or left completely sealed, as now, made of the same laced strips. It would be easy to fit one's arm through any portion of the fence, but it would be difficult to pull it down or push on it without cutting oneself on the hard strips of razor-edged bamboo.

Her view was veiled by the swirling whiteness. The track she made in passing was already filling up with windblown and new-fallen flakes. The guards' chances of noticing her, a mere shadow between two buildings across the way, were slight.

There were more guards than one would expect. Someone certainly did not wish the couple saved from their slow execution. Inside the criss-cross fence, a small fire had been built, around which squatted samurai with long spears leaning against their shoulders, hands cast forth in search of warmth. At the enclosure's entry, four men, also with spears and swords, stood conversing. Additional sentries strode about the inside and outside of the enclosure, only nominally on guard, seeming quite certain the weather had driven off the usual village spectators or anyone with a mind toward intervention.

The men did not themselves seem especially concerned about the redundancy of their post. They had learned in the past months that duties and assignments were occasionally pointless or askew, directed less by Lord Sato than by his minister Kuro the Darkness, whose reasoning evaded understanding. Most of Lord Sato's men no longer cared one way or another how things were run.

It was curious and darkly whimsical that the villagers, thanks to Priest Bundori's gossip, suspected things might be coming to an alarming point, but Lord Sato's vassals remained unready for a raid of the very sort suggested by Ittosai, Kuro's one true vassal. These samurai were almost pitiful, going aimlessly about their appointed task, knowing nothing of potential doom lurking beyond their fortress of bamboo, a doom clad in the costume of a mendicant nun.

Shinji and Otane were at the enclosure's very center and, for the moment, totally undefined, due to increasing snowfall. Then a sudden, higher wind brushed aside the veil long enough for the nun to see the couple, a sight that brought a grimace to her covered face. They were clad in peasant cottons—*mopei* knee-britches and *hapari* field jackets—clothing that the youth Shinji would have provided so that Otane might not be detected as a samurai's daughter; a failed plan.

They were mounted head-down and back to back, spread-eagle on the X of the wooden cross, bound arms and ankles by means of hemp rope. Both had long hair unbound and brushing the ground. The nun could not see Shinji clearly, for he was on the backside of the cross; but they had turned their faces sideways that their cheeks might touch.

They were stoic and silent. Their heroic love and tragedy

made them seem heavenly spirits tortured by callous hands of mortals lacking understanding of such beauty and rich sentiment.

As for the numerous vassals posted in and around the punishment-enclosure, they seemed hardly to notice their woeful wards. Whether such heartlessness was from a true lack of feeling or an emotional deadening that protected their own hearts was impossible to judge. The crucifixion itself was not an untoward event, and a samurai was rightly immune to much opinion. By contrast, an esoteric nun was free to exert all manner of fervid sympathy or response.

As the wind passed, the snowy curtains hid the sad vision once more. The bikuni rubbed sore hands vigorously to warm them. She was eager for the reaping, for surely it was a nun's duty to save such perfect beings as these who had been captured. Never mind that the young vassal samurai were only slightly less innocent, and perhaps the sadder for having never known an attachment like the one that the couple knew. Never mind that a nun performed the bidding of a dark priest. Shinji and Otane could by no means be left to excruciation and death!

Two humps of snow in front of the sealed gate moved. The bikuni realized one of those inconsequent humps was in reality the widow Todawa, who had been bowing long before the gate in abject obeisance. The other hump was her grandson, feeble-minded Iyo. Snow fell from their shoulders as they sat up on their knees, and Iyo looked to his grandmother for direction, having no idea how to behave in such a fix, having less idea why his sister and Shinji were thus maltreated. He looked confused rather than horrified and might not have a real sense of the agony suffered by the silent lovers. The father, Kahei Todawa, doubtless remained under house arrest, and so could not join the rest of his family in their prayers and hopeless pleas for mercy.

The bikuni could not see the widowed matriarch's face, but could not doubt the expression was anything but discompassionate, a mask disguising emotional turmoil. From this old woman, Otane had inherited stoicism; and it was from Otane that Shinji, usually sharp-tongued and unable to hide his feelings, had acquired a like amount of endurance, the epitome of dignity and intrepidness.

The nun had seen enough. Piqued, she stepped forward, leaving her geta a step behind, for she would like better footing since she would do battle on slippery snow. She drew steel as she took that step; but before she was out of the alley, she was momentarily blinded by an unexpected flurry of snow that had coalesced into a tiny, furious cloud before her hat. Seeing it through the loose-woven window-portion of her amigasa, the nun could not be absolutely certain she had seen, within that come-and-gone cloud, a pair of redly burning embers.

She dismissed the brief vision as a dollop of snow fallen from the eves. But as she started again from the alley, there came once more that tiny monstrosity of whiteness and red eyes fluttering before her, batting against her incognito-hat, plaguing her line of sight.

A guard circling the bamboo enclosure noticed the cream-and-charcoal shadow beneath the eaves. He started forth to investigate. The nun withdrew into the alley, for the snow-colored beast was most vexing. Her sword cut upward at an angle, then down. She heard a chirping sound as the face-flutterer struck the ground. She looked where the thing had fallen and realized it was one of Priest Bundori's albino birds. Her sword had only clipped its wing. It hopped away through the snow, complaining like a bothered hen.

The bird would freeze to death in the snow, unable to fly back to White Beast Shrine. The nun felt responsibility for its small life. She sheathed her sword, stepped backward onto her wooden geta, then turned to backtrack a ways, intending to catch the clipped bird.

The inquisitive samurai, sad to say, continued his approach, though not with much wariness. He hurried through the alley, then pursued the nun across a clearing beyond the buildings. He called for her to stop, but she increased her pace, not looking back.

He came in earnest now. He was nearly upon her. She heard his sword slide from its scabbard. In that instant, she turned to face him, her weapon having appeared in her hand with the swiftest ease. The samurai looked startled. Then he looked horrified to realize he had been gutted. Blood melted red holes in the snow.

The bikuni stood poised, her back to an ancient fir at the clearing's edge. Her sword was held at a high angle where its sweeping arc had ended, sharp edge toward the fir. For a moment the samurai looked as though he wanted to collapse. When he did not do so, the bikuni's blade twisted forward, ready to retrace its previous path and take the man a second time.

He wavered in his stance, looking at her piteously. His surprise, which had become horror, now became resignation and resolve. His sword swept forward, striving to cut her mortally, but the nun's steel was quicker, cutting at an angle across his forehead, even while she stepped aside from his assault.

Blinded by his own gushing blood, he turned toward the sound of the bikuni's footsteps. He staggered in her direction, then fell to his knees. His sword went back and forth madly, trying for a lucky contact. The bikuni lowered her sword, watching him. He fell to his left shoulder, still swinging his sword in his right hand, swinging it at nothing, at snowflakes. Then he rolled to his back, grasping the sword in a proper two-handed manner. He thrashed foolishly, grunted, hoping against all probability to slay his slayer.

His pain was evident. It would be cruel and immoral to abandon him without his coup de grace. It was this very necessity on which he placed his hopes—to cut her when she tried to get close enough to end his anguish.

She leapt forward, parrying his ridiculous cut, and buried the point of her sword in his throat.

Now, poised above him, seeing him awash in his own blood, the bikuni forgot the vision of Shinji and Otane and saw, instead, how Priest Kuro meant to use her. The excessive guard was not there to insure her failing to pull the crucified lovers from their shared cross. Rather, Kuro the Darkness had faith in her ability. He counted on her to kill all those pathetic vassals.

The horror of her dilemma was only beginning to settle in when a tall, slender woman in shimmering white kimono stepped out of wreathes of snow. The bikuni stepped away from the slain vassal, raising her sword, then lowering it, seeing the woman pale as death, eyes red as blood, one sleeve of her kimono shorn halfway through, as though by a sword's stroke.

"Has someone attacked you?" the bikuni asked.

"Someone has," the white woman said, her tone ironic. She was young and eerily gorgeous, a snowy apparition with a courtesan's coiffure and sensuously aristocratic bearing. "My name is Akuni," she said, "a friend of Reverend Bundori. He asked me to see if you were all right, so I came just now to search for you."

The white woman drew nearer the nun and the corpse, cocking her head to one side to look at the samurai and his blood. She said,

"Bundori-sama thinks highly of you, despite that you wear Buddhist garb. A little prejudice might serve him better. Why have you killed this blameless man? You will be stuck here in Kanno province forever, making stone lanterns, if you are so careless!"

The lantern was a private matter and the bikuni was annoyed to have it mentioned. "It was not Bundori's business to tell you about the lantern."

Akuni raised her pale brow, supremely arrogant as she said, "He didn't tell me! I watched you myself! In any case, if you truly wish to end the sorrows of Lord Sato's fief, you need not kill a lot of guiltless men to succeed. You need only kill the demonic Priest Kuro up there in Sato's fortress."

"You appear demonic yourself," said the nun, sword still bared and stained with blood. The white woman laughed almost sweetly and did not act the least bit threatened.

"Perhaps I am a demon after all!" she allowed, thrilled by the notion. "But there are demons, and there are demons. Don't you think so? Reverend Bundori would not like that I suggest you kill Kuro out of hand. Nonetheless, it's what I think you should do. It would be better than killing two dozen or so vassals trying to save those pitiable lovers, *neh?* Should so many die for the sake of your meddling chivalry? If you want to save your friends, why not petition Lord Sato directly? Better still, petition his daughter Echiko, who is sentimental about lovers and would be upset to find out what is going on."

The white woman laughed a final time, then looked askance at the bikuni and added, "You always hide under that hat! Don't you know everybody knows who you are? Tell them at the castle you are Tomoe Gozen, a widow-warrior and defender of the Imperial House! How can they refuse you entry? An insult to the Emperor if they fail to greet you! Use your head for once, not your steel!"

Saying this much, the white woman withdrew into thickening snowfall, holding the cut part of her sleeve to herself. The bikuni pursued a few paces, finding that the trail vanished almost at once. She could see only the hop-marks of a passing bird; and even these were quickly erased by wind and new snow.

PART TWO

The Suffering Dark

"Princess Echiko," the nearest maid-in-waiting whispered. "It snows upon the castle."

Echiko sat huddled in a corner of the room, having crawled from her bedding some while before, trying to hide from haunted dreams and memories. Her once-beautiful face was thin and sallow. There were shadows around her eyes. At first she did not respond to the maidservant's solicitous information. In a few moments, her head began to turn, slowly, painfully. She opened her mouth to reply, but said nothing.

The maid-in-waiting draped a padded winter kimono around the sickly Lady Echiko and tried to get her to stand. Other young women moved about the dark room like shades, their moods habitually dour. The youngest maidservant, scarcely more than a child, found a huge umbrella in a cabinet. Another of Echiko's companions opened a door onto night's snowy garden.

"Come and see the snow from your veranda," the maid-in-waiting whispered, her voice edged more with resignation than concern, for concern had long proved unavailing. Echiko was brought to her feet with the aid of two maidens, one of whom had put new, thick tabi-socks on the princess.

She was a ghastly thin puppet in their hands, going where they led her. Her feet shuffled past a tray of untouched food, then out of the room. At the edge of the veranda, she stepped down onto a pair of high wooden geta; one of her servants made sure the princess placed each foot properly. The geta were high enough to keep her feet above the snow.

As they took her through the garden, between stones and stunted evergreens and amidst the naked, twisted branches of slumbering trees, she went with an eerie kind of poise, an

ethereal, skeletal grace. She was like a corpse-princess on high clogs, many layers of clothing askew, hair not quite in place. She was Death's most decorative beauty. She was the consort of King Emma of the Dark Land.

The littlest maidservant had a bit of trouble handling the long-poled umbrella whenever there was a breeze. She was not concerned whether the lady's maids were struck by snowfall; nor did she regard her own chill. But she made sure the princess was protected. It was her duty, which she took most seriously, and it was her genuine desire to defend Lady Echiko from any added plight, however minor.

Soon they were leading Echiko less than it appeared, for she chose her own direction. They passed through her private gardens without once looking at the snow-softened contours of things. The mansion was built atop high stone masonry, the masonry surrounded by moats. It was a castle only in the widest sense, richer than a mere fortress, a great house built atop an artificial mountain of granite blocks. Echiko, braced by her least taciturn maidservant, went down a steep path, away from the mansion, toward a practice range where, in better times and better weather, samurai sported and trained. It was currently a flat, miniature wasteland. She and her maids-in-waiting crossed it without looking about.

They came at last to battlements on the pseudo-cliff's edge, overlooking Lord Sato's private estates. Echiko could not see far, for it was after nightfall, and there were no stars, no moon, only a sky filled with icy feathers.

She pushed feebly at the girl holding the umbrella, wanting as she did to feel snowflakes on her cheeks and lashes. The women fretted that they had encouraged their lady too far. She might let herself catch a chill, which in her weakened state would surely lead to death. But they could not force themselves on her now, for the princess was in rapture, her thin face turned toward the sky, her eyes closed, Heaven cooling her fears and sorrows.

When she opened her perpetually sleepy eyes, it was to watch her own arm rising slowly, palm upward, catching flakes as they fell. When several snowflakes rested on her hand, she squeezed them. Then she opened her bony fingers to see the flakes had melted into tears. Her weak, weary voice spoke tragically, laconically:

"Isn't life a snowflake? Aren't all of us in the palm of great, warm hands?"

She tried to see through the darkness and the falling snow, gazing uselessly across the vast Sato estates. She looked in the direction of the peasant village. On a clear, bright day it would have been there before her, small and distant. On a clear night, it would be there smokily, as in a dream. Now there was nothing.

"Has Furusato vanished?" she asked, calling it by a traditional name. "Have the peasants of Old Village ceased to be? How sad it is."

"They are there, Princess," whispered the maidservant who was always closest. "The snow and darkness hides them, that is all."

"No. There is nothing there. They have followed Heinosuke into the Land of Darkness."

"Heinosuke will come for you eventually, Princess. Please do not lose heart."

"Oh! Do you hear it?"

"What, Lady?"

"That song we heard this morning, when you brought me here before!"

"No, Lady. That was hours and hours ago. There is no music now. And we were unable to find out for you whom it was."

"I can still hear it," she insisted, dreamy eyes gazing, head turned just so, as though to capture more of the distant harmonies. The maids-in-waiting looked extremely worried. Echiko's health had deteriorated so much, she often hallucinated. "Every note," she said, "is a veiled allusion. Have you ever heard anything so sad?"

"That was this morning, Princess."

"It has a rough elegance, don't you think so?"

"Yes, Princess," said the maidservant, giving in.

"It must be a warrior's performance. It's very good. Does one of my father's retainers play the shakuhachi? It comes from amidst the vassals' estates, I'm sure."

"It came from an old pagoda," said the fretful maiden. "We found out that much for you. But that was before. It was probably just a wanderer, who has continued along the Way."

"Oh! It comes nearer! Does the player bring news of Heinosuke?"

Echiko moved nearer the edge of the wall. She lurched forward and would have vanished downward along with the snow, leaving only the echo of her plunge into the moat. But that ever-present maidservant grabbed Lady Echiko's sleeve and drew her back.

"Don't stop me!" Echiko complained, batting at her helper. "Heinosuke calls me!" The other maidservants pressed near, trying to keep their lady from struggling, lest she fall from the ledge or merely exhaust herself to the point of collapse. The youngest maiden, holding the umbrella, was struck soundly in the face by Echiko's thrashing. The little maid went off the edge, not making a sound. The other maids-in-waiting had their voices catch in their throats. They looked down to see the top of the umbrella floating away, away. Then there was a faint splash.

"A snowflake," Echiko murmured, more dreamily than ever, her hostility gone as quickly as it came, her suicidal effort ended. "A snowflake."

Chamberlain Norifune shuffled through the dark hallway. His chilly toes were curled within his tabi-socks. He muttered to himself as he went, like a man two or three decades older. He ruminated about the world and his place in it, a comfortable place but not necessarily a stable one. He could not shake the notion that everything could be turned upside down at any moment, shaking him out into a dreary place, or snatching away his very life, reducing him to a pot of ashes.

Kanno, like many of the outlying provinces, had gone largely undisturbed during the clashes between the original Imperial armies of Heian-kyo and the upstart Shogun's forces from Kamakura. The wars began and ended without much effect on such a far-flung fief as Kanno; but a provincial government could not afford to be oblivious to the changes taking place in Naipon.

The outcome of the upheavals was that Kamakura became the new capital. The Emperor was finally and ultimately a figurehead. Kamakura's governance was not yet comprehensive, which might be a relief except that it rendered paranoia two-sided and responses unpredictable.

Some domains had resident Kamakura vassals as constables, answerable to the Shogun rather than a provincial lord, serving as a check against abuse of power and to insure fealty with the

Office of the Military. Other domains, for the time being, retained the hereditarily supported Imperial constabulary, reporting to Heian-kyo, or Kyoto as it had late been called. Really these latter officials had lost meaningful contact with the throne thirty or forty years earlier, and it was this very type of weakening of authority that had caused the reshuffling of central power. The Kamakura shogunate was not about to let the situation repeat itself, laxity merely encouraging provincial lords to rise, even as the present Shogun's clan had risen with domination in mind.

Kanno was one of the domains that had only an antiquated Imperial constable. Furthermore, that constable happened to be one-and-the-same with Chamberlain Norifune, which was part of the cause of his concern. He continued to send annual reports to Heian-kyo, designed to placate rather than inform, and generally some kind of formal reply would be forthcoming from the old capital. Yet the changing world had rendered such sneakiness a pointless ritual, Heian-kyo pretending influence, her constables pretending fealty and appeasement.

The Imperial government was not precisely abolished, since the military could not be so audacious. The Shogun legitimized his rule by means of regency, not usurpation. All the same, by slow stages, Imperial posts were being undermined and ultimately displaced by shogunate equivalents. It was only a matter of time before the process reached Kanno.

A man could not remain successful if he were devoid of tactical considerations. Many of the Imperial constables throughout Naipon were eager to trade their old titles for new ones proffered by Kamakura. Norifune courted just such a notion. "If I can get a post similar to the one I've always held," he thought, "then my position will be secure." But this wasn't exactly true, he realized, for the shogunate was not the emasculated government Norifune's family had served since time immemorial. "The shogunate will insist I make reports about Lord Sato, who is a good friend nowadays." Well, he thought, it would be possible to fabricate a lot of harmless stuff, but it wouldn't be as easy.

Thus the chamberlain's plans were to be on guard for government spies; to ingratiate himself if one appeared, so that he would be able to keep his position intact; and in the meantime, to follow Lord Sato's advice and enjoy life. Didn't Lord Sato like to say, "Won't those silly peasants grow rice whether I say so or not? Don't they pay their taxes every year? That's enough for me! Things won't fall apart if we play another game of chess. Hey, send some men to turn loose that stag they caught the other day! I want to shoot it down this afternoon!"

Yet the chamberlain had to admit he wasn't such a happy man, despite all evidence of good fortune. Duty didn't mean one grain of rice to him, so he ought to be able to look at present affairs as ideal, nothing tiring, worldly pleasures indulged. Somehow he could only think how cold it was in the castle, no matter how much charcoal was put in a pot. Candles never penetrated the darkness very far. Odd he hadn't noticed it when he was a young man. Had the castle changed? Probably only he had changed, had gotten older. "If I do get appointed constable for the new government, perhaps it will entail transferral to some other province closer to the center of things." Preferably, it would be someplace warmer, where spring and summer were not so short and autumn was not a part of winter.

And he often felt depressed to realize all these self-serving plots and plans would come to nothing if, as he feared, he would not be able to impress those harsh men under the Shogun. They might see right through him and realize he wanted merely to enjoy life in Lord Sato's castle, serving minimally, participating in the hunts with his patron, relishing the prestige of titles, wearing handsome clothes. Norifune had few illusions about himself. He was not an extraordinary swordsman of the sort the Shogun's men admired. They might pass him over with scoffing laughter. Even if they did not strip him of the title originated by Emperors, a shogunate constable could very easily come to live in Kanno. Then Norifune's privileges would be as good as usurped, his position a redundancy and an anachronism. He might at least hope to remain chamberlain; but even that might come to doubt, since Lord Sato wasn't apt to impress the Shogun's men either. His fate and the fate of his patron were inextricably linked.

Norifune was diligent neither as a constable nor as a chamberlain. He could not deny it to himself, though he kept up a few public appearances. His duties had long been meted out to underlings who, one by one, came under the influence of Lord Sato's religious tutor, Priest Kuro, whose name meant "black" and who reveled in the irony of being referred to as

Kuro the Darkness. Lord Sato had similarly delegated most of his duties to vassals, who by degrees began to count on Kuro for religious and temporal guidance alike.

Had Chamberlain Norifune been a wiser fellow, he might have warned his Lord about Kuro's wheedled power. But life was complicated enough as it stood. It was easier to be blind to things, or even grateful that Kuro kept the castle affairs in order while titled men exercised prodigal freedoms.

Having arrived in his private chambers, Norifune saw that his page had already laid out a mattress. The page helped Norifune out of his hakama. But Norifune was not ready for bed and did not allow his kimono to be removed. Instead, he slouched down in front of a pot of coals and, after the page laid a rich quilt over his shoulders and withdrew into an adjoining room, Norifune picked at the coals with a pair of tongs, and continued to worry and wonder why he felt so ill at ease night after night.

He did perform a small amount of work, he reminded himself. He signed important papers prepared by others. He made a few officious commands here and there, usually with Priest Kuro's counsel. In his behavior he was not at all unlike Lord Sato had lately become; so, he reasoned, he must be serving Lord Sato pretty well since they agreed in their actions.

Much of Norifune's work had recently been geared toward readiness against any spy from Heian-kyo or, worse, Kamakura. It was his duty to hide the fact that Lord Sato had become a lazy, unthinking leader! It was in his own best interest to keep either the old or the new governments from finding out that Norifune himself was less than a skilled executor.

Life was a worry.

Lord Sato hadn't always been a poor ruler in Kanno. Norifune was smart enough to have noticed the change. He wasn't smart enough to guess some connection with Priest Kuro. Nor did he really believe Lord Sato's change was for the worse, since he'd become most congenial though somewhat dotty.

Norifune had, like his father before him, served the province in such a manner as to give the old government no cause to interfere; and Lord Sato, like his father before him, appreciated these efforts and awarded the Imperial constable a high post inside the castle. Norifune was shamelessly aware of his personal corruption, but didn't think he was a base fellow compared to some he had heard about. And if Lord Sato had become, in the last year, rather more like Norifune's indolent family and less like the clever and proud Sato clan, well, was Norifune to judge himself so badly as to dislike his own attributes when seen in his patron?

Since there was no Imperial government left (or not worth guarding against), having control of one's Imperial constable was pretty much wasted effort. But ever since Lord Sato became dissolute, he went unconcerned about the fact of Norifune's limited political value. This lack of concern suited Norifune well. He didn't think he was young enough to succeed in some other capacity if life changed too much.

Yet there remained that inescapable inevitability of the shogunate's sooner or later wanting to know how things sat in Kanno. Norifune had lived with this worry for a few years already; and still there was no indication of Kamakura's interest. Kanno had never been very important and was not a priority to the Shogun. The region had kept to itself for so long that it was not viewed as a possible threat to anyone, else the Lords of Kanno would have risen in past generations. But if Kamakura acquired the least suspicion, Kanno could find itself instantly the brunt of criticism and impositions from outside. Norifune could not afford to bide his time in the midst of such uncertainty.

Once or twice he tried to broach the topic of Kamakura with his patron, who Norifune genuinely wished to protect, this being the surest way to protect himself. But Lord Sato was scarcely a ruler any longer, wanting only to get pleasure from this life and salvation at its closing. That Lotus priest taught that excess would lead to virtue. For once a man knew he could have everything, in the long run he would prefer nothing, and thereby he would become pure. It was also fine if it took a long time to reach that point, Kuro assured, as long as one remembered to recite the Lotus Sutra on a regular basis. Sato became disinterested in governing his fief, preferring to pursue happiness. Kuro interpreted this as spiritual advancement, for power meant nothing, joy was better. To make it easier for Lord Sato to quest through frivolity on his way to enlightenment, Kuro took much of the burden of leadership onto his own back, poor fellow. But, inasmuch as Kuro was an unworldly fellow with unfathomable distractions of his own, it was not surprising that a few things would go to ruin under a priest's administration.

Thus it was small use to take the fief's problems to Lord Sato, who would only reply, "Let's go on a hunt today!" or "Let's play a game of *shogi!*" sending some page after the gameboard.

So like many others, Norifune had taken his worries to Priest Kuro and had gotten good advice. Norifune was told that spies would indeed precede an official delegation, whether from Heian-kyo or Kamakura; and these spies were apt to go around in the guise of mendicant priests or nuns, since only nameless pilgrims could travel Naipon without having to identify themselves at every border and station. Kuro had a natural antipathy for religions other than his own, but this advice struck Norifune as meritable in its own right.

Thus Chamberlain Norifune saw to it that religious travelers were denied access to the castle and, in general, harrassed and met with indifference or hostility—even from the peasants, who feared retribution from the Castle.

"I should be grateful to Priest Kuro," said Norifune to the glowing coals. "Temporal counsel must be a nuisance to him, yet he tries so hard to be of service."

Despite the recurrence of troubled thoughts and depression, Norifune did not feel the least guilty about himself. Conscience was not an issue. After all, it wasn't as though anyone were abusing the local population. It was true that Norifune and his patron had a tendency to look the other direction when something happened of its own accord, but few destructive policies were instigated. Few policies of any kind were instigated!

Nor was anyone trying to raise an army to cause neighboring fiefs a lot of trouble. Indeed, Lord Sato's army had dwindled due to attrition, desertions, and additional reasons perhaps inexplicable but easily overlooked.

So while things were unusual enough that an investigation could be catastrophic, on the other hand it wasn't as though Sato or Norifune were plotting against whoever might send spies. (Plotting against the spies themselves was a different matter.)

Norifune thought about these things quite often, reminding himself he only desired to live happily, even as Lord Sato wished to do, without having to work any harder than was necessary, and gain as much reward from life as could be found.

Too, now that Lord Sato had gotten to be so much like his chamberlain, they were fast friends. Norifune took pride in this relationship. They were genuinely fond of one another and had become two of the most useless fellows in Kanno province. And what of it? Wasn't the Emperor useless with the Shogun as regent? Wasn't the Shogun useless with regents of his own? The more important the man, the less he should have to do!

But if it were so, why was Norifune so downtrodden, especially at night? Only an hour before, he had been playing *go* with Lord Sato and feeling merry. Now, he was cooped up alone, transient gaiety forgotten, brooding about all these things, not one of which fully explained his recurrent downcast feelings. "I'm an old man," he thought, huddled near the firepot, his shoulders quivering beneath the heavy quilt. He looked at the paper lantern, its candle flickering, its light somehow wan. "But I'm not really as old as my bones feel," he added. In truth he was only in his forties, Lord Sato's age. He had a healthy paunch and only a few wrinkles. Still, since his wife had died the year before, about the time Priest Kuro came to the castle, Norifune had not found the nights reassuring. He hadn't been close to his wife, so it wasn't as though he were a grieving widower, but the night was filled with threats and ghostliness for him. He moped about the halls and his private chambers night after night, as restless and dispirited as a sick old has-been.

He might call for a maid or page to keep him warm, to cheer his night; but they always tried to make him perform in some manly way, even though he knew it didn't interest them, and it didn't interest him either.

Then he thought he might see a priest and unburden himself. But the only priest was Kuro. Kuro had come to be more like a state minister or someone like that, and was no good at lifting the spirits of a pious chamberlain. "Me a pious man!" he said aloud, and laughed snidely at himself. "If I were more pious, maybe Priest Kuro could help me. As it stands, every time I see him, I feel worse."

He shook his head. Nothing could make him feel better.

Ordinarily he would have sat thus two or three more hours before wearing out his brain and crawling off to sleep. But tonight was going to be different, filled with distractions; for Norifune was about to have some of his fears fully realized and worse fears invented for him.

His room was unexpectedly invaded by a page other than the boy in the adjoining room. The page heralded a certain vassal, then departed. The warrior who hurried in afterward was sweaty and smelled of horse. He informed Norifune that a government agent had announced herself at the bridge and was being led to the castle by several men afoot.

"*Her*self?" said Norifune, his weak chin vanishing altogether when he drew himself to full sitting posture. His coverlet fell away and he grabbed an edge of it in his fist. "A spy?"

The vassal kneeling before the chamberlain replied, "Well, she's been reported near here for several days without once announcing herself. Could have been spying. She's a mendicant nun, but insists it is no disguise but her true calling."

"Is she of Kamakura?" asked Norifune, and the vassal shook his head, quoting what he had heard:

"'Defender of the Imperial House.'"

"Well, that's something at least," said Norifune, somewhat relieved. So it might turn out to be a matter of etiquette and formal greetings—plus a cash token of appreciation, since the agent purported to be a mendicant. Quite a clever ploy to infer gifts bought silence! There would be some prestige for Lord Sato if things went well. A visit from someone connected with the Imperial house was something worthwhile, even if the agent's connection were tangential. Norifune would have to trump up some reasonable-sounding reports for the agent to carry back to Heian-kyo; but since the government that mattered was in Kamakura, the whole thing could be chalked up to a formal affair, although rather late in the night for one.

The vassal withdrew after leaving Norifune this news. Norifune's personal page helped the chamberlain change into a smart pair of hakama trousers and put on his best overcoat with lovely tassels in front. He had just about convinced himself that *this* was not going to be a fretful encounter and that none of Lord Sato's traditional positions need be compromised. He said, more to himself than to the page who helped him arrange his costume nicely, "A good excuse for a late-night celebration, with saké and many toasts to the Emperor and his agent!" He welcomed the prospects. "Gloomy night anyway. Needed something to happen, as long as it's pleasant."

She no longer wore her incognito-hat, though she had not exactly given anyone her name; and she had not brought her alms-bag, which in any case had been damaged, but mainly was inappropriate for an official meeting with Lord Sato. She was not coming for his entertainment, after all; nor should she imply that a gift or reward was sought, whether for some religious advice or performance on the shakuhachi.

She was accompanied by a half-dozen samurai, who had been among the night guard stationed at the main bridgehouse. They went half in front and half behind, four of them with lanterns hung on bamboo poles; and they made a ghostly procession upon the narrow road. To the sides of the road were open fields, vanishing distantly into darkness. The forests had been leveled long ago, for the sake of the castle's construction and to insure no timber or hiding places for foe or would-be siege. In spring, the wild meadows would be beautifully flowered; presently, it was a wasteland of frozen, twisted stems, shrouded in deathly whiteness.

The snow had grown light. There was an area of starlight toward the horizon, suggesting that the clouds might break for at least a while. The wind was a bracing nuisance. The bikuni's long, loose sleeves whipped behind her.

Lord Sato's men treated her courteously but were clearly confused by her. They were under orders to deny pilgrims access to the castle, even to harrass them anywhere in the fief and province. But no samurai could deny an Emperor's vassal the least desire. They were therefore uncertain how to proceed with matters.

She had kept them ignorant of much, including what Emperor she happened to serve: the present puppet, or the one retired. They did not merit explanations, she maintained, taking on an air of elitism that she did not feel, but that was a common trait among those privileged to serve the Mikado.

Had they balked, she might have deigned to inform them how she had been appointed the Emperor's vassal while still a young woman, before the wars of Heian-kyo. It was more or less an honorific position, especially since the Shogun's rise; and she had never in her life laid eyes upon His Augustness and only occasionally had been called upon to serve Him in one or another capacity. Thus it was only in a narrow sense that she dared consider herself the Emperor's direct vassal.

Naipon was a conservative nation and its oldest customs demanded rigid and respectful obeisance. By custom, her position was spiritually significant and more awe-inspiring than a more materially meaningful association with the Shogun's government.

As the announcement of her position set matters of prestige and etiquette into play, rather than problems of governmental interference with provincial independence, the nun dared hope her situation was not especially dangerous. A shogunate informer would be hated and feared; assassination was the best recourse. Though the Imperial family's literal power was slight, the careers of lords had yet risen or fallen upon technicalities of propriety regarding the Mikado or His holy emissaries.

Thus she felt the trepidation of Lord Sato's men as they regarded her; as they considered the import and probity of her apparent station. They accompanied her along that dark road at a willfully slow pace, so that a rider would have the opportunity to arrive in advance and announce the situation. It could be that they would still attempt to do her injury. Other vassals might pour forth from the castle to attack, if the ban on pilgrims was to be upheld even in this extraordinary instance.

She wished she could hurry the procession or demand a horse, but her situation was too uncertain. Yet every moment Shinji and Otane remained bound to the cross, they came nearer to death. Could they be strong a little while? By using wit rather than brutality to save them, it would extend their misery by many hours. At least they shared the same cross and, bound back to back, could rely on each other's body warmth. But they had been dealt the added insult of inverted crucifixion, which was harder to endure. If one or the other grew faint or succumbed to drowsiness, neither might last until dawn.

Atop the huge wall of granite blocks sat the castle. There was a gap in the granite wall which, from a distant view, appeared as a black stripe blurred by falling snow. In that gap was a long flight of stairs and a horse-slope. There were two pairs of gates: one at the bottom, one at the top. Presently the nun and her six attendants were on the long stretch of ground leading to that entrance.

The road was no longer flanked by fields of snow, but by the half-iced moat. The soil and rocks from that enormous trough had gone to fill the area between the granite walls, so that the castle was really more like a fortress atop a large, artificial mesa.

Halfway along that portion of the road that bridged the fields with the castle, two of the samurai, then the others, pointed or looked skyward. An umbrella was falling at a sharp angle. Hanging from it was a girl in court costume. What an extraordinary sight it was! In a moment, the girl struck the thin, fresh ice of the moat and vanished beneath the top layer of snowy slush.

All that remained adrift was the open umbrella. It had made the girl's plunge weirdly slow. Now it marked the place of her almost certain death. The umbrella had carried her to shallows near the outer edge of the moat. If it had not broken her fall enough, then she would have died from impact against the stony bottom, not from extreme cold or drowning.

The six samurai had watched the spectacle with a sort of detached wonder, but the bikuni had darted back along the earthen causeway to see if the girl could be saved. When it registered that their ward had fled, the samurai pursued, although they dared not act as though they were guards against her rather than an honor-escort. When the first two stopped alongside her, she gave each an encouraging shove. They went simultaneously into the frigid moat and heard the sharp command, "Save that girl!"

The other four caught up by then. When the nun made as to shove them into the water also, two acted boldly and leapt on their own. The final pair held back, taking charge of the lanterns, against which snowflakes hissed. These two made some excuse about not getting in the way of the others, but the bikuni detected their fear that she might use the emergency to run off without their seeing where.

She climbed part way down the wall of the causeway to receive the unconscious girl. The girl's hand had to be pried loose of the umbrella. The four soaking samurai were shaking fiercely, their hands and faces instantly wrinkled by the shocking cold. The nun climbed onto the causeway, carrying the girl. The two dry samurai helped up the other four.

"Bring her umbrella!" the bikuni insisted, remembering how, even unconscious, the young woman had clung to it. "It may have saved her life. She will want to enshrine it, unless she dies despite your brave efforts."

Her tone implied praise for the four reluctant rescuers, who could barely walk or breathe. The bikuni was inwardly amused that they should continue after her as though capable of a fight if it were required. Now it was she who led the party at a pace more in keeping with her own eagerness. By the time they reached the bottom of the long stairway, her hair was white with clinging flecks of powdery snow. The gates flung open at the approach. Additional samurai—chattering and flustered—joined the hurried procession upward to the castle. The girl in the bikuni's arms stirred slightly, murmuring, "Snowflake. Snowflake," while nuzzling breasts. The moon appeared at their shoulders, just as they reached the upper gate. It peered from heaven as though curious.

More guards appeared at the top of the long stair, where the gates were wide open. Everyone was solicitous rather than threatening, so the advance rider had obviously been assured that the ban on pilgrims was momentarily lifted. The four freezing samurai were wrapped in quilts and led away like invalids. "Reward those men!" the bikuni said hoarsely, as though she had such authority. Three padded kimono were brought for the girl. The numerous dithering vassals and servants averted their eyes as the bikuni swiftly changed the girl's wet garments.

She refused to hand over the maiden to anyone else's care. She demanded the castle physician be roused and some reason for the near-tragedy be sought. "I won't turn her over to you," said the bikuni, "until I am satisfied nobody tried to kill her."

By now the maiden was half-conscious and looked into the stern bikuni's face like a baby gazing at its mother. The bikuni was not in a good mood, but could not refrain from smiling at the confused young woman. "Echiko," said the maiden. "Princess. Echi . . . ko." Then she closed her eyes and slept. The bikuni called after a cluster of departing samurai, adding to their errands, "If this is Echiko's lady-in-waiting, she will want to know about this!"

Finding herself in a position to issue indignant mandates, the bikuni insisted she be led before Lord Sato at once, going so far as to refuse to leave her swords with anyone "in a hostile house." This caused the castle men to stride the halls equally armed and leery.

She took the sleeping girl in the wake of those vassals who were leading the way. The physician arrived simultaneously, his hakama trousers hastily tied, and things were quickly arranged in one open partition of the meeting-rooms. Quilts were laid out for the maiden's repose; pots of charcoal were set near to keep her warm; water was heated for herbal remedies. The bikuni sat upon her knees nearby, refusing to let the patient be removed from her view. "I will stay in this adjoining room," she said, and the door was left wide.

The adjacent room was the main part of the meeting-chamber, in which there was something of a panic in progress as a result of the emergency. Lord Sato was not there; but the bikuni was introduced to Chamberlain Norifune. The chamberlain had evidently prepared the room for a midnight feast, and done so at moment's notice, thinking himself prepared for all events. Warm saké, mugwort rice cakes, bean jellies, dried persimmons, pickled fish and other foods were arranged on small, beautifully carved and lacquered trays. Pages and maids, gorgeously clad, were lined up near the food and drink, awaiting a signal to begin serving. But instead of an instant celebration, they were made witness to the aftermath of near-tragedy; and a stern-looking nun implied by her manner and few words that someone must have pushed the hapless girl off the walls of the castle. Also, the nun insisted Lord Sato appear at once. Such impudence! But it must be suffered if she served the Mikado.

Clearly it was not going to be much of a party after all; and Norifune's preparations were meaningless.

"Lord Sato intends to greet you," promised a befuddled Norifune. "Like myself, he was awake in any case, so it is no trouble to have a late visitor. But he wanted to get dressed especially well to receive you, and is still getting ready. Tell me, how is His Augustness the young Emperor?"

"I wouldn't know," the bikuni said curtly.

"Oh?" Norifune was taken aback. "Then you serve His Augustness-in-Retirement? It makes sense, as you have become a nun yourself. How is His Grace?"

"I wouldn't know that either."

Norifune was trying to be pleasant even in the face of someone rude; but her disinterest in the Mikado's health suggested that she might have contrived this whole business in order to gain access to the castle in spite of Lord Sato's ban.

"Pardon me," said Norifune, "but may I ask to see some credential or other? A letter with the Emperor's seal or signature perhaps?"

The bikuni had previously set her sword on the floor near her right side, which was not the side of readiness; and now she picked it up in her right hand as she stood, which was not a threatening motion since a sheathed sword was useless in the right hand unless the bearer was left-handed. All the same, several vassals' hands eased toward the hilts of their own sheathed swords.

"My credentials," said the nun, drawing steel left-handed and offering it to Norifune, blade pointing upward and away from the chamberlain. He took the sword from her and, kneeling before a bright lamp, inspected the temper. His brows raised suddenly when he recognized the famous design, and he said with surprise and alarm,

"The Sword of Okio!"

"One of only two remaining in Naipon," she affirmed. "The other has been retired to the same temple His Augustness Go-Temmu now makes His home."

As Norifune handed the sword back to its owner, Lord Ikida Sato appeared with two bodyguards at his personal entrance to the greeting-chamber. All heads went down except that of the nun and the two bodyguards. Lord Sato crossed the narrow stage at the head of the room and knelt beside an arm-table, striking an exaggerated and theatrical pose of self-importance.

He was wearing garments more suited to an aristocrat than a warlord. He had powdered his face, darkened his teeth, reddened his lips, and made large round brow-smudges high on his forehead. His real eyebrows had been shaved. On his head sat an eboshi hat, tipped forward. He might be cousin to the Mikado dressed thus! It was quite audacious, though he might have learned such dress from his late wife of the royal line, or felt it was a good way to appear when His Augustness' agent was present.

It was customary not to speak until after a Lord gave permission, but even before all the heads in the room were raised, the bikuni had remarked,

"A crow plays the cormorant," an adage which could be interpreted as, "A scruffy fellow thinks he's elegant." Lord Sato's pose was spoiled by a pouty look and his cheeks puffed out; but Chamberlain Norifune went immediately to intervene.

"That poor girl in the adjoining room fell from the castle walls. The nun suspects some evil goings-on and is upset about it. She serves Go-Temmu and it is a great honor for us to greet her, don't you think so?"

The bikuni saw how easily Lord Sato was placated. He seemed a bit of a clown to her and she bit her tongue sharply to keep from saying anything unnecessary. Rather, she changed her seated posture so that one knee was up, one hand upon the floor, and her gaze fixed boldly on Lord Sato. She got right to her point.

"I am here with a peremptory request!" she exclaimed.

"Ho?" said Lord Sato. It had been long since anyone had been peremptory with him. He appeared to like it more than patronizing attitudes and conciliations. As long as it did not turn out to be too difficult, he was interested.

"There is one of Lady Echiko's ladies-in-waiting, who is the only daughter of vassal Todawa. I wish her placed in my service."

"It is not a bold request," replied Lord Sato, before Chamberlain Norifune could stop him. Norifune hurried atop the short stage and knelt before Sato to whisper something to him. The bikuni was at the same time saying,

"The problem is that she is presently bound to a cross in the punishment-enclosure near the village. I would be grateful for the loan of a horse so that I may hurry to pull her down, along with a farmboy by the name of Shinji."

As Norifune withdrew from Lord Sato's side, the bikuni saw that the powdered face appeared twisted and perturbed. But Sato's annoyance passed in a moment. He leaned forward to match the hard gaze of the bikuni. He smiled pleasantly and asked,

"Do you play *shogi?*"

"I would respectfully decline."

Lord Sato looked to his left-hand bodyguard and said, "Hey, to fix a nice room for this lady! Tomorrow she will go on a hunt with me!"

"Lord Ikida Sato!" the nun said sharply. "As you can see, I have taken vows as a nun. I cannot go on a hunt with you, for I no longer eat meat other than fish."

"I see," said Lord Sato with a pensive but lost look. "Well, then, hey, you!" He addressed his right-hand bodyguard. "Get us a *go* board quickly!"

The bodyguard did not move from his Lord's side, which suggested to the bikuni that Lord Sato's private guards were actually under someone else's orders; otherwise, even a stupid request would be seen to immediately. The nun, appalled but not quite frustrated, turned to where Chamberlain Norifune sat. His face was awash with sweat, despite the fact that the room was chilly. The nun said,

"Chamberlain, your Lord appears to be insane. If word of it gets out of Kanno province, it means the clan's downfall. Rest assured, I am not here to spy on you. My itinerary does not include any stops at Heian-kyo or Kamakura in the fore-seeable future."

She implied her silence could be purchased after all. Chamberlain Norifune began to fumble in his sleeve-pocket, where he had already prepared funds. The bikuni was about to point out that she had no interest in Lord Sato's gold, but at that moment the heads in the room again began to bow. The skeletal Lady Echiko came into the room, dragging her long sleeves and long train of her court kimono. She had been listening, along with a couple of her servants, from outside in the hall. The bikuni had heard someone there for quite some while.

Though Echiko looked as wild and mad as her father, she was entirely lucid when she said to the chamberlain, "Fool! Don't give her money! Give her Otane as she requested! Why have you punished one of my maids without telling me? I wanted her returned, not executed!"

Echiko's awkward gait brought her within reach of Chamberlain Norifune, whom she struck soundly in the face with her closed fan. He turned his cheek aside and bore it. "She ran off with some peasant, my lady!" he said, trying to justify himself. "How many sins could be overlooked? Even Priest Kuro felt . . ."

Echiko hissed at him to stop. Her eyes were almost white. She circled the room, lingered momentarily at the doorway beyond which lay the sleeping, injured handmaiden. Sanity brushed the lady's complexion and there was clearly affection between Echiko and her servants. She was guileless where they were concerned; she had no recollection of the incident on the edge of the wall.

Then she continued to circle the room, a haunting and uncomfortable sight, and collapsed to her knees beside the nun to whom she spoke imploringly: "You came to save Otane because you pity her and her lover? I'm grateful to you! I didn't know about it, please believe me!" Echiko bowed to the nun, acting like her servitor. It was difficult for the bikuni to maintain her angry and arrogant pose in view of the anguish of the princess; but the nun managed to appear impassive.

"My father will write out a warrant for their release at once," said Echiko, raising her head abruptly. She looked sharply at her clownish father, who tried to act wise and upright in her presence. She said to him, "Isn't it so?"

"Get me brush and paper!" he demanded of his left-hand bodyguard, but someone else went for it instead. Soon he was writing out the warrant of release. His arm moved with the flourishing strokes and he fixed upon his visage a look of supremely humane feeling. Then he spoiled his own theatrics by glaring peevishly at his bodyguards, as though hating that they might peek at his calligraphy and pass judgment on it.

As the warrant was being folded, sealed, and Lord Sato's signature placed hugely on the outside, the bikuni sat without noticeable emotion, scarcely breathing. Echiko was panting and could not raise herself off her hands and knees; her head was practically in the bikuni's lap.

In a voice so low that no one else could hear, the bikuni said, "Heinosuke is well. Take care of yourself for him." Princess Echiko's shoulders stiffened, then relaxed. Without looking up, she asked even more quietly, "Is he not blinded after all?" The question startled the nun, though she did not reveal any feeling. "He sees fine," she answered, which was surely true, as she had seen him with books and lists of names. The bikuni wished she could talk to Echiko privately; but perhaps it was better that she left the princess with the illusion that the nun knew more about him.

The nun did not dare say more, or ask. It was best to remain absolutely still until things were worked out between these mad people. Two of Echiko's ladies-in-waiting had been at the doorway to the hall and hurried forward to help her stand while the prisoner release-warrant was placed, by a servant, into the hand of the nun.

One of the handmaidens was head of castle women. She did not appear ambitious, preferring to stay close to her lady's side; but she was in fact in a position of power within the castle hierarchy. She quietly commanded the physician to leave and solicited the help of several servants to lift the sleeping patient and take her away to the women's quarters, where handmaidens would care for her tenderly.

Echiko was also led away. She was barely out of sight when the nun heard an unexpected gasp from Lord Sato's sickly daughter. Then a sweet but masculine voice said, "Princess, you should be resting. I will come to you later tonight to recite the Lotus Sutra." Lady Echiko choked on a stifled comment, then gave a sigh of resignation as she was led through the halls.

In the next moment, Kuro the Darkness stepped into the meeting-chamber.

Had she expected the priest to have a monstrous appearance? She should have known otherwise; for those who knew him were swayed to his will, while those who had never set eyes upon him thought his influence hellish.

Kuro the Darkness did not shave his head like most priests. His hair was long and hung loose, cascading over his shoulders in the manner common among certain of the esoteric orders, of which he was presumedly *not* a member. He wore a black gossamer priest's robe with excessively long sleeves over a white under-kimono, the hem of which hung lower than the black robe. A tubular obi was oddly woven about his waist, almost braided rather than wrapped. Long-fingered hands touched one another at the front of his belt.

He was slender and the very epitome of holy grace. His demeanor was at once proud and humble. And there was something about his attractiveness that the nun could not help but remark, for his pretty face reminded her of a young uncle who had died in the wars of Heian-kyo, or perhaps it was a girl cousin she had been fond of as a child. In fact, if she dared think about it, he looked a bit like herself. Kuro the Darkness might well be mistaken for her twin brother, though not quite an identical twin. At the very least, she could not deny, upon seeing him, that he must be a man of Heida, her own home province; a kinsman, as Ittosai had informed.

He stood inside the doorway, his most pleasant face almost shining; and the nun was infatuated by the look of him, narcistically so; and she was impressed by the apparent sincerity of his gentle bearing. How could anyone have judged him evil?

She strove to shake off the glamour of the long-haired priest, lank and lovely as a temple page. His gaze settled upon her comfortably. She sat motionless upon her knees in the center of the room, aware of his awareness of her ability to turn aside his magnetism. For a moment, she saw through his disguise, or he had revealed himself to her alone. Something sinister glinted greenly from his eyes. There was nothing in the room of that color, so it could not be dismissed as a chance reflection.

The flames of the room's lanterns grew wan. At the same time, the sinister gleam passed from Priest Kuro's eyes; and the nun felt Kuro's beauty wash over her more strongly than before, trying for her soul, gently, experimentally, not at all insistently. Totally on guard, she refused to be affected. She focused on one realization: that the spiritual coldness and gloom throughout Kanno province and especially within Sato Castle was the result of Kuro's ability to absorb all that was warm and uplifting, draw it into himself so that he alone, among all things, shone with hope and beauty against the backdrop of a cruel and relentless world.

But the actions he somehow inspired were not as saintly as his aura. He motioned with one frail, lovely hand—by no means a menacing signal, but several of Lord Sato's vassals drew steel and surrounded the bikuni; it was surely not coincidence or the idle fancy of unreliable vassals.

She rose to a squatting position, hand to hilt, but did not draw steel. She could escape the circle of men, killing all of them, she was certain of that. It was exactly Kuro's plan. Her eyes met his, and she said, "I will not kill them for you." No one in the room quite heard what she had said, except for the priest she had addressed; and he replied with sweet simplicity:

"You will."

And none heard his words either. The men pressed nearer, the points of their swords closing in. The nun slowly moved her hand away from her sword and got back upon her knees. She did not try to speak to Lord Sato, who smiled fawningly at the priest and clearly had no control over his own life or the actions of his vassals. She turned instead to Chamberlain Norifune and said, "You would have your men attack me when I have made no threat?"

Norifune stammered, not knowing why the vassals acted as they did.

"Your lord has given me this warrant," said the nun, "and I wish only to take it swiftly where it will save those two people."

Norifune did not want to see anything untoward about events, forever trying to view things in a commonplace light, despite that they could not reasonably be fitted to normalcy or routine. He looked at the vassals who were poised to slay; and he said, "Back away, men! Do not treat her like that!" Their swords wavered as though they did not know what to do. In a few moments, they slid their feet backward along the tatami mat. The nun breathed more freely. She said to Norifune,

"You seem less influenced by this priest than the others, no doubt because you were more corrupt to begin with; it makes you immune to further corruption, though by taking the least precautions, you have come under his sway. Tell me, or consider: Was Lord Sato possessed of his wits until Priest Kuro came? I've heard he was once a functioning lord. Have you tried to benefit from his weakness? Have you refused to see its cause?"

Kuro walked across the room and sat on the edge of the stage, near his patron, who continued to gaze lovingly at the gorgeous priest, oblivious to movements and conversations in the room. Priest Kuro made no effort to stop the nun from telling Norifune her feelings and suspicions. Indeed, the priest appeared amused by the nun's efforts.

"This priest is not merely what he appears," she said. "For reasons I have not uncovered, he plots the deaths of several Kanno families, to the last child. It is widely rumored that he is not even truly human, but I will not venture things so far. The families endangered are in one way or another connected to this castle; perhaps your own family is among the seven, and your own safety uncertain. Heinosuke of Omi must have solved the mystery. But no one would hear him and he was banished."

Chamberlain Norifune looked left and right, seeking some escape from the bikuni's harsh ideas. He stopped chewing on his moist upper lip and tried to sound annoyed as he exclaimed, "Nonsense! Heinosuke went mad and attacked Kuro without cause! He ran off to avoid the consequence!" His tone fell quickly from a pretense of anger to a pleading whine as he continued, "You have the warrant you sought. Why sit there and slander a pious servant like Kuro the Darkness?"

"Listen to what you call him," said the nun.

Norifune waved a hand and said, "It is only a title of ironic endearment! As you can see, there is nothing dark about him. Everyone counts on Kuro's sage advice."

"You will not see how he has affected this castle? Look at him there! How upright he appears! He is amused by the numbness of your thinking!"

"What do you expect him to do? Slap your face for lying?" Norifune was quick to the defense of the priest and himself. He said, "He is always passive as you see him. Why don't you leave the castle at once? Don't overstay!"

It was a bold thing to say to a vassal of the Emperor-in-Retirement; but Norifune was at wit's end. The nun began to stand as she replied,

"I would be pleased to go."

Priest Kuro waved a dainty hand before his nose, as though to swat aside some odor. Lord Sato's vassals blocked the bikuni's way.

"Don't do that!" said Norifune to his men. At that moment, Lord Sato took some notice of affairs and shouted, *"Iye-iye!* Don't let her go just now! We were going to have a game of chess!"

Norifune made fists of frustration, clutching and wrinkling his fine costume, looking at Lord Sato with pained expression, clearly blaming Sato's madness for every strange proceeding. "Priest Kuro," said Norifune. "Can't we let her go?"

"Who rules this castle?" the bikuni interrupted. "Who rules Kanno? That mad lord? You, a ridiculous chamberlain? Why ask a priest if I can go, when you have already commanded it!"

"Iye-iye!" Lord Sato reiterated.

"It is my liege who gainsaid my suggestion," said Norifune, still unwilling to see the obvious.

"Believe me," the nun whispered harshly, turning a final time to the chamberlain. "I am as much stressed as yourself, or I would be more deferent even in a madhouse such as this. Priest Kuro acts passive, for he thinks he has a strong weapon and needs only to influence others. He wants to use me against all of you. See how his face resembles mine? His one personal vassal, whose name is Ittosai, has informed me that Priest Kuro is a relative of mine, I hope only a distant cousin. For this reason he seems to count on me as a partner in some mission of *kataki-uchi,* a revenge-seeking of enormous consequence. I am not a willing cohort. But if I draw my Sword of Okio in defense of myself, this room will turn to crimson. It will not be my blood or Priest Kuro's that paints the walls and floors."

Lord Sato said, "That saké is nice and warm! Let's all drink together!"

He was as witless as Otane's deficient brother; but the bikuni had a glimpse of intellect locked behind those eyes. What a nightmare it must be, turned into a fool, knowing in some shadowed corner of the mind that everything you say is stupid.

"Please stay a few moments longer," said Norifune, relenting to Lord Sato's desire. "My liege wishes all of us to share a bit of wine."

Servants were scurrying about preparing drinks. The nun refused to sit. Priest Kuro stood also, stood from where he had been sitting on the edge of Sato's stage. He raised his arms, the long black sleeves hanging down, and he seemed about to pirouette; but he held the odd pose for a long time, while the light in the room began to fade without apparent cause. Kuro was drawing power to himself again, with the result that everything around him became paler and sadder.

The nun moved her hand toward her sword's hilt, planning a lunge in the direction of the priest. But the room had grown so dark that she was momentarily unable to see a thing. The lanterns still glowed in their places, but the light penetrated nowhere.

Then Kuro reappeared, more appealing and beatific than ever, an angelic presence adrift in the darkness that had filled the room. She tried to draw her sword, but it was stuck in its sheath. Kuro the Darkness spoke gently, sadly, and the nun was tempted to believe that his sorrow, if nothing else, was authentic. He said, "Every step a human takes is mistaken. There is no road. There is no Way. The bigger the step, the greater the mistake."

The words were for the nun. No one else had heard. The bikuni heard Lord Sato's voice somewhere in the dark. He said, "This is good saké! Won't you have some? Please, one cup before you leave."

Try as she might, she could not draw the blade. Apparently Lord Sato could see her clearly; or, more likely, she alone was exempt from some alternate perception woven for the others. A page stepped out of darkness, carrying a huge, shallow bowl of steaming liquor.

"Just this one cup," said Lord Sato. "Then you must hurry along your way, for the sake of my daughter's handmaiden, who will become your ward."

The priest, still holding his strange posture, was looking into the bikuni's eyes; and his expression was knowing and forlorn. He seemed to say to her, "Aren't these foolish men? You and I alone can see the sorrow of the world." She would have pitied him if she did not see so clearly what his actions led to.

"This is too large a cup," said the bikuni.

"Oh?" Sato responded, sounding as though his feelings were injured. Was he unable to see the size of the cup presented? If she drank so much, she could die of it. At the least, she would be unable to make it to Shinji and Otane. "No one has ever refused," said Sato, "a cup of saké from a lord."

"It is too large," she reiterated. "I cannot drink so much."

Now she heard the voice of Norifune issue from darkness: "Don't insult my liege. It is only a tiny cup. It is unforgiveable to refuse. Can't you see that if you humor him a little, he will not insist you play a game of chess?"

"This is madness," said the bikuni.

"We agreed not to discuss that part," said Norifune reasonably.

"I am standing here in darkness," she said. "I can see very little except Priest Kuro, who stands before me motionless, shining, arms akimbo. The rest of you are hidden."

"That's foolish," said Norifune. "Priest Kuro is still sitting near our Lord."

"No. He is not."

Lord Sato spoke again, a pouting edge to the words. "If you won't drink one cup before you go, then I will revoke the license that makes Otane your servant from now on."

The nun took the huge bowl from the page, who was ghostly and faint despite standing closer than Kuro, who alone could be seen plainly. For a moment she considered dashing the contents onto the tatami; but Sato added with petulant cruelty:

"It is not much to ask that you finish one small cup. If you fail, it can only be out of disrespect. As you can see, my vassals stand ready to kill you at my command."

In fact she could not see any vassals. She believed they were close by. She held the basin near her mouth and, before drinking, quoted the aphorism, "'When drinking poison, do so to the dregs!'"

Then she began to gulp.

Priest Kuro relaxed his posture. The lights came up as between acts of a play. The bikuni saw Lord Sato was draining his very tiny cup; he looked happy now that the nun shared saké with him. Norifune had finished his cup. He was scratching behind his ear, then scraped under one fingernail with another, unmindful of sorcery. Several vassals stood near, swords drawn, but at bay.

The bikuni finished the wine and tossed the shallow basin upon the tatami mat. "Keep your promise to me," she said, more to Kuro than Sato. "Let me go now." The wine had not yet taken effect, except for making her stomach uneasy.

Priest Kuro took another strange pose, his head turned demurely, his frail hands held forward, the thumbs interlocked, his fingers like the wings of a nightingale.

Lord Sato sighed, then said, "Now that she is gone, I feel bored."

"I'm still here," said the bikuni. Nobody heard.

"I am too wound up," continued Sato, "to consider sleep. I wish the weather were clear enough for a midnight hunt."

Even now the bikuni could not deny the beauty of the face that gazed at hers. It was her own vanity to find him beautiful. She had hated to think he might be a relative; but now she welcomed thinking it, for if he were not a man of Heida, then he was not a man at all, but some distorted reflection of herself. He spoke a few seemingly idle words, which were directed at Lord Sato, who presumedly believed the priest still sat close at hand.

"The snow has ceased falling only a little while ago, my Lord." Kuro's tone was sweet, his narrative poetic: "The wind has cleared Heaven of its clouds. The Celestial River is a bright rainbow. The moon is full, surrounded by a vast halo."

"Wouldn't it be fine," Lord Sato exulted, "to view the moon in its big rain hat!"

The bikuni heard everything, but saw nothing beyond Kuro in the resurged dark.

"A midnight hunt indeed!" said Norifune, sounding relieved that the evening's nuisances were over. "It would be a challenge!"

Priest Kuro cocked his head a bit more, increasingly sweet and, if one knew no better, utterly guileless.

Lord Sato commanded gleefully, "Turn that gray doe loose, the one who was so frisky this morning! I will hunt her to the ground!"

Kuro parted his hands. The lights came up again, but no one noticed the bikuni still in their midst. Lord Sato's body guards, who had obeyed none of his commands earlier, were now quite eager to fetch his hunting cape and hat and other garments for a mounted chase. The other vassals scurried out of the room to get their own hunting gear or to prepare the

horses. The nun had given up on drawing her sword, but thought to grapple the priest by leaping on him in a contest of physical strength. Her feet would not move in his direction. Her tongue cleaved to the roof of her mouth. Priest Kuro pointed to the door, the only route open to her. How painful was his expression!

"Each step we take," he said, "is mistaken."

Thinking only of Otane and Shinji, the nun darted from the meeting-chamber. Halfway along the halls, she staggered against one wall, feeling the effects of the drink. Her arms were light but at the same time heavy. When she found her way outside, she fell upon a snowy path and vomited noisily. A small portion of what she had swallowed came out. She looked upward at the black sky, which was not as clear as Priest Kuro had promised. Here and there were smudges of moonlit clouds rushing majestically along the curve of the Celestial River. The moon indeed had a halo. It was called a rain-hat because it generally heralded a storm. Off in the west, there were still billowing clouds, changing and roiling at a miraculous pace. The clarity over Lord Sato's castle was, then, the calm before the long-promised storm, a gargantuan blizzard to freeze Otane and Shinji to their cross.

She stumbled across the veritable mesa on which the castle was built, and came to the gate leading downward. The post was curiously abandoned. No one stopped her from unsealing the gate. She stood at the top of the long stairway, the sight making her woozy. It had been cleared of snow, though a bit more had fallen since vassals did that labor. She felt the effects of the liquor rather too much now. Her first step downward caused her a sensation of sudden vertigo. If she took each step as carefully as she felt necessary, the hunters would be after her before she was halfway down.

Alongside the staircase was a rough slope for horses to ascend and descend. It, too, had been more cleared than not, but had an icy slickness here and there. To her bothersome state, the slope appeared more manageable than the stairs; but she had gone only a short ways when she slipped off her wooden geta and tumbled face downward.

More fretful of her sword's sheath than her own bones, she protected the Sword of Okio and slid dangerously along the incline, coming to halt after what felt like a very long time. She lay on her side, feet higher than her head, feeling annoyed, and uncertain if she were injured. The saké dulled her sense of pain, but her left arm ached from the plunge.

She half slid, half hopped the rest of the way to the lower gate, which was also unguarded. She opened it without difficulty.

Hunters on horseback might pour downward at any moment. She tried to run across the moat's causeway, staggering left and staggering right, fearful of dumping herself into the frigid water. At the end of the earthen bridge, she had to stop, dizzied by her flight. Before her, the snowy sea rose and fell. The sight amused her despite her predicament: a sea of snow. Didn't it go up and down just like water? How exciting! It was slow and subtle, but definitely moving. The world had become an ocean.

Her arm definitely ached. Pain reminded her of the seriousness of her situation. How moods swayed under the influence of spiritous drink! Things now appeared gloomy and hopeless. And in a few more moments, it no longer seemed that anything mattered one way or the other.

Already she heard horses neighing as they issued from stables above, prepared by grooms for the night hunt. Would Priest Kuro's glamour be so complete that not one vassal, not even Norifune, who was more under the sway of laziness and corruption than Kuro's magic, would be able to tell they hunted no deer, but a drunken nun? She couldn't think about it. She could barely think at all. If she dwelled too much upon it, she might convince herself that she had drunk a magic potion and become, indeed, a gray deer, and the perceptions of the hunters were less foggy than her own belief in her human appearance.

More by instinct than reason—for her reason was askew— she knew not to use the main road across Sato's estates, for she would be run to the ground at once. She staggered from the road, through snow, leaving unfortunate markings to betray her passing. She saw the glistening, moonlit sea of whiteness, and a stand of trees way across the fields. Among those young trees, she might have a chance at surviving. But she had become so awkward, she might never make it so far. Night erased depth-perception and the trees were actually further than she guessed—a shadowy forest of misbegotten hope, which stayed the same distance ahead, try as she might to get nearer.

Mounted vassals clattered from the castle's height, drummed the earth of the causeway. The sound carried nicely over the quiet fields. They had directional lanterns, reflector beacons that cast long stripes of light across the snow. She heard Lord Sato's childish shout of joy as he spotted what he thought to be the deer. She heard a whistling arrow. Only by blundering face-down upon the snow was she saved, by luck alone.

She fell into a narrow ravine, so shallow that she had to tuck her head down in order to be protected. The ravine had a small overhang; and the harried nun half crawled, half loped along the narrow space where no snow had reached the ground. The ravine came eventually to an abrupt end, where snowdrifts had filled it. She raised her head and saw Lord Sato and his men far off, arrows poking upward at their backs, tall hunters' hats upon their heads, their hand-held beacons shining this way and that. They looked left and right but didn't see where the prey had vanished; from their perspective, there was no ravine to be seen.

They rode across the snowy field in the wrong direction. Some of them split into a second party and started in an even more mistaken direction. The bikuni was little encouraged by their miscalculations. The moment she were to climb from cover, they would see her; and if she remained where she was, they would eventually find her.

The two groups of hunters split up again, intending to flush the deer from whatever feeble hiding place it had discovered. The nun sat in the bottom of the ravine, back against the wall, massaging her left shoulder. She realized her fingers were stiff, either from the fall alongside the staircase or from her usual problem in cold weather.

She tried to make her wine-enfeebled consciousness think more clearly. "If I climb out, I'll be a big gray shadow on white snow. Even in the darkness, they will catch me." That was as much as she could resolve.

Her wooden geta had been a nuisance. She removed them, tied them together, and hung them from her belt. Her toe-socks would suffice against the cold, unless they got wet. She needed every edge of sure-footedness, considering her present awkwardness.

For the moment, she felt a reckless calm and did not feel as harried as she did a bit earlier. Her mind was resigned though no less befuddled. As Lord Sato's men had broken into several groups, perhaps she would have a chance against them. Surely she could devise some plan, she thought, if she sat quietly a few moments more and concentrated.

Concentration was difficult. Her mind wandered. Her arm hurt. She had, in one sleeve, a bamboo container packed with the ointment Priest Bundori had made for her. She removed some of this and put the aromatic remedy on her sprained shoulder and her stiff knuckles.

If she stayed in the ravine much longer, she would be in trouble.

But she could think of no plan.

Some of Lord Sato's hunting companions were highly skilled men who, in fact, were specialists in catching healthy beasts alive, and bringing them to the estates for their lord to hunt down. Others were not skillful men. Most rode after their prey with no sense of the untoward; with no sense of urgency; but there were one or two who sensed and appreciated the evil jest.

These latter were men without conscience who, akin to Chamberlain Norifune, were less in the weird priest's thrall, for there was less goodness in them for Kuro to suck out. In the case of Norifune, the lack of conscience made him an indifferent sort of fellow, willing to go this way or that way as the tide insists. But those hunters who suspected they were not chasing a deer, who could only half pretend to see tracks as those of a deer and not a stumbling, drunken warrior-nun . . . these men could not suppress a tight-lipped, knowing grin as they looked at their companions and their lord, wondering who else, if any, shared this macabre knowledge.

By day, nothing could hide for long in the snow-flattened fields. But by moon and starlight, something might evade them for a while. The mounted hunters danced their horses this way and that. They shined their candled beacons along the snow, but had left so many of their own tracks along the ravine's margin that they could not be sure they hadn't obscured the marks of fleeing prey.

A few shouts were passed back and forth, but nobody made a call of discovery. They began to wander further apart. The land sloped upward, affording a fair view of the dips and rises, which were few. Some of the men were highly familiar with the terrain, having hunted here often and having learned to assure Lord Sato good sport. They knew that the apparent lack of hiding places was somewhat illusory. A few narrow streams and occasional gulleys could not be seen at a glance or from a distance. The hunters began to wander further and further from one another, each having in mind this or that spot where prey had huddled on past occasions.

It was Norifune's group that passed the spot where the nun had been sitting, panting, trying to collect her wits despite what she had been forced to drink; but she had vacated the spot. None detected the sign of her having been there, or having left, except one man. He looked askance at his fellows, more and more certain that *they* honestly believed their prey was merely a dumb beast. This man searched the area with the others, and held back when they began to ride further on, going slowly, looking at the ground for evidence of a deer's passing. The straggler rode back to the end of the long ditch, shone his beacon into it, and looked pensive.

He saw the markings of human feet, naked but for tabi-socks. Though he could see where she had been sitting, he could not quite tell how she had gotten out without leaving a trail. But, since he had some sense that the prey was not a beast (the glamour had enough effect that he was not actually convinced of anything), he suspected his quarry's human cunning. Furthermore, he was aware of the methods by which a human being, though not a beast, could pass over snow without leaving much evidence. The others had not thought to check for such signs, being more fully convinced that the prey was more than two-legged.

The hunter had his horse's reins attached to the saddle and controlled the mount by knee pressure. He hooked his lamp on the saddle as well. Then he pulled an arrow through the bottom of his quiver (the arrows being kept with fletched ends down and accessible through an opening at the base of the quiver). He sat ready to nock the arrow, but had not yet comprehended the prey's location. He did have clues.

As the horse obeyed its rider's subtle encouragement, the hunter was able to locate—barely visible in the moon's glimmer—a strip of snow that had been oddly unsettled, as though someone had dragged a bail of rice over it. He knew it to be the kind of track left by someone who lies flat atop snow and inches along in a wormlike fashion, skimming the surface, leaving little evidence of having passed.

This trail ended a short ways on. The hunter became puzzled. He nocked the arrow but could not see where to aim. His companions were now quite scattered over the terrain. Lord Sato and his group were furthest off mark. The hunter knew that he alone was onto something; but, selfishly, he did not call the others back. He danced his horse around the area, trying to guess what further trick the prey had used, what direction she next had taken.

He pursed his lips and glowered downward from his mount, unable to resolve the mystery.

Without warning, a patch of snow erupted, directly beneath the horse. The nun stood, her sword bared, stabbing straight upward through the horse's stomach, pushing the stomach with her shoulder. The hunter felt the horse tense its every muscle, heard it scream, and almost simultaneously felt his rectum punctured.

As the horse went down, the hunter unleashed his arrow at random; it went deep into the snow, to no purpose. He began to shout with panic and horror as he hopped away from his thrashing horse, trailing blood in his wake. He clutched his buttocks and cried for aid, then fell, thrashing, much as the horse was thrashing. Meanwhile the nun had gone a surprising distance over the snow, though hampered by deep drifts.

Nineteen hunters were on their way, responding to the cries of their fallen companion. A barrage of arrows was unleashed. The drunken nun wheeled, staggered, made a sweeping arc with her sword, standing less than perfect for a proper *yadome-jutsu* arrow-deflection. The arrows shattered against her blade, missing their mark, but a splinter lodged in her arm. Her clogs, dangling from her obi, clattered like wooden ox bells as she dashed in the direction of the stand of trees. She heard the twang of bowstrings and turned again, deflecting death. There was small chance of getting as far as the woods. She had to consider offensive action rather than try to outrun horses and arrows. The hunters were still scattered and it would take a while longer for them to regroup. She must act swiftly.

She ran straight toward Chamberlain Norifune.

The nun looked ghastly in the moonlight, her shoulder-length hair plastered by sweat to the sides of her head, eyes maniacal rather than afraid, sword raised above her head. Norifune was completely undone! He tried to wheel his horse about, to let other men take the initiative. He shouted the order, "Kill her! Kill her!" but this confused the situation further, since the others saw only a deer blundering into better range. Norifune half-saw the illusion—a misty deer with the image of a warrior-nun superimposed—and his mind tried to withdraw from any such knowlege of sorcery. It really was a helpless doe, ripe for feathering, not a dangerous warrior.

She made a miraculous leap (must have been a deer after all!) and Norifune felt the edge of steel strike his neck. He plunged to the snow, his horse running off. He knew the blow should have decapitated him, but somehow he lay upon his back feeling good as dead but hardly headless.

The nun hovered over his prone form, point of steel to his neck; and if the illusion of the deer was utterly dissipated for him, he still would not see things as they truly were, but fancied that the nun had been the sorceress from the beginning, and led the hunters a merry chase for reasons all her own.

"Who are you?" screeched the panic-stricken Norifune, unable to move away from the threatening blade without injury.

"A lot of people want to know my name," she answered. "All right. I will tell you. It is Neroyume. It means 'sleeping in hell.'" She pressed the sword's point until Norifune was scratched the slightest bit. "You would be sleeping there just now, except I struck you with the backside of my sword and not its sharp edge. You owe me your life! Now, tell those other men to stop this business at once. I can't think so well and am liable to do something rash."

She stepped back to let Norifune stand. He was about to shout exactly the proper order, but an arrow that missed its intended target buried itself in Norifune's kneecap, and he fell back down, howling.

There were hunters all around her in the next moment. The hot breaths of horses made pungent clouds. The hunters watched her, using their horses to urge her away from injured Norifune. The men looked as though they were curious and uncertain.

"Help the chamberlain," one of them said.

"That's a funny deer," someone said foolishly. "Kind o small."

"Just a baby. Should we kill a fawn?"

"At once!" another answered.

The nun cursed, *"Kisama!"* which meant they were a asses. "Can't you see Priest Kuro brought you to this? H *saimenjutsu* mesmerising art is excellent!"

The men were startled. One said, "A magic deer! It speaks!

An arrow was unleashed and her sword swept-up to deflect it. The splinter in her arm hurt. Blood stained her sleeve.

"A weird beast, but wounded," one of them said. "Look at its reddened shoulder."

They were surrounding her. There was no chance of escape. Presently they raised their bows, almost as one. She could not deflect arrows on all sides.

An unexpected wind raised flurries of powdery snow, sufficient to keep Lord Sato's further men from finding their way quickly to reinforce the others; but it did not hinder the vision of those who surrounded her now. The panting, wild-eyed nun took her best yadome-jutsu stance, but knew it was hopeless. There was only a moment's life left to her, she was certain, but she would try her best.

The belling of a stag unsettled everyone. It was a surprising sound, barely natural; and the hunters turned their attention aside for the moment, thinking their prey's mate was dashing from somewhere to save the injured, cornered doe.

Out of the flurries charged a monstrous white buck with murderous red eyes. It charged with such ferocity that the hunters nearly forgot their original target, and unleashed arrows toward the monster instead. The buck caught the arrows in his thorny antlers, and belled again, proud of his ability.

The nun took the opportunity to escape the circle of confused and panicked men and horses. She had run some ways before the horrendous vertigo overtook her and, her foot striking a rock unseen beneath a layer of snow, she tumbled forward, and could not muster the courage to get up. As she lay there, she looked back to where the eight hunters were shouting conflicting demands of one another.

She saw that the source of their consternation was even more spectral than Priest Bundori's warring stag alone. The stag had a rider! The rider was a slender youth with a ghastly, sallow complexion and a white kimono embroidered with a yellow snake. He moved with preternatural limberness as he maneuvered a Shinto ceremonial rope as a lariat.

The lasso moved through the air like a winged serpent, grabbing men from their saddles, while at the same time the great buck ripped into the flanks of horses, his antlers a nest of knives.

Chamberlain Norifune regained enough of his wits to limp away, toward Lord Sato and other men who were approaching.

He shouted at them to come no further, declaring a ghost or monster would destroy them. The eight men fighting stag and rider were to be abandoned.

Among those eight, one gave up quickly and rode off in fright. Another, whose horse was gored and dying, fled, even as did Norifune. The other six received lassos about their throats, clinging momentarily, long enough to jerk, to break their necks.

The nun was no less confused than the others, but was grateful for the time required to scrabble for the cover of the trees. The recent carnage would certainly not end the hunt. The other men might well take it into their heads that they hunted both a hind *and* a stag, a supernatural couple who could be hunted only by night and did not exist by day. Whether this frightened them or thrilled them did not matter. They would pursue the deadly sport, no longer requiring the encouragement of Priest Kuro's mesmerism. For they could never again call themselves hunters, let alone samurai, if they let such prey escape, and left the slain unavenged.

Even now her plan was uncertain. She must make it through the wooded area to the river. If she could not locate so much as a long-disused bridge, dangerous and rickety, then the river would be nothing but a dead end.

The sky had blossomed new clouds, while high winds brought others. The moon and stars were blotted out. Snow was falling anew, with increasing vigor, hampering her vision more than did the darkness or inebriation. As she loped and slid over the terrain, her lungs felt more and more expanded. She had lost all sense of direction.

Samurai were everywhere in the woods, seeking the prey. She heard horses blowing, their hoofs kicking through the snow. She heard samurai shouting to each other, some elated by the unearthly hunt, others fearful; some were merely lost and calling for orientation. It did not seem as though Lord Sato or Norifune were still among the hunters. The chamberlain doubtless had used the excuse of the turning weather as a point to cajole Lord Sato back into the castle, either to seek instruction from Kuro the Darkness, to obtain reinforcements for the devilish hunt, or merely to hide.

The nun was spotted. Two riders bore upon her as she ran an evasive route between close trees. The trees were too young and the underbrush too slight to provide effective cover. The two samurai did not lose her. One of them shone a beacon. The other prepared to unleash an arrow.

The arrow missed, for the bikuni came to an abrupt halt. Her path was blocked by Priest Bundori's albino stag. He stood snorting and pawing the snow. The stag's rider was also red-eyed and white-haired, but not quite a true albino, having an ocher coloration. The xanthic rider's lariat reached out once. A hunter's cry was stifled. His lantern dashed to the snow and went out, the hunter dead beside it with his neck horribly twisted. The horse ran on riderless.

The archer nocked a second arrow; but with the trees, the dark, and the blizzard, he was unsure of his target. As he hesitated, the lariat reached out again, snatching the longbow from his grasp. He drew his sword; but, thinking better of the uncanny situation, he wheeled his horse about and pounded a trail toward the sound of other riders.

The stag-rider leapt onto the snow and soon stood before the nun, who was twice reprieved by the youth's efforts. The stag remained a short distance away, standing so quietly that he was nearly invisible among the trees and snowfall.

The youth's sallow face was long. He was not entirely unpleasant-looking, but he was not attractive either. His looks were somehow inhuman, even aside from his lack of proper pigmentation. His red eyes were fiery gems. When a red tongue licked white teeth, that tongue was decidedly forked. He addressed the bikuni.

"I am that serpent whose life you saved. My name is Raski. It has been my fate to follow you through many lives and serve you."

The bikuni recollected a fighting stallion by that name. She had ridden him into battle and he died courageously. She also recalled a valiant canine who had been awarded the death-name of Raski at his funeral. Both of those beasts were white-furred, though not albino. The bikuni had no doubt that there was such a thing as reincarnation; but she was unable, at the moment, to feel deep concern about the karma of a beast. It was only vaguely disturbing that a creature might be reborn with each life reduced to something lower than before.

Possibly the karma of a beast would have meant more to her had she not recalled full well the one previous occasion she had seen Shinto ceremonial ropes used as Raski used them. She raised her sword against him, her threatening pose slightly spoiled due to her intoxication.

"It was you who killed those nine men near the shrine!" she accused. "I have sworn to avenge them!"

She dashed forward, but the youth slunk backward, looking startled and abused.

"I am a serpent, after all!" he exclaimed. "I don't understand your anger!"

"Why not try to take my weapon with your rope!" she challenged. "Use my Sword of Okio against me as you used those men's swords to pin them to trees. A cruel way to kill!"

The hunter who had fled without his bow was riding back, accompanied by other men. They searched through the blizzard and among the trees for sign of the prey. An unforeseen shaft struck the serpent youth square in the back. If he could have avoided it, he did not try. The arrow's point burst out through his chest. He threw his head back as though to shout and collapse, but in a moment the look of pain passed from his face. He turned with his weird rope, sent it forth, snatching the mounted archer's sword from its sheath. The youth caught the sword and let his rope fall coiled upon the ground.

Turning to the nun, he said, "I have never learned human sentiment. For this reason my lives have been short, and I have descended from higher beasts to lower. I regret punishing those men in a manner you could not approve. I will do penance fighting these present samurai for you. I promise their pain will be slight. Then I will die with them, of this arrow through my heart. The stag is yours to ride across the river; he knows the proper ford. Please let me do this, for the sake of my future lives."

The hunters were closing swiftly. The nun could still not think clearly. She turned her mind to thoughts of Shinji and Otane suffering on the cross, and away from such a thing as the fate of humanity and beasts. She hurried to the stag and mounted. He leapt away from the circle of danger. The bikuni looked back to see the serpent youth jumping among the swirling snowflakes. As a snake from its coil, he flung himself toward a mounted samurai, piercing first the horse, to its very heart, then slicing the rider as the horse went down.

He took another arrow from behind as he was doing this. He turned to face the next attacker, now revealing two arrows rather than one poking outward from his chest, dripping serpent's gore.

The strange, yellowish-white youth hissed, leapt again, and the bikuni could see no more.

What a mad, savage ride the stag supplied! With moon and stars immured beyond roiling clouds, and the very atmosphere whirling with snow, she had to trust the stag's senses. They sped through black woods and black night, outdistancing the one or two hunters who pursued. She did not see the river until she heard cloven hoofs splash the shallows. The river would not be swollen until spring. Though it was wide and cold and swift, the ford at least was no deeper than the stag's belly. The nun raised her feet to keep her tabi-socks dry. The red-eyed buck ploughed the rapids. The spray invigorated, but was insufficient to sober the nun.

In the next moment they were on a narrow, umbral path that could have led to the Land of Roots, for all the nun could judge. It was pitch dark. Naked branches were difficult to dodge as the snorting buck leapt and ran through the wild back acres of the properties of Lord Sato's vassals.

Only once did she become so much as slightly orientated. A samurai residence, poorly lit from within, came into view. She recognized it as Kahei Todawa's residence, in which he remained under house arrest. Then the nun could see no more. The buck leapt onto some other path, without a moment's slacking.

The rider could not control the mount. She dared not try, even had she known the means; for she did not know the route. She had faith in the stag's night vision and his knowledge of the narrow paths of beasts. But she did not suppose he comprehended where his rider wished to be taken. She could only cling to his neck and give herself over to chance and the Shinto gods.

She might have ridden in this manner for eternity. She had no sense of time. Exhilaration gave way to jaded detachment. She let go of the stag's neck, clung with legs alone, and began to pick carelessly at the bothersome splinter lodged in her left arm. She did not consider how the buck was unused to being straddled and might prove deadly passage.

His jewel eyes, loathing the sun, were fine orbs for the night. He saw a fallen cedar on the path ahead, its roots a tangle of bared claws. The nun had no precognition of the barrier. He leapt fantastically, powerfully, scarcely hindered by the weight upon his back. As the nun had been worrying at the splinter, she had no expectation of the leap. Her wine-slowed brain sent messages of urgency to the wrong parts of her body. Her hand went foolishly to the hilt of her sword, responding only to a general sense of emergency.

As the stag struck the ground on the far side of the log, the nun was flung forward, nearly impaled on the antlers. The path turned sharply. The stag veered, unsettling a startled rider and leaving her upon the path.

She lay winded, having actually managed to draw the sword full length before hitting the ground. Snow spun around her face. She stood and bumbled about like a temple-clown feigning a bump to the head, amusing the novices and visiting children. Realizing how idiotic it had been to draw steel instead of grabbing the beast's neck for steadiness, she could only curse her state of intemperance. Sheathing her sword, she listened to the fading sound of the stag's pounding hoofs.

As it turned out, she was not long lost. When she stumbled from the animal paths onto a real road, she immediately saw the bridge that joined samurai estates with the peasant village. There were men posted at the bridgehouse. Pulling herself into a sober-seeming posture, she approached the guards and addressed them gruffly. She showed them Lord Sato's sealed warrant, Sato's signature on the outside.

They let her pass. She crossed the bridge casually. The snowfall had gained surprising momentum. Wind stirred snow upon the ground. When she was across the bridge and certain the guards could not see her through the thickening flurries, she gave up her nonchalance and took to her heels, passing the length of the village and heading for the light of campfires in a bamboo enclosure.

Outside the fence sat foolish Iyo and his grandmother the widow Todawa. They were still praying for the salvation of Shinji and Otane, in this life or the next. They were mainly ignored by the guards, who might hide their discomfort regarding a family's sadness and destruction.

The swift approach of the nun caused several men to gather at the gate of the enclosure. They had half expected a meddler, since so many guards had been posted at the execution site.

They were prepared to thwart any effort to free the pitiable lovers from the cruciform.

But the martial nun fell passively to her knees and held forth a letter with Lord Sato's signature thereon. The chief duty-guard received the letter, bowed to the seal before breaking it, unfolded the paper lengthwise before his eyes, and read it carefully. He then let go of one side of the letter and asked, "What's this?"

"Their release warrant!" said the bikuni.

Widow Todawa, forever disguising the least emotion, for once let slip a startled sigh. Her moment of hope was quashed when the samurai replied,

"I don't think so."

He dropped the missive. The nun snatched it before the whistling wind carried it away. She read the words herself, snow whirling about her. Her face was suddenly drained of blood. Lord Sato had written: *Save Princess Echiko. Save me.*

So his chained intellect had reached out to seek salvation from the first holy pilgrim to gain access to the castle after Priest Kuro's arrival. But how could his plea save Otane and Shinji now? It could not. The nun was too dumbfounded to feel anger or sorrow.

The chief vassal motioned several men to action. The old widow and her retarded grandson were kicked and shoved aside, minor abuse intended to save their lives. Steel was drawn at all quarters. The nun was still upon her knees, holding the useless missive in disbelief. When steel licked forth murderously, she rolled to one side, let the wind take the missive, drew her sword, and cut her attacker's leg so that it came loose below the knee.

A second samurai moved forward as the nun somersaulted backward, coming to her feet, gutting her attacker from her crouch. Then she stood—slowly. She was transformed into a frightening presence, face still ashen with disappointment, but her expression firm and resolved.

She acted from instinct. She did not think about the deeds or the skills that came into play. Her sword angled left; it angled right. Two men fell. She pressed forward but was blocked from the enclosure. Too many men had gathered there. She began to run along the perimeter of the fence, pursuers on her heels, another guard waiting for her up ahead, his spear held in readiness. She closed upon him. Her sword took him so quickly, he was dead without knowing the nature of the cut that had been his undoing. His spear lay beside him in two pieces.

Two of her pursuers caught up. She turned, cut both of them with a single horizontal slice. Then she cut twice at the fence and pressed it with her shoulder.

She was within.

She ran toward a fire. The blizzard had risen with frightful intensity; she could not immediately locate the cross. She was nearly upon it before she saw Otane's dark hair sweeping the ground, her inverted body spread-eagle on the cruciform, Shinji on the other side bound identically.

"Otane!" the nun cried above the storm as another samurai dropped before her blade. "Shinji! Otane! Brace up!"

The world was doubly blurred by her drunkenness combined with the heavy flurries. She leapt over a bonfire, cutting down the man on the other side, then danced awkwardly to one side, killing another. She reeled, spun, slew. Blood sprayed her face. Her costume was of cream and charcoal and crimson. The long sleeves of her kimono turned and twisted in the gale, making her seem an enormous crow flapping and slaying and hopping about.

Her sword arced toward the cross. The rope binding Shinji's left and Otane's right arms fell away. Shinji tried to untie one of the other ropes with his freed hand. He was as sick and weary as Otane, and could only pick uselessly at a knot.

Slice—a man fell.

Slice—another rope fell from the cruciform. Shinji and Otane hung by one arm and one leg apiece, still too helpless to do anything for themselves.

Slice—spray—death.

Slice. Slice. Now their arms were free. Then the rope around Shinji's left and Otane's right ankles fell away. The couple plunged headfirst onto the snow, heaped upon each other, moaning and crying out with uncertainty. They wept and clung to each other, but were too weak and ill to stand, to run, to do anything but hold onto one another as the nun hovered above them, slaying whoever dared approach.

What a monster she appeared! Her left arm was bloodied from the arrow's splinter taken earlier. Now she was further painted by the blood of others. Her hair was a horrible tangle plastered to the sides of her head. The incongruity of a trace of beauty only made her maniacal, drunken rage the weirder.

Samurai stood on all sides. Spears and swords pointed at her with avid intent; but for the moment, the men were unsure of themselves, reluctant to press the attack.

"Watch out for her!" one shouted.

"Not a human being!" another said, stumbling backward over the corpse of some friend. To hear their voices, to see their frightened faces, made her feel empathy for their plight. Yet, what could she do if they would not give up?

"Look at her eyes!" another said.

Someone added sharply, "Aren't they shining green?"

Surely it was the bonfire that caused the gleam in her eyes. But why would they have thought they reflected greenly? Hadn't she seen a green glint in the eyes of Kuro the Darkness? Her mind was too fogged to consider it. She was possessed of wine, not monsters. Her efforts were chivalrous though grotesque. She held her preparedness and could dwell on nothing but the defense of Shinji and Otane. Hadn't they been persecuted? What matter so many lives exchanged for two, if those two alone had meant no harm!

Someone emboldened himself to the attack and perished at once. Then the nun moved toward a trio of men, who gave up ground. Others came from behind to try to get at Shinji and Otane, to kill them or reclaim them as prisoners, probably even those samurai did not know which. The nun returned like a mad beast protecting its litter of young. Two more men were downed.

Such carnage she wrought! Rapid snowfall hid the blood, provided shrouds for the slain. The deed was hidden even from herself, as she multiplied its effect.

Otane and Shinji braced each other and clawed at one of the diagonally crossed beams of the cruciform. They found their uneasy, tortured legs. The nun cleft her way through the ranks of insistent samurai. She led her wards in the direction of the exit. Not one samurai was left standing inside the enclosure by the time the gate was obtained.

A few guards remained outside, waiting fearfully, their spears and swords not as steady as before.

Still bracing one another, Otane and Shinji followed in the wake of slaughter, trying not to witness the number of lives reaped in their behalf. Outside the punishment-enclosure, standing above two freshly slain, the nun and her wards nearly fell over the large retarded youth and old widow Todawa, who were still praying in the snow.

"Tah—neh!" shouted Iyo, his flabby features twisted upward with a combination of confusion and glee. His knees were all but frozen to the ground from the long hours of prayer with his grandmother. He tried to stand to hug his sister, but could barely move, seemed not to know why his legs were stuck. Beside him, his weary grandmother gazed upward at the bikuni. Her eyes were worshipful. In her kneeling posture, she mumbled a prayer of thanksgiving, rubbing her palms in the direction of the bikuni, as though to a Buddha.

"Don't pray to me!" said the scowling, blood-spattered nun. "I am no god!"

The old woman continued rubbing her palms in the religious fashion as she said, "To me you are a god. Goddess of Mercy."

The nun turned her head to look right, then left, men dead or writhing on every side. She said, "Grandmother, do not betray yourself to me now. Remain stoic or I will think badly of you. This has not been mercy of the slightest kind."

There was a muffled clatter of hoofs. The nun looked along the village street, but could see nothing through the blizzard. The hunters, along with reinforcements from the bridges and castle, were approaching.

"Hurry away!" the bikuni demanded. "My mind is not yet clear, for I have been drinking too much. There must be someplace you can find to hide Shinji and Otane."

Widow Todawa climbed to her feet and urged Iyo to stand also. He slapped at his legs with large hands. Then, without encouragement, he went to help Otane and Shinji remain upon their own unstable legs.

"Leave that way," said the nun. "I will stay at the end of this street so no one can pursue."

The family staggered away, looking like a group of crippled pilgrims. The nun, not much steadier, went forth to greet the riders. They came out of snowy darkness in a large group. At their head was Kahei Todawa, released from house-detention on this special mission.

"Kahei!" exclaimed the nun. He drew rein upon the street, then dismounted. Taking a few steps forward, he drew his sword and said,

"You must not meddle in my Lord's affairs. I regret it, but I am here to stop you if I can."

"Kahei!" she repeated, backing away from him. He was not a young man and had not been a remarkable warrior even in his youth. She could kill him with ease if skill was all it took. But he was the father of Otane. How could she kill him? "Kahei!" She could think of little more to say. "Think better of this!"

The other samurai remained on their horses, watching the drama, waiting to see if the nun would keep her ferocity in such a dilemma. Kahei Todawa, and not a vagrant nun, had the right to decide a matter of rebellion in behalf of his daughter.

"Isn't it for Otane's well-being?" the nun insisted wildly, backing farther from Kahei. "Wasn't Shinji your unofficial son-in-law?"

Kahei stopped. He glared at the bikuni. Her white kimono, gray hakama, and black gossamer vest were streaked with blood. Her sword dripped blood. Her shoulder was injured and bloody. She had risked a lot. She had acted with brash heroism for the sake of his family. How could he take advantage of her reluctance to fight him?

He was like a piece of metal caught between two poles. He owed allegiance to Lord Sato. He must obey his master, even if it meant recapturing Otane and Shinji and killing them at once.

He turned to face the mounted men. He told them, "It will not be said I failed our Lord. Tell him I have given him my blood in remonstration. By this act of *kanshi*, I urge him to become free of Priest Kuro's influence."

Kahei Todawa put the butt of his sword against the ground and leaned the point upon his belly. The nun ran forward to save him from so rash an act as protest suicide. But he had already lurched forward, his sword coming out at the base of his spine. The bikuni dropped her Sword of Okio on the snow and caught the falling man. "Kahei!" she cried out, as though a loud voice could draw him back from death. "It was unnecessary!"

The silent, older man in her arms rolled his eyes and died with a placid expression.

Riders surrounded her. The bikuni let spitted Kahei fall onto his side. She inched her fingers toward her sword, which lay upon the snow. A mounted spearman charged. She snatched the sword, deflected the spear; and as the horse grazed by, she reached over her shoulder and stabbed the rider in his lower back. Before he had fallen, she had already leapt toward the next man, frightening his mount so that it reared. As the rider tumbled from his startled steed, the bikuni's blade swept upward, severing one arm and half his head with one stroke. He struck the ground in parts, snow and wind swirling about a fragmented, twitching corpse.

She heard more horses, but could not see them in the night and snow. There were additional men afoot, running from she knew not where, searching for her. By now, Otane, and what remained of her family, would have found safe shelter. The nun felt only anguish about the endless slaughter. She was not eager to continue a harvest she had sought previously to avoid. Now that Otane and the others were away, there was no need to carry on.

She ran between two buildings that stood too close together for a horse to get through. Had anyone seen her? She was uncertain. Her only plan was to vanish into the hard blizzard before more vassals found her, attacked her, fell before her blade.

She crossed a small clearing and stumbled on something buried by the snow, plunging to hands and knees. Her fall uncovered the corpse of the young samurai she had slain early in the evening, the first of the many who died in the past hours.

He was frozen solid. His face was contorted, his cheeks sunken, his eyes two sharp crystals. The nun scrabbled to her feet, hearing someone in pursuit. The door of one of the buildings had been flung open. The bikuni sensed an upraised weapon and heard a strange sort of scuffing through snow. She turned, cut crosswise, then stood waiting for her latest victim to collapse.

It was a hunchbacked woman, older than even widow Todawa. Little of her visage could be seen because she had bandaged her chapped face against the weather. Her eyes were ancient and tormented.

Snow rose up around them so that in the whole of the universe, there existed none but the esoteric nun and a feeble hunchback whose stomach cascaded blood. The old woman dropped her knife, clutched at her stomach with bony fingers, and slumped to her knees.

A reedy, sad voice exclaimed, "I regret that I have failed to avenge you, Chojiro!"

The nun knelt before Chojiro's elderly aunty. If not for this one woman, the nun might never have given another thought to the chubby vassal who had begged uselessly to be spared, who had vowed to live an upright life from then on if he could be allowed to live at all. How swiftly his head dropped free of his body! How easy to kill a man! How difficult to raise him up again! What good was there in making a lantern out of stone and placing it somewhere for the sake of one man, or two, or three among the countless slain? Hers was a warrior's life, a warrior's way, a warrior's fate. She could not, in the depths of her heart, feel guilt or shame. But she could feel pity. And she cried above the sound of the snowy gale, "Aunty! I intended all along to give my blood to you! Don't give up! You can still stab me!"

Ancient eyes looked hopeful yet forlorn. She said, "You will let me?"

The nun grabbed the old aunty's knife and put it in bloodied, bony hands. "Strike deep!" she counseled. "Don't die before you've won!"

"Thank you," said the dying aunty. But as she tried to push the point of the knife into the nun's belly, she found she lacked the strength to cut so much as a thread of the kimono. The nun wrapped her own hands around those twisted, knotted hands of the aunty and helped in the performance of the revenge. The knife went deep into the bikuni's stomach; and the old woman passed gratefully into another realm.

For a long while the bikuni did not move, knowing how well cut she really was. The old aunty, though dead and staring without sight, still clutched the blade, still sat knee-to-knee with the bikuni, snow clinging to her brows and bandages.

There was only the sound of the blizzard.

The only light was that which filtered through snow from the open door of the house from which the old aunty had made her unexpected charge. Lord Sato's men surely searched the area; but they did not seem apt to find anyone in such weather.

The bikuni drew away from the old aunty, whose corpse fell backward, taking out the knife. Blood gushed onto the bikuni's lap. She stretched herself across the snow and began to crawl. She probably had not gone far when her strength gave out. The cold began to numb her body. Aching fingers closed around someone's ankle. She looked upward through whirling flakes and saw a one-eyed man, a young man who was beautiful except for the eye, which had been plucked out, which had healed with frightful scarring of the sunken lid. He gazed at the injured nun at his feet, his one eye impassive. She recognized him, although she had never expected him to have but one eye; it made an awful sense in light of Lady Echiko's inquiry about his vision.

"Heinosuke," said the nun, raising her hand toward his knee. "Help me, Heinosuke."

By morning, the blizzard had broken. The snow level had dropped from peaks to the mountain thighs, leaving no trace of autumn on high though in the lower country autumn was still young. Priest Bundori, short and bowlegged and stooped, stood upon the threshold of the shrine-house, gazing over the compound. Every bush and limb and patch of ground was covered with snow, knee-deep in places. The ponds were thinly iced. The garden's smooth boulders had been transformed into bleached skulls.

Beyond sight, but within earshot, snow shook loose from high limbs and crashed noisily toward the ground. Bundori plodded along the path toward a tool shed. After some difficulty getting the door to open, he managed to retrieve a wooden scoop with which to begin clearing the main path.

As he worked, he looked worriedly about. The labor was less fulfilling than usual. He felt more wretched than he had felt in many years. He had tended to brood in his youth, but had almost forgotten the feeling.

The white buck had gone off in the middle of the blizzard, only to return well before dawn, his white flanks stained with blood not his own. His crimson eyes were wild, as from a battle. Bundori did not know what to make of it; he certainly did not like it. When the buck returned, Bundori was quick to cleanse the blood from the beast and say prayers of exorcism, lest the blood of dead animals or men despoil the shrine.

Now, as Bundori shoveled the path, he could see the buck in his open shelter, looking innocent as he slept, his flanks shaking occasionally as he dreamed.

At the end of the previous day, Bundori had sent one of his white birds, charged with protective charms, on a mission to discover the whereabouts of the nun. As the nun had been gone the whole day, Bundori worried; but he was reluctant to put his nose in more of her affairs, since she would not count it as a favor.

Akuni had come back with a slightly clipped wing—or, rather, a cut kimono, since she had straggled home in human guise. She brought disturbing if somewhat circumspect news. She also brought the nun's incognito-hat or amigasa, and the alms-bag which had had sword-damage done to it since Bundori last set eyes upon it. Akuni said the nun had left these items outside a shuttered teahouse and then headed for the castle.

Avoiding a few pertinent queries, Akuni pled weariness and returned more eagerly than usual to her true form. She retired to her nest, aided by Bundori's hands, since her wings were unbalanced; and she snuggled with her pretty husband Udo.

Bundori was unable to sleep during that long night. By the light of the fireplace coals, and while the blizzard whistled and growled at his door and roof, Bundori sat with dry straw to repair the nun's alms-bag. When this was finished, he began to reinforce an extra pair of straw boots for her, since she had gone off in borrowed geta, not expecting a first snow or one so heavy. The straw sandals she had worn to the shrine were worn out, not to mention unsuited to the change in weather. "She'll like these," he said, putting the straw boots alongside the bamboo amigasa and wicker alms-bag.

The night had become even more disturbing when he found his white buck had run off, only to return bloodied like that. Increasingly fretful, Bundori began to invest strong Omo and lordly Guma with as strong a protective spell as he could muster. When the blizzard stopped before dawn, he sent the two birds over the snows to see what they could find out about the missing nun. If she were in trouble, Bundori would feel responsible.

As he worked upon the path, he kept watching for the return of Guma and Omo, whether flying home or returning through the snow in human forms. As it turned out, when they finally appeared, they came as humans; and they carried the serpent youth, to whom Bundori had not given much thought after the day the bikuni had brought a small white snake to the shrine.

The two man-birds carried the seriously wounded youth to the edge of the shrine grounds, setting him down at the property's periphery. Omo remained with the uncomplaining youth. Guma, looking like the moody ghost of an early Mikado, went forth to meet Bundori halfway along the path.

"Raski is hurt and may not live," said Guma. "He has caused a lot of harm in the night. For this reason I am uncertain whether you will want him to die upon these holy premises. Perhaps he is not pure and blessed as other white beasts, and his death within these grounds would be a desecration. Nevertheless, he is our friend, though we didn't know him long."

Bundori went to the rustic fence to see how Raski fared. There were two arrows sticking out of his chest and a number of sword cuts about his body. He had lost more blood than he retained. His eyes had the same wild look that the white buck had borne home. "Yes," said Bundori. "Bring him. Break the fletches from the arrows and draw the shafts on through. I'll mix a healing unguent, though it doesn't look like anything will help."

Inside the shrine-house, Guma's imperious wife Iwazu set her infant down and quickly unrolled a bamboo mat on which the man-birds placed poor Raski. They tried to get him to speak, but he would only stare wildly. His sallow face and bright red eyes were far more frightful and weird than the faces of the pale bird-folk, who were strange but oddly placid creatures.

"He doesn't have his senses," said Iwazu. "I don't think he's in pain."

Lordly Guma said softly, "We may never know."

Shiumi and her child appeared as though from nowhere, from a shadow of the room. The occult power of the birds to perform shapeshifting was enhanced by the mere fact of an emergency, and by the spells Bundori had cast before sending any of them on errands. Omo and Akuni alone did not take on human form; and even they were roused from sleeping late and peered down from the rafters. Shiumi, usually sharp-tongued when possessed of human speech, went quietly to Iwazu's infant to watch over him.

Observed by his friends, Bundori placed medicine-compacts against the terrible rents of Raski's body. "A normal youth would have died of these already," said Bundori. "I can't help him. He will die soon. Do you know what happened?"

Guma had a dour expression. Omo turned away, unspeaking.

"He helped the nun do a lot of killing," said Guma, his

voice deep and serious. "Twenty, thirty men at least. Probably more. Some won't be found until spring thaw, as the blizzard hid the corpses."

Bundori was upset. It could mean the nun was dead, the snow her shroud. He raised Raski's head and put a wooden pillow underneath. Then he bent to Raski's face and asked, "Why did it happen?" Raski grimaced, then stared blankly.

"Is he smiling?" asked Shiumi, who was further away than the rest, caring for the children. "Is he proud of what he has done?"

"It's a look of pain," said Omo, who rarely spoke. His tone chastised Shiumi. "He is not insensate, after all."

Bundori spoke abruptly, more sharply than was his usual manner. "Be birds again! Leave me for a while! I don't like what's going on and may abandon this place soon."

Iwazu said wryly, "A bad time of year to choose asceticism."

"Foolish to wait for good weather!" said Bundori. His usual humor was overwhelmed by disappointments. "A true ascetic relishes the cold!"

The bird-folk were not happy to hear Bundori threaten to leave White Beast Shrine. But they would not argue with him about it. It was neither his fate nor duty in life to make things pleasant for birds. They began to shrink away, for he had commanded it, taking on their normal forms. Simultaneously, Raski's body began to writhe and contort, shedding size and weight, becoming thin as rope. In a short time, he was only a small, brittle white snake with a faint, yellow pattern along his back and injuries from his head to his tail.

Bundori cupped his weathered hands about the snake and lifted him. "Piteous fellow," said Bundori. The snake was stiff and dead. "Maybe in your next life you will be more fortunate. I will make of you a relic and keep your remains with me in seclusion. If I had paid better attention to you, and had I not secretly wished Tomoe Gozen to do something about things in this province, then you would not be dead, nor would you and she have killed so many people."

Bundori held the ruined snake near to his heart and wept. Later in the afternoon, having yet to hear anything of the nun, the Honorable Mister Paddy-Bird began to pack the fewest possible belongings, and tied them to his back. He had dressed warm, putting his cloth-wrapped feet deep into straw boots. At the door to his home of many years, he said, "Forgive me

for not taking better care of you, my dear family. Take care
of yourselves. I've given everything up just now. I must erase
my sin!"

Then he tramped along the half-cleared path and left White
Beast Shrine forever.

Awakening, the nun had no way of realizing a number of
days had passed. She lay pondering her last of a series of
dreams, earlier ones forgotten. In the one recalled, she was
adrift beneath the skin of the world, floating in a red cloud of
murderous spirits. She was armored and armed and held her
own among the others. In this dream, she could not figure out
why they were fighting; but it was important to continue. Nobody was quite able to die in this dream. No one was capable
of winning. The red cloud rained blood upon the world below,
which was Emma's Hell. Only on waking did she know that
she had been one of many *asura*, endlessly fighting ghosts of
samurai who in life had been too cruel even for Hell's liking,
never to touch the fiery ground, doomed to everlasting battle
in the hollow sky.

Her senses came back by degrees. She was in a warm place,
wrapped in a tattered quilt. She opened her eyes, turned her
head, and did not immediately recognize what kind of building
she was in. There was a pot of radiating coals placed near her.
She remembered the old aunty whose dying deed was to press
a knife into the belly of an emotionally agonized nun. The
bikuni placed a hand under the quilt and inside her kimono and
felt a linen bandage. She dug fingers beneath the bandage,
partly out of a morbid curiosity, and felt the wound well-
scabbed and healing. Thus she ascertained she had been out
of her wits for several days.

She was stiff. It hurt every muscle and especially her stomach to try to rise. It was an incredible hardship to move. The
very thought of it started her panting.

As her mind cleared, she had vague recollections of one-
eyed Heinosuke mopping her fevered brow and propping her
up to force her to drink herbs and salty soup, which she would
spit up like a sick, helpless baby.

"Suke?" she ventured feebly, but no one replied. She was
alone.

Above her head were the workings of a mill, broken, can-
nibalized, and useless. So she was in an abandoned millhouse.

Heinosuke must have gotten her across the gorge; she was presently in some obscure place among the farmlands. It looked as though Heinosuke had lived here quite a while. He had built several makeshift shelves and gathered things to sustain himself through a hard winter. There were a few possessions, including the genealogies he had filched from various temples.

She had previously supposed Heinosuke lived in or near the Temple of the Gorge. She had left him a note to that effect, which was embarrassing in retrospect. He wouldn't live in such a place.

When she felt bold enough, she crawled out from under the torn, ratty quilt and toward the door. From hand and knees, she reached out and slid the wooden door aside. A wintery breeze took her breath. Beyond the door stretched a fallow field, unploughed for a few years. The field was covered by a lot of snow. Here and there some weedy patches poked up. There were saplings in the middle of the field, by which she was able to make her judgment that the place had been in disuse for more than one growing season.

There was no surfeit of strength in her arms and legs; but she managed to scrabble up the doorframe and stand gazing out into the cold, cold morning. Though sunlight was diffuse, the sky and ground were startlingly bright. The world had rarely appeared as white as it appeared at that moment.

A leafless, gnarled tree grew near the millhouse. Snow lay thick along its branches, making it look alive with plum blossoms. On the tree's trunk were finger-length hoarfrost crystals, glittering wondrously. A motion on the horizon caught her attention: herons passing over the roof of a forest. She saw the glaciered peaks of higher mountains and could also see the highest donjon of Lord Sato's castle. It was a long way off.

Unseen, a hungry crow went "kaa! kaa!" perturbed to find itself caught in the mountain's premature winter. He would starve to death unless he could make it to the lower lands, where there would be a lot of autumn's rubble to pick through. The bikuni felt as lost as a skinny crow of winter. How melancholy his homely sound!

There were footprints around the outside of the millhouse. "Suke?"

If he were anywhere near, she could not call loud enough to be heard.

She turned to walk carefully to where her hakama trousers

and long vest had been left, cleaned and folded. She could not consider putting them on over her kimono of raw, cream-colored silk; it was dirty and badly wrinkled from having been slept in and sweated in. She took it off and tried to do something about it, but it was hopeless. Someone had spot-cleaned the blood as she wore it, so at least there were no lasting stains. There was a small cut where the old woman's knife had gone through. The left sleeve had a tiny hole. The bikuni had a miniature sewing kit in her wallet, but lacked the motivation to worry about repairs.

Her underlinens, wrapping breasts and loin, were filthy. The wound's bandage alone was clean. Heinosuke had cared for her modesty as well as her injury, but it had left her somewhat less than sweet-smelling.

She went outside carrying her kimono, barefooted and half-naked, searching for some part of the creek that was not iced over. There were no farmhouses in sight, though she could smell fireplaces. She would be embarrassed if Heinosuke returned just now and saw her undressed. But she would be able to see him from a long way off, should he appear across the fallow field.

The mill wheel was stuck in mud and the mud had frozen solid. Sections of the wheel were filled with snow. The creek had changed its course with time, veering away from the wheel. A few paces on, the creek rushed between two snowy banks, tinkling like wind bells.

She stripped of linen and crouched naked on a tiny flat bridge to wash her things. She did not wish to bathe in such icy waters, but used some snow to scrub her body; it didn't get her as wet, for which reason the snow seemed less chill than running water. She was shivering when she was finished, but it was invigorating; it eased her aches and stiffness. Belatedly, she found a wooden bucket, and took water into the building to wash her hair.

Soon her wrung laundry was hanging from the broken workings inside the millhouse, above the pot of coals. She wrapped herself in a quilt, waiting for things to dry. The millhouse was quite small, so the coal pot was sufficient to keep the temperature pleasant.

She found things to eat, but had trouble swallowing. Her stomach hurt to be stretched even a bit. Strength was returning to her, though she would not like to get in a fight.

The Sword of Okio was leaning against a wall. She checked the blade and saw that it had been cleaned and oiled for her, though not powdered. Heinosuke's austerity left him with fewer things than a sword might require. It was audacious to clean someone's sword without permission; but it would have been terrible to have left it stained with gore while the bikuni lay fevered for days. She was grateful for Heinosuke's concern, and took his forward behavior with her sword as indication that he remembered their friendship when he was a child and was called Yabushi.

By the time her clothing was dry and she had clad herself completely, arranging the pleats of her hakama just so, and placing her shortsword through her belt, the bikuni was weary from so much exertion. She sat upon her knees near the coal pot, drew a quilt over her lap, and looked through the genealogies Heinosuke had collected.

They didn't mean a lot to her, except that it was clear they represented the lines of only seven main families. They covered a period of time that stretched back a little more than a century. The temples would have had genealogies going back much farther; but Heinosuke had placed restrictions on his interest, had devised a framework within which to pursue his research.

She wished Heinosuke would return from whatever errands he was on. She was still too weary to return to the village at random. Before she showed her face, she would like to know the outcome of the horrible slaughter.

Her shakuhachi lay upon a shelf. She was about to take it from its bag when she heard someone at the millhouse door. Heinosuke entered, stamped his feet before removing straw boots, and managed not to look at the bikuni. He wore a quilted jacket over his kimono and hakama. His longsword's handle was particularly long, his shortsword normal. He took his jacket off and moved into the interior of the millhouse in such a way that the bikuni would not see his sunken, scarred eye.

"Good morning," she said; for when in doubt, banalities suffice.

He nodded curtly. He was a pretty boy, despite the eye; but how sad he looked. He was like a younger Ittosai Kumasaku, not as world-weary and cynical as that big samurai, but equally morose.

"You're feeling better, Neroyume?" he asked.

"Neroyume? How do you know about that name?"

"You talked a lot in your fevered rest. You said your Buddhist name was 'Sleeping in the Dead Country.' A good name for an esoteric nun."

"If you're serious, I should thank you for such flattery. All the same, feel free to call me by my former name. I chose 'Neroyume' when quite beside myself."

"I studied esotericism," said Heinosuke, "before I left Omi. It is a cruel religion, and realistic. Even Kwannon, Goddess of Mercy, is viewed in the aspect of Benten, the many-armed dragon-slayer, weapons in her many hands. An esoteric nun should cherish such a name as Neroyume."

"Life exists that life may end," said the bikuni. "But I must confess I chose Thousand Shrine Sect for the amount of freedom it allowed. You know more of esotericism than do I. When we knew each other before, you were considering Zen."

Heinosuke nearly smiled, with what memory the nun could not be certain, until he said, "That was because of our mutual friend. I haven't thought of that pleasant Zen nun in years. She once said to some rude fellows, 'My friend likes to kill people.' She meant you. 'I feel sorry for her and would ask you to leave quickly for my sake.'"

"I don't remember that," said Neroyume. "It isn't true I like to kill."

"Oh?" Heinosuke's hint of smile was no longer to be seen. "Wasn't her name Tsuki? Yes, I haven't forgotten. It's too bad she died."

"She lives in a place not far from Shigeno Valley," said the nun. Heinosuke looked surprised. "She is nearly blind in one eye, but not in bad health. Your own eye is more greatly damaged."

"I thought she died," said Heinosuke, turning the side of his face more to the wall.

"Well, she didn't after all."

"But my sister died?" he said, removing the length of hair from inside his kimono, the locks the bikuni had left, with an ill-considered missive, at the Temple of the Gorge. Heinosuke sat against a beam of the millhouse and sighed sadly. "I thought she was well. What happened to her?"

"Did you know she was cast out of the Rooster Clan?"

"Was she? Well, they told me something different. I was supposedly the head of the family, but I was only a child. It was many years ago. Most of my family perished in the wars.

I liked Oshina. I liked thinking she was happy somewhere. Did you kill her?"

"Why do you think so?"

"It is your fate to destroy the last of seven families. The Rooster Clan was one. Weren't you a chief participant in the wars of Heian-kyo? My relatives perished in those wars. You did kill her, didn't you?"

"It was before the wars. After she was cast out, her life was wretched. She begged me to help her die."

"I didn't say I blame you," said Heinosuke. "The roots of this sad destiny are a century old, at least. Perhaps the Thousands of Myriads planned it at the start of time. The seven families have declined in this past century, and those who are left have come to center around Sato clan holdings, here in Kanno where it started long ago. If you happened to help things along the way, it was not really your fault."

"You know more about it than I, Heinosuke. Will you explain it to me?"

"I nursed you these few days for that reason," he said. "When you know, you may wonder why I didn't let you die. Maybe it was because of my memory of you as Tomoe Gozen. Maybe I flirt with my own doom, thinking myself dead already. Or I may have a plan that requires your famous sword, a haunted sword to slay a thing from Hell, if you can get close enough."

"You think Priest Kuro inhuman?"

"I think us all inhuman."

Heinosuke stood and went to the other side of the single room, ducking under the millworks, still trying to keep the nun from seeing his ruinous eye. He took two chipped lacquered boxes from a shelf and went with them to where the bikuni sat, a quilt upon her lap.

"Tomoe," he said, and she was glad to hear him say her name.

When he sat upon his knees beside her, he once again chose an angle that kept him from facing her directly. He took a lid from one of the boxes. A scroll, which he had drawn up, lay within.

"You have seen this once before," he said. "Please look at it again."

She took the scroll, unrolled it, saw how many names had been deleted since the first time she saw it. "So many," she said softly.

"And so few left to die," said Heinosuke. "When you've slain the last of them, Kuro's vengeance shall be met. It is the surest way to exorcise him from Naipon. For it to happen, you must kill them all."

"You have deleted your own name," she said.

"I am in your hands already. I don't mind. Without Lady Echiko, I don't see much in life."

The bikuni did not like to look at the list, would not inspect it closely. She rolled it tightly and placed it in Heinosuke's box. "If you care for Echiko," she said, "why have you abandoned her to her fate with Priest Kuro?"

"Kuro will not harm her. She doesn't know it, but I have found out she was a foundling. Not Lord Sato's family, except that he says so."

"It's interesting you would say so. Whose family, then?"

"No one ever knew. Lord Sato's late wife took Echiko in before she was old enough to speak or walk."

"You say there are seven families endangered by Priest Kuro—or myself. Could Echiko be kin to one of the other six?"

Heinosuke looked upset by this query. "An oversight," he said. "I had not considered that."

"I have seen her lately," said the nun, fixing on her chance to give Heinosuke back a reason for life, a reason to seek action. "She is not well. She starves herself. Priest Kuro chants the sutras for her nightly. If not Kuro's vengeance, then she pines for you."

Heinosuke turned his face further away.

"Do you think she could not love you because of your one eye? It's not good-looking, I'll admit. You could wear a patch. That would lend distinction. Be assured, Princess Echiko is dying, and Kuro the Darkness has some interest in that death."

"He has only done away with priests who stood in his way, and members of those seven families," said Heinosuke, pointing stubbornly at the list he had drawn from genealogies. He had gotten over thinking his knowledge of matters could be used to a good end and did not want to confront anything that would motivate him to hopeless efforts. "No infant recorded in those families might have been Echiko. She is not involved."

"As you know so much about Kuro," said the nun, "tell me who he is."

Heinosuke was glad to think of anything besides Echiko. "I was appointed Lord Sato's archivist, responsible for his family records. It was a good position. I hadn't been at Sato Castle long when I realized Lord Sato's mind was deteriorating. I had reason to suspect the priest was poisoning him. I tried to investigate. Nobody agreed that Priest Kuro's behavior was strange; he only moves about at night. I caused a lot of trouble for myself, warning people something was up. If I had kept silent, I would have been married to Echiko by now; Lord Sato favored me before he became afflicted, and Chamberlain Norifune did not change Lord Sato's policies from before. But could I protect my opportunities while watching my future father-in-law grow senile at his age? In retrospect I see Kuro toyed with me; I was part of his machinations. I became convinced that the plot worked a certain way and put my future on the line. There was no posion. I made a fool of myself; and other castle men began to spy on me.

"I had to keep out of mischief; I attended to my duties. While doing so, I found an old record, which described part of an incident from a hundred years ago. I began to suppose Priest Kuro was the descendant of a certain monk named Nichiroku, and that for some reason an old feud was being settled generations later. But I was still on the wrong track, confused for a while. I wasted a lot of time trying to find out where Priest Kuro came from. If he was a relative of Nichiroku, then he might have been born in Heida province. But I could not discover evidence that he came from anywhere at all. He might not have existed before appearing at the castle and winning Lord Sato's heart.

"His name means 'black,' but written another way it means 'ninth son.' I was trying to find out his original name and started collecting genealogies. I could not find a ninth son of anyone who was Kuro's approximate age. Finally I stopped thinking in terms of people alive today. If you reverse the two characters of Kuro's name, it comes out 'roku' as in 'Nichiroku,' the sixth light. Nichiroku was a ninth son of a Heida family, and he was the sixth out of seven disciples of Morihei Sato, who became known as Abbot Johei, founder of a Lotus sect in Kanno. I found out that the other six disciples, and Johei, represented seven families, mainly from Kanno, except Nichiroku. All but one of the disciples were of important families. The seventh disciple, below Nichiroku, was a peasant's son. That family used to farm the land around this millhouse; but there are fewer in that family nowadays.

"As I looked into the fates of those families, I soon discovered my own clan's past connection with Kanno province. All the families had something in common: they had been declining for a hundred years, as though laboring under a curse. In the past year, the remaining members of the seven clans have been especially beleaguered. This coincides with Kuro's appearance here, though a tangible connection cannot be made. The families turned to their priests for help; but any priest who looked into the matter, or prayed in behalf of those families, became himself cursed as well."

The bikuni asked, "So you think Kuro took his name indirectly from the original Nichiroku?"

"No. Kuro *is* Nichiroku, returned from the dead as a *goryu* or vengeful spirit, eager to complete a vengeance against the families of the abbot and six monks who wronged him long ago."

"An overwhelming theory," said the nun. "I still think he could be a mortal sorcerer. It can't have been easy for you to check records of men from Heida."

Heinosuke took the lid from the other box. A brittle parchment lay within. "This makes it more than my theory. I found it in a secret compartment of a chest in the Sato archives. It tells exactly what happened to Nichiroku. It is the confession of Morihei Sato, who with six disciples did Nichiroku harm. Once I knew the whole story, I understood the origin and sentiment of Kuro the Darkness. I knew that I had no allies in the castle and must act alone to save Lord Sato, his clan, and many others as well.

"I lay in wait for Priest Kuro, intending to cut him when he appeared. I waited a long time in the room where he passes his days. He keeps the place guarded well, but as archivist, I had access to the architectural records and knew of various secret corridors. When he came at last, I leapt forth and stabbed him where he stood! I stabbed his heart!

"I could not get my sword back out. He looked at me with so saintly an expression, I regretted my mistake. He bent his beatific face to see my sword stuck in his chest. When he looked up again, his perfection was erased. He was an appalling mummy, skin stretched upon bones! His eyes shone like two lanterns of green paper! Yet his voice was unchanged. It was still sweet. And he said to me, 'Don't you see too much, Heinosuke?' He reached out with his right hand, which was bony and clawed and black, and he plucked out my left eye!"

Heinosuke turned to face Tomoe so that she could see the full effect of Kuro's deed and how unfortunately it had healed.

"Yet you did not cry out," said the bikuni, remembering what Otane had said about that night. "You slipped away through darkness and came to the women's quarters to make Echiko believe you no longer cared; and you have counted yourself among the dead since then. If my Sword of Okio can do better than your common blade, will you count yourself among the living?"

"In such a world as this?" he said. "If you can exorcise him only by fulfilling his desire, will you count yourself among the living?"

"Each day comes and passes. I try to live without regret."

"I will tell you everything I've learned," said Heinosuke. "If you do not find it regrettable, then you are very different from me."

"I would like to know everything," she said.

Heinosuke placed the lid upon the second box; for he knew the tale by heart, including the words of the confession. He began, "Once upon a time . . ."

"Is it a fairy tale?"

"No. But it begins with a legend. Don't interrupt as I tell you."

"There is a legend regarding the land on which the Temple of the Gorge now stands. Long and long ago, a province had not yet been named, and there were only a few people scattered through the lower valleys. Atop the gorge, where rivers converged and leapt forth into a terrifying plunge, demons gathered on certain nights, rising from the Land of Roots, meeting to cavort with the monsters of land and air. It was a joyous occasion for such beings.

"One of the demons was Green Fire Devil, a will-o'-the-wisp who could take the form of a stooped old man. One time he was sent up from Hell to get some things in order for a festival the demons had in mind. As he was drifting over snow-coated swamps and amidst trees, he chanced to see the Snow Woman, who had wandered from the highest peak because the weather suited her. She had the appearance of sculpted ice. Her hair was like frost's etching, hanging on the air. Her eyes were piercing blue. She was vastly more elegant than anything Green Fire Devil had seen before that night.

"When he spied her, she happened to be embracing a handsome woodcutter. He was stiff in her arms, a blissful expression frozen to his face. When she let him go, he remained standing in his place.

"'Yuki-onna!' shouted Green Fire Devil, much impressed with her beauty and her strength. 'Yuki-onna, I am an old devil but robust in my heart. Come see if you can cool my flame!' As it turned out, Green Fire Devil was the first being able to withstand the cold of Yuki-onna; and she was the first being unsinged by his affection. Thus they had a long affair, despite that she was beautiful and he was homely beyond compare.

"A gathering of demons celebrated the romance of Snow Woman and Green Fire Devil. It became an annual event, for demons are forever anxious for such an excuse. Their various festivities tended to last whole nights. If there was a typhoon or blizzard, so much the better! If dawn were heavily overcast, they might prolong a party. More commonly, things ended before first light smote the eyes of night's minions.

"The place was known to men, but shunned. If people came too close and witnessed the affairs of demons, they were invariably drawn into the festival, dancing and shouting and having a good time. Afterward, they would go into the gloomy land and not come out again.

"Because the countryside was thinly populated, there were few problems. Peaceful centuries came and went. The number of festivals increased with time; whatever reason could be found, a new holiday was added. The site became famous among the denizens of Hell; for there were not a lot of places where they could walk upon Naipon's topsoil.

"During a time of incessant human wars, armies discovered an important route through the mountains, and Sato Castle was built to guard the pass. The land came to be ruled by the present lord's ancestor, Yorimitsu Sato, a strong warrior. One evening Yorimitsu went up to a high wall of the castle and chanced to look over to the gorge. He saw erratic movement and glowing shapes and suspected an enemy attack. He sent some strong men, who ended up dancing and having a good time but were never seen after that. Only one man returned a little before dawn, trying his best to convince his beloved lord to come join the thousand sporting demons and monsters. At sunrise, this man died twitching and screaming.

"Lord Yorimitsu Sato invited a certain sect of powerful Buddhists to exorcise the place. It took a long time, for the priests had to use occult means to uncover the reason for each demon-festival, then do a different rite against each type of demon and each of their festive excuses. Afterward, a grateful Yorimitsu awarded the land around the top of the falls and provided the funds to build a temple there. That temple was bigger than the one you see there today, although part of the original is incorporated into the present building.

"When the Temple of the Gorge was completed one-hundred and five years ago, it was not long before part of the ground gave way beneath it. Half the temple tumbled into the gorge. Many monks were killed. A passing pilgrim claimed to have seen a green-colored *yane-no-mune* or roof-ridge ghost dancing on the tiled peak just before that part of the building collapsed. None credited the witness. Attaching no supernatural importance to the matter, the abbot preferred to believe the error was in placing the temple on a weak fault too near the cliff.

"After proper consultations, the temple was reconstructed, giving the cliff greater berth. Yet, the following year, at the height of winter, fire broke out in the repaired part of the temple, destroying one-third of everything, including the abbot's quarters, which had been untouched the year before.

"This time they could not deny supernatural implications. The temple had burnt with the rich blue color of the fires of Emma's Hell. A stooped old man, made of green fire, was seen in the blue holocaust, wailing like a lonesome dog and jerking his body in a piteous dance.

"The next day, a woodcutter and his two sons were discovered in the snow-shrouded forest. They were standing on a path, frozen to their places, as though embraced by Yuki-onna.

"The sect abandoned the vicinity, but it was not left vacant long. Yorimitsu Sato had meanwhile died of a strange illness, and his cousin Ofuku Sato was made Lord of Kanno. Ofuku Sato had an older brother named Morihei Sato who had shaved his head, become founder of an order of Lotus monks, and changed his name to Johei, with seven chief disciples and numerous lesser followers.

"Lotus monks were generally impoverished in those days, having yet to raise up a great proponent like Saint Nichiren. This group considered it their good fortune to inherit such a large temple, due to Abbot Johei's relation to the Lord of Kanno. They were a belligerent sect then as now and boasted that the temple's past havoc had been the cause of previous monks not being holy enough. They rebuilt the burnt-out part of the temple with funds provided by Lord Ofuku Sato to Abbot Johei. They were certain they would never experience the kind of demonic persecution a less meritorious sect endured.

"Before the first year ended, Raiju the Thunder Animal came tramping across the forest roof. A hurricane tore one-quarter of the temple from its foundation and dashed it into the gorge. Many of the novices were killed by Raiju's lightning. The seven disciples had to nurse each other's injuries.

"The self-esteemed order took solace in the observation that less of the temple had been destroyed than on previous occasions, when another sect had been in charge. But to tell the truth, they were depressed fellows. Their pride had been dealt a wicked blow.

"The abbot was joined by priests of other Lotus enclaves so they might discuss the problem best. By means at their collective disposal, they discovered that the exorcisms commissioned by the late Yorimitsu Sato had caused the separation of Green Fire Devil, who was dispatched to Hell, from Yukionna, who wandered on the snowy peaks. Whenever Green Fire Devil heard his lover's sorrow, he would cause the temple harm, just by trying to get out of the gloomy land.

"The romantic ties of demons are not very common. The Wonderful Law suppresses the cruelty of demons, but regarding sentiments of love, the Law is helpless. The priests did not wish to consider the least failing in the Lotus Sutra, however, and continued to be self-assured. They drew floor plans of the temple and compared the areas variously stricken, seeking some pattern. They saw how on the first year a part had fallen away with the cliff's edge; where on the second year a part had burnt to the ground; and on the third year some of the building was snatched away by spectacular winds. Those areas of destruction overlapped at a particular point which the priests finally deduced was no larger than a trunk or a coffin. Green Fire Devil was able to ascend from the gloomy land at that spot, given the right conditions.

"Various magical rites were performed. A special tablet was made and buried deep in the ground in an effort to seal in the lovesick demon. Only when these things were completed was the temple rebuilt, the monks hardly courting the possibility that they would fail twice.

"But the monsters of land and air had consulted much as the priests had consulted; and they considered countermeasures to the efforts of the strongest adherents of Shaka's Wonderful Law. These monsters pitied the hapless couple who were being denied their meetings with one another. As a result of these unfathomable consultations, there was a fourth catastrophe at the Temple of the Gorge in the following year. It was the worst event of all.

"During an especially shocking windstorm, Raiju the Thunder Animal returned, leaping from tree to tree and snarling, a beast as big as seven horses but able to pass daintily over the forests. Large stones of ice came pounding from the sky. And the monstrous Nure-onna rose out of the mists of the gorge!

"Nure-onna the Wet Woman is like a big snail pulled out of its shell, but with the head and torso of a woman. Some say the part of her that appears human is beautiful, while others say she is horrifying at both ends. All agree she is deadly to encounter.

"She crawled up the face of the cliff, as snails can do easily, and continued right up the temple wall. She found a certain place on the roof that especially interested her, and with taloned claws began to tear away the tiles.

"Despite the sound of Raiju and the furious hailstorm, monks heard the odd scratching on the roof. They came running out under their umbrellas, but the umbrellas were beaten to pieces by the huge balls of hail. The monks saw Raiju roaring in the trees. They saw Nure-onna clawing the temple's roof.

"The monks ran about, pelted by ice-stones, not knowing what to do. Some of the novices tried to hide in the forest, but they encountered a woman made of ice, sparkling crystals whirling about her body and seeming to explode into stars. She raised her arms as though desirous of the chaste novices, and they ran back in search of their abbot, who was nowhere to be found. They beseeched the seven privileged disciples to effect some miracle, but the seven were confounded.

"The disciples were able to collect their wits enough to order the frightened novices to the armory to fetch spears. These

were soon brought, and the seven began pitching spears at
Nure-onna. The wind was Nure-onna's ally, and the spears
could not reach her, but only clattered to the roof among the
balls of ice.

"The Wet Woman remained intent upon her task of making
an opening in the roof, high above the site where priests previously divined a source of evil. When the hole was big enough,
her slimy body oozed into it. Most of the monks were too afraid
to go inside to see what she was up to. One, less afraid than
others, was called 'sixth light' or Nichiroku. His one affectation
was that he never shaved his head, and for this reason he was
called, behind his back, 'Disciple Page,' for his effeminate
appearance. He alone had the bravery to rush into the temple,
a sturdy spear his sole companion.

"Winds rose and Raiju's claws sparked, striking blue flames
to the branches of trees. Monks ran for cover in woodsheds
and the like. They could not hear anything inside the temple
and were not eager to go in and see how brave Disciple Page
fared.

"After a while, the Wet Woman squirmed up from the hole
in the roof. She went down the outside of the temple, then
over the cliff. Raiju, settling down and retracting his claws,
tiptoed over the roof of the forest, wishing to avoid the sun.
A few monks had taken refuge in an outbuilding near the cliff
and they saw Nure-onna go slowly into the mist. Certain she
would not climb up again, they hurried to the temple to see
what havoc had been wrought.

"It was dark within, except for the dim morning light showing through the ruined roof. By this light they saw a rough
opening in the floor. The Wet Woman had broken through the
floorboards and dug a pit beneath the temple. From the pit,
she extracted the ceremonial tablet, on which was scribed the
Lotus Sutra; and it lay broken upon the altar. The face of the
wooden Buddha had been scratched by the vindictive Nure-
onna's talons.

"In the bottom of the pit sat Nichiroku. His spear was stuck
through his thigh. He moaned the Lotus Sutra, but in an odd
way. The monks were afraid to help the delirious fellow, for
when he looked up from the bottom of the haunted hole, his
eyes shone like emeralds.

"Abbot Johei came at last, making no excuse about hiding
for so long. He strutted about proudly in his priest's robe, but

it was false pride and barely disguised his budding doubts regarding the Lotus Sutra. Peering into the hole, he revealed no emotion at the sight of Nichiroku, injured by his spear, mouthing the sutras strangely.

"The abbot, his faith faltering, sent the novices away, and addressed his six remaining chief disciples. They had always obeyed him implicitly. When he invented an explanation for the terrible events, they may not have believed him; but they were unwilling to express their doubts. 'The Wet Woman was trying to help us,' said Johei, pretending divine inspiration. 'A Shinto monster has shown us that a human sacrifice alone can preserve the sanctity of our Buddhist temple.'

"With dour expressions, the six disciples pushed dirt into the hole, the dirt Nure-onna had dug out from under the floor. Afterward, they made a hidden door over the spot, disguised in such a manner that none could suspect the floor was ever damaged. They patched the roof as well. Then they went about their business, pretending they had never buried one of their own alive. But you may well guess that none of them could recite the Lotus Sutra without remembering Nichiroku. In their dreams they heard him chanting. They heard the secret door open up, though it could not be opened from below, as it had heavy objects placed on top.

"When novices did their sutras, they claimed to hear Nichiroku's voice joining in. Sometimes it grew louder and louder until every other voice was supplanted by this one. Now and then, someone caught sight of a ghostly monk sitting on the tiled peak of the temple, his posture woebegone, a throaty, toadish voice whispering, 'Praise to the Wonderful Law of Shaka Buddha! Praise to the Wonderful Law of Shaka Buddha!'

"In the past, the temple had been troubled about once a year. Now it was haunted daily.

"One by one the lesser members of the temple ran off to join other orders. One or two jumped into the gorge, though bodies never washed onto the banks below. The six disciples remained longer than the others, for they well knew their own involvement, and were still reluctant to turn from Abbot Johei. But things were too much for the six disciples. Soon enough, they gave up their cleric training entirely. One returned to his family's lands to farm. The rest sought employment in the world, through the auspices of their wealthy clans. Within a year of the terrible event, there was only Abbot Johei, and he was close to madness.

"In the middle of a winter's eve, the ghost-disciple cried out to his master, Abbot Johei. Johei found the caller standing on top of the secret door, the heavy objects having been moved aside by the ghost himself. 'Tomorrow,' said the ghost-disciple, 'Green Fire Devil wishes to rise from the Land of Roots and search for his beloved Snow Woman. You thought to cure the trouble by sacrificing me, but the trouble is compounded. Had I been asked to give my life, I might have done so without feeling such an urge for revenge. As it is, I have become a *goryo*, a vengeful spirit.

"'Perhaps it is true that I am strong enough to block up the gap through which Green Fire Devil passes. But I am disinclined to be such a guardian. How can you make me do it? How can you placate this angry spirit for even one hundred years?'

"So saying, the disciple's ghost disappeared. Throughout the rest of the night and much of the following day, Johei wrote his confession of the sacrifice of Nichiroku, buried alive beneath the temple. Then the abbot killed himself upon the secret door, hoping this action would placate the vengeful spirit for a hundred years.

"The next day, Lord Ofuku Sato recovered from an ailment similar to the one that took the life of the previous Lord of Kanno. As he believed his brother's prayers had brought the miracle, Ofuku Sato sent someone to tell Abbot Johei the good news of Lord Sato's recovery. But the messenger found Abbot Johei's body, and beside it the confession. The letter was hidden away and the matter covered up. The temple was forbidden to any sect and let to ruin. Green Fire Devil has not been seen again, but those who ventured near the temple by night have reported the presence of a ghost-disciple who makes fervent prayers against those who killed him and against their progeny.

"One hundred years passed before Priest Kuro came to Sato Castle. A year has passed since then. The rest is as you've seen it."

"Do you believe it?"
"It all happened."
"What do you propose?"

"As for the means to proceed against a goryo," said Heinosuke, his manner conveying no sense of hope, "my mind is full of confusion. The tenets of kataki or revenge are as noble as sentiments of love; more noble, if the Warrior Way holds truth. This being so, it may be as difficult to defeat Kuro the Darkness as it was for the priests of old to suppress Green Fire Devil. Additionally, Kuro has convinced the objects of his revenge to chant the Lotus Sutra, thereby soliciting the Wonderful Law for achievement of his end. In this case, good and evil are one; there is no sure way against it. Only by the completion of his intent will a goryo rest. I have told you this whole story, hoping you would see some clue."

"I have faced him once," said Tomoe, "and the result was unpleasant. I think the best that I can do is to leave Kanno province swiftly, though the passes will be difficult after the blizzard. Against my will, I am Kuro's weapon. Without me, a link in his scheme will be broken."

"That would only make his vengeance linger," said Heinosuke. "He was patient for a hundred years. He can be so now."

"Yet, if I stay, I will be the one to kill those others, whose names you have compiled. I have no desire to do so. I've meddled over-much already. Pardon my saying it is your responsibility. If love between demons is a noble thing, then the love between you and Lady Echiko is twice as dear. You hoped that I could provide salvation. But I am taking a lesson from the Honorable Mister Paddy-Bird, who is reserved in matters of action. I refuse."

Heinosuke sadly lowered his head and closed his one good eye.

The nun said, "If Kuro were a common fiend, I would strive against him. But I cannot deny that he heralds from my family's line. Though he is a vengeful spirit, yet must I consider him my ancestor. Our ancestors are our gods. Our gods control our destinies. I can be of no help to you."

It was two more days before she felt sufficiently recovered to travel. The minor wound high on her arm was virtually healed; it itched a little. Her belly's injury did not seem apt to tear open. She set forth from Heinosuke's quiet retreat.

Early in the afternoon, she tramped the paths of White Beast

Shrine, sensing something sorrowful, though there was no outward sign of violence or desecration. The stag was nowhere in evidence; there were no fresh tracks and no food placed in his stall. There was a hammering sound from the rear of the shrine-house; someone was boarding up the shutters. The door had been left open. The nun thought she saw spectral activity within; but closer investigation caused the vision to resolve differently. The albino woman—who a few days earlier had introduced herself as Priest Bundori's friend—was cleaning and storing everything, as though the priest's residence might not be used for a long time.

At the doorway, the nun inquired worriedly, "Is Bundori-sama well?"

The pale woman with tracings of blue veins at neck and throat turned her face toward the nun, then looked away without replying. The nun tried not to feel perturbed by the beautiful but strange woman's attitude of disapproval; but the woman's rudeness smarted.

The nun said, "There was an argument at the rope bridge yesterday or the day before. The peasants are talking about it. The guard refused passage to a group of wealthy-appearing travelers, who could not identify themselves sufficiently. There were children among them. As everyone was albino, like yourself, I may not be wrong in thinking they are your family, and White Beast Shrine has a special importance to your kind. There was a strong man among them; a farmer heard him say his name was Omo. He grappled with the guard and threw him in the gorge. You chastised me a few nights ago for killing. But your family is not above reproach."

The woman, affecting the petulant attitude of a spoiled courtesan, spoke hotly. "Kill as many as it pleases you to kill. My only wish was for Priest Bundori's happiness. He has gone away to be a hermit instead. He left some things for you over there."

The nun reclaimed her hat. She saw that her alms-bag had been repaired. "I meant to return these borrowed geta," she said, "which in any case aren't quite sufficient for a journey through snow-choked passes."

"You might as well keep them," said the white woman, keeping to her work.

"I think so," said the nun. "He has made me these straw

boots, too; and prepared a container of the remedy for my hands. If he has left at random, I suppose it will be difficult to thank him."

"Don't concern yourself about it."

The nun tied the geta clogs together and attached them to her obi belt, then tried the straw boots on, which were the perfect size. The white woman's mate entered, as white and youthful and beautiful as she. He left slats propped against the outside wall, apparently eager to board up the entrance. "Akuni, it is about time we started for our rendezvous with the others. You've cleaned this place enough." Then he turned his attention to the nun, and addressed her with less admonishment than was in Akuni's tone. "A girl came from the castle in search of you on three different days. I don't know what she wants. Her name is Mirume if you want to find her. I think she is a servant to Princess Echiko."

The nun slipped the strap of her alms-bag around her neck, letting it hang at her front. She tied her amigasa's chin-strap, shadowing her face in the deep hat. She said, "If you don't mind my asking, are you human beings or some kind of spirits? I met a young albino man, less gorgeous than yourselves, who claimed actually to be a serpent. Are you snakes as well? I don't have a reason for asking. If it is too personal, it's unnecessary to reply."

"We are not serpents," the young man said, and immediately changed the subject rather than explain further. "Mirume was not the only one to seek you here. There were three others who came, astride thin black horses. They were well-armed and had traveled a long way. Akuni, who is clever, managed to mislead them without actually lying. If they believed her, then they've gone their way. I think they meant you mischief."

"I wonder who they were," said the nun.

Akuni, sealing a packed chest and shoving it into a closet, said to the nun, "They were women samurai, two of them younger than yourself, one older, taller, leaner, and severe. They were the wives of Yoshimora Wada, your foe of many years. As they asked about Tomoe Gozen, I said no one uses that name in Kanno."

The nun stepped onto the shrine-house stoop. She gazed back at the albino couple, seeing them through the loosely woven front of her hat. She said, "Though you don't seem to like me very much, yet I feel indebted. Thank you for your help and consideration. Whether you are human beings or devils, I don't mind. Perhaps after all there is not much difference."

With the top and bottom portions of the stone lantern strapped to her back, Tomoe Gozen started off toward the gorge, a walk that wearied her enough that she wondered if she were ready for a journey after all. The stone was heavy for someone who had spent several days convalescing.

There was an additional weight upon her. She had been blunt with Heinosuke, crushing his hope that she would strive where he had failed. There was also Echiko's handmaiden, seeking her out, no doubt, to beg intervention or succor. Lord Ikida Sato himself had managed to peer from the haze of his snared intellect and ask, however circumspectly, for a wandering nun's aid. Could she turn from so many and live her life without regret? But it was as she said to Heinosuke: No Naiponese could turn against her own ancestors. Were she bound, as in her past, by samurai mores, she might well be made to assist the vengeful spirit with conscious vigor; for duty lay with one's master, one's clan, and one's gods.

Near sunset, having rested often along the way, she arrived at the Temple of the Gorge, passing around it to the cemetery of derelict monuments, thence to the separate area of recent interments.

Everywhere among these graves, the snow was tracked and dirtied by horses and digging. A number of new graves had been dug, some not as yet receiving tenants. Even discounting the number of slain whose bodies would not resurface until spring thaw, there were yet a lot of corpses to be gathered and buried in this place. Ittosai Kumasaku had been kept busy at his hated task and had not quite caught up. The bikuni was glad not to have made better time, for she was not anxious to see doleful Ittosai, and it looked as though she had missed him by only a little while.

The western mountains sported violet halos and the first stars winked through the cedars which surrounded the insufficient graves. In the fast-dimming light, the bikuni found the one inconsequent grave among many, marked by a slat and an unsteady hand that had scribed the name of Chojiro. The bikuni supposed the unmarked graves to left and right to be the other two men she had killed on that first unfortunate night in Kanno. The majority of the newest graves were her victims as well;

yet her sympathy focused on these three men, and especially upon Chojiro, who had degraded himself in her presence without obtaining mercy.

Every other individual who stood before her blade had pursued a grim fate without her having encouraged them to do so. But Chojiro had wished to run away, and she refused a second opportunity.

She set the lantern's hefty base upon Chojiro's grave. It was not perfectly shaped. Some might say it needed more shaping. But she had gotten to the point of fearing it would get worse instead of better, had she continued to chip at it. The lantern had the kind of rustic grace of a student potter's first works, whose later pots would outshine the first technically, but never equal it in naive invention, freshness, and imagination. Not that she fooled herself that it was special. She did not expect the ghosts of these men to suddenly repose joyously because of her small labor. Nevertheless, she addressed Chojiro and the others with apologetic testimonies and begged that they accept her meager offering as a fraction of recompense.

She let the sorrow of life wash over her. For wasn't it a poetic thing in which to be immersed? She sighed heavily, and from her kneeling posture, she leaned forward to place the lantern's top upon the base.

As she began to draw away her arm, a pudgy, gangrenous hand broke the grave's surface, reaching out of dirt and snow to grab the bikuni's wrist.

For a moment she merely stared at the worm-infested hand and the vile, swollen fingers that gripped her. She pulled a bit, enough to know the hand, now moveless, was stronger in death than it had been in life. Softly, the bikuni said, "Chojiro. Your aunty said you were a good boy, despite yourself. Don't upset her spirit by blaming others for your fate."

There was no immediate response. The bikuni remained quiet and patient. At length the hand relaxed its clammy grasp. Chojiro's arm drew back into the grave. The bikuni, composed and relieved, brought forth her shakuhachi and began to play. She sat amidst those wretched, insufficient burial mounds and played a long while. The sonorous, tranquil strains rose above the cedars and were absorbed into the earth, speaking equally to Paradise and Hell. She was a noble presence in that place, the very boon for the mishandled dead, whose spirits ached with confusion and isolation.

When she was done, she went to the Temple of the Gorge, intending to pass the night spread out before the gaze of the blasted Buddha. She would begin her journey at dawn. Her coming to Kanno had raised a storm of trouble, although it did not seem to her that she had been the trouble's exact cause. However that might be, she could by no means stand against her ancestors by battling some spirit of her clan. For this reason she intended to flee Kanno, though it did her conscience ill.

The night did not pass easily, due to her uncertainties. The pride of a chivalrous streak grappled with better sense and wisdom. She awoke in the cold of the early hours, thinking she had heard a voice. She opened her eyes and turned her head; she saw the dark visage of the temple's damaged Buddha, his eyes shut against the nightmares of the world. What she had heard was the voice of a peasant lad proclaiming cruelly, "My thousand-year-love has shortened!" followed by the weeping of a girl.

It must have been a dream; for the only sound on waking was the drone of the gorge, mute and far-seeming.

She rolled forward to her feet, having no idea of the time, but feeling no longer wearied and trusting it was close to dawn. She pulled on straw boots, took up swords and hat, and went out into the cemetery. Her eyes were well-adjusted to the night. Still, shadows played tricks, and the monuments appeared to stretch across the land forever. They swept upward without reaching an horizon. The tombstones became smaller in the distance, until they turned to stars. The whole of the world and the universe was a graveyard.

She skirted the outer wall of the temple and passed through gardens gone wild, her boots breaking the crust of a snowy path that had not been used long and long. The route took her to the edge of the gorge, in which she could see naught but formless shadow.

The disturbing dream had brought her to this spot. It returned to her in snatches and replayed through her mind. An angered, vicious Shinji exclaimed, "Love you? Ha! I consider you barely human! What a sad fate to be bound thus! To roam this place forever part of you!"

"How would I be such a monster," replied the sweeter yet ironic voice of Otane, "except that you cling with so much need? What a hypocrite you must be to recant the dulcet promise, to condemn me for being only what you've made me."

"I've made you? Ha! Ho! How is it so? It is I who would be an ordinary soul but for your undesired presence! Who wanted such an amalgamation? Did I ask for it? Daughter of a samurai! Always wants her way!"

"Vile peasant!" Otane scolded. "Devoid of gratitude! I am faithful despite this unhappiness! What is my reward? One would think you loved me not!"

"Love you! I consider you barely human! What a sad fate to . . ."

The bikuni shivered at the remembrance of the nightmare, wondering what possessed her sleeping mind to such invention. She stood perfectly still, trying to free herself of the sick feelings the dream had planted in stomach and mind. She watched the shadowy mists ebb and flow in the black depths of the gorge. A fragment of shadow broke loose and lapped upward along the face of the cliff. The fragment floated and elongated and rose through air.

As it came nearer, the shape began to shine with choleric pallor. The bikuni stepped back, dropped the hat she had been holding in her right hand, thinking her Sword of Okio might be called upon to ward away the two-headed specter rising fast before her eyes!

The faces of the ghost were contorted and began to shriek from bloody mouths. The monstrously compounded fiend drifted over the gorge, a menacing duo joined at the waist, its four arms swinging wildly, as though hoping to scratch the bikuni. But it could not pass onto land. It must remain over or within the gorge.

Tomoe had never seen the likes of such a spirit. It was legless, the joined bodies ending in a single, serpentine swirl. Though there was no wind, the hair of the female part of the ghost blew as in a gale. In its bruised, death-bloated face was a corruption or likeness of Otane. The equally appalling figure joined to her was her peasant lover Shinji, hanging his head in abject misery, eyes shining with yellow malevolence.

"Otane! Shinji!" cried the bikuni. "What's become of you?"

The dual ghost ceased screeching when addressed by its two names. Otane took to weeping piteously; and what could be more piteous than the tears of a monstrosity? She squirmed helplessly, as though trying to rip free of the other half, and she whined a frightening reply.

"There was no escape. Grandmother was cut down. Iyo had

run away, confused by everything, but returned with his garden shears, bellowing unintelligibly as he pinched off the head of one of our attackers. While two others pierced my foolish brother, Shinji and I were able to get this far. But how could we go farther? Could we fly across the gorge? It was hopeless to continue."

Shinji spoke with amplified hatred, never having liked samurai, liking them less now that he was dead. "It was this samurai daughter's idea that we bind ourselves together with her obi and leap into the gorge. How heroic we felt! How tearfully joyous to know that we would at last become bound through eternity! What a wicked jest is love!"

The love-suicide ghost scratched impotently at the air, in the direction of the bikuni. They spoke with one voice, saying, "Why did you help us? But for you, we might have been separated, and pined a little while, but never suffered such a fate as this!"

"It isn't so!" the bikuni shouted, terrified less by the love-suicide ghost than by her part in such an unexpected doom. "How can I be faulted?"

The monstrous ghost began wailing from both faces, making no sense at all, and yet those loathsome faces told of their animosity. They strove uselessly to snatch the bikuni into the dizzying gulf. She had imagined something noble about the love between the peasant and the samurai daughter; how badly she had misled herself! It was easy to mislead herself, for hadn't she once loved? Hadn't it come to nothing, due to duty and honor and pride? She had lived her life with regret after all! Something in her had wished for others to find a less lonesome path; she had exerted effort in their behalf; and she had expected to abandon Kanno province with one fortunate event to consider. Now there was no fortunate memory. The lovers had been saved from crucifixion only to find themselves trapped—to take their own lives in tender double-suicide, then to discover in death that they were less enamored of one another than they had long pretended.

Dawn reddened the east. The shrieking love-suicide ghost began to sink into the mists of the gorge, its faces turned upward, arms raking at the sky. The bikuni watched the monstrosity sinking, and lamented her role in their horrific end.

One way or another, Kuro the Darkness refused to allow her the smallest victory. She wanted to turn against him, without regard for her own soul or the anger of her ancestors. But hadn't the love-suicide ghost been proof enough that she could never fathom the complexity of Kuro's plot? Anything she attempted was apt to result in the furtherance of his demented vengeance.

The bikuni felt the despair of helplessness. Though the sun began to rise, it seemed as though nothing could erase the chill that settled across her world.

PART THREE

The Flame Within

Ha-yugao, whose name means sword-edged moonflower; Kosame, whose name means little shark; and Shi-u, whose name has many meanings, came to Kanno province in search of Tomoe Gozen, following a lead they had gotten while traveling through Omi. Ha-yugao and Kosame were too young to have fought at Heian-kyo, but they had esteemed themselves in lesser battles and often defended Lord Wada's outlying holdings with valor and cunning. They were proud and spirited: Kosame, quick with biting humor; Ha-yugao, always eager for action and sharing much of Kosame's wryness. They were beautiful by any measure, though sometimes rambunctious and impolite. They rode upon their slender horses conscious of their imposing nature; and they were vain.

Ha-yugao's specialties included the use of *manriki-gusari* or weighted chain, and *masakari* or broad-axe, besides her small and large swords. Kosame was expert with the *nagamaki* strapped to her horse, a halberd noted for an exceedingly long blade and relatively short handle. These two tended to ride alongside each other while Shi-u followed, although this did not precisely reflect the hierarchy between them.

Shi-u had been named by her mother for the weather outside the birth-hut on the day Shi-u was born. The name meant "misty rain." Taken another way, the same beginning syllable coincidentally meant "warrior," and written differently, it meant "death." So her name was commonly said to mean "a rain of death." She had esteemed herself mightily in the wars of Heian-kyo and in earlier wars. She was Lord Wada's first wife, and without her he might never have risen so far, although it was rarely admitted.

187

She was a lean woman with dark skin and she sat high upon the thin black horse of a breed possessed only in the Wada clan. Like her younger "sisters," her hair was long and bound at the nape; but unlike theirs, hers was shot with streaks of white. Her face was ageless, more handsome than pretty, and she might pass as a tough youth and not a woman in her thirty-seventh year.

She bore no special weapon. Her swords were all that mattered to her, although it was widely rumored that she alone was match for Kosame if it came to nagamaki; and she alone was the match of Ha-yugao if it came to axe or chain. Where the younger women were lions, Shi-u was a tiger. Where they were falcons, she was an eagle.

At first they thought they had been misled as to the whereabouts of Tomoe Gozen. When they learned about the recent slaughter of local vassals, they knew of only one possessed of such strength and also a nun's vestment. At a teahouse, they overheard the story, Ha-yugao and Kosame exchanging knowing glances. An ear leaned this way or that way helped to inform them about affairs at Sato Castle. Apparently Lord Sato was a madman under the sway of a self-serving priest who the commoners considered a devil, literally or figuratively, depending on who spoke. A chamberlain was regent, but allowed the priest to decide much policy. The chamberlain feared that the nun would escape Kanno with information about Lord Sato's condition. This explained why the roads were blocked and the woods set with patrols, a situation that had held the three women warriors at a Kanno border-check an entire day.

It didn't concern the three that Lord Sato's secret was commonly whispered in the village or that the chamberlain's effort to suppress such information was hopeless. Such a carnage as the nun had wrought so few nights before was exactly the sort of incident to circulate from one corner of Naipon to the other, by one means or another. A deserter among Sato's vassals might carry out the news. A peasant illegally changing home provinces might do so. A pilgrim or traveling relative might let a few words slip. A spy, whether of the Imperial class or for the Shogun, might already have the story. As regarded the inevitable fall of the Sato clan, Ha-yugao and Kosame were mildly amused, while Shi-u was indifferent. If the situation could be twisted in some manner to aid their own mission, this

alone mattered. The important consideration was that Tomoe Gozen was already boxed within Kanno province and would have a hard time evading the wives of Yoshimora Wada.

Had it been known that these three were connected with a shogunate general, they would become objects of the provincial government's wise fear and impotent hostility. But, as they had no outward concerns about local affairs and were rather too obvious a threesome to be apt spies, they were not often bothered by vassals.

When approached by any of Sato's men, the women freely introduced themselves as ex-*shirobyoshi* dancers who had decided to become mercenaries and bounty-hunters. As the male-impersonating shirobyoshi were occasionally infamous, the story was believable. Thus, though outsiders, they were allowed the mobility they required to surreptitiously investigate the lay of the countryside.

Their adversary might hide in the forests for weeks without detection. There were an unusual number of abandoned temples; it was conceivable that she could move from one to the next, comfortably though furtively camped. But it would be unlike their prey to lurk about in such an unworthy manner.

It was even less likely that she was somewhere in the village, which was often searched by Sato's men. The villagers were unlikely candidates as confederates.

As for the samurai homesteads, the bikuni would be unable to find help there, unless Lord Sato had traitors among his vassals. For the time being the three women considered this a slight prospect. Or, if Sato's vassals were faithless, nothing in their manner or character suggested that their treason was due to a higher principle. They would betray Tomoe Gozen, too.

This left the farmlands beyond the gorge as the most reasonable place to seek refuge and to plan a route through difficult passes and around the patrolling vassals. There were no major bridges across the gorge, only a rope bridge, which took a lot of traffic but was only mildly guarded, as it was situated in the middle of the province rather than on some border. The upland ford was inaccessible during the mountain's indistinguishable autumn and winter, so the rope bridge was the bikuni's only route to the farmlands. It would be easy to bribe or cajole the minimal guard at that inconsequent post.

Having made these deductions, the three women set out

afoot to snoop around the farmlands. They created something of a stir among the farmers, by their manner and mere presence. The beauty and rough bearing of Ha-yugao and Kosame provoked curiosity. Shi-u, though beautiful in her inimical fashion, provoked trepidation.

Only once did a vassal become suspicious, discovering that the women had been asking after the same esoteric nun that the vassals were ordered to kill on sight. But Ha-yugao and Kosame were convincing in their wit and bravado, insisting when they found the bikuni, they would tie her up and deliver her to Sato Castle for a fat reward. This cooled suspicions and sparked amusement. The vassal said derisively, "What dozens of men could not achieve, you three will do alone?"

"No question," said Kosame, her eyes flashing. Ha-yugao fingered her broad-axe meaningfully. The vassal laughed hard and went along his way, leaving them to what he thought their folly.

They knew Tomoe Gozen would prefer not to slay her way across the border. No one could raid a border checkpoint and expect to pass unharassed among other provinces. It was a key issue with Kamakura that provincial lords show no weakness at their borders, or the larger government would send forces to step in. This being so, yet another limitation was placed on Tomoe Gozen. As they saw her options narrow, the three warriors knew the box was shrinking around their quarry.

Some clues were picked up here and there among the farmers, most of whom were reticent, but a few were eager to tell tales, especially to Kosame, who could put on a show of vulgarism that won over ill-bred commoners.

When at length the women returned to the village, where their horses had been stabled, they took a single room at an inn. Their lantern burned late into the night. Their voices spoke softly.

"She's forever clever about such things," said Ha-yugao, oiling the metal of her battle-axe and pursing her lips. "If she decided to leave undetected, she may already have done so."

Kosame, sitting cross-legged by a pot of coals, shook her head. She said, "Some gossiping farmers claimed to have seen her at the rope bridge this morning. The guard there wouldn't speak openly, but he obviously hid something. Doubtless she spoke to him gently and he thought it best to let her pass unmolested, for otherwise he would die. That means she's somewhere around here after all, perhaps in the village. Hard to say what she was doing among the farmlands these past days, or where she stayed. Probably an injury had her lying low. Now, she'll move quickly."

"That instrument-mender said she was a friend of a Shinto priest. So that albino at the Shinto shrine lied," said Ha-yugao. "When we went back there this afternoon, the place was boarded up and empty. That's strange, but a lot of holy places have been abandoned. I don't think it's connected with our business."

Shi-u sat near the lantern. She spread a map of Kanno upon the floor. Although she did not speak, she pointed at a route through Kanno that looked as though it would be dangerous in good weather or bad.

"The gorge?" said Ha-yugao, leaning her broad-axe against a closet door and scooting near to Shi-u and the map. "Look at this, Kosame! If there's some path down into that, it would be possible to walk right out of the mountains without being seen! The locals fear the place, and there has never been a good bridge across it. For some reason it is shunned, so it would serve Tomoe Gozen's purpose of escape!"

Kosame didn't bother to go look at the map. She picked at the coals with a pair of iron tongs and said, "Stupid if Lord Sato's priest or regent fails to think of it, too."

Shi-u spoke at last. Her voice was a boyish monotone. Her expression never altered. "Not stupid," she said, "if it is shunned for good reason. It's not on people's tongues today, but who knows if the gorge is wisely left to itself."

Kosame and Ha-yugao became still, thinking over Shi-u's stark innuendo.

"Stupid to follow her, then," said Kosame, breaking the silence.

Ha-yugao laughed ironically. "Since when have we been smart?"

Kosame, relenting, joined the others around the map. She squinted at it, making a sour face, then said, "Well, if she wanted to avoid the vassals, she'd probably find some way down into the gorge about here." She pointed near the waterfall. "But we can go where we want." She slid her finger along the gorge's ridge and stopped at a particular place, saying, "We'll climb down here and cut her off."

"If there's a way down," said Ha-yugao.

"We'll take ropes," said Kosame. "One way down—or another."

"Is it a good plan, Shi-u?" asked Ha-yugao; for, little as she showed it, Shi-u mastered them. To the present query, she did not answer, but leaned back on the floor with her hands behind her head, staring at shadows on the ceiling.

A lone vassal was stationed in the tiny guardhouse near the rope bridge, seated on a stool, his spear against a shoulder, his feet tapping a nervous rhythm. An iron tripod and basket stood outside the guardhouse, full of burning, aromatic wood, flames murmuring and casting unpleasant shadows. Light began to streak the distant heavens; it was not yet enough to aid vision.

Many of Lord Sato's men had died recently. The guard felt as though some war were being waged against the Sato clan by a foe able to appear and disappear at random and in numerous disguises. At this very post, a guard had recently vanished. At first it was supposed that he deserted, and who could blame him if he had; but a peasant reportedly witnessed the missing guard's fate: a family of red-eyed demons, alabaster white, noble of countenance, set upon the guard, the strongest lifting him bodily and tossing him into the crashing rapids far below!

Dawn broke and the guard's mood was relieved somewhat. He went out to stand in the warmth of the flaming tripod, striking a pose intended to be monstrous and severe, though it fell short. He stood watching hoarfrost crystals, sticking out like millions of needles or minute swords from the heavy ropes of the bridge, grow before his eyes.

He tensed at an unexpected sound: a soft wail in the distance. He listened with a sense of uneasiness, and the sound became more distinct. He started across the rope bridge, thinking the sound came from the further side.

Ghosts weren't ordinarily creatures of the dawn, but the guard's tremulousness was not markedly relieved. There were all manner of monsters who were fearless by day. The guard thrown into the gorge had apparently been attacked by daylight fiends.

Each step was made tentatively. The guard's nape was drenched in sweat as he walked along the swinging bridge.

The sonorous wail was loudest at the center of the bridge. The guard looked downward into darkness. For a long while he stood transfixed, his face tilted, his expression worried and stiff. By the dim light of the morning sun, he could see a dense fog below, stirring restlessly, lapping like a tide. He heard the roar of rapids and the boom of wave against boulder.

He heard the ghostly sound of someone playing a flute.

While pondering the unlikelihood of music from the gorge, a gorge noted for hostile spirits, the rope bridge lurched, and the guard squeaked with fright. From sheer clumsiness, his foot went through woven ropes and he nearly lost his spear. Regaining balance and a small measure of composure, he raised his spear and pointed it in the direction of three presences in the long shadows of morning.

"Hold there! Off the bridge! Who seeks to cross?"

He hurried toward them. They were the three women who the vassals were buzzing about. The lone guard found them as startling as they had been described. One stood with a short-poled halberd and a disdainful, bored look. The one beside her carried an oversized axe. The third had placed herself in a shadow; he couldn't judge her demeanor or countenance. All three bore long and short swords.

There had been no order to interfere with these women, who were rather too colorful and overbearing to be suspected as spies. But the vassal felt the perfect fool for having been frightened by their sudden appearance, and needed to save face by demanding some sort of identification and statement of business. He postured with self-importance, covertly admiring the beauty of the two women who listened to his pointless objurgations, exchanging bemused glances between themselves.

While he was carrying on and making pompous commands, the third woman, who had been standing apart, stepped to the fore and said,

"Samurai, tell us: How can we get into the gorge?"

Her rawboned tallness and the unwavering look in her eyes undid him at once. Her inconceivable query struck him mute. Who in all Naipon would go into such a place?

Ha-yugao said with a sharp sort of sweetness, "We'll obtain rope if it's the only way."

The vassal worked his mouth up and down, but nothing came out.

Kosame, her nagamaki held loosely, observed wryly, "He's quite a fellow, isn't he?"

Ha-yugao snickered; the weighted chain hung from her obi jangled when brushed by the axe handle.

Shi-u placed a strong, long hand upon the guard's shoulder. She leaned close and said, "Somehow, you annoy me."

He found his voice, though it squeaked more than he remembered it. "An old s-stairway f-far along that way! It's broken and d-dangerous!"

"Thank you," said Shi-u, drawing away from the quaking vassal. The other two women had already started along the cliff-edge path in the direction the guard had indicated. Momentarily, Shi-u followed.

Well before the wives of Yoshimora Wada imposed upon the quaking guard, while they slept at a village inn, another drama unfolded near Sato Castle. Heinosuke of Omi passed over a snow-covered field in the castle's moonshadow, himself the swift shadow of an owl against the night. He went undetected into a stand of leafless trees. Among the trees that grew along the river, he came upon an ancient cairn, built by the primitive, earlier race of Naipon. He moved three large flat pieces of shale aside, revealing a narrow black gaping hole. Squeezing into the cairn, he crouched long enough to blow spark and tinder into a flame with which to light a candle. He started along a passageway less ancient than the cairn, though more forgotten.

As archivist for the Sato clan during the previous year, Heinosuke had approached his chores with an enthusiasm unmatched by the retainers who had held that post in previous generations. In the course of arranging, sorting, and taking inventory of the remarkable collection of family records, books, and documents, Heinosuke chanced upon many foxed and mildewed maps of early Kanno, as well as the original architectural plans for the construction of Sato Castle. It was doubtful that any living individual knew as much as Heinosuke had been able to learn about the underground routes.

The tunnel went deep, deep into the ground and came out into a vast natural cavern. The floor was a rugged trail of pits, pools, and strange formations; crystalline walls glittered in the candlelight as Heinosuke passed. There was a particularly acute dampness where the cavern passed beneath the castle's moat.

Beyond this point, Heinosuke found the chiseled passage that led upward at a sharp angle, away from the vaulted cave.

The artificial mesa on which the castle was built consisted of blocks of granite and a great deal of fill. Riddling this tremendous groundwork was a perplexing maze of claustrophobic burrows, few of which were known to the present generation. Fewer still were used. Heinosuke concentrated on his memory of a specific route. It was far from inconceivable that a man could become irrevocably lost among the interconnecting and misleading passageways.

Here and there, tunnels had collapsed over the years. Others had filled with water. It was necessary to amend the route in these places, to find other ways through, so that Heinosuke became less certain of direction.

The occasional pitter-patter might have been rats or running water or something unimaginable. Sound was distorted. Time and senses were muted. Only by the fact that he had started on a second candle did Heinosuke realize that a lot of time had passed. He was uncertain of the path that lay ahead. He was more certain of his retreat. Yet, if he fled back to the cairn and the relief of fresh air, his efforts would have been wasted and Echiko would remain in danger's midst.

He had only the word of Tomoe Gozen that Echiko was abused by Kuro and his plots. As the bikuni's actions were influenced by the sinister intrigues of the revengeful spirit, Heinosuke had tried to discount the information brought by her, one of Kuro's unwitting conspirators. Yet it was true that Heinosuke, with all his snooping and research, had been unable to establish the exact lineage of the foundling princess. As the bikuni had suggested, it was possible, after all, that Echiko was related to one of the seven families that Kuro sought to destroy.

Even were Echiko not one of Kuro's objects of revenge, he might use her for the furtherance of his goal. Or it might be as simple as the bikuni had suggested: Lady Echiko pined to death; Heinosuke's pretended lack of concern was the greater curse against her.

Thus Heinosuke had set out in this endeavor, to enter Sato Castle by little-known subterranean routes, to see Echiko's condition himself. If it appeared necessary, he would kidnap her, whisk her to safety, if such a place existed. What they would do thereafter was difficult to conjecture. But he had been lax too long, lost in his self-pity, disappointment, failure, and unebbing sense of horror.

There was a movement in the tunnel, far ahead. Heinosuke pinched his candle's flame. He pressed against a shallow cavity and watched the shadow of a hulking samurai, head bowed under the low ceiling, a small paper lantern in his hand. Heinosuke was relieved that it was at least not some monster!

The thickset samurai might have passed Heinosuke without detecting him, except for the chance placement of the lantern. For a fraction of a second, the light lingered between two faces: one-eyed Heinosuke's and the dour, high-cheeked, chiseled features of Ittosai Kumasaku. In the next moment, Ittosai had dashed the lantern to the ground and stomped it into a slimy puddle. Both men drew steel in the quick and utter darkness.

Metal sparked against metal and Heinosuke's shoulders were jarred deep in their sockets. He leapt backward from the powerful opponent, panting, while Ittosai remained still and calm and could not be heard in the least. Heinosuke stamped about in mild panic, sword waving to block whatever blow might come his way. Ittosai, motionless, listened. But he did not try anything risky in the confined space.

A booming voice echoed through the tunnel, and there was a quizzical aspect to Ittosai's loud musings. "I was under the impression that only Kuro the Darkness had resolved the complexity of these passages and had imparted to none but myself a single route by which I might come to him with information or receive instructions. Now it seems as though Heinosuke of Omi knows the labyrinths, too."

Heinosuke was uncertain how to take Ittosai's offhand tone. With undisguised disdain, Heinosuke said, "You are that horrid Ittosai of the Graves! People say you serve a monster without pity or qualm!"

"If I spare you, it won't be out of pity," Ittosai admitted. "When you die, I will bury you without compunction. But it is not *my* duty to take your life. As you say, I am merely the man of the graves, though once I was noted for better things."

Heinosuke heard Ittosai's sword begin to slide into its sheath. He could not believe this devoted servant of Kuro truly meant no interference, for the man's reasoning was outside Heinosuke's sphere of understanding. Therefore Heinosuke leapt at the sound of the sword sliding into its scabbard, knowing it to be his best chance to overcome the powerful Ittosai Kumasaku. But Ittosai had moved silently to one side, and the younger man's incredible speed was wasted in the darkness. His cut went into the clay earth of a wall. Ittosai's huge hand wrapped around the back of Heinosuke's neck, lifting him from the floor.

Heinosuke felt the weightlessness of flight and the jarring impact with a wall. He landed in a battered heap, coughing, stunned, his neck sprained. Ittosai spoke without the least emotional investment in his own words: "I won't stop you from taking the Lady Echiko from the castle, if that's your plan. My master's plots are more bewildering than this labyrinth. If you leave Echiko to starve herself to death, Priest Kuro doesn't mind. If you make a chivalrous attempt, then you play into his hands in some other way. Nothing is left to chance. No option turns out well. Believe it!"

Heinosuke regained his breath, his head no longer swam, and he stood slowly. He clutched his sword in too tight a fist.

Ittosai said, "Consider life's futility, Heinosuke! I feel sorry for you. Why not do as I? Look to your own life instead!"

There was a twisted sort of concern in Ittosai's voice; but could momentary compassion be trusted in a man whose advice was selfish and inhumane? Heinosuke had collected his wits by now, calmed his thinking. He became as quiet as Ittosai. Heinosuke knew he had one skill above others: he was capable of inimitable swiftness. He knew where Ittosai stood and launched himself with silent speed. He heard Ittosai's startled grunt.

Heinosuke pushed at the huge body. By his touch, he knew that his sword had only gone into the underside of Ittosai's arm. Ittosai raised a knee into Heinosuke's stomach; and as Heinosuke bent double, Ittosai drew his sword in such a manner as to slice across the young man's lowered face.

Heinosuke tumbled backward, his hand clamped to his one eye, blood oozing through his fingers. When he moaned, it did not convey the depth of his pain and his horror. Ittosai whispered, his voice yet thunderous in the darkness of Heinosuke's world, a darkness which would now extend beyond the walls of the tunnels. "Was it your eye?" said Ittosai. "It's unfortunate. Even now, I won't kill you."

When the big man was gone, Heinosuke began to crawl, dripping gore from his sliced eye, feeling the wall one-handed. He strove to retain consciousness and reason and to bear in mind the ancient maps of the castle's deep foundation.

Neatly rolled and strapped across the bikuni's back was a traveling quilt, tattered and unwholesome. She had scavenged it from the Temple of the Gorge, where some wayward pilgrim had left it who knew how long ago, quite likely having fled the haunted place too swiftly to gather bedding. The small quilt would suffice for the few cold nights to be spent in the depths of the canyon.

The bottoms of her hakama trousers were lifted and tucked into her obi, so that she could climb where necessary. But once the floor of the gorge was obtained, there were only a few occasions that called for her to scrabble over natural monuments or the debris of landslides.

The whole of the morning she walked along the river and through persisting fog. Every sound was rendered spectacular when sight was so hindered. At times the rapids crashed with uproarious insistence against banks and boulders; at other points the river was almost quiet, so that fish (or something!) could be heard leaping.

She made excellent speed, for the river was lowest at this time of year, though still fabulous. There were dry beds of gravel softened by snow, high banks with animal trails, or swamps frozen solid enough to be reasonably safe to traverse. It was unexpectedly easy passage in all, discounting the gorge's daunting and oppressive mood.

If she thought plainly about that indefinable mood and investigated whatever presented itself from the mist, there was nothing unexpected. But, like dim stars seen more clearly from the side of one's vision, if she dropped her wariness and expectation for the least moment, formless presences became tangible at the periphery of her awareness.

She fancied herself blithely strolling along the Sandzu, Hell's river. The musky fog was a vast, amorphous entity through which lesser ghosts swept to and fro, gazing on those who passed. Finding her mind unnecessarily imaginative, the bikuni made herself increasingly uneasy. To placate, if not disperse, the spirits of the gorge, she drew forth the shakuhachi and began to play. The sound of it calmed her own spirit as well as those around her, irrespective of the unearthly manner in which the melody rebounded from unseen cliffs.

The fog began to burn away in the cold afternoon sun, revealing the looming cliffs, from which numerous projecting shapes of stone appeared eager to tumble down. The route had led sharply downward from highland Kanno, so that she was soon below the snowline, disregarding isolated isles of snow. She doffed the straw boots, which would wear out on naked rocks, and stuffed them in the end of her rolled traveling quilt. Then she donned the geta that had hung like wooden bells from the bedroll. The raucous clatter of her new footgear lent an easier familiarity to her trek, lulling her into a false security.

Near a bend, a black and leafless tree was seen to have fallen into the river. It had once made a valiant effort to root itself high upon the face of the cliff, only to be chucked down in the prime of its growth. It lay in the torrent, rocking faintly, its black limbs raking upward. The bikuni was nearly drawn into melancholy thoughts at the sight of so awesome a symbol of life's unfairness and struggle's futility.

The tree did not quite bridge the two banks. From the bikuni's vantage-ground, it looked as though the other bank might provide an easier route further on, whereas the present bank looked narrower and more rugged in the distance. It would be tricky crossing by way of the insufficient bridge; the tree was thin near the head and a leap from there might not work out well. It would be a bad idea to get soaked in this cold weather.

As she stood pondering the wisdom of climbing across the river versus the wisdom of adhering to the present course, a flash of blue cloth caught her attention. Something was snagged in the tree's submerged limbs. At first the nun approached slowly. Then, as it became more evident what it was the black tree had captured, the nun began to trot over the rocky terrain.

Her mind reeled with the recognition. All the subtle dreariness of the gorge heightened and descended upon her sensibility, as a smith's hammer pounds steel. Before she climbed out onto the tree, she first drew her sword, severed a hooked limb to be used as a tool, then resheathed. Branch in hand, she climbed toward the middle of the river.

Some of the limbs were sharp as thorns. Some were brittle and snapped against her weight. To reach her objective, it was necessary to brace herself across three limbs, none of which could hold her weight alone, and lie almost flat, hovering above clear, rushing water. She reached downward with the limb in an effort to hook onto the obi that tied Shinji's and Otane's bodies together at their waists.

They had been in the river for a week, since the night they were freed from the cruciform, only to seek a more horrible demise. They were recognizable only because of the blue peasant cottons that they had worn on the day they were captured and crucified, and by the fact that they were bound as people bind themselves when pledged to commit *shinju* or love suicide.

The hooked end of her branch caught hold of the obi. She pulled; and she whispered, "I will see you put to rest, Otane, Shinji. I have not abandoned you yet." As their bloated, pallid corpses were raised, the bikuni realized the three limbs would not take the added weight. She spread herself wider, flattened herself more, braced across six or seven limbs of different sizes. One broke and poked her. Her free arm grabbed blindly for a sturdier branch, and found one. She began to crawl backward, toward thicker limbs and the trunk, moving spiderlike, pulling the corpses with her. For a moment her bamboo hat caught on a small limb, but the twig broke and the bikuni made it to the slippery trunk.

Rapids beat against the tree. The bikuni found surer footing and pulled Shinji's and Otane's bodies from the water. At the moment of success, the tree began to shift. The bikuni was thrown backward and nearly impaled upon a sharp limb. The hooked branch she had used as a tool was broken near the end. There were terrible scraping sounds and snapping limbs against the riverbottom. Neroyume clung for the sake of her life and saw the bodies of the clinging lovers slip under the log, beyond view.

The tree found better anchor. The nun hurried back and forth along the trunk, frantic to see where the currents had whisked the two bodies. She saw them at last, among frothy rapids far down the river, bashed against a boulder, then rushed beyond sight. The bikuni despaired. She had failed Otane and Shinji again.

The tree's new position offered no hope of crossing to the other bank. The bikuni continued along the way, watching for the corpses to resurface, although there was not much hope of seeing them again.

The bikuni's inability to cross to the other bank proved unfortunate. The river widened, meeting the cliff on one side, leaving no path. It became necessary to climb the wall about a fifth of the way up, where a ledge presented itself. It was not an easy route, though it could have been worse. If she were careless, a plunge into the freezing rapids might be her last mistake. But by taking the ledge slowly, it was not excessively dangerous.

The ledge wound around a hump on the cliff's face. It was impossible to see ahead. For all she could tell, the route would only take her halfway before coming to a sudden end.

It was essential to hug the wall and find handholds wherever possible. Shale broke loose and clattered toward the river. While upon this precarious perch, the bikuni heard someone reciting the Kwannon Sutra. The rush of water blended with the chanting, lending an inhuman aspect to the litany. She clung to the wall, motionless, trying to judge where the sutra originated. It became stronger and more distinct.

"*Shin-kwan, shojo-kwan, kodai chie-kwan*...clear vision, pure vision, vision wise and full of mercy. Clear vision, pure vision, we rely upon thee ever. Thy merciful heart is a wonderful cloud/ from which falleth sweet dew extinguishing/ the flames of earthly passion. Clear vision, pure vision, vision wise and full of mercy. Clear vision, pure vision, we rely upon thee ever."

In a moment, the chanter appeared from around the curve of the cliff's face. He ceased reciting and became most quiet, glowering at the nun, the two of them standing almost side by side.

He was young, homely to a high degree, and head-shaven. His hat hung at his back and his clothing were the blackest black, his kimono's sleeves hanging below his knees.

They were in quite a predicament. Neither could continue their journey, and it was an equal nuisance for either to retrace the distance they had come.

"We're in trouble," said the bikuni, a forced smile barely showing from beneath her hat.

"I don't think so," said the monk in a holier-than-thou tone of voice. He immediately quoted: "'A monk is higher than a nun; a nun is higher than a lay monk; a lay monk is higher than a lay nun.' I cannot tell by your costume whether you are a nun or a lay nun. In either case, since I am a monk, practically a full-fledged priest, in fact, there is no confusion as to who should remove herself as quickly as possible from my chosen path."

"If we join hands momentarily," the bikuni suggested, eminently more reasonable than the stuck-up little monk, "we could negotiate the treacherous route with mutual safety and benefit."

The monk was aghast. He exclaimed indignantly, "How can you suggest it! To lay hands upon this pious and chaste friend of Buddha? Women are perverse and greedy! They are ignorant of correct conduct! Your scheme is not clever enough to take me in. What a clumsy conceit, to think you might touch so much as the hem of my vestment, let alone these hands, which perform holy works."

The nun replied evenly: "Please rest comfortably. Your attitude scarcely fills my heart with perverse sentiment."

"It is you who lack proper manners," said the monk. "How is it troublesome for you to return the way you came, then start out anew once I'm safely through? Someone instructed you poorly as Buddha's servant!"

"It is unforgivable if you cast aspersions on the old priest who instructed me," she said, not mentioning that her instruction had consisted exclusively of shakuhachi lessons. "His feelings about young monks was that they spend the first year of their study sitting and thinking and thereafter they just sit."

"If I were sitting somewhere," said the monk, "you would not be in this dilemma. What will you do about it?"

"It crossed my mind," she said, "to push you off."

The monk, ignoring the idle threat, closed his eyes, turned his face upward, and, as he waited for the bikuni to do exactly what she said, he chanted, *"Shin-kwan, shojo-kwan, kodai chie-kwan, hikwan koji-kwan . . ."*

Exasperated, the bikuni started back along the way she came. The monk followed with a smirk, pleased to have won out against her unsubtle bluff. Soon they were on a dry part of the riverbed, standing face to face. As it was nearly sunset, it would not be wise for her to attempt renegotiating the ledge until morning. At least now she could be certain it led somewhere! Despite herself, she was amused. The monk was not a strong-looking fellow and would have had the harder time starting over again.

He began to make camp. Without asking permission, she decided to share the same site. If he didn't like it, the monk changed his mind on discovering himself incapable of making a campfire from the damp and iced wood around the river. The bikuni had collected a number of twigs earlier in the day, keeping them inside her kimono, where they dried nicely. With flint and steel from her travel kit, she struck a small blaze, sufficient to ignite the damp stuff the monk had gathered.

Although the nun was not traveling without food, she had not eaten that day. The Shinto priest of White Beast Shrine had repaired her alms-bag and put a lot of millet inside; but she had nothing in which to boil the millet. For this reason she was extremely hungry. The homely monk happened to have a nice supply of dried fruit and crackers, the latter practically in crumbs. When she unfolded the wrapping paper, the bikuni sat near him by the fire and said, "This humble servant of Buddha is indebted to Buddha's friend for sharing." He was tremendously annoyed, but made no acidic reply.

In a while, he struck up a conversation, affecting a friendly tone although retaining an abusive edge to many of his comments. "So, you're running away from Kanno province, am I right? I'm going straight there myself."

"What do you know of Kanno?" she asked softly.

"No monks allowed. No nuns. The lord of Kanno is a fanatical Lotus convert. I'll cause some trouble about it."

"Maybe it's not exactly what you think."

"Can't be scared off," boasted the little monk, his chin held firm. "I'm resolved to reestablish Kwannon's worship."

The bikuni was tempted to let the overconfident buffoon find out on his own how things were in Kanno. But it would be too wicked to let him wander innocently into a different kind of trouble than he expected. She told him with stark simplicity, "Lord Sato is held under the sway of a goryo."

"Is it so?" said the monk, putting on a show of attentiveness, though the nun thought his amazement was a deception. "Lord Sato is under such a fiend's influence? So that's why priests are banned from crossing the borders!"

The bikuni nodded. "The vengeful ghost is a spirit of my

own clan. For that reason I could not fight it. You're correct to say I am running away. I cannot deny it. As you are above a lay nun, surely you will be more capable than I."

Her irony did not evade him. She was a warrior and he a little fellow. All the same, he answered with unswerving braggadocio: "No doubt you're right about that. At least I'm not his relative! Might just kick him in the shins or someplace better."

"You're a funny man, but rude," she said. "My Buddhist name is Neroyume."

"Ho ho! A fierce name! Mine is just as bad: Kasha."

A kasha was a corpse-stealing demon known to crash wakes and make off with casket and all. It was the sort of name a cynical esotericist might consider, but not a worshipper of gentle Kwannon. "Why did you choose such a name?" she asked.

"I didn't," said monk Kasha. "I've always had it."

"Your parents must be strange."

"Quite so," he said, not insulted, but taking it as flattery. "By the way, I happen to know a good story about a revengeful spirit. It's called 'A Correction Regarding the Fate of Okinamaro the Dog.' I heard it from a pious and elderly priestess who in her youth served an Empress."

"I, too, know the story of Okinamaro," said the bikuni.

"You think so? You have heard how the august cat-in-waiting was attacked by Okinamaro, how the dog was subsequently banished from the capital, but reinstated a few days later when he piteously ingratiated himself to His Majesty? The story did not happen exactly as Sei Shonagon wrote it down. When she recorded that chapter of *Makura Zoshi* she was feeling sentimental, and the sorrier truth of the event didn't suit her mood."

"In that case," said the nun, "tell me the tale."

"I would like to. Well, the august cat-in-waiting was much beloved by His Majesty, who in His devotion conferred upon the feline the title of 'Chief Superintendent of the Female Attendants of the Palace.' One day this high-ranking animal wandered out into the garden, making footmarks here and there upon the fresh-raked sand, and climbed upon a bridge to sun herself. A nurse in charge saw the august cat-in-waiting and cried out, 'How improper! Come over here at once!' The august cat-in-waiting yawned hugely and looked the other direction.

"The nurse was beside herself with vexation and called to the garden's dog, Okinamaro. 'Okinamaro!' she said. 'Go over there and bite the Chief Superintendent of the Female Attendants of the Palace at once and teach her a lesson!' Okinamaro, thinking the order was meant in earnest, set upon the august cat-in-waiting, only to get his nose injured by quick claws. The indignant Superintendent marched away, twitching her tail. She took refuge behind a screen, in the lap of His Majesty.

"His Majesty saw that the august cat-in-waiting was perturbed. Furthermore, He was alarmed by the foul-smelling slime upon the fur of the generally fastidious animal. Learning that Okinamaro had salivated on the august cat-in-waiting, He ordered Okinamaro to receive twenty lashes, which was not excessive, then to be exiled from the palace, which was a most unhappy fate.

"'Alas, poor dog!' Sei Shonagon wrote, the sleeve of her kimono doubtless soaked with tears. 'He used to swagger so much at ease. When he was led along the paths with a willow wreath upon his head, and adorned with flowers of peach and cherry, could he have guessed it would so soon come to this? At meals he used to be with us, and after three days of his exile, we missed him greatly.'

"A few days later, a dog was heard to be howling in terror. A scavenger-woman ran through the palace gardens shouting, 'Awful! Awful! Two chamberlains are beating a dog to death! They say it is chastisement for ignoring the rule of banishment!' Here the *Makura Zoshi* gets things right, for Sei Shonagon was among the witnesses who hurried forth to try to save Okinamaro's life. Alas, he had ceased howling and reposed a battered heap of fur and blood. His body was flung outside the gate.

"But after sunset, a wretched-looking dog appeared, trembling all over, his body woefully torn and swollen. 'Is that Okinamaro?' asked a maid, standing on a deck overlooking the garden. She called to him by name, but the awful-looking beast did not move.

"'Okinamaro was killed,' said another. 'Surely he did not survive such a beating.'

"Yet another maid said, 'He is too utterly loathsome to be our dog. Okinamaro always came when he was called, and hopped joyously. As this animal won't come, it cannot be Okinamaro.'

"This is where the version told by Sei Shonagon goes astray, for her soft-minded readers would not have wished to be seriously disturbed. For doesn't *Makura Zoshi* say Okinamaro groveled at the feet of His Majesty and was recognized at last? Doesn't that book assure us that Okinamaro's banishment was reversed and he was his old self in a few days?

"Okinamaro may or may not have been recognized. But he had become so repugnant that he was turned out by guards, who poked him with sticks. The dog did not once whine or grovel, as was falsely said. The guards who got him out of the garden came back sweaty and alarmed. They were certain the dog was nothing but a resurged corpse. The dog had not so much as panted, but had looked at them with eyes the shade of plum-blossoms, malevolent and weird.

"That night, a warrior broke into the women's quarters of the palace. Everyone was running around in fright and confusion. The warrior was looking for one specific woman, and it was certainly not for the sake of a discreet tryst. He found the nurse who had set Okinamaro upon the august cat-in-waiting; and he shouted at her, 'Woman! Why did you not tell them you commanded me to bite the Chief Superintendent of the Female Attendants of the Palace?'

"As the nurse was incapable of reply, the warrior stuck her through the breast with a spear and pinned her to the sliding door. By then a lot of guards had gathered in the halls of the gardens. The murderous warrior could by no means escape. All the same, he vanished somehow and was never seen again or brought to justice.

"The nurse lived a few days, refusing to die until a meeting with His Majesty could be arranged. Then she confessed that she set Okinamaro upon the august cat-in-waiting and had remained silent afterward. The corpse of Okinamaro was recovered and interred with the bodies of other palace animals, and sutras were offered. Only in a certain sense, therefore, did Sei Shonagon tell the truth when she wrote that Okinamaro was completely reinstated."

Tomoe Gozen was uncertain to what degree monk Kasha wished his story to be taken seriously. A dog's grudge against a nurse was hardly the same as the grudge Kuro felt against seven clans. Or was it presumptuous to think a limited event regarding a dog was less significant than an event of monumental effect? To the bodhisattvas and the Thousands of Myriads, Okinamaro's revenge might be no smaller or greater than a human spirit's vengeance.

Having reflected on the story in a courteous and appropriate manner, the bikuni offered a sort of all-purpose critique, since she remained uncertain of a precise moral. "Human life is a ripple behind a passing ship," she said. "The ship's port is unknown to the ripple. It dashes off the wrong direction, then disappears."

Monk Kasha laughed and waved a hand, as though this were altogether the improper comment. Belatedly the bikuni suspected the monk had teased her from the beginning. He offered the counterobservation, "Life is a cranberry growing on a mountain path. It is snatched in the beak of the hototogisu cuckoo bird."

The bikuni's complexion flushed slightly. The sky was dark and only the campfire lit their faces. "You make fun of people," she said. "Not that I mind. I will lose any contest of Buddhist thought."

"You're a better nun than you believe," said Kasha, feigning sweetness. "Which is not to say you're much of one. Even lacking pious intention, if you go down upon your knees before Kwannon or Buddha, good will come of it. Just as a meal taken abstractly nourishes the body."

Monk Kasha leaned nearer the fire, the homely contours of his face made weird by the dancing blaze. He brought the subject back to its beginning. "Say, tell me more about Kanno. Not much information gets out."

"The goryo is the main problem," she answered. "Not many of Lord Sato's men are left. By this time next year, the shogunate will have moved in to put someone else in charge of Kanno. There is a chamberlain trying to forestall it; but there's no question he will fail. He trusts the goryo, who has manifested himself as a most beatific priest named Kuro. If you and he stood side by side and several people voted, it would be decided you were the evil spirit, not he."

As she spoke to the homely monk about the goryo, he seemed to peer inward, something of gleeful expectation passing across his face. It was a strange response. In fact, the monk did not appear truly surprised or fretful about anything she mentioned. He surfaced from his inward glance and said, "What do you know of vengeful spirits?"

"What I observed in Kanno," she said. "They're strong."

"Not usually," the monk amended matter-of-factly. "They're trouble enough, like the spirit of Okinamaro, who was able to achieve his aim. But as a rule, a goryo lurks around the place of its unnatural death and can get its enemy only if that enemy comes close. It is also generally the case that a goryo is immune to ordinary exorcism, and lingers until it gets its way. Yet this one doesn't like priests. With such an excess of power, why fear a Buddhist exorcist?"

"If what you say is true," the nun allowed, "then Kuro the Darkness is exceptional."

"Well, I'll see him soon enough," said monk Kasha. "I don't think he'll escape me, in any case."

The monk curled up near the fire, wrapped only in his garments. The bikuni unrolled the musty travel-quilt and wrapped it around herself, drew her arms inside her kimono, and sat with her back against a rock. She sat watching the campfire, listening to the river and occasional gusts, thinking deeply. Monk Kasha began to snore.

She went over the history of the goryo as told to her by Heinosuke. And she considered the monk's advice on the matter, for it did seem he had meant to advise her, and had not grilled her on account of information needed for himself. Kasha knew more than he pretended. As the bikuni fell asleep, this topic was uppermost in her mind, and continued through her dream.

In the dream, the campfire did not die down, but became a brilliant shade of green, burning bright. The homely monk jumped up from where he had been sleeping. He appeared to have doubled or tripled his size but was otherwise unchanged. He kicked at the green fire and offered a lot of unholy curses. "This will fix you!" the monk said, kicking another stone into the unusual blaze. "You'll be sorry about that!" he said. "Too much trouble for everyone!"

The bikuni awoke in the white haze of morning and sat forward with a gasp, exclaiming, "I know where the goryo gets his power!" She was eager to share her realization with the monk, but he was nowhere to be seen.

She could see no evidence of his having shared the camp. The fire's remains appeared to consist of the twigs she herself had lit, with none of the wood monk Kasha presumedly had gathered. There was only a charred bit of river-rock to mark the place where she recalled a large, healthy blaze. Her stomach growled as though she hadn't eaten anything the day before. She couldn't find any of the pits of the dried plums Kasha had shared with her.

She might have dreamed him entirely! The gorge was noted for its hauntings, so it was worth considering. If a goryo was able to plot supernatural vengeance by eliciting the aid of the Lotus Sutra, then surely some other kind of spirit—god or devil—might make a new web contrary to the other, with the help of the Kwannon Sutra. When she thought it over, that monk had not looked quite human, though his homeliness hadn't been of a frightening kind. Despite his rude manner, he had cheered her heart with snooty humor; he had affected her thinking about leaving Kanno and about the powers of vengeance after death; and right from the start he had caused her to delay her flight away from the entire mess.

"What an odd man," she thought. "Picking up after himself just to confuse me."

She rolled her travel-quilt and strapped it to her back, tied her hat on straight, and considered which direction to take—back to Kanno, or away. The thought of returning revived doubts: suppose the odd little monk had been Kuro's cleverest trick to get her back! But if that were the case, the monk would not have provided her, by subtle means, with the final clues that might well be the undoing of Kuro the Darkness. It was maddening that the monk had gone off without letting her explain the theory that her conscious and subconscious had worked out. Had the monk vanished like that so she would be forced to return and personally test her theory? She would have preferred to tell him her reasoning and get his opinion. If she were wrong, it would be an error to return to Kanno, where Kuro might again manage to manipulate her actions.

As the morning was nearly as foggy as the previous morning, the nun used the lack of visibility as an excuse not to tackle the treacherous ledge. Instead, she wandered through the mists in search of anything edible growing above the river's bank. She managed to uncover a few wintering roots, which were exceedingly tough, but digestible.

Almost to spite her, she thought, the fog began to burn off early, unlike yesterday, forcing her to the difficult decision. Everything had gone badly in Kanno and she was not feeling inherent predilection toward adventure. She was mostly decided to continue her journey as far from Kanno as possible. It was wiser than risking the chance of killing others because of Kuro's influence over her.

The cliff's face was becoming visible through the dissipating haze. It was senseless to delay longer. She started in that direction, but stopped when she spied a faint figure sitting across a miniature inlet of partially iced, stagnant water. At first she thought it must be monk Kasha. A breeze swept away the light haze that clung to the figure, and the bikuni saw that it was a woman samurai. She was sitting on a rock, gazing along the river. She was armed with two swords and a nagamaki, or short-poled halberd. She was dressed in bright colors: kimono with fernbrake pattern and a quilted haori jacket in a lighter shade of green, with gold threads forming a sea pattern. In a moment, the samurai stood and faced the bikuni across the pool, apparently having been waiting for this very meeting. She had a pleasant face.

"Hey! Are you Tomoe Gozen?" the samurai shouted over the small body of water. "I want to talk to you! Come over here!"

The bikuni did not move. She knew the woman had to be one of Lord Wada's warrior-wives, three of whom had been snooping around White Beast Shrine and elsewhere in Kanno asking about Tomoe. She had no desire to admit to being the one they sought. It appeared as though this woman had come upriver, negotiating the ledge during the misty morning and waiting near the bottleneck, where it would be impossible to miss the bikuni.

"I am Neroyume!" she called back. "It isn't me you want!"

A sound of slipping gravel caused the bikuni to turn. A second woman, armed with axe, swords, and weighted chain, stood with her arms folded under her breasts. Axe handle and sword sheaths were lacquered red. Her hakama trousers were patterned with large white flowers on a black field. Her overcoat was blue-black with a moon and mist embroidered on one sleeve.

"Perhaps you're Neroyume," she said, "but you are the one we want."

She unfolded her arms and patted the axe handle dangling from her obi. The coiled, weighted chain rattled with meaning of its own.

The nagamaki-wielder was hurrying around the miniature

bay. In a moment, the bikuni realized, she would be caught between these two women. Still, she did not move.

There was a third woman. She came into view along the lower bank, carrying some of the same kind of edible roots the bikuni had found earlier. She was lean and quick, but did not come as close as the others. She stopped in front of a rotted-out stump, dropped the tubers as though they had lost her interest; and she rested her left arm upon the hilt of her long-sword in a relaxed pose. She came no closer, but observed.

"You are Yoshimora's harlots," said the bikuni.

"We are his wives," said Kosame, grinning and not affronted. "My name is 'little shark.' Across from you stands 'sharp-edged moonflower.' We're nice if you get to know us."

"Why does Lord Wada still seek me after all these years?" asked the bikuni. "I am retired and no nuisance to him."

Kosame strode nearer, the pole of her halberd tucked casually under one arm. She said, "You were the prize he missed. He is too stubborn to give up. You could come out of retirement and be famous as you were before. It is a matter of pride for us, too. Would you refuse to be our sister?"

"I am Buddha's woman only."

"How so?" asked Kosame, her eyes flashing with wicked humor. "We know your true sentiment. You could not recite one sutra to its end. Just a matter of taking off that vest and letting your hair grow longer. Then you have returned to the world. It's very simple."

The bikuni had to watch two fields, for Ha-yugao was also tightening the distance and had removed the chain from her obi. Tomoe said, "You think to threaten me, but I am harder to impress. If you intend to say it is to save face that you attack me for refusing to be added to your husband's collection of wives, please reconsider, and think of my position. Lord Wada defeated Lord Kiso a few years ago. How could I submit to my husband's foe? If I return to the samurai world, then I would also be bound to avenge Yoshinake Kiso. Hard on Lord Wada if I do."

"We can take you by force," said Ha-yugao. "I can tie you in my chain. It has been arranged for you to receive orders direct from the Shogun before submitting to our lord. You owe allegiance to the Shogun and must accept his decision."

"A nun is unallied," said the bikuni. "I adhere only to the dictates of Heaven."

Kosame did not look convinced of the nun's piety. Ha-yugao continued to speak. "Your solitary Thousand Shrine Sect could be outlawed if you refuse. It would annoy a lot of innocent travelers."

"I don't mind," said Tomoe.

"No?" said Kosame, lifting her nagamaki and seizing upon the bikuni's words. "Then you cherish your solitude and it has nothing to do with devotion to your sect. It is neither a matter of a grudge against Lord Wada, nor a matter of religion. This being so, aren't we justified in thinking it a matter of our own pride?"

Kosame took a stance with nagamaki. Ha-yugao's chain began to whirl and whirr, a sound like a cicada. Tomoe said, "Your Lord Wada may want one more wife, but he may end up with two less."

She drew her Sword of Okio.

She immediately ran off at an angle, forcing her two opponents to keep in motion, keeping them from reaching her at the same moment. She came to a sudden stop, raised her blade, and caught the weighted chain, which would have wrapped around her throat. Caught by Ha-yugao, the women were locked in a tug-of-war. Neither gave up ground to the other; but Tomoe was in the touchiest situation, with Kosame hurrying forth with her nagamaki turning like a swift waterwheel.

Tomoe took the offensive, running straight toward Ha-yugao. Ha-yugao started the slack of the chain rising and falling like a wave. A deft twist sent a loop of chain at the bikuni. The Sword of Okio caught the loop, so that once again Tomoe's neck was safe, though her sword was badly unbalanced by Ha-yugao's continuing manipulation of the chain. Holding her sword one-handed, Tomoe grabbed the chain in her other hand and gave a terrific pull. Ha-yugao slipped on an oval stone, equilibrium askew, affording Tomoe the moment she required to untangle the Sword of Okio.

Ha-yugao dropped the chain. Her axe came up with a swiftness that would have deflected the Sword of Okio if Tomoe had continued the assault; but, seeing her assault would be wasted, the bikuni veered aside to see about Kosame.

The nagamaki reached further than a sword. Tomoe ducked beneath a potentially decapitating sweep and jumped back from two excellent thrusts. Kosame was made confident as the nun was forced to give more and more ground. An overhead cut might have carved the nun from head to crotch, but the Sword of Okio blocked, and the nun lifted her foot and landed a solid kick to Kosame's fingers.

Kosame grimaced, but did not drop the nagamaki. She scuttled backward, abandoning the fight, and squatted to one knee. She placed the nagamaki on the ground with loving care. Then, drawing a cloth from her kimono, she began to wrap the broken fingers of her right hand, offering no vocal complaint.

When Ha-yugao closed in with the terrible broad-axe, the third woman, who had watched from the stump near the river's edge, shouted with authority, "Ha-yugao! She's too strong for you!" Ha-yugao could barely break momentum. By the look in her eyes, it was difficult to obey, to check herself from avenging Kosame's injury. The lean woman approached Ha-yugao and said, "Help Kosame bind her hand. I alone am match for Neroyume."

The rawboned woman was dressed in browns more somber than the bikuni's black and cream and gray. A pattern of clouds was burnished into the thread of her kimono, umber on umber. She removed a dark scarf from her sleeve, twisted it into a rope, and tied it around her hair, drawing her white-streaked ponytail into the headband so that hair would not fly about in what promised to be a difficult encounter. She pulled one arm out of her sleeve so that her arm and right breast were exposed, a breast too small to require a binding linen. Drawing her longsword, she took an excellent posture with hilt held close to her face. She said, "I am Shi-u Morita, first wife of Yoshimora Wada, and have never known defeat. If you have never heard of me before, it is only that I shed useless pride long ago, committing myself more fully to my husband's causes. As you won't give in to his wish, I am resigned to cutting off your head. It will be my trophy."

Tomoe removed her deep hat so that her field of vision would not be hampered. She said, "Now you can get at my neck better." She untied the travel-quilt at her back and let it fall beside the hat, then took her alms-bag over her head and set it down. She had not taken Shi-u's lecture as a boast. By the woman's relaxed bearing, the bikuni knew Shi-u was a woman of uncommon talent. Tomoe removed an extra under-obi and used it to tie back her sleeves. Then she redrew her sword and took a stance proper to counter that of Shi-u Morita.

Shi-u measured the bikuni's stance in turn, and changed her

own posture, inducing a new stance from Tomoe. They stood a long way apart, appraising one another's approach to each implied attack. Any stance one chose, the other knew one suitable to counter, and there was no weakness in either one's defense.

Kosame yet knelt, with broken hand clutched to her stomach. Ha-yugao wandered to the right of Kosame for a different perspective on the duel, which seemed scarcely to be engaged, yet was profoundly interesting.

Tomoe tried a posture rarely seen, but the other knew its answer. The bikuni said, "Shi-u. I often feel that it is my karma to live a long life and walk the longer road to Hell. It would be a shame for a peerless fighter to die. Can Lord Wada spare such as you?"

"I don't believe he need worry about that," said Shi-u with a calm self-assurance to match Tomoe's. But she added, "However, if it comes to such an event, he would not miss me much."

"I thought it might be so," said Tomoe. "You have been in bondage longer than these others. Very well, we fight in earnest."

She turned the dull edge of her sword outward, for she did not wish to kill Shi-u. Taking the offensive, she was impressed by the ease with which Shi-u slipped aside. Shi-u said, "If you have a chance against me, it is not by striking with your sword's dull backside. I won't hesitate. Nor should you."

"I'll break your fingers, as with Kosame," said the nun, without a trace of a boast. "Or your arm."

"It wouldn't be enough to stop me," Shi-u warned. Then her attention was drawn elsewhere and she shouted angrily, "Ha-yugao!" An axe flew through the air with deadly accuracy. Tomoe leapt away, but a lock of hair fell from her scalp. Ha-yugao followed up her attack with a headlong rush, longsword drawn. Tomoe lunged beneath Ha-yugao's bold cut. The Sword of Okio sank full length into Ha-yugao's stomach. Ha-yugao threw her own sword in the river, a startling act, then grabbed the hilt of Tomoe's weapon, refusing to let go.

"Kill her now!" shouted Ha-yugao. "I have her sword!"

Tomoe let go of the Sword of Okio and lurched aside from Shi-u's fierce and vengeful slice. Tomoe rolled across hard stones, bruising her shoulders badly, coming to a squatting position near a startled Kosame. She grabbed Kosame's nagamaki. Ha-yugao continued to stumble about the gravel, clinging to the longsword in her stomach; and she made horrible little animal noises. Kosame cried out in a mournful anguish. As the nun was standing with Kosame's halberd to hand, Kosame managed, with broken fingers, to dig into Tomoe's arm and leave long scratches.

Tomoe leapt again and rolled, coming to her feet in a perfect upright stance with the nagamaki above her head, blade tipped downward and sharp edge up. She faced Shi-u, whose dark complexion had paled and whose dark eyes revealed a pain of spirit. It was a look worth fearing.

"I had no intention of killing any of you!" Tomoe shouted angrily. "You and I were to duel fairly, but Ha-yugao interfered from behind! How can you save face after her dishonorable actions? Leave me alone at once! Leave me!"

The nun panted and glowered, excruciatingly annoyed by events.

Shi-u, stricken by the nun's words, backed away and slowly let her sword slide into its scabbard. She said, "I cannot justify Ha-yugao, but you have already punished her."

Shi-u strode to Ha-yugao, who was still standing despite the mortal wound of a sword sticking through her body. Her face was bloodless, her white lips open. Shi-u took the hilt of the Sword of Okio and drew the blade out. Then, angrily, she reprimanded Ha-yugao with one word: "Fool!" and stuck the Sword of Okio into the woman's throat. It looked cruel, but was only the coup de grace; Ha-yugao could by no means have recovered.

As Ha-yugao fell onto the gravel, Shi-u approached Tomoe and held the Sword of Okio forth, saying, "I won't fight you today. I know your intention to continue through this gorge until it comes out in the next province. Once I've reclaimed my horse from the village near Sato Castle, I will race ahead and wait for you where the gorge ends. Kosame will take Ha-yugao's body back to Yoshimora, so there will be no one to interfere with us a second time. We'll continue our duel two or three days from now. The word of a samurai!"

Tomoe let the nagamaki drop. She took her Sword of Okio, shook the blood from it, sheathed it. She did not speak as Kosame snatched the halberd from the ground and, with Shi-u's help, tied it across her back, along with Ha-yugao's fine axe. Kosame, despite broken fingers, lifted Ha-yugao's body onto Shi-u's back. Shi-u would carry their dead sister from the gorge, in the fashion of a sick old nanny, strapped with an obi. Ha-yugao's arms hung limp in front of Shi-u's shoulders. Her head bobbed sadly.

The two women started up a steep incline, managing despite their handicaps to reach the narrow ledge. Apparently they knew an easier way out of the gorge further on, and would double back to Kanno once they had reached easier ground. Tomoe Gozen watched them go, not providing them with the least clue of her changing plans. She would by no means meet Shi-u where the gorge ended. The woman was too special to fight. It wasn't that Tomoe feared losing, though in fact she was not convinced that her strength was greater. It was rather too distressing to think of Shi-u's dying; and with such an attitude, Tomoe would lose equal footing. Win or lose, the proposed duel was unappealing.

By the time the wives of Yoshimora Wada had reclaimed their horses and ridden away from Kanno, Tomoe Gozen would have returned to the heart of that very province, ready to test her theory of the goryo's source of power.

A gust whipped through the gorge, tangling the bikuni's short hair before her eyes. She watched the wives of Yoshimora Wada, small and distant, climbing along the ledge. Then they vanished beyond the hump on the cliff's face; and Tomoe Gozen would have been just as pleased never to see them again.

Tomoe's plan to turn back was far more firmly rooted than had been her intended and reluctant flight. Still, she must linger for the time being, lest Shi-u and Kosame detect her altered determination or hear of her return. She must not be seen in Kanno before the women samurai had left for good.

This dallying gave her the opportunity to truly ponder the fateful manner in which she came to be standing midway along the fabulous gorge. Danger awaited at either extremity. In one direction there was the promise of the duel with Shi-u, for whom Tomoe felt extraordinary empathy and whom she would hate to fight. As for the return route, it meant renewed confrontation with Kuro. All paths led to jeopardy. Her choice was not necessarily the safest.

The most fearful element had been the infeasibility of rebelling against a spirit from among her own ancestors. The fear of sacrilege had begun to ebb; for her theory regarding Kuro's power had occasioned a chink through which she might escape the dilemma. And she might do so by nobler means than running away.

She was convinced that the goryo was possessed by the fiend called Green Fire Devil, the cause of the fiery sheen that passed from time to time through Kuro's eyes. Judging by the story Heinosuke told, the whole affair could be said to have started well before Nichiroku was buried alive. Every anguishing event had actually grown from the insufficient or ill-advised exorcisms that had separated Green Fire Devil from Yuki-onna the Snow Woman. A temple should never have been built on land admired by supernatural agents. Once the wrong path was chosen, every additional step compounded the error.

The unreasonable death of Nichiroku had rendered him the hundred-year guardian, buried atop Green Fire Devil's doorway out of Emma's Hell. Who could say what agreement they had reached while locked in their obscure, other-world battle? Nichiroku's indentureship expired and he escaped from the pit, a foul corpse disguised as an angelic priest. Hell's crack was left unguarded. Yet who had seen Green Fire Devil adrift in fields or forests or swamps and up the sides of hills? Where was that demon if not held within Kuro himself, bestowing upon the resurged corpse its excessive power! Kuro the Darkness had formed an extraordinary league with Hell's fiery minion.

Thus it was Green Fire Devil who feared Buddhist exorcism. It was the Buddhists who had divided him from the object of his demonic lusts. A Shinto priest like Bundori was left relatively unmolested, since no such priest had ever interfered with the site of the Temple of the Gorge. Green Fire Devil worked within Kuro to rid the region of Buddhists. Kuro the Darkness in turn made use of his demonic attachment to pursue revenge against seven clans. Their aims were intertwined. Their manifestation was more perfectly unified than was the amalgamation of Shinji and Otane into a love-suicide ghost.

The bikuni reasoned thus: If she managed to free the vengeful ghost from its possession, this could be construed, if only in a semantic sense, as a service to her ancestral spirits. As a side-effect, Kuro the Darkness would become figuratively emasculated, a common goryo bound to the place of his death, capable of achieving his revenge only against those who disbelieved the curse and wandered close. This, however, need not be the bikuni's consideration. It was not her intent to harm the vengeful spirit. Indeed, with straightforward aplomb, her intent was to *honor* and defend that spirit. She would visit him when he was restricted to the Temple of the Gorge. She would light incense for him. She would pray for his peaceful repose.

If this meant dancing along a precipice of impiety, then she would have to take extra pains to avoid profaning the goryo. In devotional prayers she would never address him as dark Kuro but only as shining Nichiroku, the monk from Heida! Until then, she must set her mind upon the task of destroying the demon that possessed the ghost.

She had gathered her gear and fit her hat on snugly and was ready to head back; for surely she had dawdled enough to avoid Shi-u and Kosame. The sun peered into the gorge. The last of the mists had burned from the ground. Until she regained the snow-level, her route ought to be easy and pleasant. But as the bikuni was prepared to set off, she heard a lonesome, weird sound that was so high-pitched it hurt her ears.

It had begun long before she noticed, at too high a note to register. It modulated itself in a variety of fashions, arriving at an audible pitch by slow stages, and still experimenting, like a child with a tiny flute. Only in retrospect did the bikuni realize she had been hearing something for longer than she was aware.

The shrill, strange sound was such a curiosity that the nun began to seek it out. It echoed from the looming walls and confused her. As she strode about in idle fascination, it became evident that the whistling notes originated somewhere around the stagnant inlet off to the side of the river. There were numerous lurking-places around this pool, river flotsam and boulders strewn about. Yet she found nothing hiding. Her wary investigation led her to the conclusion that the sound rose from the tiny bay itself, as though the water sang.

During this minor quest, the note lowered more and more, though never ceasing to be shrill. It wavered more than it had, until syllables could be picked out. It was an inhuman voice, but still a voice, struggling to communicate. One syllable was *"neh"* and the next sounded something like *"ryo"* followed by a drawn out, awkward *"yiu"* and finally *"meh"* before starting anew. The bikuni had earlier been so intensely caught up in thoughts, and before that in the encounter with Lord Wada's wives, that she had been rendered somewhat mind-weary or slow-witted. She had been much too overwhelmed by everything and for this reason took a while to see the obvious. She had interpreted *"neh"* as "grass" and *"ryo"* as meaning "dragon." But "dragon's grass" was utter nonsense.

But the wailing lament was actually a beckoning cry of "Ne-ro-yu-me," her own Buddhist name. When this dawned on her, she wondered if something were trying to beguile her by its peculiar whining, befuddling her thoughts. But she was beguiled by nothing other than her own musings. Curiosity continued to outweigh any fear of what might be found.

At length she saw the very point of origin for the cry. There were two tiny nostrils at the surface of the water. The possessor of those nostrils was incongruously large. "Neroyume," it said more clearly, as though getting the feel of speech through its nose.

The face was that of a giant salamander, its wide, clamped mouth almost a smile. The creature was as long as a human body, but the limbs were minute. Fragments of broken ice floated about so that she could not quite see the whole body. She squatted and looked more closely, causing the salamander to cease its whistling cry and sink into the muck, away from view. A large bubble rose afterward, drifted the longest while, then popped.

The bikuni reached out and took an edge of broken ice, pulling a large sheet onto the bank. She saw the salamander's dark gray skin, wrinkled and undulating along the sides. Neither she nor it moved for a long time. She remained squatting as near the water as was practical, holding up the front of her amigasa so that her vision was not shaded. Finally the salamander raised its head again, its nostrils barely breaking the surface. The water was stirred and cloudy, so that the creature was scarcely more than a shadow of gray within gray. Its tiny eyes blinked beneath the surface. It watched the bikuni warily—or shyly.

Its frilled sides rippled as it moved to one side, neither further from or nearer to the bikuni. Its almost human, miniature hands opened and closed on nothing. The long, thick body ended in a stubby tail, slightly coiled.

This creature was known in many places as "the boneless man" and was dreaded, but without reason. The bikuni knew it was not a monster. It was an ordinary though rare animal. In Kai, the province of waterfalls, where such creatures were more common than elsewhere, it was called *samushii* on account of its noise, which was sad and strange.

The reedy voice emitting from the nostrils was less and less difficult to understand, though it took concentration, as when listening to an especially odd country dialect. It said, "You are fearful to . . . the spirits of the gorge."

"Am I?" she said.

"As I am an ordinary beast and unaffected . . . they have elected me . . . to say to you, 'Your sword . . . disturbs us with its holy emanations. We don't mind . . . its being haunted by its maker the smith; but the blessing of the Mikado . . . which it bears . . . is more painful than . . . sunlight in our eyes.' I hope," the salamander added, "that you are not offended. For myself . . . I am not bothered by your weapon's emanations."

"I am not offended," said the bikuni. "I will try not to disturb the spirits of this gorge, since you ask politely. But popular authority would say those spirits are evil."

The salamander, mastering its long unpracticed speech a bit better, said, "They do not mean to suggest . . . that their intentions tend always to be good ones. But repulsive creatures, too, prefer a modicum of peace. They will be relieved by your agreement. In exchange for your good favor . . . I am asked to make a prognostication . . . in your behalf."

"I did not know," said the bikuni, "that the samushii could tell fortunes."

"I am special among my kind," said the samushii in its painfully high voice. "Perhaps it comes from living . . . among spirits."

"If those spirits are harmful, as they readily admit, perhaps this renders your prognostications dangerous."

"If I may say so," said the salamander, "I have never caused the least harm . . . to anyone. I cannot state so boldly whether my vision has ever . . . helped; for everything I see, I see through water. It is small recompense to you, therefore, that I make an observation . . . in exchange for your sword remaining sheathed while in the gorge. The spirits merely want to avoid . . . a debt."

"Then foretell what you can," said the bikuni.

"My prognostications . . . are not exactly fortunes. They are things others cannot see about themselves. In you, I see this: You have hurtful karma attached to your person . . . brought from previous lives. For this reason you . . . have always been unlucky or at least reluctant in love."

"Love prophecies are the cheapest kind," said the bikuni, amused by the fortune-telling amphibian's common approach.

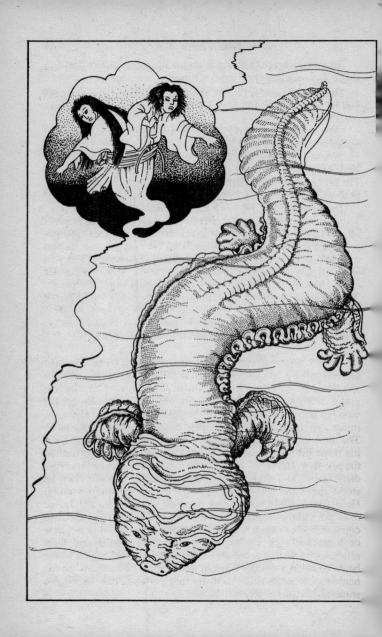

"The aura you project . . . is dangerous even . . . for lovers who come too close."

The bikuni stood abruptly. She said, "Perhaps I don't require you to tell me more." Though her tone was not angry, it was strict.

"My . . . apology," said the salamander, beginning to squirm backward in the pond.

"Wait!" said the bikuni. She sounded undecided. She said, "I have indeed been the death of at least one pair of lovers. The fate you would have me think is mine is subtle and horrific. Is there any way around it?"

The whole length of the salamander floated near the surface. The speaking nostrils reappeared. The salamander resembled, all in view, a corpse in an advanced state of decay, slimy patches of white scum exuding from the gray. It said, "You may break the chain of events when you become . . . lucky in love. It may happen in this life . . . or another; a salamander cannot know. Until then, you are the dew of Kwannon's mercy. You extinguish earthly passion. More than this . . . I do not know."

The huge, slow, primordial creature began to swim away. With heavy step, the bikuni started back to Kanno.

A big man, powerful, competent and implacable, driven or condemned by bitter ambition ironically harmonized with despair and resignation, Ittosai Kumasaku dug another shallow grave into which a fragment of his soul lay down. He set the wooden shovel to one side and wiped his forehead. His arm, injured by Heinosuke, was tightly bound and caused no pain. The atmosphere was chill, but his labors kept him heated. Near his three horses was a pile of frozen corpses. He approached the pile and took up a twisted body at random, dragged it across dirty snow, and shoved it into the fresh-made hole. Then he stood above the grave, gazing at the corpse of an old woman. He'd found her that morning beneath snow, behind a house near the village edge. He recognized her as the hag who had come day after day to pray before the grave of a son or nephew or some such; he couldn't remember what she'd said their relationship was, but he remembered telling her which grave held the chubby vassal. She put that sloppy marker up with the name of Chojiro written so badly that it looked like Tubudu or something equally absurd.

Ittosai had been burying the dead in Kuro's graveyard for months, and had become hardened to it. He felt less shame than in the beginning, and no pity. Yet the stiffened hag struck him as especially forlorn, lying in that hole. He climbed down with her, lifted her out, and hauled her toward the grave she had often prayed before. A rustic lantern had recently appeared on that grave, and Ittosai propped the old woman against it. Taking up his pick, and then his shovel, Ittosai began to dig a grave behind the one covering the old woman's last relative.

There was no sense of compassion in his conscious mind. He did not attempt to resolve the wherefores of his act. He felt only that he had to dig other graves in any case, and might as well place the hag near a relative as not. His chiseled expression never revealed the least emotion.

It was hard work, since the upper level of the ground was frozen and a lower layer consisted of thick clay, which came loose in heavy chunks. He rested often, not from weariness so much as disinterest, and for having nothing better to do except go hunt up additional bodies once this batch was interred. Villagers shunned him, naturally enough, though now and then one or another would point him in the direction of some hidden body. His task was easier in cold weather, despite hardened ground, for his discoveries never smelled, even if days had passed since death had occurred.

One of his three horses, the oldest and lately the boniest, blew and stamped with dissatisfaction. Ittosai set down his digging implements and wandered off into the woods a moment. There was a shed, hastily constructed a few months before, and filled with fodder. He went inside and grabbed a large but extremely light bag. The mildewed bag was made of straw and that straw was more edible than the bag's contents of dry leaves from early autumn. He took this bag to where his three horses stood unhobbled, and he burst it open. The oldest mare received the rice-straw container, for it was as close as she would get to good feed, and she needed strength.

Ittosai had no dealings with the villagers, who were short of feed for their own animals, and who he was too proud to approach. It would be intolerable if they treated him as an outcaste and not a samurai; he would feel obliged to kill them, though it was not his duty. He also, alas, had no access to supplies from Sato Castle, though a fraction of the feed kept there would be a boon.

Although he had planned ahead—building the shed for tools and fodder and storing additional fodder in the stable of one of the abandoned samurai homesteads on which he squatted—it was poor food in all, and his animals suffered. His own meals were dreary as well, but that mattered less to him. Soon, he supposed he must give up pride, if only for a while. He would be menacing and severe to avoid being insulted, and pry supplies from villagers. They would despise him without letting it show, but he would at least pay them for the feed, using the antique coins received from Priest Kuro for Ittosai's retainership.

As his horses ate, Ittosai sat with them. He always had his gold with him, trusting no hiding place. He removed it from his kimono and shook the bag. As he gazed at it, the first hint of emotion played across his features. The look was one of contempt, not avarice. Whether his contempt was for the gold, or himself for keeping it, was hard to judge.

The coins were minted in the continental Celestial Kingdoms, for the Dragonfly Isles of Naipon had not made its own coins before a century ago, until which time the country depended on imported coins or unminted metals. The old coins had become rare in the last decade, trade in the first place being usually in goods or rice, and native coins usurping those from the Celestial Kingdoms of Ho. Ittosai wondered at Kuro's hoard, but didn't wonder much; curiosity conflicted with his duty.

Much as he despised the truth of the matter, gold alone created opportunities for position, and a good arm merely held what gold obtained. Ittosai hoped there was going to be enough of himself left to seek advancement someday. By the time he had accumulated funds sufficient to offer "gifts" to influential men, and served out his unpleasant retainership to Kuro, perhaps the bitter ambition would be bitterness alone.

Tucking the gold back in his clothing, Ittosai stood from his rest, patting his mares, whispering to them, and apologizing for the meagerness of their meal. The bony mare shook all over, as though crawling with flies, but there were none. She had gotten senile, though as Ittosai counted the years, they were not sufficient to account for the beast's rapid decline. Life had been too hard on all of them, including himself.

When he started toward his task once more, Ittosai saw, in a deep shadow of the surrounding forest, an amorphous shape about eight feet tall and quite wide. In his stomach, Ittosai was startled, but revealed no sign of it.

The shadow appeared to shrink. The vision had been an illusion, a play of light or something. For the only thing to step out of the forest was a diminutive monk. Joining Ittosai, the stranger introduced himself. "I am Kasha, a propogator of the Kwannon Sutra." His ugly face produced an amicable grin. He said, "I see you collect dead bodies. A good trade! I approve."

Ittosai's face became flushed with anger. He suppressed it at once. He was a giant against the monk's height and could have bashed him into a tree without effort. Ittosai Kumasaku continued his endless struggle to keep hostility from seeping out, or any other feeling. Even in the face of such an outstanding insult, he would not be baited.

"What do you seek, bonze," his deep voice boomed.

"My old friend Kuro," he said matter-of-factly. "You smell like him."

To Ittosai, this seemed another insult. "Do not anger me, bonze. I may take exception."

"You think I'm poking fun? Not at all! You happen to smell like my old friend." Monk Kasha tapped his nose twice, then sniffed. "I happen to know the odor of my friends. Surely you have seen him lately?"

"I am his one retainer. You can get no other information from me." Ittosai picked up his shovel and began to cover a corpse already in a hole. Dirt and clay struck a horrific visage, then hid the arms. Monk Kasha looked on with genuine interest.

"That horse," said Kasha, "is sick."

"I know it," said Ittosai, not looking up from his task. "It's not your business."

"You should kill it," said Kasha.

"It's not your business."

"She would make a fine corpse."

Ittosai dropped the shovel. His hand reached toward his sword. Emotions battled inside, and he didn't quite touch the hilt. "You would make a better one," he said, taking up the shovel anew.

"You think so?" asked Kasha, as though he had never considered it. "Well, maybe so. It would be interesting to find out. I'm very old, you know."

"You don't look old," said Ittosai, breathing deeply, striving to master himself, to shake off feelings of hatred for the little monk. His feelings were not entirely explained by the monk's flippant remarks; and the awakening turmoil caused Ittosai a sense of mild alarm.

"Older than you think," insisted Kasha. "Older than your master Kuro. Older than these trees. Old."

"The trees are older," said Ittosai, having no idea why he even bothered to argue. He said, "You're addled."

"Maybe so. But *you're* in danger. You'd make a nice corpse, it's true, but I thought I should warn you, if only because I empathize with your job."

"How am I in danger?" asked Ittosai, his tone conveying no genuine interest, his shovel slow at its work.

"Yuki-onna lurks near," the monk said. "She is furious that you hurt someone who was admired by her friend."

Ittosai shoved more dirt onto the pile and patted it with the flat of the shovel. He turned and looked down on the little man. Kasha backed away from Ittosai's expression, leery if not afraid.

"Don't believe me, then," said Kasha. "Do as you please about it. But Yuki-onna is near." He tapped his nose. "I smell her, too."

"How have I hurt Yuki-onna's friend?"

"A friend of Yuki-onna's friend," Kasha corrected, touching his chin pensively. "It's hard to quite explain. Did you blind a young man last night or this morning? I can't be sure you did it; I'm not all-seeing. It seems to be part of why she's angry with you."

"Thank you for your warning," said Ittosai, registering neither belief nor disbelief, but only weariness with monk Kasha's uninvited presence. His disdain began to pass, and the monk ceased to matter to Ittosai Kumasaku, as so many things in life had ceased to matter.

"I'll be off," said Kasha. "Following the scent, so to speak. Goodbye. Take my advice about that horse. Cruel to let her suffer."

When the homely monk with his teasing attitude had gone, Ittosai's vexation warmed within, a hidden ember waiting to be fanned into destructive conflagration. He went across the tamped, dirty snow and stood among the horses, the last of the only friends he had ever believed in. His deep voice was gentle as he talked to them, the monolog largely meaningless. He stroked their flanks and the sides of their faces while they snuffled and blew and returned his affection. "Wait here, my girls," he said, and took the reins of the oldest mare to lead her into the woods, beyond the shed, to an area where the snow was not yet marred.

Sunlight found passage through evergreens, lighting the place. The bony horse moved slowly, her every joint stiff and pained. Ittosai dropped the reins and wrapped his left arm under the old mare's head and playfully held one of her ears. She relaxed her chin upon his shoulder. "You're my girl," he whispered, drawing his shortsword. "You're my beauty." Where the mare could not see, he touched the point of steel to her chest, but there did not seem to be enough strength in his arm to break the skin.

He hugged her more dearly, his cheek against hers, and slid the sword forward with such care that the mare was oblivious. She began breathing louder, harder. Her heart was pierced, yet death was not sudden. His bloody sword came out with equal cunning; the mare suspected nothing but her own growing tiredness. Her weak legs shook, but it was as though she were shamed by her own unsteadiness and refused to fall. She blew hard through her nostrils; blood and mucus sprayed Ittosai's back, but he was unconcerned with that. The mare's front knees buckled and her back legs followed. Ittosai went to his own knees, still holding the head. The mare rolled slowly to her side, still pumping wind, and Ittosai lay her head gently on the snow. Her round, brown eyes watched Ittosai stand; but after that, it did not seem that she could see. She blew twice more, without much blast, and offered not the least death throe, but died relaxed.

Ittosai cleaned his blade in snow then strode away, his face an unchalked slate.

Mirume, the maiden knocked from the castle's mesa wall and rescued from the moat by a passing nun, had known sorrows throughout her life. To tell them all would be too piteous and, what's more, would be too dull; for many of the most wretched lives are of a kind that hold little interest for outsiders. But it helps to comprehend her mother's acute anguish when one considers that she could give her only daughter such an unflattering name as Mirume, the same name as a female witness in Hell. Perhaps the mother thought the name was auspicious; perhaps she could think of nothing but the hellishness of the world her daughter had been born to. The name was conferred at the mother's dying breath; an eerie legacy. Mirume was to bear the burden of having killed her mother by daring to be born. A more unfilial child could not be imagined; there were those who kept telling her this was so, though if truth be told, it was desperation and not pregnancy that weakened her mother's will to live.

Her mother had been lowborn but, by all accounts, beautiful; and her beauty proved a curse. Having found herself attractive to, and attracted by, a comely samurai, she gave in without thought of the day of abandonment, without considering the cruelty of a family loath to raise a bastard. When fatherless and motherless Mirume was old enough, and it was noticed that her beauty developed along the lines of her mother's, she was hauled away to the castle and offered as a servant. "She's a samurai's bastard," they said, and exchanged her for this or that; and never after did they communicate with Mirume.

Yet life became more joyous, if only for a short while. She found herself in the employ of Lord Sato's gentle daughter, graceful and angelic (until she became ill), whose mother had been of royal extraction, descended from Amaterasu the Sun Goddess. Mirume felt only adoration for the beautiful princess; and she felt compassion, for the princess had lost her mother, too. No service was a nuisance if Echiko benefited by the least degree. The hardest task was a wonderful occasion.

Her daily company consisted of numerous castle women, some bright, some foolish, some severe. She was the junior of all of them and easily pushed about; but she did not mind. She loved her new clothing, learning proper manners, sharing and criticizing one another's poetry, the composition of which Lady Echiko encouraged. If she were looked down upon for her uncertain origins, and made to work harder than anyone else on account of her youth and willingness, this was nothing compared to the hardships imposed upon her while in the charge of lowborn relatives who despised her, beat her, and blamed her for her mother's death.

Lady Echiko was so far above Mirume that it was absurd to think of such a superior individual as an older sister. Yet secretly, she did so. This bold fantasy was built upon, month by month, in many imaginative directions. The young hand-maiden began to conceive of the princess as a glimmering presence, mysterious and seraphlike, a bodhisattva sent to Naipon for the express purpose of being patron and savior to Mirume.

She worshipped Lady Echiko, and surely this was noticed; but possibly there were those who felt it was Echiko's due, for taking in an untrained orphan.

Beneath this venerational exterior, Mirume retained, in her secret existence, the original belief that she was Echiko's little sister. Despite a humble outward attitude, Mirume was something of a megalomaniac. Sister to a goddess, indeed! Beneath her the universe depended. Her prayers were heard in Heaven more loudly than the prayers of others. Her influence was profound though so subtle none could see it.

Such egoism has few rewards, if one begins to see the shape the world is in, truly believing in one's own influence on the matter. She already felt that she had caused her mother's death; why not be the source of all pain everywhere? Mirume suppressed all aspects of her fantasy that were dark and sad. She was able to maintain a brighter perspective, an almost hysterical inner happiness, which rarely betrayed itself.

A blissful view of things was soon to become dented. A shadow fell across her world. Mirume's prayers would not disperse it. A beautiful priest named Kuro had appeared, devoid of past, and his strong efforts in behalf of ailing Echiko failed to push away the night. Rather, his presence somehow increased the world's gloom, and Echiko's sickness. Mirume sometimes looked askance at Kuro, when he came to chant the Lotus Sutra in the dead of night. He was less beatific when he didn't know that he was watched.

In her dreams, maggots seethed at the sockets of Kuro's oozing eyes. Gravesoil impacted his ears and mouth. His hands were not held in prayer and were no longer graceful. They were spidery claws picking out Mirume's hairs one by one, while she lay perfectly still, afraid to shout. From this dream she would always awake in stark, wide-eyed silence.

Lady Echiko grew pale. She grew thin. Life became cold and frightful in the women's quarters. Other ladies-in-waiting enclosed themselves in shells of quietude. Echiko was dying, but no one would admit it. The nightly services of Kuro brought Echiko no peace. Echiko was horrified by his visits, but none confessed to seeing this was so. In their minds at least, the other women had abandoned their mistress, however close they hovered. There were exceptions, especially Mirume, whom

Echiko in her weakness began to cherish most. But what could a girl do but comfort and adore? Heaven no longer listened.

Mirume was hopelessly in love with her mistress. To see the princess waste away was to see her own world melting. When came that evening when Mirume was pressed from the wall, it was almost a blessing, for Echiko had willed it. Death, thought Mirume, would be absolute. Pain would be negated.

Then she awakened in the arms of a warrior goddess. She was borne up to Heaven in those arms.

Later, when she realized she was not in Buddha's paradise, she was not disappointed. She had been resurrected. A miracle had occurred. What jubilation was in her! She alone, of all the people of Naipon, was aware that two goddesses lived upon the land. Princess Echiko was one. The other traveled in the guise of an esoteric nun.

Mirume was driven deeper into her fantasies, finding beauty where none existed.

The workings of her mind were at once unfathomable and precious. The brunt of her belief was that Echiko, a supernatural presence, could be saved from this consumptive ailment by commerce with a heavenly peer. If Mirume could bring the two goddesses together, what would be the result? Miracles, no doubt! Echiko would recover. She would ascend to Heaven on moonbeams or in a chariot of gold, drawn by seven winged oxen and a god of noble bearing for groom.

Since Mirume was to be instigator of this miraculous meeting between lady-gods—the humble candle that ignited wonderful events—surely she would be rewarded. She would be taken up to Heaven also, to sit forever at the knee of Echiko-no-kami, Goddess Echiko, Mirume's private patron.

Such fancy was never voiced and so was never contradicted. None suspected Mirume was mad. Perhaps she was not mad at first, but only distracted by personal worlds that buffered her from the reality that her own mother had been unable to face. But harmless escape grew in bounds until Mirume truly did not know where dreams began and ended. Horror might surround her and make her sad; but somehow it was bearable, and often it was rendered pleasurable. The worst event could be turned merrily askew in her reviewing of the subject.

This being so, she had a calm and, some might falsely assume, rational response when Echiko's heart's desire blundered through a wall, from a passage none had known existed.

To her mind it could be viewed only in terms of good fortune. Who else did Echiko wish to see but Heinosuke? Why shouldn't he issue from a wall if Echiko required it?

She could not help but see his eyes, one a healed and empty socket, the other freshly slashed and gory, the orb swollen in two directions. Ladies-in-waiting screamed with shock and fright over the bloody, unexpected, horrid visitation; but Mirume rejoiced. She took Heinosuke's hand and with tears of happiness led the blind man to Echiko's bedside.

Here her memory faltered. For one thing, she had no idea why no guards rushed in or why the ladies-in-waiting ceased shouting and running about, or even where they went. Everyone of lesser importance merely disappeared from Mirume's perceptions of the world. There was only Heinosuke, Lady Echiko, and their devoted witness Mirume.

The dismal reunion yet touched Mirume's heart, causing her to blush and turn away, there being things a discreet witness does not seem to observe. Echiko was heartened and made stronger. Heinosuke's plight filled her with certainty and power. She rose from her deathbed, performing this and that, Mirume could not recall what all. Though there was little muscle left between her flesh and bone, color returned to her cheeks, and a semblance of her previous beauty.

The princess convinced Heinosuke they should escape together, die together if need be. Heinosuke was pliant to every suggestion, being blind and being helpless and being somewhat crazed.

Mirume helped Echiko bind Heinosuke's injury, a clean and colorful strip of cloth around his face. How pretty it was! When Heinosuke and Echiko went into the maze beneath the castle, Mirume went after, uninvited but not told to go back. What the vassals might do come morning, finding Echiko missing, Mirume did not know, did not care. For now she fancied freedom and a wondrous outcome. Everything struck her as proceeding quite well and in accordance with a divine plan she had always known would come to pass.

Mirume's previous efforts to find that *other* goddess, who had saved her life, had been unfruitful. Now she was confirmed to greater efforts by praying intensely in whatever retreat she, Echiko, and Heinosuke might find. "Neroyume kami!" she would pray. "Neroyume kami! The Witness of Hell calls thee from thy slumber!" Surely the warrior-nun would hear, and come. Face to face with Lady Echiko, any miracle could be effected, including the restoration of Heinosuke's sight.

So much had become invested in her fanciful view of possibilities that the inevitable collapse of her imaginary world might well unleash the full measure of her insanity. For, supposing she arranged the very meeting she expected would solve the woes of the world, what could be achieved but disillusion and disappointment? The ill would remain ill. The blind would still be blind. And Mirume would witness, in the end, the immutability of life's tragedies, great and small.

Nothing could surprise her until that future moment when reality impinged. In the meantime, all things fit into her visionary arrangement. The most shocking situation could be shifted into a better light. A jumbled mass of horror, to her eyes, lacked the least aspect of chaos.

Thus it did not give her pause or wonder to pass through passages beneath the ground. Echiko acted as though she knew the way, although this could not be so; yet Mirume took it for granted that Echiko knew much. Heinosuke was utterly confused and uncertain of direction. The path chosen by Echiko was contrary to the one he had known. But in his blindness and pain, he hardly questioned how Echiko came by such certainty of their route.

The way was arduous, wearisome, and peculiar. There was no candle, no lantern, yet Echiko led safe passage. Hours might have passed; in darkness, who could tell? At length they arrived in a hollow chamber and from there proceeded upward to the light. It was well into day. Mirume saw that they had exited a mausoleum in a graveyard. Hovering before them, shrouded by mist and blanketed by snow, the Temple of the Gorge stood among sentinel cedars. In that horrid place, Echiko sought sanctuary.

At first Mirume would not enter. She stood outside, alone, calf-deep in snow, gazing at the rooftop. A chasm of suffering and realization struggled for control of her mind, but she refused to be drawn into sanity. Such sanity would not be bolstered by anything strong and would not endure; and her next madness might well be less passive and disguised.

Emboldening herself, she entered the temple and helped skeletal Echiko arrange a section in the vast hall for Heinosuke's comfort. A blasted Buddha sat at the head of the hall; it was not a comforting statue. Rubbish lay all about.

Together Mirume and Echiko nursed Heinosuke—an insufficient nursing, to be sure—and when he asked, in his delirium, "Where are we?" Echiko replied, "This is White Beast Shrine," easing Heinosuke's struggles.

Mirume had never heard her mistress lie before. She refused to hear it now. As Heinosuke fell into uneasy sleep, Mirume wandered outside into the Buddhist cemetery and strove with all her heart to see it as a Shinto garden. Whatever Echiko said, to Mirume it was truth. How horrible the garden! How horrible was Shinto! She had never noticed it before.

She ventured near the cliff and rearranged her memory so that White Beast Shrine seemed always, as she recalled, to sit beside the gorge. Lady Echiko was wandering also, leaving Heinosuke to his fevered rest and striding through the graveyard cum garden. Mirume did not see where the princess wandered. Mirume was too busy pursuing her own hopeless plan. She fell to her knees upon the cliff's edge and began to pray in a loud voice so that she might be heard above the roar of the falls. She would pray all day if she must. She would pray all night as well.

She prayed to Neroyume, begging her to wake from slumber and hurry to the aid of one and all.

Neroyume listened.

She had thought to camp the night at the foot of the cliffs, then climb to the temple in the safety of morning's light. She built a small fire to push away the mist and cold, settling against a depression in the wall, out of the snow, snuggled in the repellant quilt. Thus relaxed, she raised her right hand out from under the ratty coverlet to see her swollen knuckles and wrist. The swelling had never been so bad. Numb from cold, her hands actually ached less than she was used to; but they looked worse.

She couldn't quite straighten the fingers. She could make a fist, but not a tight one. She drew the hand under the quilt, then inside her kimono, and found a long, thin scarf. She brought this out and, with teeth and hands, tore the cloth in half. She wrapped each hand so that only the fingers poked out. Then she coddled her hands, one inside the other, hidden from her sight, against the warmth of her body. The look upon her face was one of calm relinquishment. She had passed beyond complaint regarding the impermanence of life, vigor, and her own two hands.

The drone of the giant falls engulfed her senses. As she was drifting into slumber, her eyes suddenly opened. She looked out from the cubby in the wall. She thought she had heard someone yelling. She stood, dropping her traveler's quilt, and stepped away from the base of the cliff, onto packed snow. Though she looked upward, she could see only the swirling mists of the gorge, dimly aglow. The sound of river and falls made her uncertain of any other noise.

The gorge-spirits, for fear of her Sword of Okio, had struck a bargain with her; so it was unlikely they would toy with her senses now that she was near to leaving their domain. Yet who would be shouting the name of Neroyume into the gorge? As her concentration intensified, it was more and more certain that someone had altered one or another sutra, inserting her Buddhist name into the prayer.

More annoyed than curious—for the bikuni hated to be revered—she covered her campfire with snow and took to the cliff's face. She had camped at a point of relatively easy climbing, the same place where she had descended a couple of days earlier; so the way was familiar. Yet her swollen, numb fingers were occasionally uncertain of their grip; and enough snow clung to the crags that her straw boots sometimes slipped.

Soon she came above the level of mist, as a diver rises from the sea. She saw the cliff's upper ledge against a striking, starry sky.

A young woman knelt dangerously near the dropoff, shouting her obnoxious recitation.

Tomoe Gozen's incognito-hat hung loose at her back. Her extra shoes hung at her belt. Her vest fluttered in the night wind and her swords' sheaths stuck down in back like two tails, one long, one short. Her straw-booted feet found a firm protrusion. Her hands clung to a pair of thick roots. She leaned far back in order to shout to the maiden:

"Stop that at once!"

In response, the maiden skipped a single beat in order to peer downward, then took up her chant with greater insistence, albeit with hoarse voice due to having shouted for long, desperate hours. She rubbed palms together in exceeding earnest, as though fearful Neroyume might sink again into the mist if the prayer were the least insincere or inadequate.

"I said stop it!" the nun called, climbing as quickly as was feasible. "I'm not Buddha!"

It was the maiden Mirume, who the bikuni had caused to be dragged from the moat of Sato Castle. Tomoe Gozen had hoped to avoid her, having heard a young lady-in-waiting had been asking after the esoteric nun. Whether the girl felt gratitude or required some favor, the bikuni wanted no conference. When she climbed onto the snow-slick ground atop the gorge, panting from the climb, she remained on all fours and glowered at the maiden until she ceased the prayer. Mirume pointed toward the temple, as though a simple gesture was enough to answer all uncertainty.

"Why are you here?" growled Tomoe. Mirume's eyes grew round when she heard the edge of anger.

"Lady Echiko," said meek Mirume, "brought Heinosuke."

This information explained little or nothing. Tomoe raised herself to her knees and massaged her cloth-wrapped hands. She said, "Why have the three of you come here?"

"To hide," said Mirume with stark, naive simplicity. The nun supposed this reply could be made to sound respectable, except that there were plenty of abandoned holy places where runaways might seek sanctuary. The haunted temple should be nobody's first choice.

"It would be best," said Tomoe, "if you returned to the castle. After tonight, Kuro the Darkness will be no trouble to anyone."

"You will destroy him?" the girl asked, her face brightening with hope.

"That I cannot do. He is my ancestor and I would risk my soul. Kuro is a spirit possessed by a demon. If I exorcise that demon, this would be an act of piety. It would be in service to my ancestor's restless spirit."

"You know such an exorcism?" asked Mirume, impressed.

"I know this one," said the bikuni, and touched the hilt of her sword. "This blade is blessed by His Augustness in Retirement. When it destroys the demon inside Kuro the Darkness, Kuro will become the corpse of my relative Nichiroku. Even if the corpse remains animated, he will be able to haunt only the Temple of the Gorge, where he died a century ago. That is why you must leave here, for this is the place where Kuro is bound to return."

"But this is White Beast Shrine," said Mirume, sounding certain. The bikuni looked startled by so patently false but unselfconscious a statement. Studying the maiden's face, the bikuni guessed at the madness stored within.

"That's not true, Mirume. This is a badly haunted place, and unsafe."

Mirume did not reply. She remained convinced of her own fabricated view.

The bikuni stood and began walking along the snowy path. Mirume was quick behind, disregarding the nun's advice to return to the castle. The moonlight wasn't much; but upon the whitened land, it was enough to see everywhere. Stars winked. Chill winds stirred lightly. Slender mists stalked the land.

Tomoe Gozen had intended to go directly to the main hall of the Temple of the Gorge. But her attention was drawn aside by a white specter with two horses. The horses pulled lightly at their tethers, but Ittosai Kumasaku would neither let them go, nor take them the rest of the way through the necropolis.

Puzzled by his pallor and motionlessness, the nun veered into the graveyard. Mirume continued to follow, weaving a course between old monuments capped with snow. The nearer the bikuni came to Ittosai, the more quickly she stepped.

Momentarily, she stood beside him. He was rimed from head to foot. Even his clothes were stiff and brittle. She reached out to touch the part of his arm which was bandaged. He was so extraordinarily cold that when she drew back her hand and inspected her fingertips, she saw that they were blackened, as though burned. In their numbed state, she had been unable to feel the frosty sting.

"Mirume," the bikuni whispered. "What happened to Ittosai?"

Mirume would not or could not answer. The nun drew her shortsword to cut the reins from Ittosai's frozen grip, so that his confused and impatient horses could wander where they wished.

"Do you know, Mirume?"

The bikuni looked into the young woman's eyes and saw an exceeding fright in their depths.

"Speak to me, Mirume. I insist."

"I didn't see her do it," said Mirume, unable to take her eyes away from Ittosai's iced visage.

"She? Was it Yuki-onna? It's cold enough. She might have

come down from the higher peaks."

The young woman's terror was like a strand of seaweed beneath the placid surface of a bay. Most people would not notice it, but the bikuni saw that it was there.

"What do you remember, Mirume? What have you seen?"

Her eyes became rounder still, two black mirrors reflecting the moon. She whispered, her voice still hoarse from chanting, "Death."

"Ittosai's death?"

"Death. In the castle. The maids-in-waiting, who ran about. The guards, who tried to answer. Dead." Mirume pointed at Ittosai, and said in a breathy whisper, "Like him. Dead!"

Mirume covered her eyes and began to weep. She was young after all and apt to act like a child. The bikuni pulled on the woman's arms and said, "Stop it, Mirume. Tears won't help. Was Yuki-onna in the castle? Don't suppress it any longer. People can go mad from what they refuse to remember."

When Mirume let her hands be pulled down, she looked up with eyes glassy, her features lax. She was no use now. The bikuni started to walk away, shaking her head. Mirume followed in a dreamy, mindless state, with arms hung limp. Tomoe Gozen looked back at Ittosai for a moment, saying, "I'm sorry about it. He might have found himself one day."

While the nun lamented, Mirume passed by and ended up leading the way toward the temple. Snow dropped from hovering cedars. A tiny, dark beast scuttled over the snow, then vanished into a hole at the base of a tombstone.

When they were near the rear entrance of the main building, Mirume stopped, loath of entry, half blocking Tomoe. The bikuni heard an inexplicable rippling sound. She saw that Mirume had bent her neck backward and was looking toward the ridge-roof. When Tomoe looked there, she saw a weird old man of gleaming green fire. He pranced back and forth along the top of the roof, but failed to melt the snow upon the tiles, or even to dislodge it. Wind played through his insubstantial form, and this was the cause of the rippling noise.

This was Green Fire Devil, the very fiend with whom the nun had come to do battle. He looked down at the two women, his fiery face contorted with laughter, although he made no sound beyond the rippling. Clearly he understood the bikuni's intentions.

He pounced from the ridge-roof, and Tomoe's cloth-wrapped

hand moved toward sword's hilt. She did not draw steel, for Green Fire Devil had leapt upon Mirume, and vanished, fantastically, through the pupils of her eyes!

Mirume's shoulders quivered. She reeled about to face Tomoe Gozen, eyes like green gems flashing. Her hair had come undone and moved about like serpents, animated more than wind explained. She snarled and raised hands that had sprouted sharp, black nails.

To use the Sword of Okio upon the demon now would slay Mirume as well. The nun moved backward, reluctant to fight. Mirume jumped through the air, a bird of prey latching onto its victim. She clung to the front of the bikuni, legs locked around waist. Long hair wriggled and grasped. Clawed hands grabbed Tomoe's ears and drew blood behind them.

Tomoe pushed her left palm under Mirume's chin and forced the fierce girl's neck back and back. Mirume began to shout, a sound like a beast, not a woman. She thrashed wildly with hair and arms, trying to claw the bikuni's throat. Tomoe raised her other hand to deflect the claws, then bashed the possessed woman on the side of the head with the bottomside of her fist.

Mirume flung herself away, wailing animalistically. Her leap took her up and up; she was veritably flying; and she landed on the ledge of the temple's roof. She clawed at her own hair, making herself bald above one ear. She mouthed an appalling and pitiful, "It hurts! It hurts! It hurts!" Tomoe was uncertain whether it was her blow that had caused Mirume's agony, or if it was the result of Green Fire Devil's invasion of her mind.

Without warning of relent, Green Fire Devil issued from Mirume's eyes, raced across the ridge-roof, and disappeared. Mirume collapsed upon the tiles. Tomoe Gozen looked frantically about the area for something to help climb up to get Mirume. The motionless body slipped, then slipped again, dangerously near to falling from the ledge.

The bikuni raised a thick, fallen cedar branch—almost too much to heft—and leaned it against the wall. She climbed monkey-fashion and grabbed Mirume just as one leg slipped over the edge. Mirume's glazed eyes opened halfway. She smiled with sweet trust, as on the day Tomoe carried her into the castle.

Once again, green light bathed the incline of the snow-covered roof. Tomoe did not look to where the demon reappeared. She whispered to Mirume, "Hold tight right here. Don't open your eyes or Green Fire Devil will get in." Then she climbed the angle of the roof, placing herself between Mirume and Green Fire Devil. She drew the Sword of Okio.

The fiery old man swung his arms upward at his side, flapping like a crazy bird. A tongue of flame grew out of his face, as though intending to lick the bikuni; but her sword threatened to lop off the tongue, and it retracted. Green Fire Devil leapt forward, then leapt back. The bikuni pursued him, climbing toward the ridge-roof. Temple tiles broke beneath her steps. Snow cascaded away in a miniature avalanche.

She slipped on ice, landed on her left shoulder, and swung her sword wide as Green Fire Devil tried to take advantage. When she crawled to the topmost ridge, she became a silhouette against the sky of icy stars, between the greater silhouettes of mighty twin cedars. Green Fire Devil leapt up and down and had an angry expression. He was annoyed that she straddled his favorite perch. He placed his hands upon his cheeks and pulled his lower eyelids down, a childish insult. He spun about and slapped his ass at her. She started after him across the roof, but he seeped under tiles, leaving no trace of himself.

For the moment, the night returned to stillness.

When the bikuni got Mirume into the main hall, Heinosuke stirred in the corner where he lay. His face was mostly hidden in a bloody, colorful binding. A thin straw mat had been laid over him in lieu of a quilt. As he tried to sit, he queried weakly, "Echiko?"

"It's Tomoe," said the nun. Echiko was nowhere to be seen. The nun placed Mirume on the floor near Heinosuke. The young woman appeared to sleep. The nun said, "Heinosuke, Mirume could not tell me why you were brought to this temple."

"Isn't it the White Beast Shrine?" he asked in confusion.

"It's the Temple of the Gorge. I've come to destroy Green Fire Devil. I long considered the story you told me; and as I did so, it became clear to me that Kuro is only a resurged corpse, and it is a hell-beast that empowers him to perform great evil. My Sword of Okio will lay the demon low. It will be easier if I can uncover his path in and out of the Land of Darkness. Do you know the exact location of the secret door? You said the Lotus monks built it in this hall; but the floor is vast."

Heinosuke was disoriented, lost in his own darkness, but tried to think it out. Possibly the records he had sorted through and studied never were specific about the placement of the hidden door. Before he could say anything about it one way or another, the dark hall was filled with emerald light, and Tomoe Gozen moved anxiously. Green Fire Devil peered down from the rafters. The bikuni grabbed Mirume, covering the semiconscious girl's eyes, lest Green Fire Devil try to pry them open. Green Fire Devil leapt upon Heinosuke to keep the blind man from speaking.

Heinosuke appeared to be engulfed in flame, but writhed unburnt, thrashing in agony and yelling. The monstrous entity strove unsuccessfully to find access through useless eyes.

The bikuni had flipped Mirume onto her belly and, removing one of the lengths of cloth from her own swollen hand, deftly bound the maiden's face, knotting the cloth at the back of her hair. This accomplished, she spun to confront Green Fire Devil, drawing length of steel.

The glimmering old man gave the nun a startled look; but before her Sword of Okio could scrape him, the fiend was sucked, like a fiery intake of breath, into Heinosuke's lungs. Heinosuke swelled with new vitality. He dragged himself to his feet, long-handled sword to hand. He began to swing madly in all directions, for the parasitic demon was as blind as its host.

Tomoe made a sound that baited Heinosuke away from the vicinity of Mirume, then stepped quietly from the gross, exaggerated onslaught. She was in the same fix as earlier. To kill the demon meant killing Heinosuke.

It was essential to locate the hidden door, to thrust her sword into the Pit. No hellish minion could pass fully from Emma's country, but must keep a portion of itself within the dark gate. Sheathing her sword and snatching up a vagrant length of broken staff from amidst temple rubbish, the bikuni began to peck at the floor. It looked as though she were spitefully teasing her blind, would-be slayer. He answered the tapping of her stick with wild, random swordplay. But Tomoe Gozen was merely trying to find some part of the floor that gave indications of the door that monks had made over the grave of Nichiroku, and over Green Fire Devil's entry. Because Heinosuke stalked toward each noise, her evasive measures kept her from being methodical in her search.

When she was knocking on the floor in front of the blasted Buddha, whose quiet presence dominated the hall, Heinosuke's sword dashed downward at the bikuni. As she scooted from harm's way, Heinosuke's weapon sank deeply into the wooden body of the Buddha. Golden blood seeped from the Buddha's injured shoulder. The blood flowed along the length of the sword, shining like molten metal, bathing Heinosuke's hands and forearms.

The blind man screeched and let go of his sword. From his stretched mouth, Green Fire Devil leapt out and back into the rafters. The demon passed through the roof, leaving the hall once again in darkness. The only sound was Heinosuke collapsing before the Buddha.

The Buddha's eyes were no longer closed, but white and opened. How ravaged was His face! He was a dark aspect of the Buddha, but no less holy, and Tomoe Gozen fell upon her knees before His staring visage, gazing back at Him; and the nun breathed heavily with a divine revelation of Buddha's pain, anger, and compassion. For that fraction of her life, she knew the things no mortal can long know, and saw the cruel nature of the universe. Buddha's promise of escape from the endless cycles was at that moment vastly more appealing than the beauty and terror wrought by the Thousands of Myriads.

His white eyes slowly closed against the world. He began to crumble into ash, as though He had long ago been burnt to the core and was held together only by the strength of a lingering, sacred wish.

Her moment of inspiration dwindled and the bikuni was overcome by sudden selfishness. She clasped Heinosuke's fingers, thinking the Buddha's golden blood might by some miracle cure her own weakened, swollen hands.

There was nothing but soot on Heinosuke's hands.

The bikuni sat by the young man's quietly breathing form, staving off disappointment. If no one else were involved on this night, she would have withdrawn from the temple, returning sometime when her hands hurt less or the swelling was less evident. But there were Heinosuke and Mirume to consider, both of them helpless and unconscious; and something in her felt as though her mission must meet results tonight, or never.

Untying the remaining length of cloth that wrapped her hand, the bikuni drew her sword and began to tie hand and hilt together. Thus she need not fear losing her grip by some misspent attack on Green Fire Devil. The fiend had withdrawn to lick its own wounds. She hoped the bath of Buddha's blood would make the demon's handicap equal to her own.

While the demon was gone, she could accept no respite, but must move swiftly in search of the door. She took up the broken length of wood and began, board by board, to test the sound of each section of the floor.

Rather than detecting a hollowness, the broken staff struck a place that sounded thicker. The bikuni struck all around the area, ascertaining the dimensions of the heavy, well-camouflaged trapdoor.

As her eyes quested in darkness for some hint of crack at which to pry, a frigid wind tore through the hall, then died away as quickly. When she looked up, Lady Echiko stood at the rear entry from the cemetery. Thin as she was, she might have been some awful set of bones pulled out of a grave, done up in finery as a ruthful disguise.

Echiko saw Heinosuke prone before the altar of ashes. She began to walk toward him, her gait strange and unappealing. Tomoe looked quickly to the rafters, but no emerald flame appeared. She half expected any moment to find the fiend possessing Echiko; but when Echiko's eyes turned upon Tomoe, they were not green, but glistening cobalt. Her look was one of ire, as though convinced the bikuni bore responsibility for Heinosuke's state.

The princess became white as frozen Ittosai, then whiter; and then her whiteness faded into clearness. She metamorphosed before the bikuni's stunned gaze. Skin became transparent as ice; there were no veins beneath; and bones were glassy rods, nearly invisible in the depths of diaphanous flesh. Her costume became a robe of wind and snow, constantly in motion.

Transfigured Echiko radiated radical frigidity. A faint blue glow cast shadows all about the hall.

She moved toward Tomoe Gozen.

"Yuki-onna!" Tomoe cried. "Why possess poor Echiko and ruin the love she found? It was you all along, and not Kuro the Darkness, who leeched away her will to live!"

Yuki-onna's voice was sweet and other-worldly, like bells and tinkling crystals. "I possess no one," she said. "I am who I've always been."

Her hair had become a web of icy shards cascading down

her shoulders. She was a pellucid carving in cold glass, miraculous in appearance, uncannily beautiful and frightful to behold. Tomoe held the Sword of Okio one-handed, but Yukionna feared that blade less than did other supernatural creatures. "If you cut me," said the soft, tinkling voice, her teeth sparkling with prismatic color, "I'll die like any monster. But your blessed sword will become brittle, so cold am I."

Tomoe backed against a wall. She could withdraw no further. Yuki-onna came near enough to be slashed, chilling Tomoe to the marrow; but the nun valued her sword as she valued her own life. She could not make the decision to attack.

In that instant, a longsword pierced the wall from outside, barely missing Tomoe's nape. She lurched aside. The blade retracted in order to stab through the wall a second time. Then, strong fingers dug between the siding. Some fiend was trying to enter at Tomoe's back, coming through the wall.

When the first boards were ripped away, Ittosai Kumasaku peered into the temple, thawed by the fiery demon whose inner presence colored his eyes. Yuki-onna lost interest in the nun and watched emerald-eyed Ittosai without evident emotion. Tomoe scrambled away as Green Fire Devil used Ittosai's tremendous strength, trebled by possession, to tear a gaping rent.

She started toward the place along the floor where she had previously located the hidden door. But Ittosai was at her back, forcing her to spin about and block a blow that stung her to the elbows. Ittosai's excessive power only caused his sword to break centrally. The sharp end whisked by Tomoe's face and clattered far along the floor.

She blocked another cut from the much-shortened blade. It was a less powerful blow, for Ittosai had performed it one-handed; and as the Sword of Okio blocked, Ittosai's free hand sprung forth like a serpent, latched onto Tomoe's throat, raising her so quickly that she was flung high into the air before realizing what had happened. She struck the floor at an angle and slid through rubbish, whirling to a stop upon her back, winded, vision dizzied.

Gagging and catching her breath, she found the broken tip of Ittosai's sword. She grabbed it and flung it at the big man who stalked near, taking him in the thigh.

The injury might not have slowed him even had he not been possessed with stranger strength. But this whole encounter had been observed by Yuki-onna, who moved about the periphery of the room, watching especially Ittosai with an aspect of curiosity. Green Fire Devil may not have been concerned about the broken swordtip that sank into Ittosai's upper leg; yet he turned aside to look hard at Yuki-onna.

For long moments, Yuki-onna and Green Fire Devil were locked eye to eye. Then the demon spoke with Ittosai's booming voice:

"I have striven longer than a hundred years to return to Yuki-onna. But you are not the one who was endeared to me. What are you to watch me so, if not the sweet demon I once loved?"

"I am Shin-yuki-onna," said the Snow Woman, her tinkling voice weighted with sorrow. "Your fiery lust killed my mother after all; for the half of me that is fire burned within her womb, and birthing me was her first and final agony. For long decades unaware, I lay beneath the snow, a motionless child of ice, neither dead nor living. One warm summer, the snow level rose higher than ever before. My tiny body was uncovered and began to cry. Lord Sato, upon a hunt, heard the cry; and finding a perfect white infant, recalled his beloved wife's empty womb. Soon I was placed into the hands of Lady Sato, who raised me as her daughter, teaching me human sentiment, never knowing how much strangeness was dandled on her knee.

"These things being as I have said, you can have no grudge against humanity. These long years, there has been no Yuki-onna for you to return to as a lover."

"Can my eternal Hell be made the deeper?" asked Green Fire Devil, making Ittosai's face expressive and sad. "By the testimony of my unknown daughter, I am the slayer of my love."

"You have helped Priest Kuro trouble people dear to me," said Shin-yuki-onna. "Because I could not fight my unwitting and cruel father, I pined and grew thin, shedding much of my human aspect. I struggle to remain human in my heart! The half of me that is fire is able to warm the half of me that is my mother; and my one wish has been to care for Heinosuke, who is now blinded by Kuro's hatred—and by you."

Tomoe Gozen heard this strange exchange, still dazed from being dashed along the floor. She crawled upon her belly, unnoticed by the supernatural father and daughter, lost as they were in the woes of one another.

Unfocused eyes found the place upon the floor where the

Lotus monks had made a door, had hidden Nichiroku's terrible grave. She rose to knees, using her sword to brace herself, then found unsteady feet. She stabbed downward, the Sword of Okio passing through the floor and into the pit beneath.

Ittosai Kumasaku threw his sword straight upward in an uncontrollable spasm. It stuck deep into a rafter beam. He lumbered backward, away from Shin-yuki-onna, tearing at his chest as though burning from inside. The green flame played through his eyes, appearing and disappearing, two uncertain beacons scanning wildly and finally shining upon Tomoe Gozen, who hunkered beside the secret door.

She tried to draw her sword back out; but it became an inadvertent handle, and Tomoe Gozen raised the door upon its hinge.

Green Fire Devil was too weak to escape from the big man's body. Ittosai fell to his knees with unnatural force, cracking the floorboards as though he had increased many times in weight and might sink into the world. Tomoe Gozen could not guess whether the man who had been Ittosai Kumasaku would be alive after the grim exorcism by steel. Once already he had died a freezing death. Now he might be doubly destroyed by fire.

Shin-yuki-onna's complexion became more and more blue, the light of her intensifying with upset emotions, as blood of humans reddens cheeks. Her father had caused loved ones pain; and now he was dying. Maybe she was torn between filial regret and a revenge-inspired glee that it was done.

Searing cold blue eyes turned upon Tomoe Gozen. The nun was uncertain of the Snow Woman's feelings. The bikuni wrenched her sword from the open trapdoor. Curiosity drew her attention down. There was no literal hole beyond the shallow pit from which Nichiroku's corpse had issued the year before. But there was a glimmering sort of darkness collapsing upon itself. A miniature green flame in the shape of a hunchbacked old man writhed at the center of the shrinking dark cloud. The shade of Green Fire Devil grew tinier and tinier, until he was but a pinpoint of light. And then that light winked out.

Several paces away, Ittosai Kumasaku plunged from knees to face without a sound, and lay still.

The hall remained bathed in underwater-light, the hue having changed to aquamarine. Shin-yuki-onna was a shimmering, transparent gem in the shape of a woman, cold light shining out of her. Her sweet, bell-voice inquired, "Why have you slain my father? I might have convinced him to return to Hell." Then she raised one hand above her head and held her fingers as though upon the hilt of an invisible sword.

From those fingers sprung a two-edged sword, the one edge blue ice, the other edge green fire. As she brought the sword down from above her head, she placed her other hand upon the hilt and said with a lilting menace:

"This is more purely my soul than your steel is yours. It means I have invested more into the fight."

Tomoe Gozen struggled to comprehend the full depth of meaning to each event. With a dawning which held no certainty, she said, "Do not fight me, Snow Woman. The more you use your power, the less you can remain human. Even if you kill me, you may lose. Consider Heinosuke, lying there like a useless rag. Look at moaning Mirume, who has worshiped you so long, and would serve you unto death, and after. What will become of them if there is never again a Princess Echiko? Think even of your foster-father, who loves Echiko as his own. I have slain Green Fire Devil, who had no claim on you. I have saved your truer father. At this moment, Lord Sato will be awakening from his year-long nightmare, becoming himself once more. Who will he seek first, if not his daughter, with apologies, and tears, and relief?"

"Think how you would reply," said the tinkling voice of the Snow Woman, "if you had seen me slay your sire, and I said to forget."

Tomoe backed away from the pit, ready to defend herself. She said, "I am bad luck for lovers, I assure you. It's the end for you and Heinosuke if you persist. Savor the earthly passions denied other supernatural beings!"

Shin-yuki-onna approached, her sword of fire and ice creating strange shadows. Tomoe took a ready posture, sword pointed down and held halfway behind herself. Across the room, Mirume moved one leg, then a hand went to her blindfolded face. Ittosai Kumasaku's huge body gave a lurch, whether death throe or painful spasm, the bikuni could not tell. Heinosuke was the quietest of all. Between these three people, Shin-yuki-onna and Tomoe Gozen held one another at point of sword.

The Snow Woman took another careful step and raised her

shining sword a little higher. The bikuni bent her knees and slid one foot forward the least amount, her sword still held pointing behind. She began to chant the Kwannon Sutra as taught her by monk Kasha:

"Thy merciful heart is a wonderful cloud
From which falleth sweet dew extinguishing
The flames of earthly passion."

For the first time, Tomoe Gozen knew this was truly her fate, as prophesied by the salamander. She felt that she was one among the many arms of merciful Kwannon, the hand that bore the saber. Even Otane's stoic grandmother had mistaken the bikuni for an avatar of Kwannon. Who could judge how much in error widow Todawa may have been?

The bikuni ceased her chant and said, "Yuki. Your two-edged soul is beautiful and strange, but you handle it mistakenly. If you attack, I'll destroy you, even at cost of my sword. Merciful Kwannon will dissolve your earthly passions. What will remain afterward, but everlasting emptiness in a colorless limbo outside of time?"

The Snow Woman came forth with alarming speed, snowy garments swirling. Tomoe dropped to one knee and felt the cold of mountain glaciers, and the heat of mountain bowels, sweep above her head. At the same moment, the Sword of Okio went forward in a deadly streak. Shin-yuki-onna passed on her own momentum, stopping at the bikuni's back, motionless, her strange sword melting into dew, which doused its flame.

The Sword of Okio had stroked the Snow Woman's body for the least possible moment, yet was rimed and chill. Tomoe Gozen could not remove even the hand that was not tied to the hilt, for both hands adhered by frost. The nun watched the blade, afraid that it might shatter.

The blue light behind her faded. As it did, the rime upon the blade became fluid, darkened, and dripped as common blood. At her back, she heard the rustle of court costume, not blowing snows. There was a final sigh devoid of the other-worldly tinkle, and the sound of a frail body falling. Tomoe Gozen swept her sword over her own head, flicking away blood as she stood. With slow purpose, she sheathed the Sword of Okio and slipped her swollen hand from the knotted cloth.

Mirume was crawling across the floor on hands and knees. She had removed the blindfold too late to see Shin-yuki-onna, but in time to see Echiko collapse and Tomoe sheath her weapon. The maiden crawled onto her mistress and clung like an infant to a murdered parent.

"Mirume," Tomoe whispered in the dark hall of the temple. "Your goddess has achieved perfect bliss. But you can still serve her, for she worried about Heinosuke and was sad to leave him helpless." Mirume looked up from the corpse to which she clung. Timidly, she gazed toward Heinosuke, new and stranger fantasies forming in her mind. Tomoe encouraged her. "Go to him, Mirume. Help him find his way through endless night."

The maiden struggled to her feet. She went to Heinosuke and knelt at his side. Heinosuke stirred and Mirume bent near to whisper something in his ear, which Tomoe Gozen never heard. The bikuni had gone to see about Ittosai. He breathed, and she decided he, too, had survived.

She slipped out the back way into the graveyard, moonlight paling monuments. She breathed cold air, striving to calm her spirit and her beating heart.

To her surprise, the monk named Kasha stood near a mausoleum, grinning as though he kept a funny secret. As nothing in the world was funny to Tomoe Gozen just then, she started away from the cemetery, trying to ignore the homely monk. But he ran across the snow to catch her; and as always, his manner was meant to suggest that he knew more than he could possibly know.

"I got him at last," said Kasha.

"Who?" said Tomoe, not really caring who.

"My good friend Nichiroku."

Tomoe stopped and looked the short, ugly man in the face. Kasha said, "A few moments ago, he lost his powers, all at once. He was playing checkers with Lord Sato. Was Lord Sato surprised! His religious tutor and saintly-looking friend turned into a wormy corpse before his eyes! Nichiroku was surprised, too. You would have liked it!" Kasha laughed. "Realizing that you must have slain Green Fire Devil, the pact they had forged was effectively nullified, and the goryo would have to return to this temple, never to venture from it again. But he tried a desperate action, to tear Lord Sato's throat with the gray bones of his hands. Lord Sato, though possessed of his wits for the first time in a long year, was yet confused. He knew only that he was confronted by a monstrous thing. The checkerboard was kicked over and Lord Sato scrambled toward his sword upon a stand. He couldn't possibly have made it in time, and it's doubtful that hacking up Nichiroku would have been enough. That's why I stepped out of a dark corner, quick as you please, and exclaimed, 'Nichiroku! You've evaded me a hundred years! Isn't it time you gave up?' Then I made myself ten feet tall and wrapped my arms around him and dragged him off to Hell. Just his bones, you understand. I'm not a collector of souls, just corpses. If you ever come to Hell yourself—there are stories that you've been there a couple of times already—please remember me and drop by to see my collection."

"Kasha," said Tomoe. "That's the most foolish story anyone ever told me."

"Oh? I'm sorry you think so! You would have bèen no good at all if I hadn't helped. By the way, I converted Nichiroku's spirit to the worship of Kwannon. If you feel guilty about spoiling the completion of his revenge, you might burn incense for him in various places where Kwannon's image is kept. He's around here somewhere—just his spirit. But he's feeling better now and won't linger long, not after you and I and the merciful Bodhisattva saved him from himself. Vengeance, too, is an earthly passion."

"It's too confusing for me, Kasha," said Tomoe. "I refuse to believe a word you say. I'll leave Kanno soon and in the meantime, I would like to be alone."

"How rude to say so! But all right. I'll see you again someday, I'm sure. Add you to my collection!"

So saying, Kasha sprinted ahead. Tomoe was surprised to note that he made no indentations in the snow. Also, rather than growing smaller in the distance, it seemed that he got bigger. It must have been a trick of moonlight, but it seemed as though he disappeared before she could have lost sight of him.

After scant hours sleep, she awoke beneath the shelter of an open-fronted woodcutter's shed. A winter wren called *misosazai* shared the shelter. He made a weaving-and-shuttle sort of sound and ruffled his feathers at the bikuni.

She rose, heavy and weary.

By early afternoon she had left the province, glad at least to have seen the people acting cheerier. They did not know why they enjoyed the wintery day. As crops had been poor, autumn short, and the majority of winter before them, life would not be easy between now and spring. Yet the pall had risen from the land. The atmosphere was less deathly.

She alone remained a shadow on the countryside, and even she had wandered on. When she passed the border station, there was the least possible interference from samurai who were in good moods, though they could not as yet have had news from the castle regarding the disappearance of Kuro the Darkness and the recovery of Lord Sato's intellect. But they could not help but sense that they were no longer preyed upon by something unseen. Things bright and pleasant in the world were no longer drained into some deep, dark pit.

Months later she overheard how things were in Kanno. Lord Sato, due to his lack of heir, had been coerced into adopting a boy of the Shogun's clan. This established Kanno's connection with the Kamakura military government. The benefit to Lord Sato was that he could remain the nominal ruler of the province until he selected his own time of retirement, and his clan name would survive. The bikuni could not imagine that Lord Sato was exactly happy; for he might always grieve the loss of his daughter. Yet, in the material sense, things had not come out badly for him. As for self-serving but basically innocuous Chamberlain Norifune, Tomoe Gozen never heard what became of him and scarcely cared. Ittosai, Heinosuke, Mirume . . . the survivors for whom she felt concern were unknown to the national gossip, so she had no information. An eagerness to forget Kanno altogether kept her from traveling to that region in order to learn more about their situation.

She never did decide how many of the events in that mountain region were the result of hellish magicks, and how much had been heavenly intervention. In time she clung more securely to an esoteric worship of Merciful Kwannon, though otherwise remaining partial to the Shinto pantheon. She ceased to be surprised when acts of gods and acts of devils were indistinguishable, just as the hearts and motivations of human individuals could never be completely fathomed.

EPILOG

Duel at the Beach of Tears

One spring evening in Seki province, the mendicant nun paused at a roadside shrine and knelt before the humble structure, intending to play her shakuhachi. The shrine consisted of a box with a thatched roof and stood upon four stilts. In the box was a statue of the goddess Benten, indistinguishable from certain of the many-armed aspects of Kwannon. Two of Her hands were held in prayer. In the other six She held: sword, wheel of punishment (or knowledge), bow, arrow, rope, and lotus flower. The goddess had once been gilded but only a little gold was left above Her breasts. There was even less red paint remaining on Her weapons. Her face was gentle, unlike many carvings of the dragon-taming Benten. The wood-carver must have been thinking of Senjin-Kwannon to make her face convey a kindly disposition.

Despite its age-cracks and worn appearance, the statue must have been a treasure in some temple long and long before. Now it had fallen on hard times, sitting in so rustic a shrine, a few dried out food offerings on a rock, and no recent incense.

It was the nature of the Thousand Shrine Sect that its members paid homage to the humblest as well as greatest holy places. But before she could raise the flute to her lips, the bikuni was distracted by the worn plaque hanging from the lip of the stilt-box. Carved into the wood was the simple legend:

This world of dreams
passes in a twinkling
of one's eye.

The maxim put the bikuni in a reflective mood. She could not play her instrument, for her mind was uneasy. She returned the shakuhachi to its place under her dark vest, in the back of her obi where it did not show. Holding up the handles of her

255

swords so that they would not touch the dust, she leaned forward with her free hand flat upon the ground, and remained bowed a long while in apologetic obeisance. Then she rose and started in the direction of a knoll, from whence the sea was visible beneath the evening sky.

It took a moment to recall whether it had been two years ago, or three, that she had been in the mountain province of Kanno. How time rushed by! Her life was strangely unpredictable. She could not place the chronology of several small adventures; had something or other happened before the terrible events in Kanno? or after? Well; failing to keep a travel-diary, there was much the mind neglected. She only thought of Kanno because of a Shinto priest named Yano of Seki, a hermit in some unknown hideaway, but once custodian of a large, rundown shrine. He had asked her to visit his home province someday; and here she was without having planned it.

Yano had asked her to consider the beauty of the countryside as she strolled about Seki; then, if she would be so generous, he wished that she would remember him, so that dear Seki might come to him in dreams.

A barefoot boy, small but swift, darted up the dark, steep path, almost bumbling into the nun. He hugged several dumplings to his breast, obviously stolen. He was a dirty, ragged scamp and could not possibly have purchased so many. One dumpling fell from his clutches, rolling and rolling back down the path, covering itself with dust.

A ronin pursued the brat, sword waving. He looked to be a hungry fellow, yet chasing after so small a foe with blade drawn struck the bikuni as an overreaction. Rather than keeping out of the way, she made a point of tripping the man, and his sword went flying. He jumped to his feet, snatched up his weapon, and pointed it at the nun. He gritted his teeth and winced so hard it made him spit just to breathe.

"Don't look down on children," said the nun. "Emperor Ojin, who became wargod Hachiman, ruled Naipon when younger than that boy."

"He stole my dinner!" spewed the ronin, beside himself with rage. His sandals were worn so thin he ought to have thrown them away. His clothing needed washing. He might have tried to kill the woman, but she was uncowed and well-armed. She was also mysterious, her face hidden beneath an amigasa, her posture relaxed but ready. But he was a wronged man and knew it. He would not back away. He exclaimed, "An insult to trip me that way! Make restitution!"

The bikuni reached into the front of her kimono, near her obi. She drew out a wallet, untied it, and removed some coins. These she threw at the ronin's feet. "Buy lots of dumplings," she said, and walked on up the path.

She came to the knoll's rise, the momentary incident already gone from her mind. She looked down the long slope toward a village. Cuttlefish boats were setting sail by night, torches front and back, their fires reflecting in ragged streaks upon black water. Night-fishing was perilous, especially if there were an unpredicted storm. Many fishers lost their lives each year. Deadly though their industry could be, to see them heading toward the horizon, their brands shining, and to hear their sisters and wives shouting blessings from the beach, was pleasing to the senses.

"Bundori-sama!" the nun exclaimed softly, wondering if her words would carry to Kanno on so light a wind. "Yano of Seki! Are you dreaming just now? I'm thinking of you, as I promised."

She was embarrassed to have been overheard. The rag-clad boy with dumpling on his face crept near. She turned her hat-shrouded face slightly, then said with low intonation, "Want to steal something from me? You can't have my shakuhachi."

"Thanks for helping me escape," the boy said dryly. He was pretty cocky for a dirty-faced thief. He looked the bikuni up and down as though deciding whether or not to approve of her, then said, "I suppose you saved my life. No one ever chased me with a sword before, although I've been caught and beaten once or twice."

"If you must steal, you should pick people who are better off," said the nun. "That ronin might have gone hungry because of you. A long time since there's been a meaningful war. Not much a samurai can do. You should know it, a samurai's son."

"How do you know that?"

"I guessed right? I thought so. Have pity on the men you rob."

"He bought six dumplings," said the boy, as though disgusted by excess. "He only needed one."

"How many did you steal?"

"All six. Want one?" He held out a dirty hand. "Too much for me." He patted his belly. "I ate four."

"Thank you. I will." She took the proffered dough, hand-print and all. She bowed simultaneously to the dumpling and the boy.

"There are some benches over there," said the boy. She followed him to a place intended for sitting and viewing the sea and village. Nice trees on either side held back the breeze. She sat and raised the dumpling under her hat. The boy sat rather nearer than was polite. He said, "You were talking to Yano but I didn't see him anywhere. He's a nice man. He helps me out sometimes."

"Don't lie," said the bikuni. "Yano left Seki when your father was a boy."

"I steal food but I don't lie!" The boy was indignant. "Yano lives way up there." He gestured vaguely.

"Up where?"

"Hawk crag. See it sticking above the forest? He lives half-way up."

"How long has he been there?"

"Always."

"Not the same man. The Yano I know is a hermit in Kanno."

The nun spoke without certainty. Yano had never really told her where he would be going when he left White Beast Shrine more than two years earlier. Sensing her vague doubt, the boy pried at it. "This is the Yano who wrote a book of proverbs and poems about folk dances."

"My Yano did that," the nun admitted.

"Then he's the same man. Not more than one Yano of Seki in this world, I'll warrant. I'll take you. It doesn't take long to climb up there."

The tame, rolling hills of Seki were nothing compared to the mountains of such places as Kanno and Kai. Parts were densely forested, especially around fishing villages, and here and there some startlingly huge natural monument reared above the trees. In other areas, the land had been cleared and was moist and green with spring cultivation.

Any so-called hermit living in such an excuse for a retreat, in the midst of a populated countryside, could hardly consider himself an ascetic. Still, it was conceivable Yano had become homesick and had returned to Seki for his final years.

The three-day moon, called Archer's Moon, shone high in heaven by the time they reached Hawk Crag. It was not difficult climbing. Old people could do it if they pleased. It would never meet the needs of a legitimate recluse. Built perilously near the edge of an overhang, the horrible shanty was barely visible in the moon's thin light. There was laughter coming from the place. An old man was laughing and so was some woman.

"He commits shocking sins up there," said rag-clad Hayo. "Say you! Buddha's man! Stop that!"

The bikuni said softly, "The Yano I know is a *kannushi*, a Shinto priest."

"No. He's Buddhist. Say you! Old man! Look out your door! We're coming up!"

The giggling of the girl increased. The old man was peering through one of his hovel's innumerable cracks. Whoever was with him must have uncovered a lamp, for light began to seep out from all the corners of the shack. The old man shouted, "I'm not a holy fellow! Don't bring pilgrims to me, Hayo, you dirty scamp! Who's that? Hey, ex-samurai! You a woman? Throw away your swords and hurry up here!"

She could see only the shadow of his head bobbing with excessive animation at the cracks. She called, "I'm a friend of Yano of Seki, known in Kanno as the Honorable Mister Paddy-Bird. If you're his impostor, soiling his good name, I'll have your life!"

"Ha ha! Come fight me to the death! If you have the nerve, ha ha!"

She and the boy reached the ledge on which the hermit lived. The man calling himself Yano scurried right out to greet them. He most definitely was not the Yano she had known. He wore a Buddhist vest and an oversized rosary as a necklace, but nothing else. A fat woman came out of the hovel, her kimono open in front, and began to climb down from the crag by some alternate route. Before she disappeared below the ledge, she shouted, "I'll come see you again. Have money next time!" He didn't answer, but waved behind his back.

The vile hermit picked his nose and said to the bikuni, "Well, as you can see, I'm Yano of Seki all right. But you're no friend of mine."

"Yano left this province a long time ago," said the bikuni, her voice stern with disapproval. "I happen to know he wrote a book on folk dance, but he never knew what became of it. Have you been claiming authorship? Do you use his good name to bait whores to your crooked shed?"

"You've seen through me!" said the impostor Yano, clutching a pretend arrow in his chest. "However, I've been Yano long enough that I've forgotten who else I might have been. I added some nice poems to the manuscript, so I'm Yano all right." He began to hop about in an absurd parody of a dance, and sang one of his unnecessary compositions:

"Stupid to dance!
Stupid to watch!
Stupid either way!
Might as well dance!

"Hey, ex-samurai, dance with me!"

Hayo began to dance at least, a spritely boy grabbing the old man's hands and hopping left and right with him. They were like two sporting demons. The bikuni said,

"Old man, give me Yano's manuscript at once. Tear out the pages that are yours if you want."

Impostor Yano ceased dancing. He said, "It's my treasure! People give me offerings in order to come up here and copy out their favorite ditties. How would I live without it?"

"Yano was a decent man and devoted to Shinto. He would be alarmed to find out his manuscript was ill-used by some vulgar Buddhist."

"What? You think that? Well! Well!" The hermit stamped the ground in agitation. "All right! You can have it! You think Yano was so righteous? He gave me that manuscript a long time ago! He said he didn't want it!" The impostor ran through the open door of his hermitage, then out again, manuscript in one hand, a portable lantern in the other. He set the lantern on the ground and squatted beside it. The lantern's paper walls were torn, and a black oni-devil had been painted on one side. The impostor turned to a certain page and said, "How's this one! You'll like it!

"Hopping in the garden!
Hopping to the clapping hands!
Hopping through the *ama-dera!*
Hopping on the nuns!

"Pretty good one? It's called 'Convent Dance.' This one's good, too. Yano used to sing it as loud as it would go!

"Oh, in Nikomi they dance squatting down!
Oh, in Nikomi they dance squatting down!
Whew! Stench! Don't dance squatting!
In Nikomi they dance squatting down!"

The hermit pinched his nose shut and rolled onto his back, kicking his feet in the air, laughing uproariously. Hayo hopped around him, laughing also.

"You wrote those," the bikuni said sharply. "Yano never would."

The hermit threw the manuscript in the air and the bikuni caught it. The rice paper was soft from wear and bound together with silk string. The hermit said, "See for yourself. Isn't my handwriting different? I wrote the ones in the back. Not as good as Yano's, I'll admit."

The bikuni dropped the manuscript and turned her face to the ledge, gazing across the top of the nighted forest. False Yano crept up to her, bending low like some kind of wheedling devil; and he said with odd compassion, "You're upset? Because your friend lived a different life than you expected? Yano was known as 'the lover in love with love' and 'the merry priest.' When he gave me his book, he said to keep up his good name, for he was done with it. You see? I was his friend, too. So don't go spoiling it by telling people what they already know."

She continued to stare away from Hawk Crag. False Yano said, "Don't be gloomy! Nothing wrong with having fun and being in love. Yano had a lot of lovers in his time. If I told you what all kinds, you'd be surprised. But he was never insincere, and neither am I. That fat whore of mine? I do her a favor and like her a lot. You think she has the Thousands of Myriads for customers? Frankly, we're in love. Not exclusively, mind you."

The bikuni still would not reply. False Yano made a derisive sound and walked away, saying, "A prude! Hey, Hayo! Don't bring prudes up here again! She's a spoil-sport. Takes the world too seriously, as though things weren't bad enough without posturing like that. Tch!"

The bikuni started to climb down from the hill's edge. Hayo hurried after her but she said, "Don't follow me, Hayo. It isn't necessary."

"Can't get rid of me!" he said. "Where are you going to

stay? I bet you gave that ronin the only coins you had! I'll show you a good place. I have my own house."

Hayo's home was an abandoned storehouse at the rear of a hillside estate. There had once been a habitable dwelling nearby, but it was presently nothing but a burnt-out hulk. The charred ruin, along with the storehouse, were nearly lost among weeds, vines, and tall grasses. Hayo had borrowed a flame for a pilfered candle along the way, and led the bikuni with this feeble light, his hand cupped to protect the flame from wind.

Though the storehouse escaped fire, it had subsequently fallen into a fearful condition. Even beggars found better places. The door had come off and lay among weeds, in two halves. Many of the floorboards were rotted through. A fool, but no one else, might ascend to the dangerous loft; nor would wisdom allow one to stand beneath the loft. The bikuni followed Hayo through the small interior, trusting he knew the safest places to step, stand, or sit.

He told her where to place her swords and hat as he reached into a secret place beneath the floor and pulled something out. It was a lovely candleholder of a type used in temples. He stuck the candle in this, then handed it to the bikuni, smiling hugely.

"Did you steal this?" she asked, receiving the candleholder.

"I steal everything. There's some charcoal in that corner, if you would light some for us."

As the night was not unpleasant, she used the least amount of charcoal, placed in a cracked pot. She had to go outside to find dry twigs and grass, but soon she had the coals glowing. Hayo meanwhile knelt before a pitiful reliquary, in which two funeral tablets stood side by side. He struck a tarnished brass bowl, which gave a dull ring instead of the long, pure note of better metal. He clapped his hands before the reliquary and mumbled something or other to his mother and father.

When they were spreading out infested bedding, the bikuni asked, "How were you orphaned?"

"I don't know how mother died. I was little. Father killed himself last year. I don't mind. I get by."

"He left you just like that?"

"I don't mind. He asked me not to."

"Not to mind?"

"And not to follow. He had a hard time. I get by." His face

was momentarily in candlelight, cheeks slick with tears. She thought it best not to pursue the subject, since it made him sad. He said, "Do you hate Yano? He's perverted, but nice."

"I don't hate him," said the bikuni, covering herself up. The boy fussed around her, tucking her in as though she were the child. Then he crawled off to his own blanket. The bikuni whispered her confession, "Maybe I'm just envious. My life could never be so free. Not even now, with no one to answer to."

"This sad world," said the boy, innocent of jest. He blew out the candle and the two of them were soon asleep.

The bikuni awoke in the moments before dawn. She slipped out of the storehouse, scratching at some fiendish bug which had transferred itself from bedding to neck. She carried her incognito-hat in one hand and strode to the high point of the ruinous estate, from whence to see the sky turn from deep indigo to shallow blue.

From this knoll she had a fine view of Namida Beach but could not see the fishing village. Namida was famous for a battle centuries before—yet it was forgotten what the battle had decided. A river ran into the turquoise mirror of ocean. Naku Jetty was a crescent shape creating a cove at the river's mouth.

Straight above her head, the sky was speckless, promising a pleasant day. Far out over the sea there reared a billowing cloud in the form of a great white horse. The newly risen sun gave the horse red eyes. She watched that cloud until it lost its shape and hidden meaning. Somewhere in the weeds and vines nearby, a hototogisu cuckoo, far from its highland haunts, made its song of endless, longing love.

Beneath the sky and with so much of the fresh world stretched before her vision, the bikuni felt miniscule. She felt as though the whole of Naipon—every rock and stone and wave, and the shadow which was herself upon a hill—might dissolve as do the shapes of clouds. Everything would cease to exist if she blinked her eyes once too many times, or failed to appreciate the vision well enough. And upon the world's conclusion, she would not wake from the dream, but would cease altogether to exist.

Hayo crept up behind, yawning and scratching his dirty shock of hair.

"A nice morning," she said, turning slightly his direction.

He slapped his thin belly and said, "My tummy smells something cooking way off there." He pointed down the narrow lane that was the main road to the village. "Enough for you, too."

"Please don't feel responsible for me," said the bikuni. "To tell the truth, I disapprove of your stealing, though it is not my place to chastise. Nevertheless, because I have once accepted a meal from you, I must repay or be indebted. Therefore, please allow me to show you how a bikuni gets by."

"Begging's fun too!" said Hayo gleefully. "Get better stuff if you steal it, though."

"I don't beg," the nun said evenly. "I play my shakuhachi."

"I'd like to hear it!" he said happily. "We'll beg together. I'll do a dance."

"It's not begging," she said. "A dance would be undignified. Come along and watch, but no dancing."

They went along the winding lane in the direction of the sea, losing sight of the water when bamboo groves impinged upon the road and shaded the cool morning. Somewhere to the right was the sound of young women using mattocks to dig bamboo shoots. It was hard work, but they were laughing. She and Hayo could not see them, but they chattered and made a lot of noise.

The grove came out into a scant wood. The sea remained beyond view. There were a few houses, which belonged to peasants preferring a relative seclusion over village life. One striking hut was grass-walled with a shimmering black roof. The bikuni had never seen such a roof in her travels. As they passed near, she saw the thatch was made of cormorant feathers. There was an old woman on her knees in front of the house, mashing yams in a mortar. She looked at the passing boy and nun and smiled without teeth. The nun realized she was carrying her incognito-hat, not wearing it, and was embarrassed to be caught ogling someone's house. Yet, for some reason, the morning had her feeling freer than the night before, and she returned the old woman's smile.

They could hear the sea though it was still hidden. As they topped a rise, where the forest had been completely cleared for various uses, the turquoise waters appeared suddenly. The smell of fresh-caught fish and by no means fresh scraped scales of fish assailed the bikuni's nostrils.

Women beat clothing on narrow, low docks built into a burbling, shallow river. The river spewed into the jetty-embraced cove. Beyond a bridge, she could see the rear of the sea-facing village.

The small road would soon be heavy with foot traffic: folk coming and going to and from the markets, wholesalers selecting what fish would be carted by laborers to the nearest inland towns, officials exacting taxes, random travelers and strolling tradesmen, woodcutters on delivery rounds, and all manner of people. The bikuni tied her incognito-hat on tight. She unsheathed her shortsword and handed it to Hayo, saying, "Go cut me some nice lengths of dry grass over there."

Hayo took the blade and looked at it with his jaw hanging down. Then he darted for a patch of dried grass, which he hacked, striking warriorlike poses.

They took the grass about a third of the way across the bridge, where the bikuni arranged it in such a manner that she could kneel comfortably upon it.

"Bird's nest!" said Hayo. "Ha ha!"

"It's a symbol of the noble traveler," said the bikuni, "as opposed to a dirty hobo like you. It means poverty and sorrows, but smells sweet."

Hayo plumped down on the corner, sniffing the straw. The bikuni began to play her shakuhachi, the notes sometimes wavering, sometimes long and pure and sweet. The usually rambunctious Hayo became still, his head turned to one side so that he could see under her hat. He looked dreamy and pleased. In a short while, a lot of people started coming and going across the bridge. Those who were in a hurry were apt to throw a small coin into the straw, which Hayo quickly dug out and stuck in the bikuni's alms-bag. Those who were moved by the song would linger a moment or two, misty-eyed and appreciative, then slip near when the bikuni paused. Only then would they drop some coin in the alms-bag, which hung loosely from her neck and to the side of her knee. Those who came close would hear a quiet blessing issue from beneath the hat.

In a short while she had earned several coins of low value. It was more than she usually received in so little a time, despite that these were poor people. It did not escape her that Hayo, smudged face and all, by his very presence, gave the peasants the encouragement to make offerings to a warrior-pilgrim. Ordinarily she could expect to be noticed mainly by those few who passed with weapons of their own.

At a quiet point, the bikuni took out seven coins and said to Hayo, "You're good luck for me. Generally fisherfolk think it too audacious to give something to an ex-samurai." She put the coins in his hand. "Now, go buy us something like cheap noodles. It'll be a treat for you, since you would usually lose the broth running away quickly. Don't go stealing things or I'll feel sad."

The boy accepted the seven coins and set off running, bare feet slapping over the bridge. The bikuni took up the shakuhachi anew and played with an abandoned sort of serenity. She was in good form and tried a difficult composition, which required the fullest range of notes. By blowing harder, the octave was raised; the flute could be made to sound like two separate instruments taking turns. The tune she selected was less melancholy than was commonly composed for shakuhachi. She was in too fine a state of mind to play something typically moody. The piece was titled "Mating Calls between Buck and Doe." Ordinarily it was not her favorite. Today she thought it fit the natural luxuriousness of spring emotion.

A stooped old man in peasant coat drew close when she rested. He dumped a bowl of raw, quality rice in her almsbag. She said gently, "Grandfather, I don't deserve so much," but he slipped away, happy with himself. She was about to play some other piece, but held the shakuhachi motionless a while longer. Through the small latticework of her hat, she had long noted a samurai standing near the foot of the bridge. The samurai might have been listening, or merely lingering.

Without lifting her hat, she could see only the legs and lower body of the samurai, who wore hakama trousers of a faded hue but sharply pleated, and straw sandals similar to those the bikuni wore but of a weave from a further province. A traveler: dusty, slender, and strong. This much the bikuni could tell from the waist down.

The samurai perceived the nun's awareness and, rather than continue watching, began to cross the bridge, each step slow and weighted with purpose. The bikuni held her breath and appeared ready to perform. The samurai halted with feet apart. The bikuni did not look up. In the next moment, a large gold coin dropped into the bikuni's nest of grass. It was an unprecedented sum.

"The value of your life," said the samurai, drawing steel.

Tomoe Gozen leapt backward at an angle, to her feet, braced against the bridge railing. Her sword came forth to block; but the samurai had not tried to kill after all. Having misinterpreted the hostility, the bikuni blocked inappropriately, and the samurai was able to complete a fantastically swift upward and downward double-cut. A triangular wedge fell loose from the front of the bikuni's bamboo amigasa. She gazed out from this rent in her hat. She saw the dark, foxlike face of Yoshimora Wada's strongest wife.

"Shi-u!" exclaimed the bikuni.

Shi-u's sword slid into its scabbard as she said, "Neroyume. I thought it was you. I've searched more than two years. You were to meet me at a certain place, but never came."

"I didn't agree."

"I cannot believe you were afraid."

"Perhaps you misjudge my courage," said Tomoe Gozen. "There are more things to fear than death."

"I was disappointed and thought you ignored our meeting as an insult," said Shi-u, folding her arms and turning sideways. There were more streaks of white in her long hair than there had been before. "I tried to return home afterward, but my lord wouldn't have me. Kosame's hand, which you shattered, never healed properly. She can still fight, but not as prettily. Hayugao was brought home dead. As I was responsible for them, Lord Wada shamed me. He said I could redeem myself with one thing only."

"My head," said Tomoe, pushing herself away from the railing. A number of peasants were backed up on both sides of the bridge. They were afraid to cross, but eager to see if there would be a good fight.

"I've disturbed these people," said Shi-u, conscious of her dignity. "We can't fight here."

Tomoe said, "Shi-u, why must we fight at all? Why would you try for the forgiveness of Lord Wada?"

Her low, boyish voice replied with abject simplicity.

"Duty."

Tomoe sheathed her sword and picked up her shakuhachi, placed it in a slender bag, and tucked it near her back. She untied her ruined amigasa and let it fall onto the nest of grass. All the morning's better feelings had fled so utterly that she could not remember what those fleeting moments of well-being were like. She strode from the bridge, Shi-u after, and the peasants scurried out of the way. Tomoe turned off the lane as soon as she saw a reasonable side-path. They came to a gardened viewing-station. A wooden platform, built beneath willows, overlooked a pool of iris and water lilies.

They were alone.

"A shame to fight in this place," said Shi-u. "Not much room, besides."

"I have no intention of fighting."

"I can be patient. You cannot lose me a second time."

"Shi-u, listen to something. I find this difficult to confess; but I have had dreams of you."

"How propitious."

"I've dreamed what nuns should never dream."

"Oh?"

"I've not felt such things since I was a young woman. It was a priestess then, of the Jono Cult, her face like that of a shining goddess, the opposite of yours."

"It's amusing," said Shi-u, but her dark face was rueful.

"I'm unlucky," said Tomoe. "But I won't die."

"It's not for us to decide," said Shi-u. "Our lives are over in the space of one sorrowful breath, unheard by any."

The bikuni answered, "Isn't that sad enough without our dueling besides? Can't we seek happiness now and then?"

"You think so? As our lives are of no consequence, what then of the precious moments? They are more ephemeral than life itself. They are nothing. A nobleman once said, 'The cherry blooms again, but in the life of a man, spring comes only once.' It's more true for a woman. You and I cannot be young again, Neroyume. It's more pitiful to linger. A swift end is more merciful."

The bikuni sighed with resignation. "Where would you propose we meet."

"Beyond the cove, opposite the jetty. There's a quiet shore called Namida. It means 'tears.' Will you agree?"

"I won't disappoint you twice."

"At noon, then. Neither of us will have the benefit of the sun behind her shoulder."

Shi-u wheeled about, her white-streaked ponytail swinging. She walked away from the riverside garden. Tomoe watched the water lilies. When she was certain she was alone, she drew her shortsword and engraved a poem in the bark of a willow. It read: "Frog upon a lily/ as enlightened as/ ever I shall be."

Hayo scurried up the dusty lane, a square wooden bowl of soup and noodles in each hand, slopping over the edges. When he reached the bridge, he stopped, looked surprised, then approached the pile of straw where the bikuni had been sitting. He placed the noodle-cups on the planks and lifted the bikuni's hat. It was cut in front; it wasn't difficult to imagine how. He fell upon the straw, looking for signs of blood, but apparently nobody had been injured. All he found was a huge yellow coin. He lifted it to startled eyes as though it might wither like a flower petal. Had she bought him off? Was it worth so much to be rid of a tagalong? The notion hurt his feelings.

If he asked around, he could find someone who had seen which way she went. But it looked as though she hated to be followed. Hayo was reminded of his stern, unhappy father's last words in life: "Don't follow me!" Then the ronin's knife plunged deep into his own belly, as Hayo's round, tearless eyes watched in expressive horror.

He stood, kicked the straw and damaged hat into the river, and reared back as though to toss the gold coin after. Then he lowered his arm, gazed at the coin again; and the look that played across his face suggested some odd plan. Abandoning the noodles, Hayo started back into the village.

Alone, Tomoe Gozen walked upon the shore. She had come early in order to investigate the lay of the beach. She had walked far from Naku Jetty and was already returning. The sun never quite came overhead this time of year, so noon was difficult to judge. It looked as though it were time Shi-u appeared.

Upon the lonesome beach, her senses heightened. Everything of nature was close to her awareness. Bladders of seaweed popped beneath her sandals. She stepped carefully between encrusted stones, avoiding a cluster of urchins. Sunlight undulated on the water—liquid gold or fire—and black diverbirds vanished and reappeared and made exaggerated gulping motions with long necks. Wind played through her shoulder-length hair, reminding her of childhood and her mother's gently stroking fingers, moving strands from small Tomoe's face.

A boat beyond the tip of the jetty—with one passenger and a man standing at the stern working an oar—was not enough to spoil the solitude. It was definitely noon and Shi-u's lateness was a welcome respite, although she was not much heartened and could not conceive that her opponent might fail to appear.

She spied a young sea turtle washed ashore, upon its back, in visible despair. As she approached, it flapped its winglike forelimbs, terrified, and dug its nose downward between a pair of stones, striving without success to right itself. She stood over it, let the turtle's despair become her own, and wondered if one or another god stood over her with the least sympathy. She tipped it with one toe and the turtle scurried after the tide as though convinced it had escaped some monster's bad intention.

At her back, the shore folded away into the distance. Before her was the jetty, the name of which meant "Wailing Sadness." Along the edge of the jetty, stone lanterns reared between boulders or perched atop them. They were not visible from the village or the cove, but were an important feature of the landscape from Namida Beach. They had been set as beacons for dead fishermen, whose spirits sought their homes once each year. Some of the lanterns were huge, others small. Some were no older than last summer; for only in summer did souls seek guidance, and each year one or two new lanterns appeared. Other lanterns were ages old, vanishing to the wear of the sea or beneath encrustation. Toward the tip of the jetty were a special group of stone carvings, shaped not like lanterns but scowling gods. These stood in honor of soldiers who perished in a sea battle, in commemoration of a war from which heroic names survived but not the remembrance of the reason they died.

A fishing boat drew near to the point of the jetty and a samurai stood and climbed out. The boatman immediately started away. Shi-u Morita was coming along the jetty's length, weaving between gods and stone lanterns. Tomoe Gozen removed her sleeveless vest, folded it, set it on a beached log, and placed her alms-bag and shakuhachi upon the cloth. She hitched up her hakama and tied back the sleeves of her kimono, then started along the jetty, meeting Shi-u less than halfway.

Shi-u's long, handsome face conveyed neither cruelty nor tragic sentiment, merely calm, firm resolve. Tomoe Gozen could not guess what her own face revealed. In her heart, she felt the gravest sorrow. Shi-u said, more with politeness than flattery, "I am glad to have heard you play your flute upon the bridge. For one of us, it must be the last sweet sound we hear, before the clash of steel."

A wheeling gull cried down to the pair. Tomoe Gozen wondered if it weren't a song intended to contradict Shi-u's statement that they would never hear another. She drew her sword and held it outward from her side; and she said, "Please do your best." Shi-u drew steel as well, holding the sword-guard close to her face, blade aimed straight up. The two women leapt simultaneously. Steel rang on steel. Both found new footing between crusted lanterns. Tomoe placed a foot upon a sea urchin; its spines penetrated her straw sandals. The women turned slowly to face one another again.

For a long time they did not move. When Shi-u finally lunged, Tomoe leapt back, giving up ground, coming nearer the beach and leaving the jetty and its lanterns.

The nun leapt high into the air so that Shi-u's horizontal cut missed its mark; and she kicked Shi-u in the face before coming down upon her back, hurt by a rock at her spine. Shi-u staggered backward, her nose nearly broken and swelling quickly, blood spewing horridly. Tomoe started to her feet, but was forced by Shi-u's onslaught to fall sideways over a boulder and straight into a shoal.

The shoal was thick with colorless jellyfish. Long, blue, dangerous filaments stung her as she was standing. Shi-u pursued right into the midst of the boneless fiends, causing Tomoe to give more ground, stumbling backward through shallows; and both of them plunged from the sea's shelf. Neither could touch bottom with her feet; neither could swim very well while dashing swords at one another. They sank as one beneath the waves, locked arm to arm, each holding off the other's sword. Shi-u's nose was still bleeding, a red cloud between them in the water. Tomoe pushed away, avoiding a cut only because the sea slowed Shi-u's quickness.

Tomoe gave up fighting and concentrated on getting onto Namida Beach, treading through water and jellyfish, scrabbling at stone, coughing, looking like a wet rag or an unwholesome mass of stringy seaweed. The seaweed lurched, stood; behind it, from shallows, stalked Shi-u. Tomoe spat water. Her straw sandals, soaked, fell to pieces, and she scraped her foot against barnacles. She complained loudly, "A bad choice, Shi-u! Poor ground for dueling!" She scrabbled on, not looking back, avoiding the cut behind her, trying to get above the tideline where there was a narrow margin of sand between the rocky shore and the stark, dry grasses rustling in the warm sea breeze.

Clothing hung wet and heavy. The women took up new postures in a sandy area. Driftwood, looking like the bones of monsters, impinged on three sides. Both strove for a certain dignity, despite looking like half-drowned dogs. Shi-u's white-streaked hair sported one green streak of seaweed. Her swollen nose did not bleed as much, but was horrible to look at. Shi-u bared her teeth and rushed forward, causing Tomoe to roll away through dry sand, which adhered to her costume. She came up in a defensive posture and brushed grit from one cheek, looking annoyed.

"I quit, Shi-u," she said; but Shi-u pressed harder. Tomoe blocked, spun halfway around, thrust quickly, was blocked, and had to block again. Yet Shi-u's arm had been cut, how badly was difficult to tell; it didn't bleed a lot.

They backed away from each other—Tomoe weary; Shi-u monstrous and menacing, even in momentary retreat. Shi-u put her sword's tip against a bit of wood and leaned on it, panting, watching Tomoe. Tomoe turned her back, as though bored, or simply unable to look at Shi-u's face. She heard Shi-u coming, but did not turn to face her. She heard the angle of the descending blade and moved, at the last possible moment, to Shi-u's left, and landed a cut. Shi-u's sheath saved her. Tomoe had cut through it, ruining it, and Shi-u pulled the remaining section out of her belt and threw it aside.

Tomoe crouched to one knee and held her sword, edge upward, pointed at Shi-u's belly. Shi-u held back, judging the strange posture. There was no answer to it, for it was wholly defensive, like a hermit crab drawn into its shell. "That won't do!" said Shi-u.

"If it works," retorted Tomoe.

The defensive posture could be exceedingly dangerous to anyone who attacked from above; yet the nun was crouched so low that Shi-u could not possibly get underneath the sword. Where science fails, stubborn insistence often suffices. Shi-u rushed forward in a deliberately suicidal attack. Tomoe fell sideways, for both of them would have died in the same moment if she had insisted on her tactic.

Only when Tomoe tried to stand did she realize her ankle had been cut. It was a deep cut, probably crippling. Shi-u had

been too clever. The suicidal attack had been more carefully planned than Tomoe had thought.

Moving swiftly toward the nun, who crawled backward between two bleached logs, Shi-u's downward slice missed when Tomoe rolled up and over one log. Shi-u's sword imbedded itself deep into the wood. Tomoe slammed her own sword atop the other, embedding it less deeply and insuring the difficulty of Shi-u's getting her steel loose.

Shi-u gazed at her stuck sword and began keening and pulling like a beast with its leg in a trap. To Tomoe's amazement, it came out! Shi-u stumbled backward several paces on the momentum of her terrific yank.

Tomoe slid weaponless to a seated position, her back to the log; and she waited. She said quietly, "This is the end," and at that moment, the boy Hayo appeared from above the grassy margin. He leapt, screaming, tears streaming, straight at Tomoe Gozen, and laminated himself to the front of her. Shi-u, too crazed and swift to break the attack, plunged her sword into the boy's back. Hayo ceased bellowing.

Tomoe wrapped her arms around the boy. He gritted his teeth and raised his face to look at her. He said softly, with gentleness, "I found something for you." In his dirty hand was a haircomb made of tortoise shell. It was a foolish gift for a nun with hair cropped to shoulders, but a costly treasure, beautiful, and well-intended. "Hayo," said Tomoe. "Did you steal it?" She closed her hand around the comb and Hayo's fingers. He replied, "I bought it. With the big coin you left me." He grinned, dirty-faced; then his head fell upon her breasts; and he was dead.

Tomoe Gozen pushed the small, limp corpse from herself, then clawed her way to a standing position in spite of the muscle cut near her ankle. She grabbed hold of her sword's handle and wrenched it up and down until it came loose from the log. She could not step forward, for the ankle would make her fall. She caressed the haircomb, noting its delicate carving of the hototogisu bird.

Shi-u stood in a woeful posture, staring at the child she had slain through awkward insistence. Then she looked toward the object proffered by the bikuni. "Shi-u, it has a cuckoo signifying lost love. Come see it, if you only will." Tomoe Gozen held the comb in her left hand; she held it toward Shi-u. In her right, she held her sword, raised high. Shi-u stumbled dumbly forward, dragging her sword left-handed. Her face was a horrifying mask of torment and self-torture. She reached out, clung to the comb in Tomoe's hand; and in the next instant, Tomoe's sword had cleaved her from left shoulder to heart. Tomoe waited three heartbeats before letting go of the comb and drawing her sword out from between Shi-u's breasts. Only then did Shi-u's rent body fall. Her hand, holding the comb, slowly relaxed.

Sheathing her sword, then pulling the sheathed weapon from her belt to use for a cane, the esoteric nun limped away from the Beach of Tears.

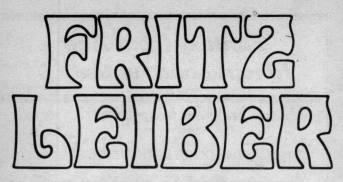

FRITZ LEIBER

FAFHRD AND THE GRAY MOUSER SAGA

Fantasy from Ace fanciful and fantastic!